RECKLESS
In RED

Books by Rachael Miles

Reckless in Red

Tempting the Earl

Chasing the Heiress

Jilting the Duke

Novellas

Charming Ophelia

Enchanting Ophelia

Spirit of Texas in *A Texas Kind of Christmas*

Published by Kensington Publishing Corporation

RECKLESS
In RED

RACHAEL MILES

ZEBRA BOOKS
KENSINGTON PUBLISHING CORP.
www.kensingtonbooks.com

ZEBRA BOOKS are published by

Kensington Publishing Corp.
119 West 40th Street
New York, NY 10018

All Kensington titles, imprints, and distributed lines are available at special quantity discounts for bulk purchases for sales promotion, premiums, fund-raising, educational, or institutional use.

Special book excerpts or customized printings can also be created to fit specific needs. For details, write or phone the office of the Kensington Sales Manager: Attn.: Sales Department. Kensington Publishing Corp., 119 West 40th Street, New York, NY 10018. Phone: 1-800-221-2647.

Zebra and the Z logo Reg. U.S. Pat. & TM Off.

First Printing: November 2019
ISBN-13: 978-1-4201-4656-1
ISBN-10: 1-4201-4656-4

ISBN-13: 978-1-4201-4657-8 (eBook)
ISBN-10: 1-4201-4657-2 (eBook)

10 9 8 7 6 5 4 3 2 1

Printed in the United States of America

ACKNOWLEDGMENTS

No book makes its way to readers without the kindness of many people. My agent, Courtney Miller-Callihan at Handspun Literary, never fails to offer smart direction and good sense. At Kensington, I remain grateful for Janice Rossi's cover design, Anthony Russo's illustration of it, Lynda Curnyn's cover blurb, and Jane Nutter's helpful promotions and advice—but most of all, for my generous and talented editor, Esi Sogah, who didn't immediately object when I told her the next romance included exploding cemeteries and grave robbers. I appreciate as well Erin Bistline, Lynn Rushton, Michelle Carlin, and Ingrid Powell for attentive readings of this novel—and Brandon Shuler, Catherine Blackwell, Keisha Mackenzie, Coretta Pittman, and Marianne Hassan for helpful commentary on the novella *Spirit of Texas* (they should have been acknowledged there!). To my nephew, whose name I have stolen, and to my mother, Mary, who never fails to have words I could use.

For technical guidance, I am indebted to Lynn Rushton, Public Art Collection and Conservation Manager at the City of Dallas's Office of Cultural Affairs, for describing the materials and techniques early nineteenth-century painters would have used to create frescos and other works of art, and to Gordon Jones, Senior Military Historian at the Atlanta History Center, for providing information about the physical construction of giant panoramic paintings or cycloramas.

As always, my deepest thanks to Miles, who reads everything with love.

Chapter One

Winter 1820

"That damned swindler."

From the office door of Calder and Company, Lena Frost could see the key, left precisely in the middle of the empty desktop. Everything else was gone: Horatio's inkwell, his penknife, his little toys, even the carved bird he'd been toying with for the last several weeks. She knew what it meant: Horatio had left. For good.

But did he take the money? She snatched up the key as she rounded the desk. Perhaps he'd left it—or at least enough to pay the remaining craftsmen and open the exhibition. *Perhaps*: the word felt hollow.

Five of the six desk drawers stuck out several inches. Horatio had left in haste. She looked through the drawers, now a jumble. Unused correspondence paper in a variety of sizes. An assortment of bills, paid—because she had paid them—to the end of the quarter. A handful of artist's crayons, almost used up. She picked up the sanguine pencil, its tip a ruddy red against her hand, then tossed it back into the drawer. Horatio was a talented artist, but his real skill was with words, most of them lies.

Nothing in the drawers was of any importance.

Only the drawer where she kept the money box was still shut. If the money was gone, her only hope would be to keep it quiet until she could open the exhibition. Subscribers had paid in advance to see what everyone was calling the most important art exhibition of the year. If she didn't open, she'd have to refund their money. If she could make it two more weeks . . .

She hesitated before turning the key, torn between needing to know and dreading the knowledge.

No. Whatever is here—or isn't—I will face it, as I always have. She turned the key. The drawer opened about four inches, then stuck. Hope bloomed for a moment. Perhaps the money box was still there, wedging the drawer in place, its banknotes and coin all still neatly arranged in divided trays. She pushed the drawer in, then tugged it out. But nothing would make it open wider.

She slid her hand in flat; there wasn't room to make a fist. Then she inched her fingers forward. She felt nothing but the wooden bottom of the drawer. When she reached the halfway point, her stomach turned sour. The box was gone. But she kept reaching, needing to know the drawer was empty before she let herself sink into the despair already pooling inside her.

At the very back of the drawer, almost past her reach, her fingertips felt the edge of a thick piece of paper. A banknote? Perhaps he had left her enough to open the exhibition? Or at least to pay her rent? Pressing the tips of her fingers against the paper, she dragged it forward and out. The note was folded over twice, and she hesitated a moment, afraid of what it might tell her.

The paper was fine, well made, one of the sheets she used to correspond with wealthy patrons and subscribers. That in itself was strange: Horatio normally wrote on paper with a large watermark of Britannia in the middle of the page. He'd play a game with the ghost image, positioning his salutation so that Britannia would look at the name of the addressee or so that her spear would intersect with his period to make an invisible exclamation at the end of his sentences. Lena had shaken her head at his games, finding it hard to remain angry or frustrated with him. But if he'd endangered the exhibition, she might remain angry with him forever.

Tightening her jaw, she unfolded the page. In the center, Horatio had lettered a single word: "RUN."

The despair in her stomach turned instantly to an unreasoning fear. Every creak, every groan of the old building sounded like a warning. *Run.*

She pushed the drawer closed, locked it, and replaced the key in the center of the desktop.

Surveying the room, she tried to imagine where Horatio might have hidden the money box. But, other than the desk, two chairs, and the old engravings stuck with pins to the walls, the room was almost empty. Everything was just as it had been for the last two years, except the money was gone, and Horatio with it.

All he'd left her was the note. She held it out, examining the way Horatio's *R* curved oddly beneath the bottom of the *U*, and the final stroke of the *N* trailed upward. An extra blotch of ink widened the line slightly before the tip, like the hand of a clock. She held the page up to the light. No watermark, no secret design that played with the letters.

She stood, her arms wrapped around her chest, the note limp in one hand. She'd never expected him to betray her, to leave her with no way out but to run. All her energy, her passion, drained out onto the wooden floor and seeped away between the boards. The exhibition would fail. She would fail. And this time she had nowhere to . . . run.

She traced the malformed letters of the note once more, then she crushed it against her palm and shoved it in her pocket.

From the outer office, the hallway door creaked open. When Horatio'd said run, she had no idea he meant so soon. Suddenly afraid, she scanned the room. The inner office door was partly open. The drop from the window to the street was three stories. She had nowhere to hide, and only seconds to make a decision.

Heavy footfalls approached. Though the crew and the ticket seller had left soon after she'd returned, the office door remained open to prospective subscribers until she or Horatio left for the evening. But should the intruder be dangerous, she would have no help. She looked down at her clothes, her best dress and coat worn to meet a publisher who'd agreed to sell engraved prints of the panorama. With only a moment to imagine a plan, she flung herself into a chair before the desk. Her only hope was to pretend to be someone else.

A tall man, strongly built, pushed the door open. Standing in the doorway, he seemed like one of the statues from the Loggia dei Lanzi come to life. And he was beautiful. His clothes caressed his form, revealing powerful shoulders, narrow waist, and firmly muscled thighs. His black hair curled in thick waves like Benvenuto Cellini's *Perseus*. In Florence, she'd marveled at the sculptures of the classical gods, their muscles detailed in marble or bronze. But she'd never realized how breathtaking it would be for those ancient heroes to come to life.

He examined the room slowly before he turned his attention to her. And when his eyes met hers, it was both exhilarating—and terrifying.

"Are you Mr. Calder? I wanted to subscribe to the exhibition in your Rotunda." She kept her tone breathless and a little naive. "I saw a panorama once when I was a child—the Temples of Greece—and I've never forgotten it, how you could stand in the middle and feel as if you had been transported to a different place and time." She spoke quickly, letting her words jumble together in a rush of enthusiasm. "I'm looking forward to seeing your painting. I've read all the clues you've advertised for deciphering the topic. I think it must be Waterloo. What else could be painted in such a grand scale? How hard must it be to paint all those figures—the horses, the flags, our men marching valiantly into battle? It must be such a glorious scene!"

"Don't forget the carrion birds and the jackals ripping apart the bodies of the dead." His voice was stern, but the sound of it resonated down the line of her spine. "Or the bodies broken apart by the cannon or the bayonet."

"Well, sir!" She rose, feigning offense. "If you treat a prospective subscriber so rudely, I will spend my sixpence elsewhere." She walked briskly toward the door. When he didn't move out of her way, she stopped just out of his reach.

He was considering her carefully, examining her clothes and her figure beneath them. Under the focused attention, Lena felt exposed, like a rabbit who'd encountered a hungry hawk.

Refusing to be intimidated, she examined him in turn. His eyes were a cold green, his chin firm. His cravat, tied loosely around his neck, made her wish it was tied even more loosely. Her fingers itched for her sketchbook and pencil. Oh, that he would be just another would-be subscriber! Then—perhaps—she could convince him to sit for her. She pushed the thoughts away. He might be handsome, even devastatingly so, but if he were Horatio's enemy, he would likely be hers as well.

He remained in the doorway, and his stare intensified. She felt the heat of it along her neck and cheeks. Her stomach twisted, but whether in attraction or fear, she couldn't be certain. The silence between them grew, and Horatio's message echoed in her ears: *Run.*

"Will you at least be a *gentleman* and remove yourself from the doorway?" She pulled her shoulders back, as she did with suppliers who wished to take their fee from Horatio instead of from her.

For a moment, he looked abashed, as if he hadn't considered that his behavior was ungentlemanly.

"It appears we both have business with Calder, and we are both disappointed." He stepped away from the doorway, giving her ample room to escape.

Then, as she passed, he offered her a low bow, as if she were a princess or queen. She felt his stare on her back as she walked purposefully, but not too quickly, to the outer office door. She refused to look back at him, afraid to reveal her fear—or her interest.

When she reached the outer door, she allowed herself one last look at her Greek-god-come-to-life, but he had already moved into the office and out of sight. She stepped into the hall, listening. A subscriber likely wouldn't wait too long for Horatio to return.

She heard the desk drawers open and close, and papers rustle. Not a subscriber then, and her disappointment felt like a rock in the pit of her belly. She waited another minute, but when she heard him wrestling with the stuck drawer, she finally took Horatio's advice. She ran.

Hurrying down the two flights of stairs, she found the ticket office door standing open, and she ran through it without stopping. Her fear tasted like metal on her tongue.

In the narrow alleyway leading to Leicester Square,

she kept to the deepest of the shadows, grateful that Horatio had refused to paint the building walls a bright, inviting color. "No, my dear"—Horatio had gestured dramatically—"our visitors must walk through the shadow of the towering Rotunda and down our dimly lit hallway. That way, when the door opens into the vast space of the panorama, they will feel as if they have stepped into a different world!"

Ahead of her, crowds of fashionable men and women jostled past. Leicester Square catered to the needs of the wealthy. Those with ready money or easy credit found a range of luxuries: from silks, laces, and furs, corsets and trusses, real ostrich feathers and artificial flowers, to wine, imported carpets, specially made fancy trim for the drawing room, and guns for hunting in the country and duels in the city.

She flung herself gratefully into the crowds. In her best clothes, she looked like one of the less-well-to-do shoppers.

The crush of bodies carried her along into the square. A stream of curricles and coaches pressed slowly forward, windows open, allowing their occupants to see and be seen. To her left, a lone sedan chair lurched slowly down the square, its occupant, an elderly lady in the height of fashion, waving directions with her fan. Lena hid behind it, following until she reached the opposite side of the square, then cutting through until she reached the inter-section of Princes Street with Coventry.

There she hesitated. The coaches pushed forward too fast. Usually, she waited patiently for a break in the traffic, thinking of her paints and images. But this time, she inched forward, muscles tensed and ready, as if for the start of a race.

If she could reach her boardinghouse at Golden Square, she would be safe, or safe enough. Her landlady, for all her lace and ribbons, took after the troll in the old Norse story: no one could pass without paying a toll.

She looked over her shoulder, watching for the broad shoulders and the curling hair of her *David* come alive. How long would it take him to realize her deception and come looking for her? Was he already wending his way behind her, following her steps, as he pushed his way through the crowd?

The crowd concealed her escape, but it also concealed any pursuit.

She waited, tapping one foot unconsciously until the brown-haired street urchin beside her looked up at her speculatively. She was attracting attention. She needed to move, but to where?

She knew this part of London well. The side streets, the alleys, the apparent dead ends. She even knew which cemeteries she could cut through and not end up a corpse herself. But all her options required her to cross this street—or return the way she had come.

She looked over her shoulder again. Horatio's boarding-house was nearby on Gerrard Street. Perhaps he would be there, nursing his sorrows in a bottle of gin, hoping to avoid admitting that he'd taken the money to appease this or that gambling debt—or spent it entertaining one of the craftsmen who applied to work on the Rotunda. He had to be in distress, or he wouldn't have taken the money, not when he knew how much it was needed to open the panorama.

If Horatio were in residence, the doorman would let her into the drawing room. The house was filled with male artists and often with their female models, so, once inside, no one would notice if she slipped up the stairs, and if they did, no one would care. She'd often had to come drag Horatio to this or that meeting. He wanted to be famous—Horatio Calder, impresario of the Rotunda—and she'd made him earn the name. But what if Horatio wasn't home? What if he were hiding out somewhere from whatever danger he thought he should warn her about? Then she would be left standing on his porch, visible to any who were searching for him.

No, her rooms were best. She clenched her hands and watched the traffic. A nearby man hailed an approaching hackney. It slowed to collect him, and she took her chance, weaving her way between coaches, carts, and wagons until she reached the opposite side. She followed the streets almost mechanically, and at each street she checked behind her, praying she had escaped.

At her boardinghouse, she would slip through the basement door and up the back staircase, trying to avoid her landlady, Mrs. Abbott, who would expect next week's rent. Once in her rooms, she would lock her door, stoke a small fire, drink a cup of tea, and wait until morning. Then she would return to the Rotunda, give the men their day's directions, and plan how she might still open the exhibition without any funds.

It was strange to long for the safety of her rooms when for months she'd wanted other lodgings. When she'd leased the Rotunda, she'd planned to live in one of the empty rooms above the ticket office, but Horatio had objected strongly. "It's not seemly, Lena-girl. You living there, and all those men in and out of the building. If rumors were to circulate, we'd lose our subscribers in a flash." Horatio had snapped his fingers, then smiled, knowing nothing mattered more to her than the exhibition.

With each street, each turn, she made it closer to home. She kept to the middle of the crowds, letting the pace carry her along. When one group of pedestrians thinned, she rushed forward to the next, her progress measured in the fits and starts of a hundred shoppers and vendors.

Eventually she turned north, away from the safety of the crowds at Piccadilly and Haymarket. The streets narrowed, sporting less fashionable but more useful shops. She could map her progress down the streets by how each shop smelled. Ink and paper led to saddle leather, and burnished wood to varnish, until she reached the end of Great Windmill Street where the hint of stale blood signaled the surgeon, and sweet rushes and rosemary, the undertaker. At night, when the gaslights were dim, she often traveled the last blocks more by her nose than by her sight. She checked off the streets on her mental map, feeling safer with each block she passed, until she reached the chemical smells of Silver Street, with its soap makers, haberdashers, wood and furniture dealers.

When the thick, earthy fragrance of chocolate met her at the northwest corner of Golden Square, she was almost home. The grocer there—a jovial Mr. Krause—had expanded his business to include a chocolate shop. Just one more street, and she'd be safe in her rooms.

Safe.

She stopped short. The crowd pushed and jostled her before splitting on either side, as if she were a rock in a stream. When she'd hurried out of the Rotunda, she hadn't been thinking about a plan or the implications of Horatio's note. She'd simply run, as Horatio had instructed. But he likely didn't mean to her boarding house.

Stepping into the doorway of Krause's shop, she scanned the crowd. Surely, her intruder hadn't followed her so far? Needing to think—and hide—she stepped into the shop itself, never taking her eyes off the road. From inside the shop, the proprietor, Mrs. Krause, a ruddy German woman with bright eyes, called her name and motioned her to find a seat. Lena complied. She chose a single seat in the back corner against the wall. From there, she could watch the door and the street, and if the need arose, she could escape through the kitchen into the alley.

A few moments later, Mrs. Krause delivered a cup of steaming chocolate. "Ah, Miss Lena, we haven't seen you at all this week! When Mr. Calder traded Herr Krause tickets to your grand gala in exchange for a weekly cup of chocolate, I thought it was a bad trade. But my Pieter has been practicing his waltz for weeks. He comes into a room and dances with me like the old times. And that, my dear, is worth everything. We are going to be the best dancers at your opening, you will see!"

Lena forced a smile. Mrs. Krause was kind, but her shop was well frequented. One careless word about Lena's predicament, and the rumors would spread across fashionable London within hours. Krause patted Lena on the back as she left to serve other customers, and Lena wrapped her fingers around the warmth of the chocolate cup.

She took a sip. Normally she would close her eyes and focus on the thick, warm silk of the chocolate. But not today. Though the chocolate felt soothing and warm, she wondered how much it would cost to repay the Krauses for six months of it. The gala had been Horatio's pet idea: an exclusive party for London's monied classes held the night before the exhibition opened, with dancing on the observation platform—and a ticket price at quadruple the regular admission. "Have no worries, Lena dearie," he'd promised. "I will take care of every detail." At first he had told her all his mad ideas to make the exhibition a success, from the musicians playing

martial tunes from beneath the stage to the children
dressed as banner bearers, who would guide the visitors
down the darkened hallway to the panorama itself. But
lately Horatio had been uncharacteristically silent. She'd
imagined he was working on the gala and his other
schemes to promote the exhibition. But what if it had been
something else? What if he hadn't been working on the
gala at all? Despair pooled into a hard ball at the base of
her stomach. Not only was the panorama itself unfinished,
but she had no idea what remained to be done on the gala.

Her heart pulsed hard against her ribs. She was afraid,
and more so for not knowing why. Certainly, Horatio was
a rascal—some might even call him a scoundrel—but he
wasn't an alarmist. If anything, Horatio underestimated
risks, always finding room for a bit more mischief before
he finally abandoned a scheme. But for all his tricks and
games, he would never intentionally endanger her or her
work. Or would he?

And why now, of all times, just two weeks before the
grand gala and the opening of the exhibition? Three years'
work, too much to lose all because of one of Horatio's
foolish schemes. She closed her eyes. If she gave the
panorama up now, she'd be worse off than when she'd first
arrived back in London after a decade abroad. Then, at
least, she had hope and confidence and a bit of money in
her pocket. No. If she left now, the panorama would fail,
and her with it. She would have to reinvent herself again.
The very thought of it made her almost weak with despair.

For the first time in months, she wished she had never
left France. She'd survived the war years by hiding her
nationality, transforming the solid Englishness of her sur-
name into the gliding French *givre*. Lena Le Givre. Lena
Frost. She could still see her mentor, Vigee Le Brun, at her

easel, laughing, when she'd announced the name she'd chosen.

"But *ma chère, le givre* is cold, so cold. In changing one's name, one should make a grand statement. Lena d'Or! Lena d'Argent! What man could resist a woman of gold or silver? Or perhaps you should choose a color—I am Le Brun, the brown. Look here: you could be L'Ecarlate!" Vigee had pointed to a rich red, almost scarlet, that she'd just applied to the canvas. "It matches the warmth of your spirit, the generosity of your affections. Lena L'Ecarlate!"

Her mentor's patron, an Austrian count who had lived in England and understood better the nuances of the language, had shaken his head. "Oh, no, my dear, our Lena is too young to be a scarlet woman." So Lena Le Givre it was. After the success of her first salon exhibition in Paris, Lena Le Givre had become a rising star, a portrait painter capable of competing with her mentor's own skill. Her commissions had been steady, and she had begun to build a life in France.

Lena drank another deep draught, her mind returning— without wanting to—to the reasons she'd left France.

For the war years, she'd hidden in plain sight, believed to be French, except by her closest circle. Then the empire fell. Almost overnight, the climate changed. Hundreds of French monarchists that Napoleon's edicts had forced to remain in England flooded home, and the English occupation forces, once welcomed, now found themselves hissed and booed all the way to the docks by the resentful lower classes. Soon the backlash extended even to those like her who had lived in France since childhood.

With every new report of hostility or of property seized, she'd begun to plan for the day that she too might need to leave. She'd quietly gathered letters of introduction from her dearest friends among the European aristocrats, gaining some commissions from minor English aristocrats before she'd ever left France. She'd purchased an open ticket for the English packet and sewn her jewels and money into her clothes. She even stored several trunks of her possessions in a friend's attic. Even so, when the tide had turned against her, she'd still been caught off-guard. She'd barely had enough time to escape by the night packet, with one lone trunk and a basket of artist supplies, believing, from the number of her advance commissions, that she was already on her way to a career at least as successful as the one she was leaving behind.

Classically trained, she was adept in a variety of methods and genres. But after her first flush of success, she found that the English were not as open to talented women as the French, and she lost commission after commission to less talented men. Her only inroads were among the gentry and wealthy merchants. The most lucrative commissions with the bon ton remained outside her grasp.

Lena had soon decided to cast her fate on more popular tastes. And nothing—except perhaps the re-creations of Admiral Nelson's naval battles at the water theater at Sadler's Wells—excited the general population more than a monumental painting of a historical scene. Such works always garnered the greatest critical attention, receiving the loudest accolades at exhibitions and in galleries. In a gallery, a monumental painting might fill only a wall or ceiling. Panoramas took that scale and expanded it tenfold, with the circular painting standing as high as a building.

Lena had told the truth when she'd confessed to her handsome burglar that she'd fallen in love with panoramas— she had seen her first in London, a depiction of the classical world, with all the architecture and temples re-created intact and the statuary in color as the ancients would have painted them. When her childhood world ended abruptly, she had spent her last penny to take refuge there, and instead of ending, her world had expanded. She'd met Vigee Le Brun, an internationally famous portrait painter, who, estranged from her own daughter, had taken Lena as her pupil. Under Le Brun, she learned how to master the little details that could transform a canvas: the delicacy of lace lying along a wrist, the gentle taper of slender fingers, the fire in a jewel or in an eye.

After three years, her panorama was almost ready to meet the world. When she closed her eyes, she could see it all: the rounded walls of the panorama, the stage that jutted into the center where the viewers would stand, and the middle space between the canvas and the stage filled with objects that would make the viewers feel part of the scene.

She watched the painting take shape again in her memory. On the primed white of the empty canvas, she and Horatio had sketched charcoal outlines for the shapes of the background, then landscape and perspective painters had provided the broad sweeps of the background: the valley battlefield, the hills beyond, the sky gray and brooding. Then tents, wagons, and artillery had transformed that natural landscape into a human one, where hundreds of men stood in battle formation. The animal painters had filled in the camp animals—horses, nostrils flaring at the smoke and noise, mules, oxen, chickens, and geese—alongside the animals brought by instinct to the battle—vultures, crows, ravens, and eagles, foxes, and jackals. Lena, however, had merged the sensibility of a portrait painter to the requirements of a giant story. Though she'd hired dozens of painters, she'd kept the panorama from becoming a hodgepodge of various techniques by requiring all the craftsmen to adopt a common style.

In the last month, portrait painters had given distinctive faces to each enlisted man, minor officer, and woman. But for the faces of the major officers—on all sides—she'd wanted to be accurate, so they had taken the faces from printed engravings, other paintings, or personal knowledge.

When some of their painters had disappeared, one after another, in the space of a week, Horatio had promised to finish the dozen or so faces that remained. But whether he had completed them or not, she wasn't sure.

It had been painstaking, exhausting, exhilarating work. And for what? If she abandoned the panorama now, she would have no way to repay the subscribers. Though she could hide behind H. B. Calder and Company and say that the failure was all Horatio's, she'd still bear the blame. She, not Horatio, had written letters to the members of the aristocracy to explain their project, visiting their drawing rooms and collecting their money. She, not Horatio, had negotiated with booksellers to carry engravings of the giant painting, and in recent weeks, she, not Horatio, had ordered and paid for all their supplies. No, she might blame the invisible Horatio, but everyone knew her face. She would have no future as a painter in England, just as she no longer had one in France. And worse yet, where would she run? Even in India or New England, the failure could follow her. She forced the thoughts away, feeling the hard pulse of her blood. She wanted to hide or run, and she couldn't do either.

I will not be afraid. I will not be afraid. She repeated the sentence to herself.

She forced her mind away from the thoughts, pressing the warmth of the mug against her lips. She concentrated on the rich, thick flavor, forcing her mind to what remained to be done at the Rotunda.

If Horatio's faces were finished, she could remove the scaffolding and begin filling the area between the painting and the observers with the sort of things one would find on the battlefield—wagons, artillery, clothing, tents, even a cannon Horatio had rented for the purpose. That middle space would give viewers the illusion that they were on a battlefield and give the right perspective to the painting itself. She felt the tightness in her chest return. Without the objects filling the middle ground, the illusion that the painting was a real scene would be lost. But how would she pay?

She set the cup down, but too sharply, and it clattered against the saucer. The coffee-shop patrons looked at her. *Careful. Careful. Don't attract attention.* She forced an apologetic smile, and they looked away.

She made herself breathe slowly, pulling the air deep into her stomach. At least she had a little time. She paid the crews at the end of every week and her suppliers at the end of each month. The next payment to the suppliers would fall after the opening of the exhibition. As long as none of the suppliers discovered her money was gone before the opening, all could still be well. The risk lay with the news getting out, and the suppliers canceling her orders or, worse yet, taking back their wares. To avoid that, her remaining crew had to get their wages on time. Some might be willing to wait until after the opening, when new visitors would bring new revenue. But even then, one careless word could reveal the Rotunda was in financial straits, and skittish subscribers insisting on the return of their funds had ruined more than one project.

She had only a week—maybe two—to find Horatio and

get the money back. Otherwise, the panorama would be ruined, and she with it.

She reached into her pocket for Horatio's note and her last sixpence. She'd intended to collect her own wages when she'd met Horatio at the offices that morning. She fingered the coin without removing it from her pocket. Even if she could return to her rooms, she didn't have enough for another week's lodging. And Mrs. Abbott was unlikely to extend her credit.

She examined Horatio's note. No signature, no indication that the note was for her, but she knew it was, just as she knew Horatio had written it.

She drank down the rest of the chocolate. The last time she'd had a cup of hot chocolate she had been telling her friend Constance about how optimistic she felt about the opening of the exhibition. The empty place where her optimism had been now felt like gall.

But, Lena realized with relief, Constance would take her in, if only for a day or two. And Constance's shop wasn't too far, perhaps a mile at most. All she had to do was travel north. Her burglar didn't seem to have followed her, but even so she would be careful. She drained the last drop and slipped quietly out the back door.

Chapter Two

"I had the most interesting experience not two hours ago," Clive Somerville announced to his supervisor, Joe Pasten. Somerville removed his greatcoat, hat, and gloves, and laid them across a nearby desk, almost oversetting a pile of reports.

Joe shook his head in amusement. "How is it that your everyday clothing is purely utilitarian, but when you dress for your class, you transform into a dandy, all narrow trousers and ruffled lace?"

"I'm expected at the Ainslie ball this evening." Clive looked down at his suit. His high-waisted tailcoat of blue wool was decorated with velvet lapels and velvet piping at the wrists, while his gray wool trousers sported velvet stripes down the seams. Under it, he wore a sunflower-colored waistcoat, crisp white shirt, and a cravat embellished with gold medallions. "After the Sinclair trial, everyone lectured me on my lack of morals. Montclair suggested that by dressing with restraint, I made myself appear amenable to weighty conversations."

"So, you took his suggestion to mean you should dress like a peacock?" Joe observed. "Had your brother Edmund made that recommendation, I'd assume he was in league with your new tailor, but Montclair is too upright for that."

Clive ran his finger along the velvet edge of his coat sleeve. "Montclair was right: when I dress like this, no one bothers trying to redeem me. Besides, there's something pleasurable about the texture of the velvet."

"Ah, there's my honest Clive under all that frippery." Joe picked up a divided wooden box. Inside, pins with painted tips were segregated by color. The pins designated the various enterprises that their very secret division of the Home Office managed. The blue-tipped pins indicated groups or individuals engaged in suspicious, but perhaps not illegal, activities. The green-tipped pins signified an agent of the Home Office, either a trusted local or an officer—whether in disguise or not—dispatched to watch over the area. Joe carried the box toward a large map of England laid out on a table. "Back to your interesting experience this afternoon: is she pretty?"

Clive followed Joe to the map. Clive quickly considered his last ten encounters with women in the bon ton. Dull, duller, and exceedingly dull. Perhaps that explained his attraction to the young woman in Calder's office. "Do all my interesting experiences involve a woman?"

"Does this one?" Joe held out several green-tipped pins.

Clive, avoiding Joe's question, turned all the sharp ends to point in the same direction, then returned the pins to their compartment in the divided box.

Joe smiled. "You and I are the only ones who arrange the pins in that way."

"When I was a student, one of my teachers cut his finger during an autopsy and died within a week. No one could determine why it killed him, but it's made me cautious of cuts or pinpricks." Clive was oddly relieved that Joe had allowed him to turn the conversation. Something about the young woman made him wish not to examine his reactions too carefully.

"Even if you weren't a surgeon, it would offend your sensibilities to put the pins in willy-nilly." Joe held out his hand. "Four blues, please."

Clive counted out the blue-tipped pins. "Don't ask for any blacks, and I'm free to hand you pins all day." Clive hoped to keep Joe from returning to the question of the interesting woman.

"All day? Then after this, perhaps you could devote yourself to some record keeping." Joe waved toward a desk in the far corner. "You will find the relevant forms stacked neatly on the desk you share with your brother."

Clive refused to look, taking another set of pins from the box and turning them all neatly in one direction.

"Silence may be an effective skill in managing your family, but it only piques my *interest*." Joe emphasized the last word. "Is she pretty?"

Clive groaned inwardly. If he were not careful, Joe would ferret out his unexpected response to the young miss before he'd had time to analyze it for himself. He made his voice light and jovial. "I'm not being silent. I'm being deliberate. I'm certain that once or twice my intriguing experiences didn't involve a pretty woman."

"Ah, another deflection. That in itself is . . . *interesting*. But I'll allow it. Besides, you didn't say *intriguing*. For you, *intriguing* means some discovery that changes your idea of an assignment. *Amusing* usually describes some sport, frequently including your brother, fisticuffs, and battered limbs."

"At least it's our opponents who end up battered." Clive straightened his shoulders. "To be fair, though, the opponents usually start out as Edmund's. I merely provide a useful confusion."

"A useful confusion." Joe paused, a bit of a smile playing along his mouth. "That could describe most Somerville gatherings. But *interesting . . . interesting* always means a woman."

"Then I meant both intriguing *and* interesting." Clive gave in: Joe would not be deterred. The memory was still vivid. Clive could see the young woman once more, her face turning toward him as he entered the room. When her eyes met his, even in memory, he felt the same punch in his gut that he'd felt before. "I found her in the office of Horatio Calder. You remember him, the owner of that new panorama opening soon at the Rotunda."

"Ah, so this interesting woman is tied to those murders you keep promising to solve." Joe didn't look up from the map. "Six bodies to date, still warm, all bought by one of your colleagues at the surgery schools. Where do we stand on the investigation?"

"Barkus bought the last body for seven pounds." Clive shifted his tone and manner to give his report, ignoring Joe's suggestion that his young miss might be involved. "A child no more than five showed him the location. A woman this time, reeking of gin—Barkus says she was suffocated."

Joe shook his head slowly. "Bad business, this. What about Calder? What's his involvement?"

"I'm not sure. He left a key on top of his desk. It led me to this." Clive removed a carved bird from his valise and held it out. "It was hidden in the space behind the locked drawer."

Joe examined the bird, noting several deep impressions

marring the base of the carving. "These marks here? Do you think they mean anything?"

"I'm not sure. They may simply result from it being wedged between the drawers." All the same, he took the bird from Joe and examined the marks again.

"Sadly, that sort of carving is somewhat common." Joe returned to his map. "Old soldiers, seamen, even beggars on the street whittle to pass the time."

"You underestimate our craftsman." Clive turned the carving over. "This one is exceptional—delicate but sturdy. The only mistake is in the color of the heron. It should be more gray than blue. But why would Calder leave it for me?"

"Would the girl know? You remember—the *interesting* one."

"I don't think so. She was waiting to pay her subscription for the panorama. Pretty in a breathless sort of way." Clive didn't mention that he'd been captivated by her lips, flushed and full, wondering if they would taste as sweet as they looked. "She could have been prying about in his desk, but she didn't take anything away with her. She didn't even carry a reticule."

Joe looked up, meeting Clive's eyes. Shaking his head, he turned back to the map. The silence drew out between them.

"Damn." Clive brushed back his hair. "If she had no reticule, where did she carry her subscription money?"

"Caught up in a pretty face and missed the big clue. If the key were in plain sight, could she have found something before you arrived? Something that she didn't need a reticule to carry away with her."

"That carving kept the drawer from opening more than a couple of inches. But her arms were slender. I suppose she could have reached in far enough to remove something small."

"A pretty face and slender arms." Joe shook his head slowly. "You broke the first rule of investigations."

"I discounted her." Clive leaned back on his stool. "She appeared to be frightened. I thought *I* had scared her."

"Could she have been afraid of something else?"

"That's why I said *interesting*. At first I thought she was dim, but then she stared me down and demanded I let her pass. It should have struck me as incongruous at the time, but I was too interested in why Calder wasn't there to meet me . . . and in the key. I could see it from the doorway."

"What about Calder?"

"I'll see what I can discover at the Rotunda tomorrow. If he's not there, we might consider adding him to our list of missing persons."

"We'll hope that his body doesn't appear at one of the surgery schools." Joe brushed his hands on his trousers. "To change the subject, have you seen your better half?"

"As I haven't a wife, I'll assume you mean Edmund."

"Ah, precision. The bane of creativity. Do you have more than one twin?"

"When I saw him last week, he mumbled something about work in the country. I assumed he was working for you. Do you need him?"

"No, your skills are the ones we need at present. But Edmund made me a wager, and I want to see if he's lost."

"Wager?" Clive looked at Joe more intently. "Edmund never bets unless he's sure he can't lose."

"In *interesting* matters, both you and your brother are equally dim. But I'll leave him to tell you his tale of woe." Joe looked up at the clock. "Ah, I must go. I have a meeting with Mr. James to discuss the status of our operations."

"Someday I would like to meet Mr. James." Clive took advantage of the opportunity. "It's odd to work for this division, however irregularly, and never see the man in charge."

Joe looked at him sternly, and Clive raised his hands in acquiescence. "I know. I know. *It's vital to the security of the realm for Mr. James's identity to remain a secret.*" Clive recited the sentence he'd heard for years. "But Montclair has met him, and, as agents go, I'm at least as good as Montclair."

"It isn't an issue of your quality as an agent. Montclair simply worked on a plot that required access to Mr. James's expertise." Joe's stern look had turned hard. "He wasn't supposed to speak of it."

"No, no. Don't blame Montclair. He's never said a word. I once saw him come out of Mr. James's offices."

"Ah, I understand." Joe paused, choosing his words. "Mr. James was much injured in the wars, and his appearance is somewhat shocking. He finds it easier to keep to the shadows where his scars do not distract others from the vitality of his mind."

"I'm a physician. I might be of help. And by oath, I cannot tell what I see or hear. In the original Greek, my obligation is called a 'holy secret,' making it a religious oath as well as an ethical one."

Joe's face softened, and he patted Clive on the shoulder. "If ever we are in need of a physician, I will remember that."

"Ah, Somerville, I knew I'd find you here!" Adam Montclair strode into the room and picked up Clive's hat, gloves, and coat. "I'll play your valet, but you must come along. There's twelve and six in it for me, if I deliver you to your crew of surgeons within the next hour."

"Twelve and six?" Clive sighed, looking at the wall clock. "I'd pay you to pretend you didn't find me, but that's too rich merely to gain an hour." Clive allowed the other investigator to help him into his greatcoat. "But we must stop by the duke's; he's agreed to look over some information related to the case."

Joe nodded support. "Perhaps Montclair can offer his wisdom as well. But before you go, answer this: would you recognize that interesting young woman, if you saw her again?"

Clive remembered her open face, slender waist, gentle bosom, and felt again the same unexpected pull of attraction. "In a heartbeat."

After Lena left Mrs. Krause's, she followed a narrow passage behind the shops. When she crossed back onto a main road, she made her path an obscure one. She hid in shop after shop, returning to the street only when it was clear or crowded. In places where she knew a corner shop or tavern had entrances on both streets, she took her way through, hoping to make it hard to trace her movements.

Though the trip could have taken half the time, she reached her destination an hour later. The sign over the store entrance showed a dark-skinned man holding both a pen and a book; the glass window was lettered THE AFRICAN'S DAUGHTER, BOOKSELLER AND STATIONER.

A bell jingled as she opened the door, and Lena breathed in the calming fragrance of books, paper, and ink. Lena had taken refuge at the African's Daughter before. In the long weeks after she'd arrived in London, friendless and alone, she'd spent her evenings at the bookshop. The dramatic rise in the population of the country's capital after

Waterloo had thwarted all her attempts to find rooms in a boardinghouse, and she'd quickly run almost through her reserves staying at the only reputable hotel with rooms available for an unaccompanied young woman.

Over several nights of frequenting the shop, she'd found in its proprietor, Constance Equiano, a kindred spirit. When Constance had discovered that Lena needed more permanent lodgings, she'd used her network of neighbors and friends to find Lena a respectable boardinghouse with an open flat. In gratitude, Lena had painted Constance a whimsical frieze that ran along the top of the store's front wall above the windows—a fanciful landscape mixing people and events from Constance's favorite books.

In furnishing her bookstore, Constance had placed large convex mirrors in its upper corners, allowing her to see her customers from almost any location in the store. Passing the tables holding new books at the front of the store, Lena stopped before the first section of sturdy bookcases and used the mirror to search for Constance. She found her friend near the middle of the shop next to a comfortable seating area, where a group of women had gathered around the large central table. When Lena had questioned why Constance had sacrificed so much shelving to conversation, her friend had laughed. "The men have their clubs and coffee shops, but we women have the African's Daughter!"

As Lena walked deeper into the store, Constance hurried to meet her, arms open. "Lena! Welcome." As they embraced, Lena could feel the tension in her back and shoulders release. She was safe. For now.

Constance, always compassionate, studied Lena's face intently. "What's wrong? Has something bad happened?"

"I needed to get away from the Rotunda for a few hours."

She stepped deeper into the shop using the bookcases to hide her from view. "I couldn't think of anywhere else to go."

"You are always welcome here. The African's Daughter turns no one away."

"I . . ." Before Lena could finish her sentence, the sound of women's laughter made her stop. "I can wait in your office until your customers are gone."

Constance gave her hand an encouraging squeeze. "They are friends as much as customers. I can leave them to their own devices. What is troubling you?"

"Horatio. He left me a note." She wanted to explain that he'd taken all the money remaining from the sale of the advance tickets, leaving her with only a sixpence left, not enough for rent or dinner. But she couldn't take the risk, and more than that, she couldn't find the words. It was all too overwhelming. Instead, she pulled Horatio's note from her pocket and held it out for Constance to read.

The woman's dark eyes widened. "'Run'? As in abandon the exhibition?"

Lena nodded, knowing that if she were to speak, she would weep.

Constance put her arm around Lena. "He should know you've worked too hard to let it go now, and he should know you would not give up." The group of women burst into laughter once more, and Constance inclined her head toward the laughter. "Do you trust me?"

"I came here." Lena held up her hands in a gesture of futility.

"Then I believe my friends can help." Constance smiled comfortingly.

"Your friends?"

"Every month the ladies of the Muses' Salon meet

here. We have tea and cakes while they discuss a book they have read. My patron, Lady Wilmot, began it as a way to bring customers to my shop, but it has become a pleasant habit."

"But an expensive one for you. How much profit do you lose serving tea and cakes once a month to a dozen women?"

"None at all. Lady Wilmot provides everything—the tea, sugar, and cake," Constance said. "This week, the Muses, as I call them, are quite dismayed by Samuel Taylor Coleridge's recent revision of his *Rime of the Ancient Mariner*."

"It's a book club?" Lena pulled back. "A book club can't help me."

Constance patted Lena's shoulder gently. "It's an unusual book club, filled with women who are committed to helping those who are in need. Come along—you can at least meet them. Then after the Muses leave, we can talk about your response to this." Constance handed back Horatio's note. "Given Horatio's message, is it safe for you to return to your rooms or even to the Rotunda?"

"I had intended to wait until after dark," Lena admitted.

Constance squeezed her elbow. "You will stay with me tonight. I have a spare cot in my apartment upstairs. It will be no trouble."

"May I?" Lena breathed out in relief, the last of the tension leaving her shoulders. "I *am* afraid to go to my boarding house."

"Then it is decided." Constance took her hand. "But in exchange, you must meet my friends. You'll be surprised how useful they can be." Constance pulled Lena toward the women, and after a second's hesitation, she followed.

In the middle of the store, six women—all dressed in

the latest fashions—sat around a table, intently debating. While they stood to the side, listening, Constance quietly identified each woman. "The salon is primarily made up of women from two families: the Somervilles and the Gardiners. Sophia Gardiner, Lady Wilmot, is the patron, both of my store and the salon. Those three to her left are her late husband's sisters, Ophelia Mason and the Misses Ariel and Kate Gardiner. The two to her right are related to her fiancé, the Duke of Forster: his elder sister, Lady Judith, and their newest sister-in-law, the former Lucia Fairborne, Lady Colin Somerville."

For a few minutes, Lena and Constance stood to the side, listening to their conversation. Whenever she met so many at once, Lena played a game to remember names: she would imagine how she would paint each person.

Ariel Gardiner—a serious woman in her early twenties who reminded Lena of Joan of Arc, champion of France— brandished a smartly bound copy of *Sibylline Leaves,* Samuel Taylor Coleridge's latest collection of poetry. "I still don't understand why Coleridge took nineteen years to revise a poem he already published. Which version does he expect us to read?"

"This is certainly a more complex poem than before, particularly with all these notes in the margin." Lady Wilmot, an elegant woman with nut-brown hair, suggested. Her serene expression reminded Lena of the Virgin Mary's patient cousin Elizabeth.

"For me, the marginal notes simply muddle things up; in several places, they even contradict the poem itself. What do you think, Judith?" Ophelia Mason waved her hand dismissively. With her lustrous auburn hair flecked with gold and red and black, Ophelia was easy to imagine, not as Hamlet's betrothed, but as Titania, Queen of the Fairies. But Lady Judith posed a puzzle for Lena's game. From her slight stature and bright eyes, Lena would have normally painted her as one of Sandro Botticelli's sylvan sprites, but Judith's serious expression refused the portrayal.

Lady Judith spoke after a few moments' silence. "Perhaps the marginal notes aren't Coleridge-the-author helping us understand his poem; perhaps they are another character, a reader, like us, who makes mistakes." Hearing Judith speak, Lena settled on Leonardo da Vinci's Mona Lisa, whose enigmatic smile hinted at a thoughtful nature beset by sorrow.

"The notes remind me of a medieval scribe explaining a manuscript in the margins, and doing a terrible job." Kate Gardiner's heart-shaped face and generous smile would be well suited for Botticelli's Venus rising from the waves. "So, I read Coleridge's literary essays, the *Biographia Literaria*, hoping they would help explain the poem." Kate put her hand on the two volumes in front of her.

"Only my sister would read three hundred pages of philosophy to understand a twenty-page poem," Ophelia teased.

"I'm most interested in the Mariner's journey." Lady Colin Somerville, a woman with curling black hair tied back in an indigo oriental scarf, spoke softly. "He catalogues the horrors of travel; in the end, though, he's a lonely survivor, irreparably damaged by his experiences."

"Lady Colin came home from living on the Continent to discover her aunt had been murdered," Constance whispered. Lena decided Lady Colin would be perfect as the heroine in George Gordon, Lord Byron's *The Bride of Abydos*.

Judith patted Lady Colin's shoulder comfortingly.

"The poem does suggest that when one lives through horrific experiences, one can only tell the story at particular moments."

Lena wanted to add, *But telling one's story never resolves anything. Even when the Mariner tells his, he remains alone.*

"This is our chance. Come with me." Constance stepped forward to the table. The women looked toward them, all curious. Lena forced herself to appear at ease. "Ladies, may I introduce my friend Miss Lena Frost. You know her as the artist who painted the frieze on the front wall. Lena, these are the ladies of the Muses' Salon."

Lady Wilmot gestured Lena to one of the empty chairs and introduced her friends, who welcomed Lena in one voice.

"I must say, Miss Frost, your frieze is quite delightful, particularly the decorative border that runs down both sides of the window frame." Mrs. Mason gave a welcoming smile.

"My sister isn't being particularly honest," Kate interjected. "Herself a redhead, she likes most that Rapunzel has *red* hair."

"It's more than that." Ophelia Mason ran her finger down an escaped wisp of auburn hair. "Have you noticed how Rapunzel's curls at the top transform along the side of the window into the green tendrils that grow up from Jack's beanstalk at the bottom? It's a delightful expression of great skill."

"I had excellent teachers." Lena deflected the praise, having learned that for a woman to accept a compliment of her skill directly, even among other women, was often interpreted as an unbecoming pride. Lady Wilmot seemed an unlikely patron for the sort of painting Lena had done for Constance's shop, unless she—like every other lady of the ton—wished for Lena to paint her nursery. In the past year, she had given up hope of gaining any but the most mundane commissions from the ton, and she had pinned all her hopes of fame and stability on the panorama.

"Though our Mariner's lessons can only be learned through trial, excellent teachers can lead a student far, especially when a student already shows talent." Lady Judith tapped Coleridge's book.

"My only talent was persistence. If I drew a line wrong—and I drew a great many lines wrong—I practiced until I drew it right," Lena offered with a smile. "But I was lucky in my teachers. They let me draw the line wrong as many times as I needed to, but guided me in how to do it better."

"Then you had exceptional teachers." Lady Wilmot leaned forward, giving Lena an appraising gaze.

"Any teacher is exceptional who can help a child see herself anew," Lena corrected mildly.

"Then perhaps you might be willing to meet my daughter. She has an interest in drawing, and though I dabble in the art, I am not a good teacher for her."

At the word *daughter*, Lena groaned inwardly. She knew all too well what "an interest in drawing" meant, and it wasn't talent or skill. No, it meant—as Lady Wilmot described herself—a dabbler. Worse than a nursery painting! Every aristocrat wanted daughters to know the fundamentals of drawing, but few had any interest in a girl developing real skill. Typically, Lena refused such offers by setting her rates so impossibly high that she would be quickly replaced with another teacher, but she could hardly afford such scruples now. "Though I must confess that I lack the skill of my own teachers, it would be my pleasure to meet your daughter."

"Then we must talk before I go." Lady Wilmot smiled broadly.

Constance, knowing how Lena disliked private lessons, intervened. "I should have also mentioned that Miss Frost is the mastermind behind the panoramic painting at the Rotunda in Leicester Square."

The women burst forth in animated conversation.

"It was a brilliant idea to advertise the subject of the panorama in weekly clues." Ariel tucked her book in her reticule.

"My partner, Mr. Calder, thought it would generate interest in the exhibition," Lena explained, willing to give Horatio credit for his idea.

"Interest!" Kate laughed. "Your topic has its own entry in White's betting book."

"Does it?" Lena found the thought simultaneously thrilling and horrifying, a sign of the possible success of the panorama and a reminder of how much scandal failing to open would create.

"Until that last clue, everyone thought that it was the Battle of Waterloo," Lady Colin added.

"And what do they imagine now?"

"No one can agree any longer," Ariel explained. "Some cling to antiquity and argue for the Battle of Troy or Thermopylae. Others are convinced it's the Battle of Hastings. A smaller group argue for the Battle of Bosworth Field, as described in Shakespeare. A few, and I am in this group, still believe your subject is the Battle of Waterloo, but others object, claiming no art can depict it."

"Having been at Waterloo, I would agree." Lady Colin shook her head. "A painting could replicate the *scene* of the battle, but none could depict it in all its horror. From the camp hospital, I didn't see the battle, but even miles away we could feel the boom of the cannon—and none of us could forget its aftermath." Her voice trailed off.

After a moment, Ophelia Mason filled the silence. "As for me, I haven't any interest whatever in the subject. It's the presentation, the theater of it, that interests me."

During the discussion, Kate's attention never left Lena's face. "You are quite an actress, Miss Frost. You never gave any reaction to our suggestions. Either you are exceptionally good at concealing your emotions, or we haven't yet discovered the subject for your exhibition."

"I would say that each of your suppositions shares characteristics with the actual painting." Lena chose her words carefully.

"A diplomatic answer, to be sure." Ophelia rose as did her sisters. "It's delightful to debate the merits of Coleridge's poem and to predict the panorama's subject, but we must be going. We must collect Mr. Mason at Whitehall." She kissed the other women good-bye, then took Lena's hand. "We will see you, I hope, at our family dinner on Saturday. Constance has promised to come, and you must come as well. We are in Kensington at Birch House."

Lena hesitated, uncertain of what the appropriate response might be.

Kate began to laugh. "Our Miss Frost can maintain the most stoic face on the subject of her exhibition, but our Ophelia has stymied her. It's the idea of inviting strangers to a *family* dinner, isn't it, Miss Frost?"

"I must admit it is," Lena acknowledged carefully.

"Ah, then you don't yet know our Ophelia," Judith explained gently. "She defines *family* quite idiosyncratically, but her instincts are infallible."

At the front of the shop, the bell rang, and soon a handsome young man with hair the color of wheat in sunlight joined them. Lady Colin's face, still clouded by thoughts of Waterloo, brightened immediately. "Miss Frost, may I present my husband, Lord Colin Somerville?"

"The pleasure is mine, Miss Frost." Colin gave Lena a half bow. "I've come to collect my lovely bride *and* my terrifying sister."

Judith batted at his shoulder. "My siblings pretend that I'm intimidating, but no one believes them."

"I do," Ariel whispered loudly to Lena's left, and Judith shook her head, laughing. Ophelia and her sisters made their way to the door, followed by Lady Judith.

Lena regretted that the party was already breaking up. She had felt safer in the group of women.

Lord Colin Somerville, his wife on his arm, turned to Lady Wilmot. "Will you come with us, Sophie? We've promised to escort Great-aunt Agatha and one of her friends to a viewing of some Old Master paintings slated to be sold next week. As a result, we can return you to your house or to the duke's, as you prefer."

"No, your brother should arrive at any minute. We are going from here to Mr. Aldine's. Besides I have business yet to discuss with Miss Frost." Lady Wilmot embraced the couple good-bye, then returned to her seat at the table.

When the shop door finally shut behind the last member of the Muses' Salon, the bookstore grew quiet.

"I love the bustle and noise of customers." Constance stacked the books left on the table into neat piles by genre. "But when they are gone, I always find the silence restorative."

"I often feel that way when my children walk in the park with their tutor." Lady Wilmot smiled. "I love them madly. I just seem to love them more after a half hour's respite."

"I feel that way when my craftsmen return home in the evenings," Lena contributed. The three laughed at the shared sentiment.

"But as to my business with you, Miss Frost. Your frieze for Constance is quite lovely. I especially like the panel where the Red Cross Knight from Spenser's *Faerie Queene* rides into battle with Don Quixote."

Lena groaned inwardly. Private lessons *and* a nursery commission. What ancient gods had she offended? Perhaps, if she were lucky, this time she might be asked to paint something whimsical for a *summer house*.

"I should have realized earlier who you were."

Lady Wilmot's words twisted in Lena's stomach. She studied Lady Wilmot's face intently, wondering if they had met before and where. Suddenly, the thought that Lady Wilmot only wanted her to paint a nursery wasn't so unappealing.

"I have had very few commissions in England," Lena admitted carefully.

"But the scenes of the Italian countryside you painted for Lady Eremond are stunning. When my husband was alive, we lived outside Naples for many years, and your view of Vesuvius from the Fort of Granatello made me long for our palazzo there." Lady Wilmot looked wistful. "Looking at your painting, I could almost smell the spice of a Neapolitan summer."

Relieved, Lena felt the compliment deep in her chest. "Thank you, my lady. The view of the bay from the fort was one of my favorites."

"Then we have that in common." Lady Wilmot's wishful expression turned animated. "If it were me, I would have been quite disappointed Lady Eremond chose to hang my paintings in her country house where few can see them."

"Though any artist longs for people to see her work, Lady Eremond prefers the country, and I saw it as a compliment that she would wish to have the series near her. Besides, she was an easy patron."

"What does that mean?" Lady Wilmot quizzed good-naturedly.

"She is knowledgeable about art. She knows what pleases her, and she seeks out artists whose style and media suit her taste. At the same time, she also trusts her artists to transform her wishes into something unexpected and pleasing."

"That sounds more like a fruitful *collaboration*."

"Fruitful collaborations are always preferable to the alternative."

Sophia laughed. "Then perhaps we could see if a fruitful collaboration is in our future. I have a ceiling to be painted. I imagine something in the style and manner of Lady Eremond's series, but with the cleverness of your frieze here."

"A ceiling?" Lena hesitated, but kept her face neutral. "Perspective can be tricky in a ceiling just as it is in a panorama. If the space is large, it could take a month to erect the scaffolding, and the Rotunda will require my constant attention for some weeks yet."

"Of course. To begin, could you complete one smallish piece—a portrait—as a surprise present for my fiancé's birthday? I would need it in two months' time. Finding a gift for a duke is difficult enough, but finding one for my fiancé is almost impossible. Lady Judith has resorted to giving him oddly shaped rocks for his curiosity case."

The bell rang, and the mirrors showed a dark-haired man striding purposefully to the seating area.

"Ah, that should be him." Lady Wilmot picked up paper and pencil, as the duke strode into the open space, his bearing decidedly aristocratic. Lena imagined him as a sixteenth-century Flemish aristocrat with stern features set off by a ruffled collar.

The duke surveyed the table. A plate of leftover tea cakes was surrounded by piles of books and empty teacups. "I see your muses have decimated Miss Equiano's table." He kissed Lady Wilmot's cheek. "I hope you have recompensed our Constance for her patience."

"Enjoying the lively debates of her ladyship's salon requires no patience at all," Constance objected genially. "I learn something new each time they meet."

"Then I stand corrected." The duke appropriated two of the tea cakes. He examined one intently, and Lena suddenly imagined him fifteen years younger, tossing biscuits in the air and catching them in his mouth. It was as if her baroque gentleman with the stiff collar caught her eye and winked.

"Darling, this is Miss *Lena Frost.*" Lady Wilmot emphasized Lena's name, as if the duke would recognize it. "Miss Frost, meet my fiancé, Aidan Somerville, the Duke of Forster."

"Ah, so you have found her." The duke turned his attention fully on Lena, examining her as a natural scientist might an insect or a moss.

Lena straightened her shoulders under his gaze. "It is my pleasure, your grace."

"No, the pleasure is mine, Miss Frost. At the encouragement of Miss Equiano, I have purchased tickets to your exhibition for my siblings, their families, and the whole lot of my London servants."

"He's also bought tickets to the opening night gala for ourselves and all the members of my salon," Lady Wilmot added.

Lena's gratitude was balanced by a dose of nausea. To have gained the attention of a duke—for good or for ill— was a considerable thing.

"I'd like to know one thing: did you or Mr. Calder choose the exhibition's subject matter?" The duke spoke in a rich baritone.

Lena paused, uncertain of the import of his question. "Mr. Calder tends to be the public face of the operation, rather than its hands or feet."

"A diplomatic answer." Lady Wilmot smiled knowingly. "Many women of my acquaintance describe their marriages in the same way." The women laughed, as Forster shook his head in mock disapproval. "You needn't worry about the duke's questions, Miss Frost. He is merely trying to gain the advantage in a bet." Lady Wilmot turned to the duke, placing a gentle hand on his arm. "Darling, now that I've found her, I've been trying to convince Miss Frost to come see my ceiling." Lady Wilmot scribbled a note and handed it to Lena.

"Found me?" Lena examined the pair carefully, remembering Horatio's warning.

"Lady Eremond gave me your name, but in its French version. I'd quite despaired of finding you until Ariel realized my mistake when she was reading the advertisements for your panorama: Horatio Calder and Lena *Frost*, proprietors. We visited your Rotunda the very next day, but your partner refused to tell us where we might find you. '*No, no, no, my lady, Miss Frost takes no commissions.*

She is entirely devoted to the panorama.'" Lady Wilmot mimicked Horatio perfectly. "I almost had to resort to bribery."

"You did bribe him." The duke's face was forbidding, but his voice was kind.

"No money changed hands." Lady Wilmot waved a dismissive hand, looking for a moment entirely like a woman who had lived for a decade in Naples. "Therefore, it can't be a bribe."

"Odd. I distinctly remember that the second time we visited his office, your footman strained under the weight of a large basket of Cook's best productions. In legal circles, that would constitute a bribe, especially given the glee with which Mr. Calder fell on the roasted duck."

"Mr. Calder was too hungry to recall Miss Frost's address, and we have a moral obligation to feed the hungry." Lady Wilmot raised her chin with a look of righteous indignation. But when the duke raised a single eyebrow, Lady Wilmot broke into laughter.

"The second time?" Lena watched their interaction with interest and suspicion: might Lady Wilmot or the duke have been the reason that Horatio had warned her to run?

"Yes, we were there just yesterday."

Lena's stomach clenched.

"I believe you are frightening your painter, my dear." Forster smiled at Lena, and his face lost its aloofness. "Miss Frost, it is *my* ceiling, though my fiancée thinks it is hers already."

"As I remember, the duke gave it to me on my birthday." Lady Wilmot raised her chin for mock emphasis.

"I gave you the *room* for your salon," the duke corrected.

"Well, then, when I am done with it, I shall give it back to you," Lady Wilmot teased.

Forster turned to Lena, putting his hand over his heart. "I had no idea that she was going to remove the paintings. All quite fine, late-Renaissance Italian and French, some quite valuable. The whole lot relegated to the attic. Some day we will go up to the attic together, and I will show you my poor ancestors. Perhaps you can plead their cause with her ladyship."

Lena, knowing her place as neither servant nor equal, merely nodded.

"The duke is in a teasing mood, Miss Frost, so pay him no mind. He won his house and all its horrid paintings in a bet. *His* ancestors hang in the ducal residence in Grosvenor Square, which he shares with his siblings when they are in town. It is currently occupied by three of his brothers and his termagant great-aunt with her five cats."

"Four. The orange tabby discovered that nine lives was less a promise than a general estimate," the duke observed with mock solemnity.

"Cats aside." Lady Wilmot touched the duke's arm. "Like much of the house, the paintings were in terrible disrepair, though we salvaged as many as were worth the trouble. But more to the point, every image in the room was of a man, every one." She shrugged. "As a result, all were unsuitable decorations for *my* salon."

"Ah, yes." Forster smiled, raising Lady Wilmot's hand to his lips for a chivalrous kiss. "The Muses' Salon, a gathering of clever, capable—mischievous—women."

"I know that you are quite busy with the opening of your panorama, and I'm sure it will be a tremendous success. But will you at least see my ceiling?" Lady Wilmot touched Lena's elbow briefly. "The duke and I have an appointment with our solicitor now, but we could meet you at his house this evening."

Lena looked at Constance, who nodded her encouragement. She thought of Horatio's warning and the work she had yet to do on the panorama. Lady Wilmot's ceiling might provide her with the means to survive the next month. Before Lena could agree, Lady Wilmot spoke again. "If your panorama is half as good as the rumors suggest, you will be flooded with commissions the day after it opens, and I was hoping to be first in line."

Flattered, Lena opened the note that Lady Wilmot had handed her. "Cavendish Square. I will come by later this evening."

Lady Wilmot smiled broadly. "That would be lovely."

Chapter Three

Traveling to Cavendish Square had taken her far from the Rotunda or her boardinghouse, but even so, Lena maintained her vigilance, watching the others on the street on the odd chance that her handsome burglar might appear.

Typically before she interviewed for a commission, she learned all she could about her possible patrons: what they liked and disliked, their habits, and most importantly, whether they were likely to pay. But Lena knew little about Lady Wilmot or the Duke of Forster. Though Constance had offered a strong endorsement of the pair, her bookshop had grown busy, and Lena had withdrawn to Constance's apartment to hide.

If Lady Wilmot had been looking for her, why hadn't Horatio told her about their visits? Of course, knowing Horatio's fondness for good food, he may merely have wished to prolong his access to Lady Wilmot's cook. Lena could easily imagine Horatio as a fat-bellied Falstaff, pulling out a handkerchief and using it as a makeshift bib while he dug heartily into the meal Lady Wilmot had brought him.

But Horatio had left her a warning. Had it included

Lady Wilmot and her beau? Or was Lena supposed to run from something else entirely? She shook her head, caught between frustration and fatalism. For all his crusty charm and secrecy, she cared about the old man. But if he—and by extension *she*—were in such danger that he had time only to steal her money and scribble a quick note, couldn't that note have included a few more words?

She knocked on the duke's door decisively, looking over her shoulder at the street. Behind her, even in this fashionable neighborhood, the street was full. But no one seemed to look her way. The door opened almost immediately, and she hurried across the threshold, hoping that whatever threat Horatio had warned her against remained safely outside.

The butler escorted Lena through opulent corridors befitting a duke's home.

With a sort of flourish, the butler pushed open two double doors, giving her a view of a large hall, undergoing renovation. Even in disrepair, the room was majestic. To her right, along one long wall, large windows looked out over the parterre. To her left, in the center of the room, fire blazed in a giant fireplace, and in front of it stood an ancient table, long and wide, its wood polished and gleaming. Along the walls, fine dining chairs waited to be called into use.

But the ceiling caught her attention—and her breath. Arched beams divided the ceiling into six wide, rectangular sections, all empty of decoration. Along the edges of the room, where the ceiling curved down to meet the walls, carved wooden frames created spaces for portraiture and other scenes. Nine of the spaces were already filled with images of women, and Lena realized that the portraits depicted the women she'd met at the bookshop.

It was an exceptional space, the sort of commission that could make a reputation. A commission like this one—in *addition* to the panorama—might be the very opportunity she'd been working toward, showing the range of her skills and abilities. Immediately her mind began painting the ceiling's spaces with scenes, their subject matter drawn indiscriminately from mythology, history, literature, and her own imagination.

Lady Wilmot approached from the center of the room, extending a welcoming hand. The duke followed closely behind. "Thank you for coming, Miss Frost. As you can see, our ceiling needs a painter of imagination and skill."

Lena tore her attention away from the ceiling. "It's stunning. I mean, it *will be* stunning in the right hands."

"That's why after I saw your work for Lady Eremond, I was so insistent to find you," Lady Wilmot explained. "Originally, I'd hoped that the painter who had completed the portraits would finish the whole. She had been in exile here during the wars, but when the way to return home became clear, she took it."

"She cannot help but be disappointed," the duke objected. "Time only stands still in our memories."

"She might discover she would have done better to stay here in the life she had made rather than try to regain the life she'd left," Lena agreed.

"Was that your experience, Miss Frost, when you returned from the Continent after the wars?" Lady Wilmot looked curious and sympathetic.

"I was so young when I left England that I had few expectations of what English life would be like on my return." Lena delivered the answer matter-of-factly, having practiced it a hundred times. "I had little choice but to return. The French government pardoned the French who had fled the wars to live in other countries, while it grew less tolerant of the English who had lived the war years in France. But I wish your painter well. Many who took that journey discovered either that there was nothing left to return to or that they were as much an exile at home as they had been abroad."

"But one must still take the journey." Lady Wilmot's voice held a hint of sadness.

The duke put his hand on Lady Wilmot's shoulder. "I must take your leave, my dear. I'm to meet Clive in my study within the hour."

"Tell your incorrigible brother I expect a full report before he goes. I haven't seen the rascal in weeks." Lady Wilmot touched the duke's arm before he walked away, a gentle motion that Lena admired. "Come this way, Miss Frost. From the center of the room, you can imagine my design best. The previous owner's grandfather had an affection for all things Venetian. He moved this ceiling from that republic more than fifty years ago. The beams are original to the room, but the wooden medallions between them and the frames around the edges of the walls are all imported. The portraits, commissioned this past fall, have only recently been installed."

"Nine portraits." Lena examined the portraits carefully. "All women and all in classical dress. Constance called your book club the Muses' Salon. Are these portraits intended to depict the classical muses?"

"Yes and no. Each of the classical muses embodied and inspired a particular area, so I determined they would be my models. Too often we see even the most unaccomplished men commemorated, yet truly exceptional women go unacknowledged and unadorned. I'd like this room to pay tribute to women of great talent, so I began with the women of my salon." Lady Wilmot pointed to the portrait to their right. "Ariel is our scholar, so there she is dressed as Clio. Can you identify the next?"

"A painter learns mythology as part of the stock and trade," Lena demurred. "Is that Lady Judith looking up into the stars as Ourania? Meeting her briefly, I didn't find her a star-gazing type."

"Ah, if I could only encourage Lady Judith to abandon practicality for daydreams!" Lady Wilmot was quiet for a moment, then continued. "Lady Judith can tease out the components of a scent or a food, a skill well represented by Ourania's focus."

"Your sister-in-law is Terpsichore. Is Mrs. Mason an adept dancer?"

Lady Wilmot laughed. "Mrs. Mason navigates the currents of society with an unerring good humor and discretion, so it seemed appropriate to portray her as the muse of dance. In these portraits, the relationship between the classical muse and my modern ladies is more evocative than exact. But each of my salon's muses has special talents."

Lena examined the other portraits. "They seem to be interesting women. Perhaps I will have occasion to learn more of them."

Lady Wilmot considered Lena carefully. "They are valuable women to know."

Lady Wilmot's gaze, kind though it appeared to be, made Lena feel that her secrets were written clearly on her face. Even so, she refused to appear ill at ease.

"Might I ask some questions?" Lena waited for Lady Wilmot's nod before continuing. "Do you wish to memorialize only living women or those from any age? And only English women or those from any land?"

"Whatever the land or time, I wish to picture women of

accomplishment. Perhaps each section could illuminate a different category of women's achievement: rulers like Sheba, Cleopatra, or Russia's Catherine the Great; discoverers like Caroline Herschel with her comet; or explorers like Sacajawea." Lady Wilmot listed the names with enthusiasm.

"What of women of letters? Perhaps poets like Sappho or Charlotte Smith or novelists like Frances Burney or Elizabeth Inchbald? Or a historian like Catherine Macaulay?"

"Ah! An artist with the soul of a scholar!"

"No, I'm merely an avid reader with a friend who owns a bookshop."

"Then I must loan you two of my books, both quite old. I have been collecting women's books for some time. Do you know Marguerite de Navarre? She modeled her *Heptaméron* on Boccaccio's *Decameron*. Such lusty tales! Or Christine de Pisan? Her *Book of the City of Ladies*— much like my ceiling here—argues in favor of women's accomplishments."

"I would be honored to borrow them."

"I will have them here when you come next. Now that you know the purpose of my ceiling, let me show you my sketches of some possible versions." Lady Wilmot led her to the table. "I was inspired by your frieze at the African's Daughter. Here my woman warriors, Boadicea and Joan of Arc, fight side by side on the shore, while Artemesia of Caria commands the Persian fleet, as described by Herodotus."

Lena picked up one of the sketches: Lady Wilmot had a discriminating eye and a subtle taste. "You are a talented artist in your own right. The lines here are fine and the coloring skillful."

"I prefer botanical illustration, though I occasionally dabble in portraits of my family."

"We could integrate botanical illustrations here or here to good effect." Lena pointed at one of Lady Wilmot's designs, watching as Lady Wilmot's face shifted from rejection to consideration. "Then the Muses' Salon would be decorated in part by one of its Muses."

"That's an interesting idea . . . and not altogether unappealing." Lady Wilmot looked from the design to the walls themselves.

Lena reconsidered the room in light of Lady Wilmot's ideas. A series of historical paintings focused on the acts of women—it wasn't merely a lucrative commission, it would be a tour de force. But even after the opening, the panorama would require her presence. Lena felt the gnawing anxiety return. Accept. Refuse. Run. Her options had been reduced to single words.

Lady Wilmot studied her face. "I know that you are devoted to your panorama, and Mr. Calder explained that you already have plans for a second to follow on the success of this one. But surely between the opening of this one and the next, you will have some months to fit my ceiling into your plans."

Lena began to speak, but stopped. She wanted both: the panorama and the ceiling. If Calder hadn't abandoned her, she would have managed, but she was alone, with little resilience to manage both projects. But perhaps, if she could set up one canvas at a time on the Rotunda stage, she could paint while monitoring the final progress of the panorama. At the least, she could begin.

"We've also crafted a budget. With the help of our previous painter, we estimated the cost of one section of the central ceiling. But of course you will have some alterations, according to your preferences for specific workmen." Lady Wilmot held out a ledger sheet.

Lena took the list. Her stomach twisted at the first item: "a plaster worker for lathe and burlap." Lady Wilmot didn't want her to paint on panels that would be affixed to the ceiling. She wanted her to paint directly on the ceiling in *buon fresco*, embedding the ground pigments into a layer of wet plaster to create a single surface. Unlike oils, which would take days to dry, plaster—and her work— would set quickly, testing her skill and precision. She swallowed once, then twice, then continued reading.

The upper part of the list addressed the materials needed to construct the scaffolding and other equipment necessary to paint such a large project. Wood. Nails. Tarpaulins. Silently, Lena read each item in the long list, comparing Lady Wilmot's list to a similar one in her mind. All in good order, thorough and detailed.

The lower part listed the pigments she would grind in water, then apply directly to the wet plaster. The colors tore at her heart with mingled despair and desire: raw and burnt umber for the earth tones; yellow ochre to add depth; caput mortuum for dark and light flesh tones and for folds in drapery; florentine chrome oxide for the greens; and a dozen others. Each name bloomed a color in her imagination. The pigments were followed by ground minerals she would use sparingly for rich accents: malachite for a luminous green, azurite for an azure blue, and lapis lazuli for a brilliant one.

"You will need a red," she said half to herself.

"I'm sure there are other pigments we will need as well." Lady Wilmot spoke softly, as if knowing that Lena was struggling with the decision. "But to make this room a showplace, both for my salon and for your talent, then we should use the best materials."

Lena returned to the list. The next section outlined a timetable, beginning with several rounds of sketches to finalize the design. Below that, at the bottom, was the estimate of her fee. She caught the gasp before it left her lips. A generous estimate. No: a more than generous estimate, particularly if it were only for a single section. She multiplied out the cost for the whole ceiling, and she felt faint.

Lady Wilmot spoke quickly. "I estimated the length of time you would likely need for one section of the room—and I wanted for you to have no need to take other commissions while painting for me. I believe it is a fair figure per section."

"More than fair. But . . ." Lena looked back at the list, calculating out how many months the project would take from the completion of the scaffolding to the end. Had Horatio known how much Lena would profit when he refused the commission? If she believed Horatio's warning, she should refuse and run. Her stomach felt leaden. It felt like a cruel joke: to be offered such a commission at the very moment she shouldn't accept it.

"Look at the room again before you say no. Paint the walls in your mind's eye, and see how beautiful it will be."

Lena picked up Lady Wilmot's sketches. Looking up, she imagined each one on a different section of the ceiling, filling each scene with the rich, vital colors Lady Wilmot had listed. Lady Wilmot's sketch of the women warriors came alive in umber, ochre, blue, and green, the blood on the fallen soldiers an oxide red. Lady Wilmot waited quietly. Completing the circuit, Lena faced Lady

Wilmot, the pull of the ceiling too great to resist. "Yes. I will."

Lady Wilmot smiled broadly, then spontaneously embraced Lena. "I'm so pleased."

"Perhaps you should wait to see if I'm a competent workman, timely in the discharge of my responsibilities."

"I have no fears. Lady Eremond said that you were prompt and efficient. And Mr. Calder—well, his praises would fill a book." Lady Wilmot opened a folder on the table, removing a banknote. "This is a retainer for your first set of sketches." Lady Wilmot pressed the note into Lena's hand. "I prefer to pay for each stage, so that you are always appropriately compensated for your labor. Before the duke returns, I was hoping we could discuss the timing of the portrait I mentioned at the African's Daughter."

Lena resisted looking at the note, though she was desperate to know if the retainer would give her enough to pay this week's craftsmen. The closer she could get to the opening ball, the more likely she would be to succeed. "Of course."

"The duke and my daughter Lilly share the same birth month, and they have grown in the last few months quite devoted to one another. I would like to have a portrait of her to hang there next to the others." Lady Wilmot pointed to a location in the center of the long wall, between two of the portraits of the salon members. "She is only eight, and I would like you to depict her as a young Persephone."

"Persephone? The most beautiful woman among the gods, stolen by Pluto and taken to the underworld as his bride. Wouldn't you prefer a wood sprite or a fairy for a young girl?"

"Oh, she is already a beauty . . . and, I should perhaps warn you, a bit of a hellion."

"I could have been described in the same way when I was a girl." Lena felt an immediate connection with the girl, coupled with a bit of jealousy. Her father had not been so accepting of his daughter's exuberance.

"I refuse to stifle her spirits; a girl needs a bit of spunk to survive in this world," Lady Wilmot explained. "What resonates for me in the Persephone story is her mother Demeter's grief, so profound that it causes her to withdraw all warmth from the earth."

"But summer returns when Persephone rejoins her mother," Lena filled in part of the story.

"And winter returns when she rejoins her husband." Lady Wilmot's expressive face changed to pensive, and her voice to confidential. "You must understand: I almost lost Lilly some months ago, and in those hours when I didn't know if she were alive or dead, I tasted that grief. So it seems an appropriate emblem for her."

"You said 'hang,' so I'm assuming I can sketch her here, then paint in my studio," Lena asked hopefully.

"Of course—it would be hard to keep the portrait a secret otherwise!" Lady Wilmot affirmed. "And your lessons with Lilly will offer us a perfect way to conceal your sketches."

"Certainly." Lena had hoped the lessons would be forgotten, but Lady Wilmot seemed to have imagined the whole scheme quite thoroughly. "If it suits your ladyship and your daughter is here, I could meet her before I leave, and perhaps even take a likeness or two today."

Lady Wilmot beamed. "Yes, that would be lovely! I was hoping . . ."

At the same moment that Lady Wilmot agreed, Lena saw the duke enter at the far end of the salon, followed by two other men. The three sat at the end of the long table, deep in conversation.

She recognized her burglar immediately. In his earlier drab clothes, he could have filled any number of professions. But his current attire left no question that he was a member of the aristocracy.

Even so, she knew him: the same look of intense concentration, the same confident stance, the same hair black as jet, curling in a thick mass almost to his shoulders. Though the flamboyance of his dress surprised her, the fit of his jacket and the colors of his attire suited him perfectly. She felt his presence as a shiver down her spine. If she were to paint this version of him, it would be as Adonis, Aphrodite's strikingly handsome lover.

Was he the duke's incorrigible brother? The rascal from whom Lady Wilmot wanted a full report? On what? Her? What he'd found in Horatio's office? Suddenly, the duke's house felt far less safe, and Lady Wilmot's friendliness less sincere. Had Lena walked unwittingly into the very situation Horatio had warned her to avoid?

Lena turned her back, hoping her Adonis might not notice her across the long hall. She might have fooled him in the Rotunda office, but even there, something in his expression had suggested he wasn't completely convinced by her performance. She'd never been able to simper for long, much to her father's dismay. And something about her Adonis's manner—and the depth of interest in his eyes—made her fear he might be exactly the kind of man who could see through all her protections.

Lena fingered Lady Wilmot's banknote. Surely Constance wouldn't have vouched for her ladyship if Lena should be wary of her. It was a situation in which she couldn't win. If she refused Lady Wilmot's commission and gave back the money, she would certainly lose the exhibition. If she kept it, she might be putting herself in danger. At the same time, by becoming valuable to Lady Wilmot, she might gain some information about the character and intentions of her burglar. As a female English painter working in Napoleon's France, she had learned that mutual self-interest was always more reliable than friendship.

"Miss Frost." Lady Wilmot's face was concerned. "Are you ill? Your face has turned quite pale. The duke's brother is a physician, and quite a talented one. Would you like for me to send for him?"

Lena studied her ladyship's face. Horatio, who had been her friend when she was friendless, had abandoned her. But Lady Wilmot—who might be the enemy Horatio had warned her about—had offered her hope. Lena leaned in, hiding both her face and Lady Wilmot's from the men's view. "No, I'm well. If I can borrow some paper in the nursery, we can have our first lesson today."

"Yes." Lady Wilmot beamed, wrapping her arm in Lena's. "Let's surprise my sweet Lilly."

The nursery was four flights up, and Lady Wilmot chatted brightly about her children as they climbed. Lena listened with half interest.

Each flight put more distance between her and the burglar she now knew was associated with the duke. She was certain, or at least partially so, that her burglar had not seen her face before she turned away. Could she remain in the nursery until he had likely left? Or would it be better to face her fears and find a way to learn more about him, his intentions, and his character? Anxiety, more than the stairs, made her blood pulse hard.

The nursery itself was painted a warm terra-cotta, a color she'd seen often in Italy, and the walls were hung with drawing after drawing by an unformed but talented hand.

At the center table, two dark-haired children sat engrossed with a set of playing cards, supervised by a young man who resembled them. A cousin, perhaps?

Seeing Lady Wilmot, the young man joined them at the door to the nursery.

"Ah, Luca, you have returned!" Lady Wilmot embraced him. "Why didn't you come to me?"

"I brought the duke my report just an hour ago. But he is engaged with Lord Clive, and you were busy in the salon, so I came here with a new geography game I found in Portsmouth."

Lord Clive. Lena tucked away the name.

Lady Wilmot turned to Lena. "Miss Frost, may I introduce Luca Bruni, my ward."

The young man bowed graciously over her hand, his charm decidedly Italian. A young Casanova, perhaps, if she were to paint him.

The two children rose from their game and stood by Lady Wilmot's side.

"Miss Frost, my children: Ian Gardiner, Lord Wilmot, and Liliana Gardiner."

The young Lord Wilmot outstretched a solemn hand, already aware of his role and obligations.

"Darlings, Miss Frost is going to paint the salon ceiling. And she has agreed to give Lilly lessons."

"Lilly likes to draw landscapes. Those are of Italy." Ian pointed to a series hung on the wall. "That's Vesuvius."

"When I lived in Italy, I spent some weeks in the countryside near the volcano." Lena drew close to examine the image. Though the hand was untrained, the eye was good.

"These flowers in the foreground remind me of the coast."

Lilly, standing partly behind her brother, smiled broadly.

"Lilly and I were born in Italy. We returned to England after our father died." Though the boy spoke well, Lena could still see the touches of grief around his gray eyes.

"Your sister remembers the land of her birth well, Lord Wilmot." Lena smiled encouragingly at Lilly. "Miss Gardiner, this green here is perfect." The child turned shy, slipping her hand into her brother's.

"Speak up, Lilly," Ian prodded. "If you want lessons, you must speak to her."

"Hello, Miss Frost." The slightest lilt of an Italian accent softened Lilly's vowels. "Sophie said to draw better I must be a good pupil."

"Do you wish to be a good pupil?" Lena suddenly wished she had arranged to meet the child more privately, giving Lilly more space for confidence.

"I like to draw. But I grow frustrated when I can't draw as well as I would like." The girl's thick hair fell in rivulets around her face.

"We all grow frustrated. What matters is how you manage that frustration."

"I used to throw my pencil on the table, but then I broke my favorite one, and I stopped doing that."

"That's very wise," Lena said gently.

"Papa couldn't draw, but Sophie can. I would like to be like Sophie. She's very brave."

The child had called Lady Wilmot by her first name twice, while referring to her father as Papa. Lena noted the distinction, but let it go. She'd known French aristocratic families with far stranger arrangements.

"I still dream sometimes of Italy. My papa—our papa—would walk on that hill with us before he died." She pointed to a drawing close to the window. Lena moved to take a closer look, glancing into the carriage yard below. No carriage waited before the house. Had her Adonis—Lord Clive?—already gone? Surprised at her disappointment, she turned to Lilly's drawing. "Let's begin with this one. Tell me the parts that frustrated you."

Chapter Four

Clive spread out a hand-drawn map of London on the table, using two candlesticks, a nearby book, and an apple to weigh down the corners. "I was hoping you might see something I've overlooked. I've put boxes around the surgery schools and circled the cemeteries and church-yards. The hash marks represent the numbers of bodies reported stolen." Clive pointed to examples of each notation.

"I had no idea there were so many." The Duke of Forster leaned forward, examining Clive's marks.

"Cemeteries, schools, or stolen bodies?" Adam Mont-clair looked on as well, his face inscrutable.

"Each, I suppose. It would seem so easy: cemeteries don't have enough space, and doctors don't have enough bodies to practice on. But no one wants grandmother disinterred to solve the problem." The duke tapped his finger on Clive's map. "You say that the last body was found near the Royal College of Surgeons?"

Clive nodded, then set a sketch of the woman's face before his brother. "She was likely an actress; she still had paint on her hands and face as if she'd walked off the stage and into the hands of her killers."

"The Royal College is near both Drury Lane and Covent Garden," Montclair added.

The duke studied the sketch intently. "You are certain she was murdered?"

"The hand prints were still visible around her neck."

"Talk to Ledbetter, the doorman at the Drury Lane. If she was an actress, he'll know." The duke placed the drawing back on the pile. "Sophia and I are going to the theater on Thursday. If you wish to join us, you can interrogate the doorman at intermission."

"I don't interrogate," Clive corrected. "I merely ask questions."

Montclair stifled a laugh, but Clive ignored him. With attention, he'd grown adept at reading the subtleties of social engagement among the ton. But it was wearing to pay such careful attention to every nuance and personality, except somehow when he was in pursuit of an answer—whether in his laboratory or his investigations. He straightened the papers before placing them in his valise. "When Montclair and I arrived, Sophia was speaking with a woman. Do you know who she is or an address where I might find her?"

The door at the end of the hall opened, and Lady Wilmot approached them. Forster waited to answer until she came into earshot. "I can't help you, Clive. I simply carry Lady Wilmot's reticule when needed." He winked at his fiancée.

Sophia batted Forster's arm. "My reticule, is it? I will remember that."

"Sophie, who was that woman with you before?" Clive added quickly, before his brother could continue his jest.

"Frost. Miss Lena Frost of Calder and Company."

"She's an artist?" Clive felt the tip of his tongue sour.

Somehow she'd deceived him. He'd have to set aside his attraction and be more attentive at their next meeting.

"Yes, and a talented one. She just finished her first drawing lesson with Lilly. I invited her to stay for dinner, but she had other obligations." Sophia studied his face carefully. "What is your interest, Clive? You rarely notice the women who visit me, unless of course you believe they have some deadly illness."

"Lady Pelart *did* die," Clive objected.

"Yes, but did you have to tell her she had only months to live *over soup*?"

He shook his head. "Even I know better than that. No, I sent her a note, asking her to meet me at midnight in the summer house. I simply didn't anticipate she would expect a different sort of conversation."

"Ah, let's see . . . The very eligible son of a duke invites a recent widow to meet him at the witching hour for a private assignation." Montclair held out his pocket watch to show Clive the time. "What else would she expect?"

"I was younger then. I wouldn't make the same mistake today." Clive attempted to shift the conversation back to more solid ground. "Besides, Miss Frost appears to be in perfect health."

"I'm glad to hear that. But as Miss Frost has accepted my patronage, she is off-limits for seduction." Sophia stared hard into his eyes.

"Seduction?" Clive made sure not to look away. If Miss Frost were not a criminal and were willing, he saw no obstacle to a mutual liaison. But that was no business of Sophia's.

"Don't sound so innocent. I know that look in your eye. It's the avaricious one you and your brothers get when they are pursuing some desired object . . . or woman."

"My interest in Miss Frost is purely professional." He was surprised at how easily the lie slid off his tongue.

"Excellent," Lady Wilmot said. "Make sure it remains that way—and arrange no assignations in my summer house."

Chapter Five

After making her good-byes to Lady Wilmot, Lena hurried as quickly as was seemly down the porch steps to the street. She paused at the gate, looking back at the duke's imposing home.

Had the duke's incorrigible burglar seen her?

If he had, there was no advantage to running. He had only to ask Lady Wilmot who she was, and the answer would lead him back to the Rotunda. But she didn't have to wait for him to find her. For the moment she had the advantage; she knew who he was—or at least who his relatives were—and he might not yet know any more about her. And she wanted—no, needed—to know more about him.

She looked for a place to observe the duke's property without being seen. She found it across the street in the park, where a large equestrian statue allowed her to observe the front of the duke's house without being noticed.

Taking the paper on which she had made some preliminary sketches of Lilly, Lena seated herself comfortably and began to draw. A long time later, when her stomach was about to send her back to Constance's for bread and cheese, the door to the duke's house opened. Carrying a valise and with a book tucked under his arm, her burglar stepped onto the porch accompanied by a man in dark clothing. His companion pointed at his pocket watch, and her Adonis nodded in agreement. The men shook hands before parting.

Again Lena noticed how well his frame fit his clothes, the way that his waistcoat hugged his abdomen and his breeches revealed the shape of his legs. She doubted that pads were responsible for the appealing curve of his calves or thighs. In the office, she hadn't allowed herself to examine him fully. But this time, unnoticed and un-known, she allowed herself the pleasure of watching him. His body was lean; his movements were economical, no motion any larger than it needed to be. But under that facade of economy and reason, she had seen hints of a man of passion. He descended the steps quickly, but with an easy grace, suggesting a strength and power ready to be unleashed. Like a mountain lynx or brown bear—other things she wished to paint or sculpt—he was likely best observed from a safe distance.

At the bottom of the porch steps, he stopped, opened the book, and began to read as he walked. Curious. She would not have pegged him as a bookish man. The duke had indicated that his family residence was in Grosvenor Square, but Lord Clive Somerville (if that's who he was) turned east. Rising, she folded her paper into a small packet and put it back into her reticule; she stuck the stub of pencil behind her ear, hidden under the edge of her bonnet. She stepped back, letting the statue hide her, then when he had passed, she stepped out of the park some distance behind him.

He was easy to follow; his head rose above those of

most of the men on the street. She kept him in view, letting a half dozen other pedestrians walk between them. But eventually she gave up even that pretense. His nose in the book, he was completely unaware of her. Surprisingly, the pedestrians parted for him, as if familiar with his pattern.

At Lincoln's Inn Fields, he cut across the fields, heading, she thought, toward Sir John Soane's Museum. But he soon turned south toward a Greco-Roman style building whose broad portico was held up by six large Corinthian columns. He took the stairs two at a time and disappeared inside.

She waited in the crowded fields, with flower girls, orange merchants, and boys holding advertising boards all peddling their wares around her. Eventually, she drew close enough to read the building's name: Royal College of Surgeons of London.

A doctor? So her burglar *was* the duke's brother. She shook her head, puzzled. What would a doctor have to do with Horatio?

She patted her pocket, feeling the firm paper of Horatio's letter through her skirt. Then she waited again, except this time, he never came out. At dusk, she made her way to Constance's, certain she would see Lord Clive Somerville again, and this time, she would be prepared.

Clive approached the table where his friends had gathered. Roland Langdon and James Battenskill, also younger sons of the aristocracy, had been his friends since boyhood. The three had pursued careers in medicine, rather than in law or the church, after hearing John Hunter lecture on anatomy. During their medical studies, the three had enlarged their circle to include Arthur Carlin and

Robert Garfleet, both sons of wealthy merchants, and John Stillman, reputedly the bastard son of a famous member of Parliament.

"You're late," Garfleet chided. He filled his glass of claret, holding the bottle at its base, a trick he'd learned selling wine in his father's warehouse. "You've missed Carlin's objections to some art dealer selling Old Masters taken from the collections of continental nobility."

"Late or absent, that's Somerville." Langdon, his cravat tied in one of his valet's more elaborate configurations, leaned forward to take Garfleet's bottle by the neck and pour himself a splash. "Good thing that cadavers don't watch the clock."

"Good thing Montclair always manages to find him." Carlin opened the cover on his pocket watch and read the time. "Somerville's great-aunt Agatha has probably told him all about this dealer already. Unlike her friends, she declined to purchase any of his stock."

"I predict that Somerville has no idea where his great-aunt goes or even who her friends are." Garfleet shifted his chair over to make room for Clive. "The exception would be if one of his great-aunt's friends ends up on his table, then he will insist on knowing everything about them."

"Here. Here. And when he misses our weekly dinner, his excuse will be that he's been about some very important business." Battenskill, famous for his ability to charm investments and patients, pushed a platter of bread and cheese toward the empty space Garfleet had created. "But he won't tell us a thing about it."

"If Carlin has Aunt Agatha's agreement, then he is almost certainly right." Clive pulled up a chair to sit between Garfleet and Stillman. "Have you saved me a glass?"

"Against our better judgment." Carlin tucked his watch

into his waistcoat pocket and pointed at the mantel where a single clean glass waited. "Langdon's feeling flush, so he set one aside for you there."

Garfleet poured Clive the last of the wine. "Battenskill's promised his sister we will arrive sober, so he's limited us to two bottles."

"This year's matchmaking mamas are only bearable if one is half foxed," Langdon grumbled, rubbing his temples with one hand.

"Ah, the troubles of the monied classes." Stillman, the plainest dressed of them, held up his glass in a mock toast. "But one can hardly blame the families: so many men died in the wars."

"If my mother grows much more desperate to see my sisters 'settled,' I'll have to serve you lot up as sons-in-laws." Langdon shrugged. "And that includes you, Stillman: your income makes you a perfectly acceptable choice for one of the younger girls."

Stillman, true to his name, made no reaction.

"Well, if I must be married to one of Langdon's sisters," Garfleet took up the conversation, "I choose Jane."

"Why Jane? She hasn't paid you the slightest attention," Langdon asked.

"That's why I admire her." Garfleet tore off some of the bread. "She respects herself enough that she has no interest at all in me."

Clive found himself only half listening. He'd dressed for Lady Ainslee's ball with special care. Battenskill's sister had a particular fondness for inviting women of good family but reduced circumstances, and he'd hope he might see Calder's dark-eyed beauty there. Her walking dress—tasteful but a few years out of fashion—had suggested she fell in that category. But then he'd discovered that Miss Lena Frost was not a member of the distressed gentry or nobility, but a woman in trade. He rarely made such a misstep, and that made Miss Frost all the more interesting.

"Come, Somerville, give us some news." Stillman turned the conversation away from Langdon's sisters. "We haven't seen you at the surgery since last week."

"I've been about some business for the duke."

"Do any of us believe that?" Garfleet looked around the table.

Each man shook his head.

"Somerville never reveals his hand outside of his family." Carlin tipped his glass, drinking the last drop of wine off its brim. "We, his best friends, must wait until after the fact to learn the delicious details."

"I called on you immediately after the incident at the wharves," Clive interjected. He'd borne his friends' good-natured complaints more than once.

"That's true: when he doesn't want his family to know how badly he's injured, he trusts us more than any other surgeons in London," Battenskill added.

"Or outside it," Clive added, grateful to turn the conversation.

"You've never been stabbed outside London." Carlin pushed back from the table.

"That we know of." Garfleet shook his head dramatically. "He might well have a band of surgeons in every region of the land, waiting for him to need shelter, succor, and secrecy."

"If I were stabbed outside London," Clive interjected, "I would refuse all help until you lot arrived to save me."

"Excellent choice." Battenskill laughed. "I've investigated the quality of medical services in the provinces, and it's not encouraging."

"I defend Somerville on this." Stillman leaned in

confidentially. "Whatever his *other* faults, he's never refused me—or any of us—help. Not even when I was in Cornwall, and he had to travel all night in a stolen carriage."

"I did not steal the carriage; I merely borrowed it," Clive corrected. Typically his friends would tease for a few moments, then move on to more interesting topics. One had only to wait out the conversation.

"Well, he's refused me help." Garfleet grimaced, and the group looked surprised. "At Lady Ainslee's *last* ball, the Rirkenby heiress pursued me quite relentlessly, and, despite my every signal, Somerville took up a spot on the balcony and watched."

"It was the best theater I've seen in months," Clive quipped, but made a mental note that in future he should interpret Garfleet's odd hand gestures as a plea for help.

"Ah, it's time." Battenskill rose, and the men followed his lead. "But I must warn Somerville and Stillman that my great-aunt will be in attendance . . . with her companion."

Both men groaned.

"Is that the one she described as "a woman without the luxury to scruple over the character of any suitor of suitable means or good family?" Carlin mimicked Battenskill's great-aunt perfectly.

Battenskill nodded.

Stillman finished his wine. "It's always instructive to see which wallflowers will dance with me, but not with Somerville—or with Somerville, but not with me."

"Do any dance with *both* of you?" Battenskill raised an eyebrow to see if Clive was disturbed by the direction of the conversation.

Clive shrugged genially. Carlin and the other men knew his character better than his own family, and if they wished to tease him for sins, real or imagined, he wouldn't object.

"Predicting it is a bit complicated, but I will give you this much: desperate women dance with me, and a woman with secrets is always attracted to Somerville." Stillman rose, and the other men followed his lead.

Chapter Six

The next morning was cold and rainy. Clive rose early, but his "early"—after a long evening at Lady Ainslee's—began later than the rest of the city's. He'd spent the evening dancing with those who would dance with him, mostly spinsters considered to have no other prospects. But while his feet were performing the steps of each dance, his mind was replaying his interaction with the clever Miss Frost. In one country dance, he'd even imagined Miss Frost was his partner and balked visibly when the gregarious Miss Alcorn reached out for his arm. His friends had quickly intervened. Stillman and Carlin had ushered him out of the hall, while the smooth-tongued Battenskill claimed Clive had fallen prey to a fever. And it was a fever . . . of sorts: Frost had such alluring dark eyes.

Clive dressed quickly, wearing, as he had the day before, clothes that marked him as a middling clerk or ordinary tradesman. He intended to arrange another meeting with Calder, but if Calder were not available, perhaps he could match wits again with the clever Miss Frost.

He arrived at the Rotunda to find a long line of customers, umbrellas in hand, waiting to buy advance tickets.

The secrecy surrounding the exhibition had pushed public interest into a near fever pitch. One had to admire Calder's ability to garner so much interest in the exhibition of a painting—albeit a very large one. It was rumored that the craftsmen worked only on portions of the panorama at a time and that only Calder himself knew what the whole painting depicted.

Clive made his way down the narrow alley to the Rotunda offices, ignoring the glares of those in line. The passage dead-ended at a ticket window and door to the upper offices. Clive had hoped to reach the upper offices before anyone could object, but the door was locked tight.

"No one goes upstairs today," a wizened old woman at the ticket window called out. "Calder says."

"Calder's here?" He felt pleased. Finishing his business with Calder would put him one step closer to a private conversation with Miss Frost, perhaps one leading to dinner.

The ticket taker shrugged. "May be, may not be. I sell tickets and keep that door locked." She exchanged two pence for four tickets. The two daughters—clearly from the country—smiled and tittered when Clive looked at them, but the mother bustled them away.

"What if I have business with Calder?"

"Those who have *business* with Calder know to go round back." The woman looked him over. "*You* don't have business."

Clive started to mention that she hadn't done a very good job of keeping the door locked yesterday, but he decided against it.

A heavyset man dropped his ha'pence on the counter, positioning his body to break Clive's conversation with the ticket seller. "One ticket, and make it quick."

Clive surveyed the area, looking for another window on the street level, but he found none. Behind the ticket offices, he could see the Rotunda itself, filling the space behind the street-facing buildings that would otherwise have been the backyards or mews. If there was another entrance to the Rotunda, he would find it.

He returned to the street and turned right, examining the buildings facing the street, and searching for a way behind them. Nothing in the first set of shops. He turned right again at the next corner. There, halfway down where the small shops became smaller dwellings, Clive found a narrow alley, leading to the inside of the block and the Rotunda yard. Across the yard, standing at the back entrance, a severe-looking guard examined each workman's invoices.

Keeping out of the view of the guard, he waited for an opportunity to enter the building. He didn't have to wait long. The morning rain still puddled slick and treacherous on the cobblestones. Three workmen, shouldering a long roll of canvas, struggled not to fall.

"Ho, there, keep steady, Owen," the leader called out, when the man behind him lost his footing. The roll, dangerously off-balance, tilted toward Owen, alone on his side of the canvas.

"Whoa, Ben, grab it, grab it," the leader admonished fruitlessly. The roll listed to one side, then to the next.

Clive, taking advantage of his good luck, stepped behind Owen and lifted the roll to his shoulder. "There. I have it."

"We appreciate the help." The leader waited, while Owen shifted forward to bear the weight more evenly.

"I'm happy to be of service. Where are we going?"

"That door on the left," the leader directed. "Walk

steady. Not fast. We can't afford to bring the canvas in wet or damaged."

"Right you are there, John. Bring in damp canvas, and Frost will have your head," Ben, the older man behind John, jibed.

"That might not be such a bad fate." Owen chuckled in return, and Clive debated whether he should ignore the rude comment or knock the man flat.

"Left, now, steady," John directed. "Come around right. Slow. Stop, men." John retrieved a slip of paper from his pocket. The guard read it, then inspected the four men and the canvas. He stood beside Clive for an especially long time, and Clive kept his face turned into the canvas.

"He's with us," John interjected. "Besides, Harald, it's going to rain. You know Frost don't want damp canvas."

The guard waved them into the Rotunda's dark interior.

"Step easy, boys. Let your eyes adjust." The leader led them forward slowly. "Remember: the exhibition stage juts out from one wall and ends about fifteen feet from the painting at the front and sides. We'll be walking underneath the stage. It's packed pretty tight with supplies and stage sets, but there's a path between the supports. I'll lead you straight, so don't step out of line."

Clive followed the other men carefully, avoiding the sturdy beams that held up the observation stage. Above them, the stage floor echoed with the workmen's heavy footsteps. Clive listened for the sound of bowing wood. If the stage collapsed under the weight of the visitors, the injuries would be severe, even deadly. The stage, though, only creaked in one or two places. Sturdily built then. At least Calder's panorama considered safety as well as profit.

Keeping his paces even, Clive counted off the distance

from the door to the opposite side of the room where the stage above them ended.

"Leave it here, men, in the wagon bed."

The men heaved the canvas roll on top of other soft goods. The other men turned back to the entrance, but Clive stepped out of sight behind a tall pile of boxes, waiting and watching.

In between the stage and the wall, ranks of scaffolding circled three-quarters of the way around the inside of the Rotunda. Through the lower ranks of scaffolding, he could see the very bottom of the painting—a fine depiction of dirt and grass—but nothing else. He needed to get onto the stage above him: that's where Calder would be, directing the workmen.

He skirted the stage's edge, looking for a way up. Eventually, where the stage attached to the wall, he found an open doorway and a staircase beyond it. Looking around quickly to see if he was observed, he hurried up the stairs onto the stage.

Standing in the shadow of the door, he took his bearings. Next to him was the large doorway through which the patrons would enter from the offices. Nearly straight in front was the panoramic painting itself, a three-story-height canvas, extending up to the ceiling of the Rotunda and down below the stage where he had just been. The scaffolding stood half-height tall, but a giant theater curtain hung in front of the canvas, hiding all but the painted sky from view. Where the canvas met the ceiling, a short curtain was in the process of being tacked to the ceiling around the skylights. Once in place it would hide the top edge of the panorama, obscuring where the sky ended and the painting began.

"Steady, men, steady." The voice called out from above

him. He looked up. There above the doorway entrance was another platform, its ladder a series of boards nailed into the wall. The voice was a woman's, low and full. It sounded like chocolate, thick and rich and warm. He couldn't see her face from his position, but he felt drawn to her, as if she were one of the ancient sirens, pulling men to them by their voices alone. He began to climb the wall ladder. No one stopped him, so intent were the men on their various tasks.

When he reached the top, Miss Frost was directing some men working on a scaffold to the immediate right of the entrance. Behind her, painted on the wall, was a grid filled with instructions and, tacked beside it, a set of very detailed plans for staging the middle ground, complete with coordinates for where each object should be set. Below the plans sat a stool and a low bench, and beside them a long cloak hung on a peg.

"Raise it slowly. Ben. Tom. That's it: you've got it off the floor." Using a series of pulleys, the men were raising a sturdy bar onto which was sewn a long section of painted canvas.

She reminded him of a conductor at the opera. Her arms directed the men's actions in precise, even economical motions, and her voice was strong. Her instructions, both specific and clear, suggested some degree of formal education. But beyond that, she was clearly a woman in her element, capable, even powerful. How could he have thought even for a moment that this woman—this interesting, intriguing woman—was breathless or dim? For an investigator who prided himself on careful observation, he needed to learn why he'd misjudged her so thoroughly.

"Pull it up evenly. Both ends at once," Frost called out, and the men pulling the rope followed her direction without question. The line of the rope led up to the pulley and from there to the top of the scaffold. There two men lay belly down waiting to affix the canvas panel. Suddenly it became clear. Once the canvas was in place, it would hide the scaffold as well as obscure the edges of the painting. She fell silent, watching the men inch the canvas up the height of the scaffold.

He stopped a suitable distance from her, then coughed to attract her attention. She remained fixed on the movement of her men. He coughed again, and her back stiffened, but she did not turn. Finally, he called out, "I'm looking for Calder."

"He's not available." Frost waved him away without turning, issuing another set of instructions to the crew to her right. "Steady, steady, men. Let the canvas unfurl slowly."

"I have pressing business with him," he repeated, hoping his insistence would move her.

"Then you are unlucky." She watched the men intently. "Jess, your end is too high."

"What about this, Miss Frost?" the workman responded.

"Almost there: lower it another hand span. That's it. You're level now."

"Where might I find Calder?" Clive stepped closer until he was almost to her side.

"Try the most disreputable tavern you know, then look at the bottom of a bottle." She didn't turn to face him. Her voice was flat, even unemotional.

"Isn't he the foreman of this crew?"

"Those who have *business* with Calder speak to me." With slight emphasis on that one word, she distinguished between his inquiries and the actual affairs of the Rotunda. .

And by refusing even to look his way, she'd given a slight that even Clive could not misinterpret. Though known for his patience, he wanted to provoke her, to force her attention.

"You?" He gave the word all the disbelief he could muster. "A woman?"

"Woman or man. If you need Calder, it's me you talk to." She refused the bait, never taking her attention off her men. "John, pull your end up. A little more on the right there. That's it. There."

He would *make* her look at him. She was clearly a competent woman, so he chose words that would offend his sister Judith, the most competent woman he knew. "Why does he leave you in charge here?"

"My. Good. Man." Her words were clipped and precise, but she turned to face him. "I'm more qualified than any man here, and they know it." As she looked him over, her expression changed from annoyance to recognition to something he couldn't quite identify. "Besides, I pay them. Any man will prefer a woman in charge if it means he goes home with his wages."

When she looked at him, he felt the same jolt of awareness he'd felt the day before—the awareness he'd puzzled over instead of paying attention to his dance partners. There was something luscious about her: thick hair plaited into braids barely concealed by her mob bonnet, wide eyes, her face set in belligerent lines.

He nodded acquiescence. "I wasn't suggesting that you aren't qualified—I was merely expecting Calder."

She raised one eyebrow, as if to tell him she saw through his game, then her expressive mouth turned under in annoyance. "What is it you want? I mean, other than to search our office." Her voice cold, she turned her face back to the men.

He decided truth was the only course. He stepped forward, pitching his voice confidentially. "I'm Clive Somerville, a surgeon, investigating a death for the police. Calder had some information for me." He looked over his shoulder, making sure that none of the workmen were listening.

"Ah, and you were to pay him for the information." She stared at him.

"Well, not exactly pay." Looking into her dark eyes, Clive felt the world had somehow tilted off its axis. He tried to focus solely on her words.

"But Horatio—Calder—would have expected something: if not money, then a favor." Lena paused, then continued, "Have you much experience with men like Horatio? Charming, glib men of many gifts, a good number of them illegal. Are you always so gullible?"

"I've never been called gullible." Clive paused, trying to get the conversation back on track. "Calder said he'd traced a murderer to London and a local tavern. Calder saw him here—at the Rotunda—twice last week."

"Last week." She sighed, but whether in frustration or sympathy he couldn't tell. "If it's a craftsman, that narrows your search to about fifty men, women, and children in the last week alone. But we also had deliveries from at least thirty companies, and some of those more than once. Our office looks down into the yard, so it might have been one of them. Or—and this is equally likely—it could have been one of the dozen sightseers Harald, our guard, turns away each day. Tell me, sir: what does this *murderer* look like?" She whispered the word as he had done. Her tone indicated clearly that she wanted nothing to do with him or his searches.

"Calder was to give me more of a description. All I know is that our murderer likes his drink."

"A distinguishing fact, that is." She all but rolled her eyes. "No, sir, I know nothing about murder or Horatio's information. If you are looking for a drinking man, I suggest visiting Mr. Whitbread's brewery." She turned away to consult the plans tacked to the wall.

He had been dismissed. But his curiosity wouldn't let him go. Her relationship with Calder made her his closest thing to a clue. But something else attracted him to her: the unruly wisps of her hair escaping her bonnet, the paint in splotches all over her skirt and apron, the straight set of her shoulders. It wasn't just the murderer. No, he wanted to know more of *her*.

As if noticing that he had not gone, she pointed to the plans. "Even if I wished to help you, I haven't time. Today, we must clear out all the scaffolds but these two." She motioned to the structures standing to either side. "Then tomorrow, we must convert the gutter—that's the space between the stage and the canvas—into the foreground of a battle scene . . . carrion birds and blasted bodies alike. As you suggested when we met before, this will not be a painting for the faint of heart."

"I must give you credit. Not many people fool me, but you did. I sincerely believed you were dim."

This time her smile was genuine. "Not much use to the police then, are you, if a simple *woman* can deceive you so easily?"

He almost objected that he was rarely deceived by women. But he didn't want to quarrel, not if it meant risking that brilliant smile.

"I have a feeling that nothing is simple where you are concerned." He motioned toward the theater curtain hung over the canvas. "Why all the secrecy?"

"Whatever Horatio's other sins, he is a brilliant showman. Make it a game. Make it secret. Make people stand in line to see it." She turned her attention back to the workmen. "No, Joe, move it a little to the left."

"Tell me something about yourself, Miss Frost. It is *Miss*, isn't it? You haven't made up a husband to use *Mrs.*, have you?"

"Perhaps I had a husband, but I had him killed to steal his money." She turned back to him, her eyes inscrutable, but even so, he felt drawn to her.

"Perhaps." He offered his most winning smile. "You strike me now as a very capable woman."

"Now?" She tucked a wisp of escaped hair behind her ear. "Ah, yes, as opposed to *yesterday* when you thought I was a dim-witted enthusiast."

"I've admitted you fooled me." He held out his hands, palms up like a penitent. "But that only makes you more interesting."

"I have no desire to be interesting." She looked directly into his eyes, as if to warn him off. "In fact, I'd prefer you find some other pursuit, perhaps a horse race, or a boxing match. Surely you find those sorts of sports entertaining."

"Ah, Miss Frost, you crush me." He put his hand over his heart and gave her his sincerest look, the one that always put him in good stead with his companions.

"I doubt that," she said flatly, and her eyes moved back to her crew.

He looked around the exhibition hall, knowing that soon she would call one or more of her very sturdy crew and have him removed from the premises. Her premises, her exhibition. Suddenly he knew what would make her talk to him. "Why all the scaffolding?"

"The scaffolds are constructed to serve as our horizontal lines, and the plumbs you see every five feet are our verticals. It's how we get the perspective right, even with a concave surface."

"Concave? How does it work? The panorama, I mean. How do you make it . . . stay up?"

"If I answer your questions, will you *go away*?"

"I'm more likely to go if you answer, than if you don't."

She sighed in a sort of defeat. "There's a segmented pipe shaped into a semicircle running along the top and the bottom. The canvas is sewn on to the top first, then the bottom."

"I can't see any sign of sewing."

"I hired ship riggers. For fine sturdy stitching in tarpaulins or canvas, there's none better."

"Then what?"

"To give the canvas tension, we weight the bottom with stacks of bricks every few feet. But because the shape is a semicircle, the pull makes the canvas concave. So we have to account for that in the design of the image, and we have to hide the edges on the sides here. That's why we're covering these two scaffolds with painted panels. Does that explain it?"

"Yes. Tell me—how do you know Calder?"

She sniffed in derision. "I placed an advertisement in the London *Times*. 'Wanted: journeyman painter, who perfectly understands his craft and whose character will bear the strictest enquiry.' Clearly I failed to enquire strictly enough."

"You placed an advertisement? I thought Calder was in charge."

"I am here. Calder is not. Which of us looks to be in charge?"

"When was the last time you saw him?"

"Wednesday." She looked distressed for a moment. "He was planning to go to Tattersall's, and he needed to make a withdrawal from his account."

"Who holds his account, a banker, a solicitor?"

"I do. I kept—keep—all our funds in the office. Calder spends his portion on credit, then criticizes me for not doing a better job of keeping him from his money."

"He sounds like a difficult master."

"Another master might insist on being in charge. So I keep him . . . for now. This show"—she gestured at the walls—"will make the name of the company and me with it."

"You seem to have great confidence."

"I know my audience. The public loves a spectacle; the ton loves a success. All I need is one of the two." She turned back to the workmen. "Wait, Hedley, don't tie that off. The hills in your section should line up with the hills on the canvas. I made a mark on the wall to your right. Give me a moment, and I'll tell you how much it needs to lower." In an instant, she was climbing another wall ladder, this one leading from her observation platform all the way to the ceiling.

Clive's mouth grew dry at the height, wondering how often each day she climbed that ladder. Miss Frost's skirt divided to reveal wide-bottomed pants cuffed at the ankles like those Clive had seen in engravings of Turkish women's costume, the only difference being that instead of slippers, Frost wore low-heeled leather boots. She climbed almost to the top, then stopped, using her new position to gauge how well the panel corresponded to her mark.

She hung there for several minutes fifteen feet above him, one arm holding on to the next rung up, her toes tucked into the space between the slats and the walls. He wanted to call out for her to be careful, but he knew the advice would be unwelcome.

"Raise your end a bit more, Hedley." She pointed with her free hand. "Another hand span. Just a bit more. Perfect. Tie that up."

The sounds came to him all at once. The nails creaked as they pulled from the wall, and the wood slats snapped as they broke under her weight. Frost scrabbled to find new footing, but gasped—along with her men—as she fell off the ladder down to the stage. Somewhere in the midst of those sounds, Clive moved. He positioned himself as best he could below her. She twisted as she fell, like a cat trying to find her feet. She angled past him, and he threw himself into her path, catching her and turning a deadfall into a rolling jumble of limbs. All the while, he held her in his arms, never letting go. Afterward, they lay on the platform, knocked breathless by the fall and by fear.

He could hear his heart beat and, where he still clutched her to his chest, hers. But when she raised her head and looked directly into his eyes, the deep color flecked with green, gold, and bronze, he thought his heart had stopped altogether. She didn't speak, and neither did he. They merely looked into each other's eyes. In her pupils, he saw his own reflection. Had she stolen his soul? Was it looking back at him?

Eventually, his heart found a more stable rhythm. She opened her mouth as if to speak, but instead moistened her lips—pink and full—with the tip of her tongue. He breathed in her scent, lilac water with a hint of paint. Irrationally, he wanted never to let her go.

The world came back into focus in an instant. Her men, climbing over the platform and up the ladder, arrived in a rush of sound. Suddenly Lena was gone, picked up off his chest by her men, and he was left lying on his back, looking up at a circle of concerned faces. He closed his eyes, testing his body for anything broken or strained. He would ache tomorrow, his muscles stretched and jarred by the fall to the floor and Miss Frost's weight. But it would be no worse than his aches after any dozen sports he'd played with his brothers. The workmen began to talk about him as if he were deaf or dead.

"Anyone know who he is?"

"I've never seen him before, but he saved Miss Lena."

"It's a miracle, it is. She never lets anyone up here when she's directing."

Clive opened his eyes and sat up. The men immediately patted the dust from his clothes and asked him to move his arms and legs. One man handed him a wooden cup, and he drank, the gin burning a line to his belly.

"Give the man some room. He might need some air."

Clive started to say something, but decided against it. He struggled to his feet.

Lena was sitting on a stool. The men were flanked around her, close but not crowding her. One placed a comforting hand on her back and said something in her ear; Lena responded, both of them watching him approach. Their solicitude surprised him, but he couldn't consider it now, not when he felt like he'd been run over by a horse at Tattersall's. The crew stepped back as he drew near.

* * *

In the second before the rung broke, Lena had been considering how to send Lord Clive Somerville away without losing Lady Wilmot's or the duke's goodwill. She'd used all of Lady Wilmot's advance to pay her craftsmen for another week, and she couldn't give it back. Clive was the kind of man—she could already tell—who didn't let go of an obsession easily, and she had no intention of attracting his further interest.

But that was before the slat had broken.

She'd flailed desperately to find another foothold, but the wood wouldn't hold. And as she fell, she knew she was already dead, if not from the fall, then from her injuries.

The seconds had drawn out forever. All her losses, all her regrets, had played across the stage of her memory, including one regret that she hadn't yet recognized. At the end of her memories, she saw only one image, the face of her burglar-Adonis.

Then he caught her.

She'd opened her eyes—still alive—to find his studying her. She breathed in his scent, a woody, clean, comforting scent with pine and a hint of musk.

In that moment, she'd imagined she could see into his very soul. She'd wanted that moment, when their eyes met, to last forever, but the world had returned to its normal speed. As her men lifted her up, she'd felt bereft, of him and the unexpected kindness in his eyes, as if she'd finally found a safe place, and it had been denied her. The vulnerability of that moment shocked and disturbed her, making her ill at ease and suspicious.

She was obligated to him now, though strangely, the thought wasn't wholly unpleasant.

"A good man puts himself in danger to help another." Louis remarked from behind her shoulder.

"You sound like Horatio."

"Horatio is at heart a good man, but he is thwarted sometimes by circumstances."

"Are you saying I should trust Somerville because he caught me?"

"I'm saying that you are alive and unhurt because he didn't hesitate. He didn't measure one action against another. He merely acted." Louis patted her shoulder as Somerville pulled himself to his feet and approached.

He knelt in front of her. "I'm a physician," he announced to the men, giving his attention to Lena. "Are you hurt?"

"I feel like an elephant dropped me on my head."

"An elephant?"

"I rode one once when I was a child."

"Did he drop you on your head?"

"No. But if he had, this is how it would feel."

The men laughed. "That's our Miss Frost, always a clever one."

"Stretch out your arms." She complied, but only because her men were watching. Clive tested the movement of her wrists and elbows, then turned her palms up.

He grimaced. The skin on her palms was badly torn and raw, and her fingernails were jagged and broken. "A pumice stone will even your nails, and some calendula salve will help with these abrasions." Then, taking care to acknowledge her authority, he asked, "There's an apothecary down the street. Can one of your men gather some materials for me?"

She nodded and called to one of the workmen, giving his name—Louis—with a French inflection. An older man, gray-haired and lean, listened carefully as Clive gave him instructions on what to purchase. When Clive pressed a half-crown into his hand, Louis hurried away.

"Let's see to the rest of you." Stepping behind her, he placed his hand on her upper back and thumped it with his first two fingers. The remaining men looked confused.

"Whatever are you doing?" Lena's voice was returning to its normal state of annoyance.

"It's called percussion." Clive thumped again.

"I'm not a drum."

"Yes, but your chest is." He tapped his hand one last time, listening to the sound her chest made. As a doctor, he should be paying attention only to her heart, but his attention kept drifting to the rise and fall of her bosom, and the pinkness of her lips. "It's a technique from Vienna for diagnosing ailments of the chest. Sometimes a fall can injure the lungs, so I wanted to listen. Can you stand?"

Lena rose, stepping a little gingerly, then more solidly.

"Does that ankle hurt?"

"A little, but not so much that I can't stand."

"Can you walk on it? Try from here to the front edge of the platform." Clive stepped back. When he leaned against the wall next to the Rotunda plans, looking every bit a Greek god, Lena forced herself to look away.

She surveyed the concerned faces of her men, then stepped forward decisively, to prove to them that both ankles were fine. Her right ankle pinched when she stepped on it, but not so much that she needed to limp to protect it. She made it to the edge and back without incident.

Clive studied her intently as she moved, watching— she knew—for the slightest sign of pain. Soon, she would have to send him away. He was too observant to keep close for long. Still, if he were successful in finding Horatio, he might solve all her problems.

When she walked back to the group, her crew exhaled in relief and began to disperse back to their work.

Soon Lena and Clive were left alone on the platform.

"Now for your hands." Clive gestured for her to sit on the low stool, but she tucked her palms against her belly, regarding him suspiciously.

Before she could object, Louis returned with a packet from the apothecary and a bottle of gin.

"Let him help you, Miss Lena. He's already saved your life," Louis insisted.

Lena shrugged acceptance and sat down on the stool.

Clive pulled the low bench forward. Beside him, he set the gin and the apothecary's packet, which contained calendula salve, willow bark, a roll of linen, a pumice stone, and a needle. He gave her some willow bark to chew.

She unfolded her hands slowly and held them out. Her fingers were long and slender. Her skin was soft in his hand, making him wish that he was holding her hand under more private circumstances.

He wet some linen with the gin and soaked her skin, then carefully he teased out each splinter with the needle. "It wouldn't do to leave a splinter to fester." Helping the stubborn Miss Frost captivated him. Even when her men had rallied around her, she had seemed unaware of the depth of their support and affection. It was as if she had lived a long time without a community—or a community whose care she could count on.

When he'd removed all the splinters, he eased the calendula salve onto her broken skin, then he picked up the roll of linen to cover her wounds.

"Must you bandage my hands? I have too much yet to accomplish today." Her dark eyes met his, pleading her case, and he found himself unable to refuse.

"The salve needs several hours to work. But if I wrap

the linen thus"—he began at her palm, then tied off the bandages at her wrist—"you still will have good use of your fingers and hands."

She flexed her fingers, testing the bandage's limits. After several second of silence, she spoke.

"I should apologize for my rudeness before." She glanced at the broken ladder. "I haven't seen Horatio for days. I'd intended to search for him later, after we finished today's work. But if you wish, I could show you the way to Horatio's boardinghouse." She paused, clearly unwilling to leave before the work was done.

"I can wait here until your work is done."

"Are you certain? It will be some time."

"I am even willing to help."

She smiled, a wan smile laced with disbelief and a hint of suspicion. But, taking him at his word, she moved to complete her day's business. She even allowed Clive to remain on the platform with her.

Clive watched Lena direct the men. Though he couldn't be certain, the men seemed to be working especially hard to finish early. When she moved to the front of the platform, Clive inspected the broken ladder. Though his muscles ached with every pull of his weight, he kept climbing, noting the condition of each slat before he shifted his weight to it. At six feet up, the nails appeared to be loose, growing looser the higher he climbed. Standing eye level to the slat that had collapsed under Lena's weight, he noticed sharp cuts on the bottom edges of the wood. As far up as he could see, each board was damaged, with the greatest damage in the highest levels. He pulled on the next slat, and it cracked under the pressure, the nails releasing easily from the wall. Someone had been intended to fall from a great height and be badly injured. But was that someone Miss Frost or Calder?

He looked down. Lena was standing in the same spot, favoring one ankle. She had lied when she said she wasn't hurt. He climbed down to take her a stool.

When he reached the bottom of the ladder, however, Louis stepped to his side, speaking low. "Billy checks the slats every week, and he says they were well nailed and solid just this past Tuesday."

"The rungs near the top are sawn near through," Clive answered, but added, "Is there a reason he checks every week?"

"For months now, we've been plagued with little accidents. Tools and supplies going missing. The worst was like today: part of a scaffold floor broke when one of us stepped on it. Luckily Ted's a big man and got stuck in the hole without going all the way through. Since then we've been looking before we step, and checking the rigging before we trust a rope. We wondered if it was one of the temporary craftsmen Miss Lena brings in to do a specific job. One crew in particular disappeared before their work was done, and the trouble stopped around the same time. We've kept most of this from Miss Lena. She's worked too hard to see the exhibition fail so close to the opening."

"Can you think of who might have wanted to harm the exhibition, Miss Frost, or Mr. Calder?"

"Not a man here would hurt Miss Lena. She works as hard as any of us, willing to climb the scaffold or sew a canvas or even skin a rabbit when we need the glue. We've even kept the topic of the painting secret, though we've all had ample opportunity and plenty of incentive to tell."

"Incentive?"

"Ah, yes, we've all been approached by young toffs wanting to win some bet in a book and willing to pay for the privilege. But we send them away with no answer, and if they won't accept that, we give them a wrong one."

Louis looked up the ladder. "The door by the ticket office was unlocked this morning when we arrived, and the main entrance door as well. We speculated that Calder forgot to lock them when he left, but perhaps someone else was in the Rotunda instead."

"Does Calder often work alone in the Rotunda?"

"He used to be here every night, painting his part into the wee hours, but not recently."

"His part?"

"He has a memory for faces, and he spends the day collecting them. He likes nothing better than to go to some club or gambling hell and memorize the lines of every face in the place. Then he would come here and paint through the night."

Clive wondered if Calder's talent for remembering faces had put him in the path of a murderer. If he only knew which clubs Calder haunted, he might be able to find the murderer without the showman's help.

"Is there any particular place Calder likes to go best?"

"Some tavern near the wharf. He says the faces are raw there, from the weather and the weight of the work."

"Do you know which of the wharves?"

"No, but if I think of something specific, I'll let you know," Louis promised. "But we're grateful you were here. We know what a fall like that could do—Miss Lena knows too, though she'll never admit it. And it's time Miss Lena had a champion." Louis patted Clive on the shoulder. "If you need anything, anytime, you let one of us know. We take care of our own."

Lena called out for Louis to retrieve some goods from under the platform, and the man met her at the ladder, taking the steps down first to ensure each one was safe.

Clive watched her, admiring her strength and determination. Few women in the ton, having sustained such a shock as the fall, would have pulled themselves together so quickly. He watched her move, and even favoring her ankle, she was lithe and graceful. When she returned to the platform, he turned his attention to the long curtain that obscured the painting, wondering what secrets might be revealed when the curtain rose.

Chapter Seven

A few hours later, Lena stood before her plans, checking off items on the giant schedule she'd painted on the wall.

For most of the morning, Clive had worked silently beside her. Typically she allowed no one to remain on the platform with her, needing to concentrate while she coordinated the movements of the various crews. It was like a great dance, and she was its conductor. Clive, surprisingly, seemed content with saying little, and she found his silence easy, even reassuring.

But at midmorning, he'd broken their silence. "I'd like to repair your ladder. I might not be here to catch you next time a slat lets go." She'd looked up to find him, cravat loose, shirt untucked, carrying an armload of slats, a hammer, and a bucket of nails. She'd forced herself not to stare: his clothes in disarray revealed even more the strength of his shoulders, the lean muscle of his chest and belly.

Though she would have normally objected—she could manage her own affairs—she'd nodded agreement. He had been too affable, too good-natured, to refuse, and she was not altogether certain that the broken ladder was an accident.

At the same time, she found herself distracted by Clive, high on the wall, repairing her ladder. Surrounded every day by strong men, she rarely noticed anymore how their bodies looked as they worked. But she found herself stealing glances at Clive. His arm arched powerfully as he set nail after nail, revealing the strength of his torso. And with each glance, she chose a different way to sketch him: Odysseus tied to the mast, listening to the sirens without wrecking his ship; Hercules, diverting the rivers to clean Augeus's stables; Hermes, the god of cunning and mischief, carrying the messages of the gods. She'd worked her way through all the classical heroes, until she cast Clive as Poseidon, trident in hand, raising a storm. Of all the gods, she'd always liked Poseidon best.

Unwillingly, she pulled her attention away from her handsome rescuer and studied the sky through the high windows. Winter days were short, and typically her crews worked long after darkness fell. But it was still light. If she let the crew go for the day, she and Clive would have several hours to search for Horatio. She sighed. So much still to do, and her time dwindling every day.

"You can mark those off as well." From behind her shoulder, Louis indicated several items on the next day's list.

She stared in wonder and gratitude. "How?"

"We want you to rest in the morning. Until you arrive, we can clear out beneath the platform and build the sets."

"Thank you—to you and all the crew. I promise to move slowly coming in." She placed her hand on Louis's forearm. "The crew has done so much—tell them to go home while there's still daylight to enjoy."

The old man patted the hand she'd placed on his arm. "I'll let them know."

Clive joined Lena at the grid, as Louis left. "Are we ready to hunt down Calder?" His voice was like rich cream. She wished he might be—like Louis—the sort of man she could rely on, but it did no good to wish for something she couldn't have.

"Yes." Lena removed her heavy hooded cloak from the peg, and Clive caught the edge, holding it up for her, smiling.

"Allow me, my lady. I am at your service."

His words felt like soft fur. It would be too easy to curl up in them and find warmth and solace there. But she knew better. Just as she knew it was best to draw the lines between them clearly, especially after her accident.

"I put on my coat without assistance every day." She kept her tone mild, but it was still a rebuke. "And I am no one's lady. I am simply Frost—as you would designate any of your servants or your merchants."

"Or my friends." If anything, Clive's smile only deepened. "As for your capability, few men could lead this crew with greater skill."

Lena knew she should accept the statement as a compliment, but the pull to trust him was too great. She let her tone shift into derision. "Only men?"

"My sister is more capable than any man I know, including the duke. I learned early never to discount a woman." Clive continued to hold her coat out.

She looked up at the sunlight. There wasn't time for dispute. Conceding, she held out her arms, allowing Clive to settle the coat around her. His hands brushed her neck, turning her collar down, and she felt a thrill at his casual touch. She shook off the sensation, but it warmed her more than the coat.

Clive added, "Besides, when I was young, I had a snapping turtle as a pet."

"Whatever does that mean?" Lena tucked her hands deep in the fur-lined pockets, grateful that she didn't need to pull gloves over her abraded palms.

"Sometimes a sharp bite is the best protection."

Lena started to object, then decided not to. She'd gained some distance between them, even if she would have preferred the luxury of keeping him close.

Clive and Lena followed the crew out of the Rotunda, as Harald counted the men off to ensure no one was left behind.

"How many entrances are there?" Clive asked as she directed him the several blocks to Horatio's boardinghouse.

"Two. The back door for those who work on the exhibition, and the main entrance for visitors. The main hallway leads in one direction to the office stairwell and in the other through a narrow passage onto the exhibition stage."

"Is there no other way in? Windows, perhaps?"

"No. All the Rotunda windows are at the ceiling. That allows their light to diffuse through the exhibition space, without interfering with the viewing of the painting."

He nodded, listening carefully to her explanations.

Why did he wish to know about doors and other entrances? But she was unwilling to ruin their amiable silence with questions. Soon they reached Horatio's boardinghouse.

"This one here. Horatio's landlord knows me." She rapped the knocker.

"Calder's gone." The landlord opened the door slightly, then wider when he saw Somerville. "Who's he?"

Lena was uncertain how to introduce Clive. Burglar? Investigator? Rescuer? Physician?

Clive spoke up. "Lord Clive Somerville, brother to the Duke of Forster. Might we come in? Mr. Calder left some materials for us to collect." Clive held out his hand.

After shaking it, the landlord pocketed the coin Clive had passed him. "Certainly, my lord. Miss Frost knows the way. The key is above the lintel."

Lena shook her head in mock dismay as she led Clive to Horatio's second-floor accommodations. The stairway was narrow, forcing them together, and she breathed in the scent of him, clean and comforting, even after a day's work. "He would have taken less. Besides, what materials do you expect to find?"

"I have no idea. But if we find something we want, we'll have no trouble taking it away now."

They reached Horatio's room. Clive ran his hand across the top of the door frame. "No key."

"It's unlocked." She pushed the door open and started to step inside.

Clive put his hand on her shoulder, sending a frisson of energy down her spine. "Allow me."

Calder's sitting room was comfortable and well appointed.

And cold.

"Horatio always has a fire." Lena shivered.

Clive almost pulled her to his side, but, not knowing what she might have heard or read about him, he gave her his greatcoat instead. He needed—no, wanted—her to trust him. He wanted her to look at him with confidence, as she did with her foreman Louis.

The two large windows facing the street were open

wide, and Clive looked out before latching them shut. The windows were too high for a man to climb in, but low enough that a man climbing out might escape a broken leg or ankle by hanging from the sill.

An interior door led, Clive assumed, to Calder's bedroom, but it was shut. Leaving it for later, Clive examined the room where Calder hosted clients and friends. A heavy table stood in front of the small fireplace. A bookcase near the door was laden with books, and a cupboard sat in the far corner. It was the sort of residence one imagined a successful, unmarried man of business would keep.

Small paintings of various subjects hung in rows along the walls, signed by Calder himself. Clive took the first painting off the wall to see if the frame hid any secrets, but saw only the back of the painted board. He looked behind the second.

A thud drew his attention. Then another. Lena stood before the bookcase, pulling each book off the shelves. Her face was intent, her movements efficient, and, for a moment, he stood merely watching her. With each book, she examined the flyleaves and the spine, then turned the pages down and ruffled through them, dislodging anything stuck between them. A small pile of paper and other objects grew on the floor beside her.

"Any luck?" He wanted to move to her side, but he held himself back.

"A bill from his tailor—unpaid. A note from a lover—unread."

"How do you know it's from a lover if it's unread?" Clive stopped working entirely, mesmerized by the way Lena held the corner of her mouth between her teeth as she concentrated. If Lena were his lover, he would never leave a letter of hers unread.

She dropped another book into the growing pile at

her feet. "A lock of hair is knotted under the seal, and the paper is perfumed." She picked the next book and began her process once more. Three slips of paper fell to the floor.

"Why are you emptying the books? Could we learn something by their location in the book? Or from his notes."

"Horatio carries a book because he believes a man of a certain class does, but he uses it like a magpie, slipping in whatever receipts, letters, notes to himself he has at hand. Though I've seen him reading, I've never seen him make notes in a book." She dropped another book on the pile.

"Would you mind if I look?" He stepped closer, near enough to catch a hint of her lilac water perfume.

"Certainly." Her voice was more teasing than critical. "Would you prefer to search his cupboard yourself as well?"

She carried all the scraps of paper, letters, and receipts to the table. There, the remains of three lemons, the juice squeezed out of them, sat beside a small bowl with pulp stuck to its edges.

"What would your partner do with so much lemon?"

"He's an odd man, and he does as he pleases." She picked up a rind and turned it over in her hand. She reached into her pocket to pull out Horatio's note, then changed her mind. "I might know what he's done with the juice. But it will have to wait."

She moved to the cupboard, opening the doors, searching the corners. "There's nothing here."

When she looked up, Clive was seated on the floor, carefully leafing through each book. "Do you intend to read them all?"

"I am looking for marks or other symbols." His eyes met hers, and she felt like the world had contracted to just the two of them. "If I see something on a page, I tend to remember it."

"Tend to?" Lena stopped, watching him work, his fingers gently caressing the pages of the book as if each one were precious, and she wondered how it might feel to be the subject of such care and attention.

"I can see it again." He turned another page, then looked at her, smiling. "In my mind's eye I mean. It's an odd quirk of mine."

"I suppose that proves useful sometimes." She wanted to sit beside him and examine the books together. Instead, she turned back to the cupboard.

"Sometimes." He turned back to the books as well.

"There's nothing here. I've pulled out all the drawers and looked behind them," Lena announced when she was done.

"It's a very clean room for a man you describe as a magpie."

"No, I said he picks up information like a magpie. He's otherwise quite neat." She walked toward the closed bedroom door. "Never a hair out of place or so much as a speck of dirt on his clothes." She opened the door and stopped short. "Until now."

Horatio's bedroom was in disarray. The bed was unmade, as if Horatio had just risen out of it, and the bedclothes in a twist. The wardrobe was open and empty, the drawers hanging out. A hatbox, also empty, lay open on the floor. A chair lay on its back near the open window, the curtains pulled through and out. Even so, the room still smelled faintly of damp, and rot, and something else.

"What is it?" Clive joined her at the bedroom door. Lena began to enter the room, but Clive stopped her. "Wait."

He took several steps in, watching attentively, as if he

were a cat on the trail of a mouse. On the other side of
the bed, he stopped and stared at the floor. "Well, now
we know why the windows are open," he said, almost to
himself.

"What are you looking at? What's that smell?" She
stepped toward him, but with the same catlike grace, he returned to her before she was two steps from the doorway.

"It's time for us to go." He turned her back toward the
sitting room.

"What?" She struggled against him, twisting to face
him.

"We need to put you in a safe place." His eyes were
sympathetic. "Then I'll return and call for the magistrate."

She looked past him, seeing for the first time a red
stain on the edge of the sheets. She pulled out of his arms
and rushed around the bed.

A man lay on the floor opposite, clearly dead. His face
was already a gray white, the sort one would find in a
mannerist painting. His blood formed an alizarin crimson
pool around his head. She turned away, the color burned
into her memory.

Clive was there, burying her face in his strong arms.
"I'm sorry. I know you were fond of him."

She pulled away slightly. "Him? I don't know *him*."

"That's Calder." His voice was surprised.

"No. It's not. I don't know who he is—I mean, was. But
he's not Horatio."

"Most people faint or vomit when they see their first
murdered body."

"I'm only a bit overset from having thought it would be
Horatio. The blood doesn't bother me. Dried, it's always
the same color, caput mortuum. The actual color of blood
doesn't look real enough at a distance and in large format,
so I've made adjustments. A little more alizarin and a little

less iron oxide. And a battle scene needs a range of bloods, vermilion for the fresh wounds and madder lake when the blood has dried."

She was chattering, and she knew it, but somehow it helped to overcome the shock of finding a dead man in Horatio's room. Had Horatio gotten away in time? Was he the man's killer? It was hard imagining the dapper old man as a killer, but then she hadn't imagined he would steal her money and disappear either. She'd believed he was fond of her.

"Let's go back into the sitting room." He led her to the bedroom door.

"No." Her eyes swept the room, avoiding the dead man. "If something here explains why Horatio left and why that man is dead, we must find it before you call the magistrate."

He pulled out a chair for her to sit. "Whoever was here before us—perhaps that man on the floor—has already searched the bedroom, and we have just searched this room. Unless you know of a particular place Calder might have hidden something, we should leave before someone finds us here and assumes we are the murderers." He returned to the bedroom and came back with the hatbox. He set the box on the floor before the bookcases and began opening the books and emptying their contents into it.

"I see you have come to appreciate my method," Lena observed.

"I've come to appreciate that we have no time to dally." He placed Lena's pile of notes and objects on top and shut the box. "Can you think of anywhere else we need to search?"

"Horatio's painting box. But it's not in here." She looked toward the bedroom, then steeling her courage, she rose.

"His what?"

"He has a box of sorts, with paper and brushes and small pots of paint. If it's here, he'll return for it. If it's not . . ." She stood at the door to the bedroom, giving the room a careful examination. When she was satisfied that the box was gone, she walked to the other side of the bed, and from a distance carefully examined the man's face. Though it was unlikely she would have forgotten his appearance, this time she looked beyond the colors of his wounds to the structure of his face. She needed to remember the narrow scar along his hairline, the broken blood vessels on and around his nose, the cyst forming a knot in the middle of his eyebrow.

"What are you doing?" Clive held the hatbox under his arm. "We need to go."

"I'm remembering." Lena turned away from the body and walked to the bedroom door.

"Most people would want to forget this." He let her pass, then pulled the bedroom door shut behind her.

"When we find Horatio, he will want to know who was lying dead in his bedroom."

"Was the box there?"

"No. He doesn't intend to return here."

"Then we need to slip away quietly as well." He took her arm gently. "I will take you to my brother's house. You will be safe there until I return."

"Return?" She examined his face, his jaw firm and honest. "From where?"

"Once you are safely situated, I will call the magistrate and sort this out with him."

"I will go with you." She lifted her chin in determination. "Perhaps the magistrate can help discover Horatio's whereabouts."

"The magistrate's first suspect will be Calder, but he needn't suspect you as well."

"Me? Why me? I haven't killed anyone."

He looked exasperated. "You *must* understand how this looks. You are a woman visiting a man's boardinghouse accompanied by a man you barely know."

She felt a prick of alarm. Had she trusted him too soon?

"Your business partner has disappeared, leaving a dead body in his rooms. This could only be worse if Calder's absconded with all the money from the Rotunda. Then you would also have a good motivation for killing your partner."

She forced her face to remain impassive. "But, I've told you, that man isn't Horatio."

"Without the windows open, this room would be dark. You mistook him for your thieving partner and killed him by mistake."

"What role do you play in this story of yours?"

"It's not my story. It's the story the magistrate will spin the minute he sees you here, and in it, I will be cast as the lover."

"Mine or Horatio's?" she asked, letting sarcasm inflect every syllable.

"In cases of murder, either will do, though, given a choice, I would prefer to be yours."

The room grew small around them. She noticed the warmth of his hand on her elbow. And his eyes. His irises were more green than blue, more vibrant than celadon, but lighter than viridian. She stared into their depths, wondering if it were even possible to paint that color and the flecks of gold in the centers. Then soon all thought disappeared. The seconds seemed to stretch out infinitely, as they studied each other's faces. She leaned forward. He placed his hand on her upper arm, and desire, shimmering like gold leaf, warmed them both.

A sound in the hall broke the moment. She stepped back, and Clive let his hand fall to his side.

"I will wait for you at my boardinghouse, or, if you prefer, I can visit a friend who owns a bookstore." She walked decisively toward the hall door. "I'll give you either address, and you can find me there."

"You are a capable woman, Lena, fully able to manage your own life. But, given the accident at the Rotunda and the body in the next room, indulge me by visiting my brother's house. This week, my sister Judith is in residence with her foundlings, along with my great-aunt, at least one of my brothers, and, I believe, several of Lady Wilmot's cousins."

Lena rubbed the pulled muscle in the bottom of her thumb, trying to ignore the fact that for a moment she'd very much wanted to kiss him. He waited quietly for her decision, and his patience swung the balance.

"I need to retrieve some things from my rooms first."

Clive waited for her to walk through, then balancing the hatbox, pulled the door shut behind them. "Let's go."

Chapter Eight

On the street, she reached for the hatbox, but he refused. Raising a finger, he signaled to a street urchin, then paying the child a penny, gave instructions on where to deliver the box.

"You should have tied it shut. This way, he'll stop halfway to your brother's and see if there is anything worth stealing."

"Had I tied it shut, he would have been certain the box held something worth stealing. As it is, he will find scraps of paper and a wood carving or two. Besides, I told him that if he delivers the contents intact, there would be a penny in it for him tomorrow."

"That's a pretty two pennies for a hatbox I could have carried."

"That boy will have food today and tomorrow earned from honest work." Clive matched his stride to hers.

"That boy will be laughing with his mates at the toff who doesn't know the value of a penny." Lena's words alone could have sounded like a rebuke, but her tone was tender as was the slight touch she gave to his arm.

"Toff? How do you know such street slang?"

She ignored the question. "I'm three flights up in the corner house." She gestured toward a run-down but respectable house on a run-down but respectable street.

"You're in the attic?" Somehow from the way Lena carried herself, he'd expected her to choose a better class of lodging.

"No, that pleasure belongs to my landlady's cousin, a mean-spirited spinster who makes my landlady seem like an angel."

"But she isn't?" He followed her toward the house, admiring the purposeful efficiency of her stride.

Lena shrugged. "It's forty-six steps from the front door to my room. Most days if I can get to step thirty-eight, I can escape without any engagement."

"What about the other days?" He followed her to the front door, all the while admiring her graceful carriage and easy movements.

"I speak in broken English, with a heavy infusion of French. Lately, to reduce my interactions, I speak almost entirely French," she said matter-of-factly. She put her hand on the doorknob and turned back to face him. "I'll need five minutes, ten at the most. I haven't much here, but some things I'd rather not leave. If you hear me speaking French, add fifteen minutes."

She opened the door, and he followed her into the dimly lit hall. "I'll accompany you."

She shook her head, nodding toward the landlady's room. He put his hand on her shoulder to stop her from ascending the stairs.

"I will be happy to speak to your landlady to explain why I need to accompany you to your room. I will of course stand in the hallway while you get your things."

"Do you have sixpence?" She slipped out from under his hand and began climbing the stairs quickly.

"Of course."

"That's all you'll need." She stopped briefly at the landing. "Sixpence for a male visitor to go up the stairs."

"What does she charge for coming down?" He took the steps between them two at a time.

"Coming down is free." She resumed her climb, moving quickly and easily up the steep stairs. "But if you cross the threshold to my room, it will cost you another ha'penny."

"A ha'penny to enter a woman's room. Is this a house of ill repute?" He whispered so only she could hear him.

"Ill repute?" Lena laughed. "My, aren't you prim? Ill repute goes a bit too far. It often serves as a house of assignation. But Mrs. Abbott ensures that she fares as well as any man's mistress, though—I'd say—with less effort."

"Are you concerned that living here will damage your reputation?"

She paused on the stairs for a moment, weighing him against some internal balance. He submitted to her gaze, wondering how he had fared in the assessment.

Pitching her voice low, she continued to climb. "I have a great regard for my *reputation*. I provide my clients with fine work at a good price. I pay the laborers I hire a fair rate. I give to those who are in need." Each phrase was punctuated by her ascent of another stair. "But like every other man of your rank and class, you don't mean my reputation as a painter, or as an engraver, or as a businesswoman. Instead, you ignore all those measures by which you would judge a *man*, and you reduce my worth to a single criterion: my chastity. That sort of reputation is of concern only to the landed classes, meant to ensure that

the heir to the land is the actual child of the landlord. And
by child, of course, we mean son."

He felt himself color. When he was pursuing an inquiry, he asked such questions without thinking to learn
someone's opinions. But he should have considered that
posing it to Lena under these circumstances would make
him sound like *that* sort of man—the sort he avoided at
his club. He started to object, but stopped himself. As an
investigator, he'd learned to listen, both to what was being
said and what wasn't.

"In your world, a young lady's sole ambition must be
to marry well, but in this neighborhood, marriage is more
often a handicap than a luxury. I have only one use for
your sort of reputation: to have enough of it so that if the
queen ever needs a painter, I am not ineligible."

At the third floor, she looked down the hall in both directions before moving quickly from the stairwell to her
door. "That's odd: usually by step twenty-six either my
landlady or her cousin has come into the hall to watch me
pass by." She opened the door with a key tied to a string
inside her waistband. "I leave a lantern inside the door, but
at this time of day, we may be able to do without it."

The sickly sweet smell of decay met them, blossoming
through the open door. In Horatio's rooms, open windows
had carried away most of the smell, but Lena's rooms had
been closed up tight for two days and a night.

Lena recoiled backward into his chest. He held her for
a moment, her back against his chest, his strong hands on
her shoulders, reassuring her. "Stay here."

This time she did exactly as she was told. She waited
by the door, the memory of the body in Horatio's bedroom

still too fresh. Had Horatio been hiding in her rooms, waiting for her to return? Was he dead here, lying in his own blood all the time she'd been cursing him?

She watched Clive's strong back as he crossed her small sitting room in four long strides. He stopped at the open door of her even smaller bedroom.

"It's a woman. Not too long dead by the look of her." He stepped out of sight. "Describe your landlady."

"Quite stout. Gray hair, almost white. She pulls it back tight."

"Gray hair, yes. But not stout."

"Is she wearing a dark gray dress with lace at the wrists or a blue walking dress designed for a much younger woman?"

"Flowers embroidered down the arms."

"That's Mrs. Paxton." She pressed her hand to her mouth to hold back her distress. The first body—a man she didn't know—had startled and sobered her. But she'd kept her mind on Horatio and on hoping he had escaped unharmed. This time, the body was a person she had known, someone she saw almost every day. Even if she didn't like the woman, she did not wish her dead.

"She let herself in; a set of keys are on the floor beside her."

"She snoops. Snooped."

He backed out of the room. "It's time to take you to my brother, then I'll return with the magistrate." He stepped toward her, his expression equal parts determination and concern.

"I can't simply walk away from this. These are my rooms. I knew her. The magistrate will want to talk with me." She stepped forward, challenging him.

From the main hall, heavy knocks at the front door

were followed by the sound of the landlady's voice, sharp and shrill.

"Is there another way out? Through the attics perhaps?" He looked around the room as if a way of escape would magically appear.

"Not that I know of . . . I usually only sleep here, so I always used the doors."

"When did you leave this morning?"

"I stayed last night at a friend's. But lately, I've been leaving slightly before dawn. Horatio and I used to divide the labor of managing the exhibition, with him opening up for the craftsmen, and me closing. In the past several months, I've taken care of both."

The voices—two men and the landlady—climbed the flights of stairs slowly.

"Luckily, you've been with me all day. Think quickly: what things did you wish to take?"

"There's a carpetbag already packed behind the cupboard. It's already tied to a rope. You can lower it out the window there to the left, then at the end of the rope, let it drop."

He didn't ask questions. He merely went to the cupboard, withdrew the heavy bag, and lowered it through the open window to the ground below, then dropped the rope to the ground as well.

Clive had already returned to her side, when the two men—one apparently the magistrate, the other a younger beanpole of a man, clearly his subordinate—reached the landing outside her flat. They were followed by Mrs. Abbott, who looked surprised to see Lena home.

"Are you Miss Frost?" The magistrate, a dour-faced man, wiped his brow with a handkerchief.

"She understands you well enough, but she only speaks French, that one." The landlady spat out the words.

Lena swallowed, then addressed him politely in English. "Yes, sir."

"I'm Thacker, the magistrate. This is my assistant, Mr. Dean. We've received news of a murder in your rooms." He shoved the handkerchief up his sleeve and sniffed the air. "That's the smell of blood all right." He looked at Lena's hands, still bandaged, and raised an eyebrow. "Do you wish to confess?" Thacker's partner, Dean, positioned himself as if Lena might run.

"I didn't kill her. I returned home only a few moments ago. She was dead already."

The landlady's eyes grew wide. "You hussy: your English is as good as mine!"

"She?" Thacker ignored Mrs. Abbott. "Do you know the woman's name?"

Lena looked at Mrs. Abbott apologetically, then answered. "She is Mrs. Paxton, Mrs. Abbott's cousin."

Mrs. Abbott's face turned from shock, to anger, to a sort of pleasure, to avarice, all in the space of a heartbeat. She began to wail, beating at Lena with closed fists. Clive stepped immediately between them, the blows falling on his chest and arms, until Dean pulled Abbott back.

At Thacker's signal, Dean shepherded Mrs. Abbott, flailing, farther down the hall. Her cries soon became words: "Murderess. Murderess. I know who you are. You will pay for this."

Clive pulled Lena, unresisting, against his side. She leaned into him, feeling his presence warm like sunlight.

"Wait here." For the next eternity, the magistrate examined the body and Lena's rooms. Lena stiffened when the magistrate leaned out the open window, but he returned to question them before he looked down.

"She your lady love?" He lifted his chin to indicate Lena.

"Miss Frost is a friend," Clive answered firmly. Thacker needed to believe that Lena had friends—solid, well-connected, *English* friends—or she might end up sleeping in a cell.

"I'll take that as a yes." The magistrate looked Clive over. "And you are?"

"Somerville. Lord Clive Somerville." He waited to see if the magistrate recognized his name. If he didn't, Clive could always invoke his brother, the duke.

"Somer . . . ville." The magistrate paused over the name, then considered Clive with renewed interest. "Are you the Somerville who works for . . ."

Clive cut him off. "*Teaches at* the surgery school."

"Right. *Teaches*. At the *surgery* school." The magistrate caught the hint, his voice shifting to a more deferent stance. The wails of Mrs. Abbott grew louder, and the magistrate motioned Clive and Lena down the hall.

Clive led Lena to the stairs leading to the attic. "Sit here for a minute." She acquiesced, sitting on the steps and leaning against the wall. She crossed her arms in front of her body as if holding herself safe.

Thacker pulled Clive away several feet. "You vouching for her?"

"Miss Frost is the proprietor of the new exhibition at the Rotunda. She's been there since before dawn."

"I can speak for myself," Lena objected, her voice uncertain.

"Yes, and I'll talk to you next, miss." Thacker's voice had turned almost kind.

Lena nodded her acceptance.

The magistrate pulled Clive farther away. "You certain Frost couldn't have killed that one before she left?"

Clive shook his head. "The woman hasn't been dead long. Two hours, perhaps three."

"And Miss Frost never left the Rotunda, after you arrived?"

"I visited the Rotunda on business early this morning, and I've been with Miss Frost constantly since."

"Business?" The magistrate raised an eyebrow and waited.

"Yes."

"*Surgery* business?" the magistrate prompted, using the euphemism Clive had given for his official inquiries for the Home Office.

"Perhaps." Clive shrugged.

The magistrate stared at him for a moment, then conceded. "I have your word that she's innocent."

"Yes."

"Her hands. Why are they bandaged?"

"An accident today at the Rotunda." Clive considered telling the magistrate his concerns about sabotage but decided against it. He needed to investigate more himself before he gave the magistrate another line of inquiry. "I saw it happen, and I tended her wounds."

Thacker fell silent, looking first at Lena, then toward her room. "Messy situation this one. The message we received was very specific."

"What did it say?" Clive inflected his voice as his father, the late duke, used to do when he expected compliance or information.

"Her name, her address, killed a woman in cold blood. Hit her over the head with a mallet." Thacker answered promptly.

"A mallet?"

"Yes." The magistrate nodded.

"And in cold blood?"

"Yes."

"A mallet's an odd choice for a woman to have at home. Did you find it?"

"No. But we'll search. Miss Frost is lucky you spent the day with her."

Clive ignored the insinuation. "I predict that mallet is going to be found in a place connected to Miss Frost."

"I would think so. You'll send for me when it does."

"Of course. Likewise for you."

Thacker indicated his acceptance. "She can't stay here, not until we've done a thorough search. But that one"—he pointed at the wailing Mrs. Abbott—"isn't likely to give her another room."

"Miss Frost will be staying at my brother's house in Mayfair."

"Your brother?"

"Forster. The duke."

"Ah. Right." Thacker nodded understanding.

"I'd like to see what the body can tell us. Can you arrange to have it delivered to the Royal College of Surgeons?"

Thacker pointed toward the landlady. "If that one agrees, Dean can manage it."

"I'll speak with her." He crossed to Lena. She was staring at the floor in front of her feet. When she lifted her eyes, they were filled with despair. His heart tightened. He wanted to wrap her in his arms and comfort her. Instead, he whispered next to her ear, "Stay right here. Say nothing." If the action suggested they were lovers, so be it.

Lena nodded, lowering her gaze back to the floor.

* * *

Dean had positioned his body—thin as it was—to separate the landlady from Lena and her rooms.

Abbott was putting on a good show at grief. As Clive approached, she punctuated her howls with more accusations against Lena. "Murderess!" She spat between wails. "French whore."

"Mrs. Abbott." He spoke gently, as if he believed her grief was sincere.

Her wails only grew louder: "You will lose your head for this, you will!" She beat Dean's chest with renewed vigor. Out of patience, Dean grabbed her wrists and held them tight.

"Mrs. Abbott!" Clive let his voice go hard. Abbott grew silent at his show of strength. "Miss Frost did not kill your cousin."

"She did. A murderess she is. But she won't get away with it. Not this time. Not here." She pulled against Dean's unexpectedly strong grip.

"Your cousin has been dead only a few hours, and Miss Frost has more than twenty witnesses to her alibi." Whatever he said was unlikely to matter, but he wanted information.

"Other foreigners like her, I bet, pretending she was one place when she were another."

"I am one of those witnesses."

"Under her spell, are you? Lying to protect her? You'll find out she's a treacherous one. She killed my cousin—God rest her soul—because Gertrude discovered what she'd done."

Clive shook his head at Dean, who still held Mrs. Abbott's hands tight.

"Besides you and your cousin, who has been in the house this afternoon?"

"No one. No one came through the front door or went up the stairs."

"What about the back entrance?"

"Locked, and I have the key." The landlady glared at him. "Ask *her* what she did in France." Abbott would be no help.

"Mrs. Abbott, which undertaker do you wish to care for your cousin?" The question of funeral expenses might divert the landlady's attention.

The woman's face turned grim as she considered the cost of her cousin's funeral. He waited, knowing what little real grief she might feel would not survive her greed. In an instant she began to wail again, burying her face in a handkerchief. "No undertaker. I haven't the money for it. She only lived here on my favor. It will break my heart, but she must be carried to the pauper's graveyard."

"Even the pauper's yard is not free." Clive waited as Abbott calculated the cost of a pauper's funeral. When she pursed her lips together in displeasure, he took his chance. "If you would allow your cousin's body to go to the surgery school, it would be a great service to medicine, and the school offers a stipend for grieving families."

"How much?" Her eyes glinted with avarice.

"Seven pounds and the cost of burial in a regular cemetery, not the pauper's field."

"I want her clothes back. I can sell them." The landlady brushed her eyes, still dry, with her handkerchief. "She would want me to do that. Precious soul, my cousin."

"As for Miss Frost's rooms . . ."

Abbott turned mercenary once more. "She has no place in my house, not with her rent past due. And she knows the rules about men up the stairs."

"How much?" Clive hid his annoyance.

"It will take a man richer than you to pay for her sins."
The woman crossed her arms over her chest and scowled.

"How much, Mrs. Abbott?" Thacker lent his authority
to Clive.

Abbott cowed a little under the magistrate's attention.
"Bob a week for the rent, but I'll take nothing less than
a month in advance. Then there's the fee for him"—she
pointed a crooked finger at Clive—"going upstairs and
into her room."

"That would be four shillings, sixpence, and a
ha'penny." Clive added up the amounts.

"I won't take less than a guinea." Abbott folded her
arms across her chest.

"My God, woman! That's robbery." Dean spoke at last.

Abbott returned to wailing.

"I'll pay the guinea." Clive reached into his waistcoat
pocket. "But it will pay for two months' rent and a sheet
to wrap your cousin in."

Abbott snatched the coin from his hand.

"That's settled then." Thacker eyed Mrs. Abbott. "Two
months' lodging for the lady and a bedsheet."

"She's no lady." Mrs. Abbott spat on the floor. "I'll get
your bedsheet." She descended the stairs followed by Dean.

Thacker watched the landlady until she was out of
sight. "You may have bought the *room* for two months, but
I warrant Abbott will take anything of value before this
night is out, even if she has to step through her cousin's
blood to do it."

"Could Dean see that Miss Frost's belongings are sent
to the Duke of Forster's house in Mayfair?"

Thacker nodded at Lena. "You certain she isn't the
murderer."

"Certain." Clive looked at her, arms still folded over
her chest in protection. Whether she wanted it or not,

she needed his help, and he would have her somewhere safe soon.

"Dean has a new wife and a babe in arms; he might welcome a chance to pack a trunk for a coin or two . . . as we search for the mallet, of course."

"Of course." Clive pulled a second guinea from his pocket. "A gift for the infant and its mother."

"Mrs. Abbott may be greedy and unpleasant, but she knows this neighborhood and the people in it." Thacker pocketed the coin. "How certain are you of Miss Frost's character?"

"Abbott's story troubles me." Clive ignored the magistrate's question. "She lives at the base of the stairs. She claims the rear door was locked. But she heard nothing. No one coming in, or going out, or going upstairs."

"You think she's lying." Thacker looked down the stairs ⁓d Abbott's rooms.

"I think she has something to hide, and she's taking advantage of the fact that her cousin's body was found in Miss Frost's rooms."

"And her aspersions divert our attention to Miss Frost." Thacker studied Lena, sitting on the stairs. "Given Miss Frost's alibi, I'll look elsewhere for the murderer, but something about your Miss Frost troubles me."

Clive waited, encouraging Thacker to continue.

"It's that big, expensive French trunk in her bedroom, almost empty. She doesn't have much in her rooms, not nearly enough to fill it. The way I see it: your Miss Frost is in a bit of financial trouble, and she's been selling her belongings. But why keep the trunk?"

Clive, thinking of the carpetbag, kept his face impassive. "Perhaps it has a value more sentimental than practical."

"Perhaps." Thacker sounded unconvinced. Dean returned with a torn strip of bed linen, not even wide enough,

Clive suspected, to wrap the body, and Thacker handed him the guinea coin. "If that mallet shows up, you'll let me know."

"Of course." Clive held back his relief; Lena wasn't out of the house yet.

Thacker followed Dean into Lena's rooms, but stopped. "There'll be an inquest. If she wishes to leave London or if she takes up lodgings somewhere other than at the duke's house, you'll keep me informed." It wasn't a question. Thacker was already shutting the door between them, but Clive nodded yes all the same.

Clive stood for a moment, thinking. The magistrate's questions had rubbed against a memory he couldn't quite retrieve. But, looking at Lena, still sitting quietly where they had left her, he brushed the feeling away. After each upset—her fall, their discovery of the dead man, and even the presence of a dead woman she'd known in her rooms—she had recovered her equilibrium quickly. But Mrs. Abbott's hateful aspersions had struck some wound deep in her core. She hadn't withdrawn until then.

Lena looked smaller now, younger, no longer the visionary whose dream was taking shape at the Rotunda or the respected leader who had managed more than a dozen men at their work all day. Something about her stillness— as if she thought that by not moving she might avoid the tragedy mounting around her—evoked his sympathy and his desire to protect.

Even so, the implication of Lena finding the bodies hadn't escaped him. Mrs. Paxton had clearly been uninvited, but what of Calder's guest? Clive hadn't admitted it to Lena, but he had known the dead man *as* Calder. He'd recognized the man's shock of gray hair at the temples and his secondhand coat worn through at one elbow. He'd met the man only last week. Clive had circulated inquiries

about one of the dead men at the surgery school, and
Calder had responded with a note setting a meeting for a
local tavern. Calder had been early, and he'd talked for
more than an hour. Calder had provided enough details
about the murders that Clive had been certain he would
soon solve the case.

Clive rubbed his hand across his forehead. A fine mess
it was, and one Joe Pasten would likely never let him
forget.

Tomorrow he would examine Mrs. Paxton at the surgery school and see what tales her body might tell. Then,
he would find a time to confess to Joe his mistake—that
the man he had believed was Calder was not Lena's partner, but was instead most likely one of the very murderers
Clive had been investigating. Worse yet, by not realizing
it, Clive had perhaps caused two more people to die.

But first he needed to convince the duke to welcome
Lena into his home and allow Clive to remain nearby.

Chapter Nine

Lena tried to hear what Clive and the magistrate were saying, but the words were too indistinct. She closed her eyes, letting the warm low tones of Clive's voice resonate in her chest. In her mind's eye, she could still see Mrs. Paxton, lying on the floor, her wound hidden by her bonnet.

At least, she wasn't having to convince the magistrate she hadn't murdered Mrs. Paxton. But how would the magistrate respond when Clive reported the body in Horatio's rooms? Two bodies, not one.

Her fingers traced the edges of Horatio's note in her pocket. If she believed Horatio's letter, she shouldn't trust anyone. She opened her eyes and stared at Clive. His back and the magistrate's were turned toward her. She traced the line of Clive's hair, the curve of his neck, the breadth of his chest, the strength of his arms.

In an instant she was falling again, the boards cracking under her weight, her skin tearing as she fell, the panic bitter on her tongue. He had saved her then, protecting her even when her fall had forced him to the floor and knocked the breath from their lungs. And he was saving her now, defending her to the magistrate and stepping between her and Mrs. Abbott, bearing her landlady's blows in her place. It had been so long since she could rely on another person to care for her. No, Clive couldn't be the man she was supposed to run from. Why would he save her or protect her, if he were? She wouldn't—couldn't—believe he intended her harm.

Or had he done it all merely to gain her trust? If being at the Rotunda all morning was her alibi, it was Clive's as well.

Her thoughts were disordered, jumping from one possibility to the next. Clive had been honest about his interest in Horatio and about working with the police. Hadn't the magistrate's tone changed when Clive introduced himself? No, Clive was exactly what he seemed to be. She was certain of it.

If she had come home earlier—if she hadn't spent the night at Constance's shop—would she be dead instead of Mrs. Paxton? Had Mrs. Paxton interrupted a burglar? But nothing had been out of place, and her carpetbag had still been tied shut when Clive removed it from the cabinet. Or had someone been waiting in her rooms? Someone who thought nothing of killing those who got in his way? Someone who would kill her as well if given the chance? The knowledge settled heavy and dark in the pit of her stomach.

She couldn't stop the questions. It was a puzzle, a dangerous, terrifying puzzle, and she had to solve it, or hers might be the next murdered body. And she couldn't face her unknown adversary alone.

She shook her head in her hands. *Oh, Horatio. Where are you, and what have you done?*

Clive's conversation with the magistrate grew louder. She could make out a few of the words: *mallet, trunk, stairs, lodgings*. But little else, and she didn't want to know. She simply wanted to sit, unmoving, conserving her natural spirits for the next challenge. She felt empty, as if all her strength were puddled useless around her shoes. After weeks of sleeping only in bits and snatches while she pushed to complete the panorama on time, she'd been unprepared for the shocks of the past day. Had it only been a day?

She closed her eyes again and waited.

"Come along, Miss Frost."

Lena opened her eyes to see that Clive had extended his hands to help her up.

"I've told Magistrate Thacker that if he needs to speak with you, he may find you at the London residence of the Duke of Forster."

She wanted to object, but she couldn't find the words. Her mind felt thick.

When she didn't respond, not even to take his hand, Clive looked surprised, but after a moment's pause, he continued gently.

"You needn't worry: our great-aunt Agatha maintains an apartment in the ducal residence, and the duke himself rarely stays there. Though the duke is too polite to ever admit it, I believe he lives in that ruin of a house off Cavendish Square to avoid Lady Agatha's management." He paused, as if he'd used too many words and needed to replenish them.

She searched his eyes. She found only kindness.

"Mrs. Abbott will find it difficult to push for your arrest if you are a guest in the home of a duke." He waited for her response, but getting none, he continued. "I've already sent a runner to Forster, informing him that you will be his guest for the next several days."

She could hardly argue, particularly if she didn't wish to offend the duke or, more importantly, his fiancée. Accepting Clive's argument, for now at least, she placed her hands in his. He helped her rise from the stairs.

"News of Mrs. Paxton's death will spread quickly once the magistrate leaves with the body." He stood quietly, examining her face as if he'd never seen her before. Then he raised her shawl from her shoulders, pulling it forward over her head until the sides partially obscured her face. The tenderness of the gesture caught her breath, and she wondered what he'd seen in that long gaze. She said nothing, afraid her voice might reveal too much of her fears, apprehension, and longing.

Taking one of her hands, he directed her away from her rooms. "Follow me closely—and quietly. Without the magistrate to intervene, we should avoid another engagement with your landlady." Lena followed Clive down each flight of stairs, not letting go of his hand. His touch was a comfort to her, a salve against the noises of the house that seemed amplified. The clatter of a pan, the sound of two women talking, the creaks in the stairs Clive didn't know to avoid. Each one seemed to yell out her escape; each one made her cringe. She couldn't bear the thought of another round with Mrs. Abbott; the vitriol in the landlady's words had burned and stung.

At the main floor, the door to Mrs. Abbott's lodgings stood open wide. Clive motioned her to stop. He leaned forward, looking into the landlady's rooms, then he positioned his body in front of Mrs. Abbott's open doorway and waved Lena to the other side.

At the front door, Clive tried to slide the bolt quietly, but the lock scraped against the plate, then stuck. Lena watched Abbott's door, fearing that the landlady would reach them before they escaped. Clive tried again, and each attempt sounded like a gunshot, or seemed to. The heavy beat of the landlady's cane announced her approach.

Lena stepped closer to Clive. "Hurry," she whispered.

Clive responded by pulling her into the side of his body. His strong arm around her shoulders comforted her, and she wanted to lean into the warmth of him, if only for a moment. But it wasn't wise. She held herself apart, perhaps only by a fraction, but enough to convey—if not to him, but to herself—that she could still manage her life as she always had: alone. He turned his attention back to the lock.

He twisted the bolt once more, pushing the door into its frame at the same time. The bolt released. The sound of Mrs. Abbott's cane grew louder, accompanied by renewed cursing. Lena hurried out onto the porch, Clive close behind, pulling the door shut behind them.

Outside the boardinghouse, the world was turning dark. The winter sun sought its bed early, leaving London's residents to find their way through a city dimly lit by gas lamps or torches. The streetlamp in front of them created a puddle of light. Pedestrians passing under the lamp's light became visible for a moment, then disappeared back into the dark.

Lena studied the crowd, looking for those who might recognize her. She pulled her shawl farther forward; even in the dark, she had no wish to be recognized. As if reading her thoughts, Clive pulled her toward him again, placing his arm around her shoulders and turning her body sideways into his chest to protect her from view. She allowed the intimacy. But she refused to think of how it might feel to be encircled in his arms if he were interested in her alone, rather than in how she might lead him to Horatio.

Together they hurried out to the edge of the street. There, a hackney pulled to meet them almost at the very moment of his hail. Somehow she wasn't surprised: hadn't the crowds parted for Clive as he'd walked to the surgery school?

He handed her into the coach, his strong arms almost lifting her off the pavement. She tucked herself into the far corner of the forward-facing seat, taking comfort from the wall at her back and side, leaving him plenty of room. But he didn't follow. Instead, he shut the door behind her, and the latch clicked into place.

Past the window she could see the lamplight indistinct, but inside the carriage, the dark settled heavy around her. Suddenly the old fears returned. In an instant, she was a child again, trapped alone in the cold and dark. Her breath felt tight, as if she couldn't open her lungs fully. Her heart thudded hard in her chest.

She tried to think her way through the panic. She wasn't alone: Clive would return in just a few minutes. And she wasn't trapped—she placed her hand on the door handle. The carriage hadn't begun to move, so she could still get out. She didn't even need the stairs.

In her work dress with its combination of skirt and trousers, she could merely open the door, sit on the carriage floor, then slide down until her feet touched to the ground. No, she was simply overtaxed, her nerves frayed by the events of the day. But her body wasn't listening. Her heart beat fast, and her breath felt tight. Her hand clasped the door handle tight, and it took everything in her not to open the door and run. They were old fears, rooted in a long ago past, one she had worked very hard to forget. She had conquered them before, and she would not yield now.

She took her hand off the door handle, then very deliberately lowered the window. With the dark outside and in, she was unlikely to be seen. Even so, she sat far back in her seat. She closed her eyes and focused on the calls of the vendors, still hawking their wares. "Ready money for old clothes." "Brick dust. Sell your brick dust." "Songs, penny a sheet."

To calm her mind, she played an old game, imagining how each of the vendors looked, then painting the scene mentally in the style of a famous painter. When she wasn't in the grip of a panic, she used the game to remember a scene in meticulous detail, but when the panic took her, as now, it was a way to come back to herself. The carriage grew colder, but she ignored it, focusing on her imaginary drawings. Surprisingly, in every one, Clive somehow became the central figure, performing some act of generosity or kindness. When the potato vendor's cart was toppled, he bought her damaged wares, and when the chimney sweep's boy collapsed of fatigue, he paid the boy's wages for the week.

She wasn't certain how long Clive had been gone, but by the time he returned with her carpetbag, she was breathing more easily. It would take hours before she felt free of the last bits of her fear. But at least Clive wouldn't know how anxious she'd been.

He put her carpetbag on the rear-facing seat. "Is there a reason you have decided to take a perfectly cold carriage and turn it into an icehouse?" He reached past her to close the carriage window, then sat beside her, not touching but still close enough. She could feel the warmth of his body and smell the crisp notes of his cologne. She breathed it in, letting the scent fill her senses. He tapped the roof to signal the coachman, and the carriage lurched its way forward.

"That's a fine rope. A resourceful tenant could even use it to effect an escape from a hideous landlady. But I must ask: how did you get such a length of rope into your rooms without being seen?" He waited for her answer, forcing her to speak.

"It's part of the rigging we used to raise the canvas sections." She felt as if she were speaking from a long distance. "Mrs. Abbott attends services on Sunday afternoons—I believe there's a man she is hoping to ensnare—and Mrs. Paxton would take that occasion to escape to the park. I always felt sorry for Paxton, or rather I felt the sort of compassion one feels for a caged snake: if the snake were free, it would enjoy biting you, but it's still sad somehow that the snake is denied that pleasure."

Clive laughed, a big hearty, generous laugh. Somehow, as nothing ever had before, his laughter made her remaining tension melt away. She breathed in a long, deep, full breath.

"You haven't answered what you intended to do with such a rope." His voice was filled with concern.

"Exactly what I did." Her relief made her willing to talk. "I didn't intend to kill myself, if that's what you are wondering. I could do that with less effort and more effect at the Rotunda. As you saw today, all I'd have to do is to step off the highest scaffold, and I'd be dead or soon to be. No, early on, I learned that Abbott makes the excuse of some debt or other to claim something from your belongings, and the rope gave me a way to protect my possessions."

"By hanging them out of the window?" His tone mixed surprise and admiration, and she could imagine his face as he said it. She was beginning to know something of his face and its moods.

"I screwed a bolt into the wood beneath my window, and anytime I heard her at the door, I hung my bag from it. Then after she'd claimed her penalty, I'd retrieve the bag. I tucked an assortment of trinkets in my wardrobe as if they had value to me. It was always best to make Abbott think she was taking something you valued, or she would find a way to claim a bigger penalty the next time."

"That's appalling—Mrs. Abbott's behavior, that is. *Your* solution was quite resourceful. But why didn't you merely find another place to lodge?"

"Few places—respectable places, I mean—allow a woman to live alone. I'd intended to live in the rooms above the offices, but Horatio refused."

"Well, you don't need to worry about Mrs. Abbott's penalties. The magistrate is delivering your belongings to my brother's house. Our murderer might have been able to find his way into a boardinghouse, but it's unlikely he will be so lucky with the home of a duke. You should plan on remaining Forster's guest until the murderer is discovered."

His voice was so serious. The corners of her eyes grew wet, but she wouldn't cry. How could this stranger who knew nothing of her invite her so easily into his brother's home? How could he want to protect her, when those most obligated to care for her had cast her out? She already trusted him too much, and that wasn't wise. "I understand that the magistrate needs my flat for tonight. But could I not slip back tomorrow or the next day? The murderer has already been to my rooms and not found me there. In my view, it could be one of the safest places in London."

"But now your landlady wishes you ill." His tone was kind, as if she were a bit dim.

"Abbott wished me ill long before today."

"The death of her cousin will likely harden that resolve."

"Don't let Abbott fool you; she hated her cousin." Lena reached forward and removed a long, knitted wrap from inside her carpetbag. "Abbott will only miss her cousin when she has to hire a cleaning lady to do Paxton's work." She placed half the width of the wrap over her knees and offered the other half to Clive.

He stretched out the remaining fabric over his lap. "If you opened the window to have the excuse of sharing a blanket, I'm afraid the blanket has failed you. I have only enough for one leg and a bit of a second. I suppose I'm lucky you didn't open both windows." His voice teased her gently.

"Please take more." She reached across his body to pull the wrap farther over his legs, just as he leaned forward. In the dark, their bodies collided. Her elbow met his gut hard. Then, trying to right herself, she pulled her body back at the same moment that he leaned forward instinctively over his belly. Her head hit his nose.

She heard the crunch as well as felt it. Without thinking, she put her hands up to touch his face. His cheeks, shadowed by the growth of evening whiskers, felt rough against her palms. "Please forgive me. I meant only to give you more of the blanket. Are you hurt?" In the intimacy of the dark, her fingers traced the line of his nose. Captivated, she followed his cheekbone down to his jaw, memorizing the lines of his face as if she were blind.

He placed his hand on hers, but instead of stopping her exploration, he let his hand follow the line of her arm up to her neck, then to her chin. She sat still, wanting to lean her face into his palm, but holding herself back.

"I could ask the same of you." His voice was lower, almost husky, the rough edges of it resonating in her belly.

His fingers found her lips, and she let them trace their fullness. "Are you hurt?"

The tension that had shimmered between them all day flared gold with sudden intensity. She let it pull her toward him: she had no will left to resist. With one hand on her cheek, he let his other slide over the fabric of the blanket, brushing the side of her leg down to her knee.

He leaned in, closing the space between his mouth and hers. His breath felt warm on her lips. She refused to wonder if kissing him would be a good or a bad decision. She leaned forward slightly, invitingly, and waited. She could imagine how it would feel—the touch of his skin against hers, tasting each other for the first time. Her anticipation grew each second that he delayed. But she would not close the distance.

The moment drew out long between them. Then, abruptly, he pulled away. "Thank you for sharing your blanket. I find myself quite warm."

Longing still arced between them. She could hear it in his breath and in the cadence of his words. She wished she could see his face and read his expression. But she would not pursue a kiss, if he were not willing. Besides, a kiss would endanger everything. A kiss would mean she trusted him. Even so, she felt unaccountably disappointed, knowing it was for the best, but regretting it all the same.

"The blanket is quite lovely, if you could see it." She filled the uneasy silence with words, but nothing eased the tension between them. She wondered what had made him change his mind. "When I first returned from the Continent, I worked for some months in Ireland. After the commission was finished, I studied with a master weaver, learning how to make dyes from her garden, then how to spin the wool into thread and how to work the loom."

"My brother's house is only a block away." His voice had returned almost to its natural timbre. "Does your weaving tell a story? Or is it only a pattern?"

"It's the story of Orpheus and Eurydice." She tried to focus on something other than the rise and fall of his breath, or the feel of his leg touching hers. "I'm sure you know it."

"Remind me." He shifted his leg away from hers.

"Orpheus was the son of the muse Calliope. At his songs, even the gods would weep or sing. But after the loss of his wife Eurydice, he refused to play, and Zeus allowed him to travel to the underworld to ask Hades for his wife's return."

"Ah, yes, I remember. Hades agrees to let her go, but stipulates that she will follow Orpheus silently through the underworld until they both reached the land of the living. Orpheus was required to trust the god and never look back. If he did, then he would lose her to the underworld forever."

"And he succeeds. He reaches the upper world but he forgets that Eurydice is several steps behind him. She hasn't entered the land of the living yet, and, when he looks back, he sees her disappear."

"Lost to him forever. What made you choose to weave such a sad story?"

"It's not sad, exactly. It's a story about the nature of love. We all die. We all grieve the loss of those we love. But sometimes—in a great love—a lover can seek to be reunited with his beloved, even if it means finding her in the underworld."

The carriage turned into the drive of a large, well-lit house. She lifted the wrap from their legs and folded it deftly away. "And they *are* reunited. In one version of the

story, Hades allows Orpheus to visit Eurydice for some
months each year."

"Perhaps you will show the blanket's design to me tomorrow." Clive tapped on the ceiling. "We have arrived."

The porch and exterior of the duke's Grosvenor Square
residence were well lit, and through the windows, she
could see evidence of a robust staff, all in the ducal livery.
The house itself was large, built—she guessed by the
architecture—early in the previous century, mixing elements of the heavily ornamented baroque style with the
ruled lines of the new Palladian fashion. To have approved
such a design—and kept it, as fashions changed—showed
that the Dukes of Forster were men of thoughtful taste.

"My great-great-grandfather built it." Clive took her
elbow. "It's a moldy old pile, but I've always loved the way
it looks, all flats and curves together."

"The combination is quite striking, evidence of what
a discerning hand can do with discordant elements." His
touch—even through gloves—renewed the sense of connection she'd felt before. She should be wary; she already
trusted him too much.

"Or to please a duke who wants one style and a duchess
who wants another. Apparently there were great rows
over the design, but they were reputed to have adored one
another, and this was their happy compromise." Clive
squeezed Lena's elbow as he led her forward. "Speaking
of couples who are besotted with one another, my brother,
the duke—if you meet him—is only terrifying *before*
sunset. After that, he's typically with Lady Wilmot, his
fiancée, and he appears suddenly quite human."

"I should have told you. I don't know why I didn't."
Stopping before the door, she faced him. "But I have

already met the duke and his fiancée. I would never have agreed to your plan of me staying here overnight if I hadn't."

"I see." His face remained unreadable. "As for your staying here . . ."

At that moment, a smartly dressed man held the door open wide to greet them. "Lord Clive, welcome. And this is your guest, Miss Frost, I assume."

"Miss Frost, this is Barlow, my brother's valet."

"It's the butler's half day off." Barlow ushered them into the house, with a pert nod of the head.

"I thought the duke was staying in Cavendish Square." Clive sounded confused.

"The duke has decided that Lady Wilmot's destruction of his Cavendish Square house will be best effected without him present." Barlow added, "His lordship has yet to learn not to wager with Lady Wilmot. In this last one, the prize was that Lady Wilmot could renovate the master suite."

"Destruction?" Lena questioned, thinking of Lady Wilmot's restrained designs for the salon. "Lady Wilmot didn't strike me as the renovating sort."

"Ah, but you have not seen the master suite, Miss Frost. If Lady Wilmot had not intervened, I would have been obligated to take a blacksmith's sledgehammer to it myself. The previous owner had a remarkable affinity for ornate wallpapers in contrasting colors and patterns. The master suite looked a bit like a bordello designed by Lady Macbeth and Kubla Khan."

Lena immediately imagined a discordant mix of tartan plaids next to delicately rendered cherry blossoms.

"Other than Lady Agatha and the duke, which of my siblings are in residence?" Clive returned the conversation to its purpose.

"Your sister Lady Judith and the newlyweds, Lord and

Lady Colin. Lord Edmund was here yesterday, but he left again this morning, and Lord Seth is expected this evening."

"I see." Clive looked thoughtful. "I assume the duke indicated that Miss Frost will be staying for several days. Given the number of my relatives here, is the Rowan suite free?"

"The Rowan, my lord?" His tone was quizzical, as if Clive had just asked for a monkey or pet eel. "Of course it is free. That is always the last suite given out."

"Miss Frost will take the green bedroom and sitting room." He explained to Lena, "When so many of my relations are present, the Rowan suite is the best in the house. A late addition to the house, it connects to the guest rooms and the family wing by a rather circuitous path, but it has easy access for the servants by way of a dedicated stairwell."

"I will have the housekeeper prepare those rooms." Barlow looked her over carefully but not unkindly, then said to Clive, "I assume you wish to call for a warm bath in advance of dinner."

Clive nodded, and Barlow withdrew.

"Kubla Khan?" she whispered.

Clive laughed. "Barlow is a voracious reader, and he's particularly fond of William Shakespeare and Samuel Taylor Coleridge. He can recite the whole of 'Kubla Khan' for you, if you'd like."

The sound of hearty laughter coming from behind a door at the end of the hall drew their attention. Within moments, the door opened, and Lord Forster and his fiancée, Lady Wilmot, entered, still smiling. The duke had his hand on the small of Lady Wilmot's back. The pair were clearly in love.

"Ah, Miss Frost," Lady Wilmot greeted her graciously. "We have only a moment. Luca and Ian will be dressed well in advance for tonight's dinner, but my Lilly still needs a parent's encouragement."

Lord Forster laughed, shaking his head in mock dismay. "Our little hellion has become quite particular about her clothes. But there's no predicting which dress she will like or hate. She simply refuses to wear some and won't let go of others."

Lady Wilmot nodded in agreement. "But given the difficulties of her last year, we have determined that letting her pick her own dresses isn't too much of an indulgence."

From behind the pair, servants appeared with the duke's greatcoat and Lady Wilmot's fur muff and heavy cloak.

"I was like that as a child. I hated the feel of anything that was too heavily starched." Having met Lilly, Lena felt somehow obligated to help her. "But the starching happened before the clothes came to me, so I couldn't explain why one dress felt fine and the other unbearable."

"That's a fine observation, Miss Frost." The duke tucked Lady Wilmot's reticule under his arm and held out her cloak. "We will test your theory this very night."

"As to dinner, we are so pleased that you've decided to join us this evening at Mrs. Mason's." Lady Wilmot fastened the brooch that held her cloak in place. "How did Clive convince you?"

Lena searched her memory for an invitation. With chagrin, she realized that Ophelia Mason had invited her to a family dinner when they met at the African's Daughter. If she were staying at the duke's house, it would be difficult to refuse, but even so, she could hardly accept. "I am afraid that I haven't anything appropriate to wear for a dinner at Mrs. Mason's."

Lady Wilmot studied her for a moment, taking in her odd work clothes, smeared in places with paint, pausing at her bandaged hands. "Knowing Clive, he has already considered the problem of clothes." Lady Wilmot patted Clive's arm. "Haven't you, Clive?"

"Of course." Clive spoke without hesitation.

"Excellent. The duke has left instructions for the large family carriage to collect you two, Lady Judith, and Boatswain around seven. Lord and Lady Colin have already ridden over on their new matched pair. As I understand, they are remaining several nights with the Masons." Lady Wilmot bid them farewell in continental fashion, kissing both their cheeks. "Barlow will send a maid to help you dress."

Lady Wilmot and the duke left arm in arm.

Once the door shut behind the pair, Clive looked Lena over, head to foot, as if he hadn't seen her before. Under his attentive gaze she suddenly felt exposed and vulnerable— she liked neither feeling. His tone, when he finally spoke, was somewhat cautious. "You can leave the matter of your dinner clothing to me."

"To you?" Lena bristled, knowing it was unreasonable. But he might have asked if she had a suitable dinner dress pressed down tight in her carpetbag (though of course she didn't). She'd had clothes before as beautiful as Lady Wilmot's, and on the Continent she'd danced with dukes. Of course, those dukes were in exile, but they were dukes nonetheless.

"Or rather you can leave it to my family. Lady Judith is too short to be any help, but Lady Colin likely has something appropriate for you to wear. Alternatively, if you prefer, we can call on Lady Wilmot's modiste. She always has a few dresses ready for situations such as this."

"I have no money to buy a dress, and I don't wish to be indebted to the duke." She raised her chin and straightened her shoulders. Unfortunately that placed his all-too-inviting lips at her eye level.

"I'm not a dependent, Lena. I have my own funds," he corrected, studying her face as if she were his patient.

"You live in his house." She seemed to have little control over her emotions this late in a long, difficult day.

"I live at my club. I teach at the surgery school, as I told you, though I do at times work for the estate as well." His voice was calm and even, and that annoyed her.

"What does *work* mean for the son and brother of a duke? An hour or so, here or there, when you find yourself at loose ends?" She glared at him, a foul mood swirling unpleasantly in her belly.

"My work . . ." His eyes flashed with frustration, and she waited, prepared to object to whatever he said. As the clock counted the passing seconds, she tucked an errant curl under her cap with her bandaged hand, and Clive's face changed in an instant.

"I must apologize. You are the most resilient woman I have ever met."

"That's an odd apology." She stared into his face.

"I am a physician. I know—or I *should* know—that fear or fright commonly produces a disorder of the emotions. Today you have met with three frightening experiences, but in each instance, you have rallied admirably. To help you recover, I should have provided you with a quiet residence, not a house filled with interfering strangers . . . and family dinners." He paused again, but Lena said nothing. "I'll have Barlow escort you to your room, and you can at least have some quiet before our trip to Kensington."

His explanation, awkward as it was, soothed her worn nerves. Though she wouldn't admit it, she did need some quiet to gather her thoughts and energies, but at the same time, she didn't wish to be left too long alone. "What will you be doing while I . . . rest?"

"I will be searching for clothing that hasn't been heavily starched."

When Lena reached her rooms, the fire was already blazing, her bath ready before it. A tall screen separated the fire and tub from the rest of the room, creating a warm oasis for her bath. A maid stood by to help her out of her clothes. She hung her outer clothes over the screen, stripping to her underwear. Stepping behind the screen, she changed into the shift provided for her to bathe in. She heard the maid shut the door.

The tub was large and deep, obviously made for the Somerville men. She dipped her hand in the water. Warm, oh-so-warm, almost hot. Perfect. Next to the tub was a pot of soap, scented with lemon and rosemary, and a hand mirror. Catching a glimpse of herself, she gasped and touched her face and hair.

How had Lady Wilmot *not* commented on her appearance? A bruise darkened on her forehead and temple where her head had hit one of the boards as she fell. Her mob hat was ripped on one side, and her hair stuck out at odd angles. One long hank of hair appeared to be painted a rich scarlet. Her color was muddy, and her cheeks were sunken.

As if on cue, her stomach rumbled and twisted. When had she last eaten? She thought back. A slice of bread and cheese with Constance before retiring for bed the night before. Then nothing. Horatio had eaten the food they kept at the Rotunda before he scampered, and Lady Wilmot's advance had gone to pay her crew. It wasn't the first day she'd gone without food, but it felt longer. Suddenly, she was less averse to a family dinner with free, well-prepared food.

She twisted the scarlet strand between her fingers. She

would have to apologize to Clive. He had been generous, helpful, and conciliatory, while she had been consistently suspicious and irritable. She pulled off the mob bonnet, removed her hairpins, and began to unplait what remained of her braid. Her dark-brown hair fell long around her shoulders. She hadn't intended to wash her hair. But now that she'd seen herself, not to do so would be inconsiderate, particularly to Clive, who would be her escort. She considered her hair in the mirror. A low bun would be suitable for a family dinner, and it would require little extra time and no help from a maid.

Lena pulled off the shift. She hadn't had the luxury of immersing herself in a warm bath since she'd left France, and she wanted to be nude.

She stepped into the tub slowly, then settled under the water. She couldn't imagine how much it cost to draw and heat so much water. At Mrs. Abbott's, a bath cost more than a man going upstairs *twice*, and the water was never warm. Lena had to be satisfied with a hand bath, using water in her basin and pitcher, and, in the winter, when it was especially cold, she'd heat the water in her fireplace. But Mrs. Abbott was stingy with the water in the basins as well, and Lena had learned to be circumspect.

She closed her eyes and reclined in the tub, letting her weariness melt into the water. Prompted by her appearance in the mirror, she paid attention to each part of her body, cataloging her wounds. Her ankle was swollen and sore, but not badly hurt. The muscles in her back and shoulders were tense and tight. Her hands were still bandaged, the linen stuck in places to her wounds. She held them under the warm water until the bandages loosened and were easily removed. Her palms were badly abraded, but the scrapes had all closed up, and nothing yet was red or festering. They looked—and felt—better than she'd expected. She let herself drift, thinking of nothing, until time itself seemed to slow. Some time later, refreshed, she began to wash her body, letting the scent of lemon and rosemary invigorate her senses.

She submerged under the water, wetting her hair through, then she washed it, one section at a time, with the deliciously scented soap. Rinsing it, she sunk down in the water once more, letting her hair float out from her head. Did she look like Caravaggio's *Medusa*? Or would Barlow say the mad prophet from Coleridge's "Kubla Khan"? In an instant, she could see Horatio, declaiming Coleridge's poem from the Rotunda platform. When she'd asked what he was doing, he'd explained, with arms extended wide, "It's a stage, my dear. We must learn how the sounds move in this space, so that we can manage them."

Oh, Horatio, where are you?

She opened her eyes in alarm. Horatio's note. She'd left it in her pocket. She scrambled out of the bath, looking for her clothes. She'd hung them on the back of the screen. But they were gone. Given her own appearance, she doubted if the maid meant only to brush them. What if it were laundry day?

Still wet, she pulled on the shift, trying to imagine a way to retrieve Horatio's note. The linen stuck to her wet body. She looked for some other covering, but found only a thin towel. She couldn't wait. She wrapped the towel around her shoulders like a shawl and pulled the clinging material of the shift away from her body. If she used the servants' stairwell, she could perhaps avoid a scandal: once below stairs, she would call out from behind the half-opened stairway door for someone to assist her.

She opened her bedroom door and rushed into the hall, just as Clive emerged from the main stairwell.

The thin shift, still wet and clinging to her body, revealed as much as it concealed. Clive stopped abruptly midstep. He stared. But whether he felt shock, dismay, or desire, she couldn't tell.

Her feet felt as if they were part of the floor. She couldn't speak.

Clive recovered his words first. "Lady Wilmot has sent word that she has two or three dresses that might suit you. Her house is only a block or two away." He held up a folded piece of paper. "I was about to leave a note under your door, telling you that I'd be back before you finish . . . your bath." He swallowed visibly and looked down at the floor. "Are you in need of something?"

"The maid. She took my clothes." Lena's words came back in a rush.

"Yes, we are in luck." His eyes continued to examine a spot on the floor in front of his boots. "It's washing day below stairs."

"No!" She rushed forward, then stopped before she reached him. "There's a pocket sewed into the side of my skirt. In it, there's a note. It's important to me."

"There should be a blanket in the wardrobe of your room. You can wear it until your clothes arrive." He looked pained. "I'll see if I can retrieve your note." He turned on his heel and ran away.

Back in her room, she found the blanket as Clive had indicated and wrapped it around her shoulders in anticipation of his returning. But he did not. Instead, several moments later, a maid brought her two notes on a silver tray. Horatio's was still folded into a small packet. She clasped it to her breast. The fire was still blazing, but there was no time to examine the note again. She opened the second. The handwriting was a firm round hand, distinctive for its lack of embellishment: "Perhaps a red dress—to go with your hair. Clive."

After a tap at the door, the housekeeper, Mrs. Tracy, a slender, blond woman with a placid face, entered, followed by a battalion of maids, carrying dresses, headdresses, reticules, slippers, and finally irons and cosmetics. The silence of the maids surprised her, so unlike the servants she had known. But this was a duke's home, and it clearly operated by a different set of rules.

Under Mrs. Tracy's quiet direction, each pair of maids displayed a dress for her consideration. Each dress was more beautiful than anything she had ever owned. Each one—even the ornate, silk confections rich in ribbons and bows—was fit for a princess. Nothing was overblown or tasteless. Even the large feather in one of the hats seemed a fashionable statement rather than a pompous display.

Hoping to please Clive by taking his recommendation (it was the least she could do given her earlier ill temper), she tried on Lady Wilmot's coquelicot velvet first, hoping the rich soft dress might work. But it and her Pomona green silk were far too long (both without hope of pinning). Lady Colin's jonquil evening dress was too short and the fabric scratchy, and the cut of Lady Judith's severe slate gown was wholly unflattering. She began to feel like the intruder in Robert Southey's children's story of the three bears: too big, too small, too everything. Nothing came close to fitting.

With each dress that the maids removed, Lena's spirits drooped just a little lower. If it weren't a dinner party and if her hosts were not a duke and his relations, she could ask for one of the footmen to retrieve one of her business dresses from the Rotunda. But that dress would be equally as inappropriate as the work dress Mrs. Tracy was having washed. The prospect of appearing at the party in inappropriate—

or ill-fitting—clothes made her wish she could run away in her shift and hide.

Eventually, only she, the housekeeper, and two maids— Trudy and Elizabeth—remained. Mrs. Tracy, taking on the expression of a solicitor examining a particularly complicated legal document, looked her over carefully. "Turn around now, slowly, let me see your figure."

Lena obeyed, trying not to wonder at the whispering behind her back. By the time Lena had made the full circle, the maids were gone.

"It's obvious you are no society miss," Mrs Tracy said mildly. "No one gets strong arms and a firm middle without work—and a bit of hunger."

Lena wondered if she should be offended, but Mrs. Tracy's tone was matter-of-fact, not critical. All such considerations were quickly lost, when Elizabeth returned, followed by two footmen. One carried a tray full of ham, bread, cheese, biscuits, butter, pots of various jams. The other a small tea service suitable for one. Wordlessly, they set both on a nearby ottoman, then retired.

"Mr. Barlow is a fine valet, but the butler would have noticed that you needed a bite to eat. And don't hesitate to eat your fill: Mrs. Mason lives in Kensington, and unless Lady Judith drives, the travel alone will take the better part of an hour."

"Perhaps it would be better if I declined the invitation," Lena said, surprised at the depth of her disappointment.

Mrs. Tracy patted her arm. "We still have an hour before you have to leave. I'll send your measurements to Lady Wilmot's modiste to see if she has something suitable already made." Pulling a measuring tape, pencil, and piece of paper from the basket of cosmetics, Mrs. Tracy scribbled on the paper.

Trudy returned, speaking low in Mrs. Tracy's ear. The

housekeeper nodded with a slight smile, handing Trudy the paper with Lena's measurements.

"Eat now." Mrs. Tracy patted her arm reassuringly. "We'll have a dress for you before you finish your tea." As the housekeeper and the maids left, Lena wondered if there were a school for housekeepers that taught them to respond to each crisis as if it were nothing more significant than a bit of dusting.

"Are you superstitious, Miss Frost?" Mrs. Tracy entered the room, wearing her typical placid expression.

"I don't believe so." Lena considered whether it would be rude to eat the last biscuit. "But I suppose everyone could be, given the proper circumstances. Why?"

"I've found a dress or two that I believe will suit your frame and coloring."

"What does that have to do with superstition?" Lena gave in, spreading the biscuit with marmalade and taking a bite. She let the flavor settle on her tongue before taking a sip of tea.

"Some people wouldn't wish to wear a dress associated with a public scandal," Mrs. Tracy said, pitching her voice confidentially.

Caught by surprise, Lena almost choked on her tea. "I suppose it depends on the nature of the scandal and what role the dress played in it. At the same time, I would be foolish to refuse a dress, however scandalous, when I have need of one."

Mrs. Tracy seemed pleased with Lena's answers. "I have been authorized to tell you the story, though certainly the story is already well known. It was five years ago, not so long ago that the dress will be too far out of fashion."

"Before or after Waterloo?" Lena wondered if the scandal had involved officers returning home.

"After. That fall." A distant look crossed Mrs. Tracy's face, then disappeared. "Lady Agatha had agreed to chaperone two debutantes—twin daughters of her dearest childhood friend, who had died some years before. The girls found it amusing to have all their clothes made exactly to match, so that they could always claim the other was the culprit in whatever game they were playing. Lady Agatha quickly intervened by having their dresses made in different-colored fabrics. But the girls would simply fool their suitors by exchanging dresses in the withdrawing room of whatever ball they were attending. Lady Ida Talmere discovered their ruse at her birthday ball, but instead of giving up their game, they knocked Lady Ida to the floor, tied her up, and gagged her with the ribbons they tore from her dress, then shoved her into the withdrawing-room closet."

"How terrible!" Lena shook her head in dismay. "Was Lady Ida hurt?"

"No, Lady Ida eventually managed to escape from the closet. She accused the girls in the middle of the ballroom floor. It was apparently a scene suitable for Shakespeare: Ida with her hair disheveled and clothes torn, raising an arm of accusation before the watchful eyes of the ton."

"What happened next?"

"The girls each pretended the other was at fault. But Lords Clive and Edmund—who, as you would expect, could always tell them apart—confirmed that the girls had indeed switched dresses after they had arrived. Lady Agatha sent them back to the country that very night, refusing them any item that they had received while in London, including the full wardrobes the duke had bought them. Lady Agatha says you may use the wardrobe as long as you wish. So the decision is yours."

"We should begin by seeing if any of the dresses fit." Lena rose from her meal.

"Good girl," Mrs. Tracy beamed. She opened the door to let in Trudy and Elizabeth. The maids carried a single dress with its accompanying wrap. The dress was a deep scarlet silk, with three narrow rows of gray-green ribbing at the bodice and ankles; nearest the floor were two narrow rows of a cream-colored flounce. The sleeves were long, with the same detailing at the wrists. The wrap was a cream silk, with a wide border of gray and scarlet, with tiny scarlet pompons tied closely to the fabric in neat rows. "If this one doesn't suit you, there are several others."

"It's lovely, more than lovely." Lena touched the fabric in awe. She didn't have the luxury of caring about fashion; she had a French dress she wore for meeting partners or clients as well as two dresses for working at the Rotunda. But this dress was more beautiful than any dress she could ever hope to own. And for some reason—she didn't pursue why—she wanted Clive to see her in it.

"It will be more than lovely if it fits." Mrs. Tracy waved the maids forward to help Lena into the dress.

Lena stepped into the red silk, wishing—if wishing would help—that it would fit. And it did. Perfectly. In every detail the dress looked bespoke: from the curve of the bodice to the length of the arms and skirt. It fitted her perfectly. She imagined Clive seeing her, his eyes widening in appreciation, and the thought pleased her as much as the dress.

"I thought this one might fit. The twins were country girls, used to doing for themselves, even if that doing was mischief. We'll move the rest of the clothing into your wardrobe while you are at dinner."

"I hadn't intended to stay but a day or two, so I hate for you to go to the trouble."

"Lady Agatha has kept the clothes for just such an occasion as this."

"Will Lady Agatha be going to the Masons' family dinner? I would like to thank her."

"Lady Agatha does as she wishes. If you wish to write a note, I'll convey your thanks to her. If she chooses to see you, she will send you a card," Mrs. Tracy explained. "Now slip off that dress while Trudy dresses your hair. Elizabeth and I will find you some slippers and a suitable hairpiece."

Lena began to object, intending to point out that a low bun would be perfectly suitable, but she stopped herself. Mrs. Tracy had been so kind already that refusing her help would be simply ungrateful. And truth be told, she wanted to see what miracles Trudy and Elizabeth might be able to perform.

Chapter Ten

Clive waited for Lena in the entry hall of the duke's house. She wasn't late: he was merely early and anxious. He felt out of control, and he never felt that way.

Since he'd caught her, he felt a natural concern for her well-being. Simply that. He'd remained by her side to ensure that she came to no additional harm, especially while she helped him search for Calder. It was a gentlemanly, *disinterested* concern, he assured himself, one no different from what he would feel for the workhouse poor, an orphan child, or a mistreated animal. Certainly he could have found Calder's lodgings without her help, but it would have taken time, and he would have thought the dead body they found was Calder's. He'd already sent a note to Thacker, the magistrate, giving him Calder's address and telling him what he would find there.

He touched the scrape to his own hand that he'd hidden from her. Not nearly so bad as hers, it reminded him how things had very nearly gone wrong. He didn't blame himself for not noticing the damage to the ladder, but if Calder had disappeared, Clive should have anticipated that his business partner could be in danger. Others had already died—he didn't know how many—at the hands of this gang of murderers, resurrection men who made their own dead bodies rather than go to the trouble of stealing them. Whether she realized it or not, Lena knew something vital—the murder in her rooms confirmed it. But she didn't yet trust him.

"What does work *mean for the son and brother of a duke?"* He'd heard some version of her accusation his whole life. As the youngest brother of a duke, he was not guaranteed a living or even a livelihood. But few occupations were open to him: he couldn't become a cobbler or a tailor, a blacksmith or cabinetmaker, an apothecary, or a baker. While privilege gave him opportunity and connections, it was irrevocably tied to expectation. And that expectation identified as appropriate a particular set of occupations. Their eldest brother Aaron—long dead and largely unmourned—had chosen reprobate, a common enough career for the heir-in-waiting. Benjamin, Aidan, and Colin had chosen soldier, but after Benjamin's death, his father had refused to send any more sons to war. That left the clergy or the bar, and Clive refused both.

From his boyhood, he'd devoured tales where ordinary men alleviated the wrongs of the day. His brothers—if asked—would say that Clive chose medicine—or rather medical researches—because he'd read *Don Quixote* too often in his boyhood. What else was medicine but a fight against the windmill of death? And death was always the victor.

But Clive was interested in the skirmishes rather than the war. He wanted to improve life as people lived it: each day. If he'd learned anything from *Quixote*, it was that impossible battles were the only ones worth fighting. So, he welcomed each windmill as an opportunity to change the world, and he focused on that world writ large. Clive's favorite imagined future was one where the wrongs of disease had long ago been righted, where no more children were crippled by rickets, or blind from measles, or deaf from mumps. To achieve that future, he and others had to discover the mechanisms by which a body worked, how it fell prey to diseases, and doing so, learn how to cure them.

That same optimism—or idealism rather—led him to help with investigations for the Home Office—or the secret part of it that employed him occasionally and his brother Edmund more regularly. Drawing on his understanding of the ways the human body died, Clive had found another way to right a different sort of wrong.

His favorite translation of *Quixote* described the man who fought injustice as a gallant "chevalier in shining armor." Sometimes, when an experiment went particularly well, or Clive solved a perplexing case for the Home Office, he could imagine himself as that itinerant knight, battling for the health of all men. Sadly, confined to his surgery, his researches rarely included a grateful damsel in distress. Though Lena's troubles made her seem to fit that role, she didn't need saving—she was independent, strong-minded, obstinate, and altogether fascinating. Though he could help her through a difficult situation as an episode in his quixotic adventures, he resisted the idea that she might be the whole romance.

Even so, they had almost kissed. She was a beautiful young woman who made it clear that she wished to kiss him. For a moment, he'd been tempted, but he'd decided against it. She was overwrought and vulnerable. Besides, he knew better than to discount Sophia's injunction not to seduce her painter.

But then he'd seen Lena rushing headlong into the hall: hair long and wild about her shoulders, eyes wide with concern, those perfect lips rosy with exertion. She'd worn such a look of panic on her face that he'd feared her enemies had somehow found their way into the ducal residence. It hadn't mattered that she was undressed, that her shift clung to her body still wet from the bath, that he could see all the evocative parts of her. Standing there, his heart racing in his chest, he realized his desire for her went far beyond a simple stolen kiss. In that moment, he made a lover's inventory: slender ankles, muscular thighs, ample hips, narrow waist, lush breasts, wide shoulders, determined chin, cherry lips, and soulful eyes. He added to it less obvious characteristics: a strong will, a quick wit, and a confidence he had rarely encountered in a woman outside the circle of strong women his family clearly valued.

He'd never received any letter that had meant so much to him that he would risk certain scandal to retrieve it. And he found himself jealous that she cared more for a folded packet of paper than for him. He had collected it from the laundry maid just as she was about to immerse the whole in the bath, and he had inspected the outside carefully, hoping to find a name or address that he could investigate on his own. But he found no clues, nothing at least without unfolding the letter, and that went too far, even in the name of protecting her. At the same time, he wanted to open it. He wanted to find that it was the last message of some dear friend who had recently died, or a communication with information vital to the success of her enterprises. The last thing he wanted to consider was that Lena had no need of his help because she already had a man she loved.

He consulted the hall clock. Five more minutes.

He looked around the entry hall of the duke's house, trying to see the residence as Lena might. The entry alone was larger by far than the whole of her boardinghouse rooms, and the boardinghouse itself could fit in a quarter, or less, of the ducal mansion. He wondered whether her current lodgings, dingy and cramped, were like those she'd had in France. And he wondered where she had lived before that, though he knew already that she was unlikely to confide such things in him. And it only made him want to know her more.

Barlow entered the house from the front drive. "Lady Judith wishes for you to know that she is already in the carriage."

"Should I ask why?"

"Given that we do not know if Miss Frost gets along with animals, Lady Judith determined it would be best to have Boatswain calm and settled before you and Miss Frost arrive."

"Is it working?" Clive loved the dog as much as anyone in the family, but he understood his sister's concerns for Lena.

"Fletcher has contrived a wall of sorts in the well between the seats to help contain Lady Colin's giant puppy, and the hound seems to be quite contented. He has already chewed half through one of the bars, and I predict there will be none left by the time you reach Hyde Park. Lady Judith is seated beside him on the forward-facing seat, and you are to sit opposite her, so that when Boatswain escapes his cage, one of you can intervene before he reaches Miss Frost."

"My sister has thought of everything."

"As is usual, my lord." Barlow would never admit it, but, after the duke, Lady Judith was his favorite of the Somervilles.

"Can I ask why we are transporting the pup? Or would it be best not to know?"

"There's no harm in knowing . . . this time. The newly-weds are staying a few days with Mrs. Mason. They wished to ride their new matched pair, but of course that meant that one of the servants would have to deliver Boatswain—or the newlyweds would have to travel separately."

"Given how reticent Lady Colin is to be too long apart from Boatswain or her husband, I see the problem," Clive filled in. The family understood that Lucy's reliance on the pup went beyond mere affection.

"So your sister offered to bring the pup with her tonight, but that was before we knew that you and Miss Frost would be attending, and with all your siblings currently in town, every other carriage is in use."

"With Lady Judith and me as a barricade, I'm sure that all will work out well." He looked at the hall clock again: one minute until departure.

Barlow followed his gaze. "I'll gather your coat and one for Miss Frost."

Clive stared up the stairs. Mrs. Tracy had promised to escort Lena to the front of the house, and Clive was grateful. He knew that his hesitance to see her again after their encounter in the hall signaled a particular kind of cowardice. But when he remembered her standing there, barely clad, her body revealed imperfectly under the wet shift, he again wished he had not promised to resist her.

Just as the clock began to chime the hour, Lena appeared at the top of the stairs. Lena barely clad reminded him of a goddess, but wearing clothes, she was equally stunning. The red gave color to her cheeks, making them seem fuller, healthier, than before. The gray-green ribbing caressed the gentle swell of her bosom, and the fabric itself fell gracefully to her ankles. He found himself dumbstruck, wishing to compliment her, but uncertain what sort of a compliment would be welcome.

"You wore red." Even to his ears, the words sounded bald and foolish.

"How could I resist, when such a delicious gown was offered to me?" Excited, she turned a circle to show him the dress. "It's *vermilion* actually, but *red* is fine for a layman."

"Your hair isn't red anymore." He fumbled for better words, but couldn't find any.

"I was able to wash the paint out." She touched her hair where the red had been. "What do you think?"

He paused, taking in the full effect. Her coiffure was quietly elegant, her hair brushed up and back, her low bun coupled with an understated braid, the whole wound in place with black pearls. Suddenly he was glad neither of his unattached brothers were expected at Ophelia's dinner. But as he gazed at her, she seemed to deflate a little, as if she expected him to criticize.

He spoke quickly, his words stumbling out in a rush. "You look stunning, simply magnificently stunning."

Her smile started as a glimmer, then broadened slowly, until it transformed her whole face. It was a smile that caught him in the gut, and he realized he might never be the same again.

"As you can see, our cousin has no fear of the current taxes on windows and glass." Lady Judith pointed at a well-lit house in the far distance. The oil lamps in the front windows looked like stars. "Sidney Mason inherited a family industry in perfume, but he contributed to that enterprise an interest in soap."

"A very profitable interest in soap," Clive added. "You have likely already enjoyed his produce: no one in the family—and certainly not in the duke's house—uses any soap but his."

Lena thought of the delicately scented lemon and rosemary soap that accompanied her bath. "Then I have. It was delightful."

"You must tell Sidney. After his wife and his heir, he loves nothing on earth more than someone enjoying his soaps." Lady Judith patted her arm encouragingly.

The Masons' Kensington home was set well back from the road on a substantial acreage, and Lena watched the house, glittering in the distance, until the carriage turned into the long lane that led to the residence. The house in the distance and the curving avenue that led to it, bringing the house in and out of view, made her think of other homecomings when she was a girl, all more troubled than happy.

She'd been barely ten when her father had sent her away. How he'd chosen Mrs. Edstein's Finishing School for Young Ladies, she'd discovered later when she'd found a stack of letters, bound in scented ribbon, from the headmistress to her father. The first had arrived shortly after her mother's funeral, claiming an old friendship with her mother and recommending herself—a widow—as a suitable ear to his grief and sorrow. Some months later, the letters had shifted to the trials of rearing a motherless child, offering her skills as a childhood monitor—all for only sixteen guineas a year. Since all Edstein's boarding students were orphans, Lena wondered if the headmistress had carried out similar letter-writing campaigns to all their fathers, grieving or not. Lena's father, a weak man, not unkind, but self-absorbed and willful, had been particularly susceptible to the attention. While alive, Lena's mother had directed him quietly, making him useful where he would otherwise have been dilatory, and generous where he would otherwise have been profligate. Mrs. Edstein, in letters, presumed to take the place of her mother, directing his decisions as if she were his wife.

Lena could still remember her final visit home. She'd looked forward to the visit for weeks, having found boarding school repressive, and Mrs. Edstein vindictive and cruel. Lena had believed that in person she could finally accomplish what her begging letters had failed to do: convince her father to bring her home and hire a governess. She'd run to the carriage her father had sent for her, only to find her headmistress already inside. No one had told her Mrs. Edstein would be spending the vacation with them.

The long ride home had been filled with silence when Edstein slept, and recriminations and threats when she didn't. But even so, Lena hadn't anticipated her father's hearty welcome of her headmistress. Intent to show Edstein his house and lands, he'd handed her down from the carriage, then walked away before Lena reached the stairs. And he'd said nothing when Edstein had instructed the servants to take Lena's bags to the nursery, or when she had taken for herself Lena's mother's room, which Lena had made her own after the funeral. On dark nights when she felt alone, Lena still felt the betrayal deep in her belly.

Without thinking, Lena tucked her foot around Clive's ankle. With the help of a bag of broken biscuits provided by the cook, her rescuer was attempting to teach the dog some trick. But at her touch, he paused and winked, his kindness displacing somewhat her old hurts.

"I think he has it now." Clive tossed a broken bit of biscuit into the dog's mouth. As predicted, the big puppy had chewed his way through his makeshift pen by the time they reached Hyde Park. But he was a gentle dog and eager to please.

"See if he will do the trick without the biscuit. That's the test." Judith took the bag out of Clive's hand.

"Yes, try it without," Lena agreed, hoping she hadn't been lost in bad memories for long.

"As you wish, my ladies." Clive gave the command and held out his hand. The pup looked suspiciously from Judith—holding the sack of biscuits—to Clive, but eventually decided to obey the command, putting his paw in Clive's hand.

Lady Judith and Lena praised the dog almost in unison, and the pup wagged his tail happily.

"That's a great trick, but perhaps you should have taught him how to wait while we descend from the carriage." Lady Judith handed the pup a bit of biscuit. "I'm afraid that if the footman opens Lena's door, Boatswain will make a leap for the door and ruin both our dresses."

"I had a dog once, and I found that it was simply best to give the dog precedence and let him descend first," Lena suggested. "That realization saved me repairing many a dress."

Clive raised an eyebrow, and Lena realized she had unwittingly given him more information about her past than she'd intended. But he said nothing, merely tossed the pup another biscuit.

The carriage slowed, pulling under a porte cochere where a brigade of footmen waited.

"Yours seems like sound advice, Lena," Lady Judith acknowledged. "As soon as the carriage stops, I will let Boatswain out on my side."

"If I may add to my sister's earlier advice about the Masons, you will find our cousin Ophelia unabashedly good-natured. She is naturally sociable, with a talent for designing easy gatherings filled with laughter." Clive paused.

"But?" Lena prodded, studying his face while he searched for the right words.

Clive looked to his sister, but Lady Judith shook her head, refusing to help him.

"Ophelia loves science." He shrugged. "She styles herself a chemist."

Lena studied his face, uncertain how to interpret his comment, but she saw no resentment or revulsion. Other than his first annoying comment about women's capabilities at the Rotunda, Clive had shown himself to be remarkably open to her expertise. Was he generally uncomfortable with knowledgeable women, or merely with Mrs. Mason's particular expertise? She knew she should let the comment pass by, but, if she were to continue to trust him, she needed to know.

"If an interest in chemical reactions is a fault, then I bear the blame as well," she said. "In the *buon fresco* paintings Lady Wilmot has commissioned, the pigment will bond with the lime, making the images both durable and vivid."

"I didn't mean to suggest it's a fault to have an interest or a passion. It's simply that when Ophelia's gotten a new chemistry book, she can talk of almost nothing else until she's worked out all the experiments in her laboratory. Last week, her husband bought her *several* new books."

Lena wanted to ask more, wanted to tease out how Clive felt about women who could talk about nothing but their passions, but at that moment, the carriage stopped fully, ending their conversation, as they both watched Lady Judith reach to unlatch the door nearest Boatswain.

The dog watched Judith's every movement, his tail a

metronome of his excitement. When the door swung open, the dog—seeing Lady Colin standing on the porch—let out a wailing howl, then sprang from the carriage and ran headlong toward his mistress. Having protected hers and Lady Judith's dresses, Lena wondered if the reunion was going to spell disaster for Lady Colin's instead. But as Boatswain reached his mistress's feet, Lucy gave a hand signal, and the pup slid into a sit, wagging his sturdy tail in time with her petting.

Clive jumped down, stepping aside for the footmen to place the steps. As Lena descended, Clive held her hand a moment longer than necessary, squeezing it as he let it go. Lena assumed it was a sort of apology for their unfinished conversation, but she wished it might be a promise instead, of what she wasn't sure.

On the porch, Mrs. Mason held out her hands in greeting. "Ah, Miss Frost, what a pleasure! Miss Equiano should arrive shortly. I must say that I'm indebted to you, my dear." Seeing Lady Colin and Lady Judith deep in conversation, Ophelia Mason led Lena into the house with Clive following. "Cousin Clive has missed almost all my family dinners this fall, claiming that his research couldn't be left."

"Says my wife who has spent every afternoon this week staring at the contents of a beaker." An average-looking man, impeccably dressed, joined them. Ophelia, taking his arm, introduced him as her husband, Sidney.

"Beaker?" Lena prompted Ophelia to discuss her work, watching Clive carefully for his response to the conversation.

"My beloved Ophelia is an alchemist, Miss Frost." Sidney Mason smiled broadly. "Some years ago, she promised that if I would keep her well-equipped with beakers and other chemical apparatuses, she would reward my investment by converting various crude metals into gold or silver. Thus far she has not fulfilled her part of the bargain."

Ophelia shook her head in mock dismay. "Sidney is teasing you, Miss Frost. My experiments are purely chemical, not *al*chemical. I'm currently interested in breaking down common components into their most basic parts and learning their attributes. Thus far, my fellow natural scientists have discovered one hundred elements, and I'm hoping someday to discover one myself."

Lena paused, grateful to meet another woman of intelligence and ambition. "That's an admirable goal."

"More than admirable," Clive said with obvious pride. "If anyone can do it, it's our Ophelia. I've made her promise to name the first element after me."

"I promised you the second; Sidney will be first." Ophelia swatted Clive's arm. "He bought me two works for my birthday, both in foreign tongues, so my experiments are moving a bit slowly." She added to Lena, not-so-confidentially, "Sidney has made me promise to have my son's tutor confirm all my translations before I try any of the experiments."

"Let me be clear, Miss Frost," Sidney intervened. "My wife's command of German and French is quite strong. But one of the books I bought her describes experiments with volatile compounds, and I wish for her to confirm her translations to ensure that I will have a house and family when I return from Whitehall each evening."

"What books has Sidney bought you?" Clive winked at Lena from behind Ophelia's head, encouraging the conversation Lena had started. The wink as much as his prompting made her belly flip.

Ophelia beamed. "I can always count on Clive to show

an interest in my researches. One—as Sidney described it—is a book on volatile compounds; the other is a pharmacopeia by the Swiss chemist Jacob Berzelius."

"I see." Clive nodded sagely. "If Miss Frost wishes to create any of a dozen poisons, she'll know to consult you. But make sure first, my dear cousin, that I'm not on the list of recipients."

"He has not yet given me reason to poison him." Lena met Clive's eyes. He was studying her intently, and his gaze held both a dare and a promise.

"Give him time," Judith chimed in from behind the group.

Lena wondered if conversations in the Mason household were always so unusual, but she found participating quite delightful. "I do have a question for a chemist, if you wouldn't mind."

"Of course!" Ophelia beamed. "If I cannot answer it, I likely know someone who can. I'm a member of the corresponding society of chemists."

"I walk past a cemetery where the stench—particularly at night—is so awful that the gravediggers say they must be drunk to withstand it. Last month they discovered one of their own, unconscious, in one of the deep grave pits, and the man who offered to retrieve him fell unconscious as well. By the time the others could retrieve them, both men were dead. What makes the air in a cemetery so dangerous?"

"That's quite easy to answer, though a bit complicated," Ophelia answered. "It's related to a highly volatile gas that Alessandro Volta discovered in a marsh at Lake Maggiore. He even developed a tool in 1776 to show its combustibility—a *pistola di volta*."

"A pistol?" Lena asked.

"A glass pistol. One chamber held the gas, the other a

projectile. To expel the bullet, Volta ignited the gas with a charge of static electricity." Ophelia grew thoughtful, then turned to her husband. "Sidney, darling, if a glass blower made us a *pistola di Volta*, I could demonstrate ignition as part of our son's education."

Sidney Mason groaned. "Perhaps I should reinforce the walls of her laboratory—or move it farther from the house."

"It's already at the very bottom of the garden, darling," Ophelia reminded.

"Then I need to purchase the land adjacent to the garden," Sidney joked. "To pay for it, I'll create a new scented soap, something a bit grassy called 'Ophelia's meadow.'"

"Or something that smells of sulfur and called 'Ophelia's experiments gone awry.'" Clive played along.

Ophelia rolled her eyes. "As to your question, Miss Frost. As bodies decay, they produce Volta's marsh gas. In city cemeteries, the bodies are so densely packed that the gasses build up below the surface." Ophelia's tone turned serious. "If cemetery ground looks like it's bubbling, you must be very careful."

"Bubbling?" Lena questioned.

"Gurgling, spongy, marshy—any of those is a sign to avoid that area."

"Why?" Clive asked, clearly interested as well.

"That's a sign that the gases have built up to dangerous levels and might very well explode! Curates often drill a hole in coffins to release the gas slowly. If they don't . . ."

"I know the answer to this: the coffins explode!" Clive placed a hand under Lena's elbow, and she relaxed into the warmth of his touch.

"Clive, given your avocation, you must treat this seriously," Ophelia insisted. "If you experience any of the symptoms of marsh gas poisoning—an aching head, a taste of metal, nausea, or trembling—you must find good air very quickly if you wish to survive."

"What distinguishes between good and bad air?" Lena was fascinated, and a bit concerned. More than once in her studio, she'd felt exactly as Ophelia had described.

"In chemical terms, it's very simple. Marsh gas is almost pure hydrogen, just one part carbon to four parts hydrogen, while the compound we need for healthful respiration is—as Joseph Priestley discovered in 1775—one part oxygen to two parts hydrogen."

"So, that's why the men in the graveyard died? They breathed in too much hydrogen, and not enough oxygen?"

"Exactly what role oxygen plays in human respiration is still under debate. But the exploding part—everyone agrees on that." Ophelia smiled.

"While Miss Frost appears to have enjoyed her chemistry lesson, Phee, I believe you promised to feed her," Clive intervened gently.

"Of course! Until dinner is served, you'll find hearty refreshments in the salon. Clive will introduce you to the other guests—all family in one way or the other." The bells of another carriage rang, signaling the arrival of more guests, and Ophelia took their leave.

Lady Colin, her big dog following at her heel, and Lady Judith arrived at Lena's elbow as if on cue.

"We are quite a scientific family." Lady Judith directed Lena toward the salon. "Both Ophelia and Clive study the natural world by way of experimentation—Ophelia with a microscope, Clive with a scalpel."

"Studies? I thought he was already a physician." Lena looked over her shoulder at Clive, who followed behind attentively. He merely shrugged.

"He is," Lucy clarified. "Our Clive is an anatomist. He

traces the workings of the muscles and organs as William Harvey traced the circulation of the blood."

Clive interrupted, "I am interested in research, but Lucy is our nurse, treating our wounds with skills honed at Waterloo."

"You were at the battle?" Lena examined the woman more carefully, her attachment to Boatswain coming into a different focus. In France, she'd known many battle-worn former soldiers who relied on the comforting presence of a dog.

"In the hospitals, there and before. My father was an officer." Lucy, apparently caring little for her dress, picked up the giant puppy and nuzzled him. "It was kind of you to indulge our Ophelia; outside our community, she doesn't often find the pleasure of a willing audience."

"No, the pleasure was mine. It was the most fascinating conversation I've had in some time. We began so mildly with scented soaps and ended explosively with bubbling corpses!"

Clive shook his head. "You are an odd woman, Miss Frost."

Lena smiled broadly, surprisingly happy to be with him and his family. "That's one of the finest compliments I've had in some time."

Chapter Eleven

Lady Judith and Lady Colin introduced Lena to the other guests, leaving Clive to trail behind somewhat uselessly. But he still remained near her, not wanting, even in a place as safe as the Masons' Kensington home, to risk an accident, or an attack. He was pleased that Lena had taken to Ophelia's conversation on chemistry so well. Perhaps she might be equally willing to hear his thoughts on medicine. He had certainly found her brief comments on painting and its chemical reactions fascinating. And then there were her eyes, deep as the sea. . . .

The group was typical of Ophelia's gatherings. She'd invited any family who might be close by, which tonight seemed to number nearly two dozen; a handful of dear old friends from the neighborhood; one or two of Sidney's oldest customers; and his grandfather, who sat in state at the head of the table, enjoying the gathering, particularly the company of Lady Judith, who shared his passion for scents.

"You've arrived just in time for the first game." Lucy grinned.

"Game?" Lena had little experience with games.

"I should have warned you." Clive leaned forward.

"Ophelia loves games, and she fancies herself proficient at making them up, though they are usually embarrassing."

"Embarrassing?" Lena studied Clive's face.

"Yes. She makes us reveal something or tell a truth that we would prefer to keep hidden." Clive shrugged. "But it's all in good fun."

"There seems to be a great deal you should have warned me about," Lena, suddenly wary, whispered.

Lucy continued, explaining, "Tonight's game is called suspicion or superstition, I can't remember which. But she's spent hours creating it."

"Are we to tell ghost stories around the fire?" Lena asked.

Lady Judith opened her mouth to say something, then reconsidered.

Clive, however, filled in. "Not ghosts, though Ophelia claims to have seen one once."

"How does she reconcile that with her reliance on logic and reason?" Lena asked, and Clive simply shrugged.

At that moment, Ophelia clapped her hands to attract the attention of the group. "Choosing a game is always difficult for a family dinner. Living in community as we do, we know well each others' quirks and tricks, truths and evasions. We even know which in our company is most likely to cheat at cards." The group laughed.

Ophelia continued. "As a result, tonight after dinner, we will all be actors in a sort of play, or if you prefer, a game of logic." A footman began to distribute sealed envelopes to the company. "When you open your envelope, you will find information on the character you will play in our game. It includes your occupation, suspicions, and beliefs, as well as several details that you must reveal if asked."

"What's our purpose?" Lady Judith prodded.

"Ah, yes, our purpose: to discover who has committed

a crime. Unless you are our criminal, you must answer truthfully any questions that are put to you. But all of you have secrets, and part of the game is deciding which secrets are criminal!" Ophelia beamed. "Since Miss Frost and Miss Equiano are at a disadvantage, I've provided advice to help them navigate our community."

"Which means what, Phee?" Clive called out.

"We all have revealing little quirks, and Ophelia has made a list of them," Sidney Mason explained.

Each of the company opened their envelopes, some grimacing, others laughing out loud. The conversation began immediately, stopping only briefly when the butler called the company to dinner.

Which of us aren't criminals in some way or other? Lena asked herself. Though she was reticent to play, she recognized that the game—by allowing her to ask impertinent questions—might help her to determine if Horatio's message was meant to include Lady Wilmot and her circle. Lena opened her envelope. According to the game, she was a rich heiress who had taken on a disguise to test if the man she loved was true or a fortune hunter. Her character was suspicious of those who wished to be her friends, always questioning their motives, and she resented being told what to do. Perfect: some of that would require no acting at all.

Ophelia's hints on how to interpret various people's mannerisms were strange, but enlightening. Now at least she knew how Lady Wilmot felt when she rubbed the outside of her ear, and not to trust Lord Forster when he tapped the tip of his chin. But there was no information on Clive, and the omission disappointed her.

What had she hoped for? To find that he laughed when he was pretending to agree with something she said? Or that he shuffled his feet when he wished to kiss her?

"Come along, Miss Frost, we must join the game." Clive took her elbow, and they joined a group comprised of the curate, the local brewer, and Lord Forster.

Everyone threw themselves into the game. She had expected to feel out of place and out of sorts, but the people were so genial, and the conversation so amiable, that she had an unexpectedly engaging time. For most of the game—or at least until it was clear she had no need of him to navigate her way—Clive remained at her side, solicitous, kind, and thoughtful. Though it surprised her, she found him a soothing presence. Likewise, the evening was very different from her prior experiences with English country life, perhaps because she was now older and master of her own fate, or as much a master as any human could ever be.

Clive watched Lena for the better part of an hour, moving from group to group, avoiding individual conversations, listening for a time, then moving smilingly to the next group. Just as at the Rotunda, she held herself apart. Yet hers wasn't a natural reserve—that he of all people would have understood. Instead, it was more like a wounded animal's reticence to accept help, or a starving one's unwillingness to accept food. In either case, he was liable to be bitten if he frightened or alarmed her. But whenever she would let him in, even a little, he discovered more to Miss Frost than he had imagined. He finally cornered her near the long windows that led to the garden. "You are good at evading questions."

"I've answered every question posed to me, and honestly." She didn't meet his eyes but rather looked into the night, the moon outlining the shapes of the beds and hedges.

"Yet in playing, you've managed to ask questions but not be asked them in return. Of the four questions you've answered, the most challenging was about your occupation— to which you answered *shepherdess*." In the moonlight, he watched her face in profile, hoping he might read something there that would help him to understand her better.

"It seemed an appropriate answer for the role I was given." She passed it off lightly, but the corners of her eyes tightened briefly. "Rich heiress in disguise, suspicious of others."

"Your role in the game, you mean," Clive prodded, waiting for her reaction.

"Of course." She lifted her chin defiantly. "What else could I mean? You've seen my rooms. If I were rich, I'd have escaped from Mrs. Abbott long ago." She looked away from the garden.

"Even so, you aren't used to being obligated to others." Clive leaned his back against the frame of the window.

"I have many obligations: to my work, my crew, my subscribers, my patrons." Her eyes scanned the room.

"But not like here." Clive gestured to the laughing company. "Here family and friends lean on one another. Tonight we are playing foolish games simply to please one of our own, but tomorrow we might be sharing a sorrow instead of a joy. You, however, hold yourself apart, and not merely here in a company of strangers, but even at the Rotunda."

"At the Rotunda, I am the foreman, the owner, and the artist, all in one, and each role requires a different sort of distance." She danced around his words. "Is this part of the game? Are you asking a question?"

"No, it's not the game, and yes, I'm asking a question. Today you let me help you, but under duress, and I have the impression you would have preferred not to have needed help, and that as soon as you can, you will refuse my help again."

"That wasn't a question, but I'll answer it, lest you think I prefer evasion." She looked directly into his eyes, as if to confirm that she was being candid. "I prefer to hire help when I need it, and I prefer to be responsible for myself. If I own a hammer, I like to know that when I put it down, it will be in the same place when I return."

"At some point, you'll have to ask for help when you can't afford to pay for it."

"Perhaps. But the disadvantage of a community like this is that people come to believe that they can use your hammer with perfect freedom. And if they break it, an apology sets things to right again. At least my way, I'm rarely disappointed." Her face was serious, but a smile played at the edges of her mouth. "Besides, if I need help in future, I have you to call on."

Clive began to respond, but decided to let it go. If she hadn't sent him away by the next time she needed help, perhaps it would mean she'd come to trust him.

The sound of Ophelia clapping drew their attention. "As one would expect, our magistrate, Squire Brookings, has discovered our crime and our criminal."

"Lord Forster, former circus performer. Burglary," Lena whispered in Clive's ear a moment before Ophelia made the announcement.

"You knew?" Clive was surprised, and yet he wasn't. "For how long?"

"Since about five minutes into the game. Ophelia provided the very clue I needed to decipher the puzzle. But she would have been so disappointed for the game to end so early."

"Ah, Miss Frost, be wary. Already you begin to act like one of our company." He held out his hand. "Might I escort you to our dinner?"

After dinner, Lady Judith, Lena, and Clive were waiting for their carriage to be pulled round, when Lucy approached them. "Judith, you must stay: Squire Brookings has given us permission to ride again over his lands. The scenery—and the speed at which you can go over open country—is exhilarating! Ophelia says you may take her bay, as she intends to blow up this part of Kensington tomorrow with her experiments."

"Did she say that?" Lena asked with a bit of alarm.

"Ophelia said she intends to experiment. Lucy added the destruction to Kensington herself—a comment that shows she and my brother are well matched." Clive offered a mischievous grin.

"When do you ride?" Lady Judith, who had been pulling on her gloves, hesitated.

"At dawn. There's a spot about a mile from here where the views at sunrise will be spectacular. Ophelia says your room is ready, as usual, and your riding habit needs only to be brushed."

Lady Judith resumed pulling on her gloves. "I will return early and join you. I'll tell Fletcher to hold a carriage for me."

Lena examined their faces, disappointment obvious. "Lady Judith, am I the reason that you are returning to London only to come back here a few short hours later?"

Lady Judith began to demur, but Clive interrupted.

"Our Judith takes her obligations as elder sister—and your chaperone—very seriously."

"There's no need, Lady Judith." Lena touched Clive's sister's hand. "Lord Clive and I have already spent the whole day together without a chaperone, and I doubt he will give me reason to regret another long dark ride alone with him. Besides, it's been a very trying day, and I intend to fall promptly asleep, waking only as we arrive at the duke's residence."

"Listen to Miss Frost, Judith." Clive gave her a kiss on the cheek. "You do love a good race at sunrise."

Lady Judith stood quietly, looking at Lena, then Clive. At some point she decided. She began to remove her gloves. "Then, if you are certain I am not needed . . ."

"Certain." Lena and Clive spoke almost in unison.

Clive handed Lena into the carriage, once more the consummate gentleman. He had been altogether perfect at the party: quietly attentive, ensuring that she felt welcome and at ease, while leaving her the distance to forge her own conversations. He'd neither suffocated nor managed her, as she would have expected from a man of his class. But he consistently surprised her. He was accepting of both her help and her objections, and he seemed genuinely interested in her opinions and expertise. In fact, the only moment in the whole day when he had been *less* than perfect was when he hadn't kissed her.

She touched a gloved hand to the spot where she imagined his lips would have met hers. She remembered how it felt to have him near her, his breath soft on her mouth, his body so close that she could relax into the warmth of him. Her body, at the memory, felt the same swell of frustrated desire. It was a reminder that she should be cautious. They were only temporary partners, thrown together by forces neither understood, and that partnership would end as quickly as it had begun.

With the remains of Boatswain's barrier removed, Lena could sit wherever she wished. To avoid complications, she sat near to the far door. In a coach that could seat eight, her choice would convey that she had no wish for another *almost*-kiss. But it was cold in the carriage. The footmen had placed tin foot warmers firmly in the middle of the coach, and they were too hot to nudge closer to her seat. So, she hugged her arms to her middle trying to keep herself warm.

She was torn between desire and caution, wishing he would sit close beside her, and at the same time, hoping he wouldn't. Whatever her reservations and fears, she was already half enamored with him, or more. And a kiss would be lovely. But it might prove *too* lovely—something she couldn't forget when it came time to part. As a woman outside his class, it would be reckless to love him, and even more reckless to let him see her heart.

Clive climbed in and took his seat firmly in the middle, placing his feet on one warmer. "The duke's coach maker crafts the doors and windows to seal perfectly. Even so, it's still warmer in the middle." Lena didn't move.

Clive leaned forward and lifted the top of the opposite seat to reveal a large compartment. He removed a woolen blanket. "If you won't use the foot warmers, at least use the blanket. It's not as pretty as yours, but it should prove as serviceable." He unfolded it, handing her half. Wider and longer than hers, the blanket reached from one side of the coach to the other. Disappointingly, she had no need to move closer to him.

"Thank you." Her voice felt uncertain.

"You told Judith we are nothing more than business

associates." Clive angled his body to face hers. Even in the half-light provided by the moon and the embers, she could trace the seductive lines of his body. "But I assure you: I rarely kiss my business partners."

"We didn't kiss." Her objection carried more force than she'd intended, and the memory filled the space between them.

"No, I suppose we didn't." He spoke in almost a whisper, and she couldn't tell if she heard regret or acquiescence in his voice. "But I've wondered all day, why shouldn't we? A kiss, nothing more."

She sat silently, weighing her options. Refuse him and always wonder? She thought of the dog Boatswain, leaping out of the carriage on just a glimpse of his mistress, his joy at the reunion unalloyed by questions or fear. Could she leap?

She slid across the seat until she was in front of the other foot warmer. There was still more than adequate space between them. He waited. She moved closer, setting her hand on his knee. She turned her face toward his, lifting her lips toward his. He waited, making her decide, making her act. She breathed in the scent of him, so new, yet so familiar. She placed her palm against his cheek, and he leaned his face into her hand. She let her forefinger trace his lips, the curve of the top, the fullness of the bottom. She paused, waiting for her heart to overcome her mind. Then she leapt.

Her lips pressed against his, softly. Her action spurred his response, and he returned the kiss, gently. Her blood rushed in her ears and her chest. The kiss blossomed, moving from tentative to certain, eager to greedy.

His hand moved from her knee to her hip, pulling her toward him. "Ah, Lena." Her name on his lips sounded like a prayer.

She wanted him, his lips, his mouth, his hands, and he gave them to her, tender, demanding, generous.

One kiss turned to two, then a dozen, each one as sweet as the one before. Reckless. Delightful.

Eventually, she interrupted their kisses, covering his lips with her fingers. "This is wonderful."

"It is." He kissed the inside of her fingers, each one, sweetly.

"I . . ." She pulled back, and he let her.

"Having you sit beside me is enough." He opened his arms, and she leaned into him, her back to his chest, wrapping his warmth around her. She rested her head on his shoulder, feeling safe and warm, and refusing to think of anything but his kindness.

Chapter Twelve

"Swan and his crew have collected another five bodies." Flute placed the note open on the desk.

"Cadavers, Flute. We call them cadavers." The man known as Charters closed the ledger he kept for their gambling hell and picked up the one he used for managing their resurrection business.

"The men say *cadaver* is just a big word for a dead body." Flute, a strong, wiry man, pulled a piece of wood out of his pocket and began to whittle.

"All the same, *cadaver* emphasizes that the bodies were dead *before* we received them. Of course, if you prefer, we could merely call them *merchandise*." Charters opened the ledger to the appropriate page and dipped his pen in the inkwell.

"Call them what you will." Flute shook his head. "I don't like trafficking in bodies."

"We only traffic in the dead, and there's little harm in that. In most cemeteries, once the family leaves, the cadaver is thrown into a mass grave, and the coffin sold for firewood. For that disservice, a churchyard like St. Clement Danes charges a pound seventeen for an adult, and a private cemetery charges fifteen shillings. But the surgery schools will pay ten pounds for the cadaver, more for one in fine condition. If we fill all the requests we've received, we'll be distributing a thousand cadavers a year, and the cemeteries will still be overfull. Isn't it better for those bodies to perform some useful service, rather than moldering cold and low with a dozen strangers?"

"Some sects believe the body will be resurrected on the day of judgment." Flute turned over his carving and began to shape the other side. "They might not appreciate finding their bodies have been dissected."

"How are we doing them a greater ill than an undertaker filling a mass grave? Eventually all those bodies will be reduced to a jumble of bones. I suppose the righteous dead will have to trust their god to sort out the parts." Charters watched Flute silently shape a bird out of the wood. "I've finalized agreements with the newer burial grounds."

"Bribes, you mean," Flute corrected, but without rancor or even dismay.

"To our partners, I call them *stipends*." Charters returned to his ledger.

"I never thought that selling bodies could be lucrative enough to justify the trouble." Flute looked up from his wood carving. "But if ever a man could make money from the dead, it would be you."

"It's a fine market, but it won't last. Eventually Parliament will regulate it. But we will have built good networks of trade we can use for other enterprises. In the meantime, we know who to call when we need a body buried or a leg set." Charters waited for Flute's nod of agreement. "How did Swan describe the quality of the cadavers?"

"Three are workhouse bodies, sold to us shortly after death. The workhouse gets its money, even when you're dead." Flute leaned forward to read the note. "The other two were in the ground, a day, maybe two."

"Did the workhouses indicate the causes of death?" Charters held his pen ready to log the information.

"They wrote it all down for you."

Charters took the sheet and began transferring information into his ledger. "Hartley pays a premium for good condition, and he's built a stable to conceal delivery. Give him all three workhouse cadavers. Tell Swan to deliver them in the black closed carriage. What about the remaining two?"

"Both women from the Rookery. Cholera."

"Lamp's been getting extra stock from independent resurrection men, so he'll get nothing more from us, until he commits to us as his sole suppliers. Send those two to the new surgery school near the Inns of Court."

Flute harrumphed. "I thought after the wars we would need fewer surgeons, not more."

"Yet the schools can't grow fast enough to accommodate the students. And we barely keep up with the demand." Charters pulled a note already sealed from his desk drawer and placed it on the edge of the desk. "At the new surgery school, Swan should ask for Slice and give him this note."

"Slice?" Flute laughed out loud. "That's unfortunate."

Charters shrugged. "Most people feel some obligation to the name their parents gave them."

"Except you. How many disguises do you have now?"

"Well, there's Charters, of course." He tapped the brown wig with the pigtail he wore and gestured at his blue-colored glasses resting on the desk. "Then Charters's aging clerk, Georges."

"He's my favorite. A nasty bugger, even under all that lace and embroidery."

"Mr. Jenks, our bank examiner, and Mr. Worth, our

avaricious country squire." Charters rose and opened the locked cabinet that held his costumes. "And two or three I've been testing in various contexts."

"Have you retired the old drunk without a name who used to haunt the Blue Heron?"

"Ah, no! How could I forget our veteran, cast aside by the nation after his service in the wars, forced to live on the street and forage for his food." Charters touched the worn jacket associated with the drunk. "For all the information he's brought us, he deserves a name. What do you think of Captain Timpson, late of her majesty's navy?"

"If he were a captain, he'd have half pay."

"True. Midshipman then, never promoted to captain. Perhaps he'll come by the Blue Heron this week."

"Make it his birthday, and I'll give him a drink and a seat at the bar."

Charters grinned. "An appealing offer, Flute. We shall resurrect our man Timpson."

"Speaking of resurrection men, Sparks and his men are outside. They wish to meet with Charters."

"Do they?" Charters returned to the desk, turning the ledger's pages until he found the one for Sparks's team. "Perhaps they wish to apologize for not meeting our expectations for good stock."

"More likely they wish a larger percentage of the profits. Will you see them?"

"They should meet with Georges. If there's dissension, he settles it best." Charters rose and returned to the wardrobe, Flute playing his valet. In a matter of minutes Charters had applied the face paints to make himself appear older, transforming completely into Georges, an aging fop who still wore the white-powdered wig of his youth. His suit was richly embroidered with matching waist and tailcoat, dating from at least twenty years before, and his wrists and neck were surrounded by a heavy lace. As Georges, Charters struck a theatrical pose for Flute. "Do I look like myself?"

"You will once the door opens, and your face settles into Georges's terrifying calm."

Charters held back a laugh. "It's delightful to have a partner with no fear of me."

"We have taken each other's measure. I think our men Barnard and Clifton should follow them in." Flute pushed the carving into his pocket, but kept his small carving knife in his hand. It would serve as a threat, even if a small one.

"The bodyguards are your domain, Flute. Act as you see fit."

Flute opened the door and nodded the crew in. The men—three of them—followed their leader, Sparks, a small man with quick fists and a temper to match, into the center of the room. Standing before the desk, they held themselves puffed up, as men did at a tavern when anticipating a brawl. Behind Sparks's crew, Barnard and Clifton—broadly built men who had been Flute's former comrades at sea—took their places on either side of the door.

Flute stepped to the side of the desk to stand at Georges's left. He held the knife openly enough that two of Sparks's men's eyes widened, then he removed his carving from his pocket and began to carve.

Georges sat without speaking, waiting for their bravado to fade in the face of his silence. After almost a minute, the men began to shrink back to their normal stances. Only Sparks was unaffected.

"We came to meet with Charters. Where is he?"

"Ah, so sad." Georges's voice was lisping and affected. "Mr. Charters, he is not available at present. But I am here.

And we think so much alike, he and I, that many find it is like talking to the same person."

The men shifted their weight, looking to Sparks for their cues. Sparks examined Georges, his eyes focusing on the man's lace and ornate clothing with the eagerness of a thief who had identified his mark. "We've worked for Charters for almost six months now, and we want a bigger cut of the profit. We take all the risks, and you sit here with your lace and flounces, making lists."

Georges flipped the lace at his wrist and took a stick of pumice from the desk drawer. "Let me explain our expectations, as I'm sure my colleague Charters did before." He pitched his voice soft enough that they had to be silent to hear him. "We are all businessmen. When you proposed to join our resurrection scheme, we outlined the market and your place in it. We build relationships with our partners to gain the best merchandise at the least risk."

"There's plenty of bodies just waiting to be taken. We lose money with every *relationship*."

"Yes, but if we buy cadavers rather than steal them, our partners do not call the watch when we dig." Georges filed the nail on his forefinger in six swift strokes.

"We dig; you don't," Sparks objected, but Georges ignored him.

"You were to partner with the local cemeteries to build a steady, reliable stream of cadavers with no provenance and no relatives. Paupers, prostitutes, orphans. From those partnerships, you were to mine fifty bodies a week, prepare them for our clients, then deliver them discreetly to the addresses we provide. We equip you with linen for wrapping, a cart for carrying, and a small fund for bribes and other essentials. But, sadly, Mr. Sparks, your crew hasn't met our goals in any week so far."

"There's no need to *pay* the undertakers when we can just look for newly filled-in graves."

"But after you identify the graves, you must dig up the body, undress it to leave the clothes in the grave, then remove any hint of earth, and, if you misstep, you must deal with the watch or the magistrate. Our method typically requires only pickup and delivery. Of course, you may increase your profit by cutting the hair and selling it to the wig makers. That was our agreement, was it not?" Georges flipped the lace on one wrist.

The men stood silently, looking to their leader.

"That was our agreement." Sparks looked confused, as if the conversation had gone awry with no warning. "But we want a new one."

"If your team cannot meet the demand, I have other crews who would welcome more territory." Georges waved his hand in a slow, definite flourish, slightly moving the lace around his wrist.

Sparks fisted his hands at his side. "You can't get rid of us. We know how many bodies have come out of the gambling hell below and we know who killed 'em."

"Ah, gentlemen, you may have a number, but in British law, a conviction requires a body. Besides, if you are correct, would I not find it easy to dispose of four more *cadavers,* should that become necessary?" He rested his hands carefully on the desk and paused, letting the silence draw out until even Sparks seemed subdued. Then Georges leaned back, steepling his fingers before his face. "Twenty cadavers this week. If you do not meet that goal, then we will reconsider the terms of our agreement." He paused. "I recommend you meet the goal."

Georges turned his attention to the ledger before him, silently writing notes as the men stood waiting. After several minutes of ignoring the men completely, Georges looked up. "Flute, please see Mr. Sparks and his men to the hall. They have *merchandise* to collect."

Sparks spoke. "We might have a bit of a problem."

"Problem?" Georges set his pen down slowly, then looked up at the group. The three shuffled their feet in response to his gaze, but Sparks remained silent.

In the face of Sparks's silence, the brawny member of his crew with the pockmarked face spoke: "Just a bit of a tussle—nothing we couldn't handle—but a man got killed. We got rid of the body. Took it right down to the surgery."

"Likely, no one even knows he's dead," the third man offered helpfully. "He was one of them French e-me-grays, no family, no friends."

"Then why do you bring this *tussle* to me?" Georges picked up his pen and returned to his work.

"We thought the building was empty, but another man was there." Sparks, now a petitioner rather than a champion, twisted the brim of his hat between his fingers.

Georges set his pen down with an audible tap, then rose, leaning forward over the desk, both hands flat on the surface. "And this man may have seen you commit murder. For it was a murder, wasn't it?"

The men looked sheepish. "Some surgeons want a better sort of body, ones that died of something other than syphilis or cholera or by hanging at the crossroads."

"So you decided to harvest a body before it was dead. And you may have a witness." Georges sat back in his chair. "Here's the rule, men. You kill no one that I haven't given you the word to kill. You steal no bodies that I haven't given you the word to steal. You work for me, not for yourselves or for the surgeons."

"Yes, sir," the men answered in unison. "What do we do now?"

"You find your witness. Then you bring him to me, and I will discover what he does and doesn't know."

"And if he saw us?"

"Then he will join his friend at one of the schools. And you will make it up to me that I've had to go to such trouble. Now out, all of you. And before I see you again, I expect you to have collected the bodies waiting for you at the pauper's field."

The men trailed out, one behind the other, and Flute's men followed them, pulling the door shut behind them.

Charters nodded to the seat beside his desk. "Do we believe them?"

"I think they are confessing because they believe they were seen." Flute settled in.

At a tap on the door, the men grew silent. One of Flute's men leaned his head in. "They took the tickets for the Blue Heron."

Chapter Thirteen

Lena refused to wake up. In her dream, she was nestled in a vast delicious pillow under a feather blanket, both light and oh-so-warm. When she awoke, her feet would be so cold that she could no longer feel her toes, and her back would ache from the sagging bed. When the cries of the vendors selling their wares told her the day had begun, she'd rush to the Rotunda, meeting her crew just as dawn spread across the sky, and they would work until past dusk. But at no point in the day would she be warm—not like now. She clung to the dream, snuggling under the covers, sheets so soft that they could only exist in a dream—or the house of a duke.

The day came back to her in a rush. Her accident. The bodies. The magistrate. Clive. Strong and kind. Every time she had faced trouble, he had acted to help her. But not just her; he'd paid a street beggar extra so the child would have something to eat.

Under the covers, she stretched out her arms and legs. After her day's adventures, her muscles should be stiff and hard, but they felt supple and rested. She couldn't remember arriving at the duke's house or undressing for bed, but her night shift—she almost hoped *he* had put her in it—was a delight. At least she had fallen asleep in his arms.

Clive. Eventually his attentiveness would chafe, but not yet. For now, she would enjoy his gentle presence . . . and his glorious kisses. She warmed at the thought of his hand cradling her neck, her lips devouring his.

Did any painting convey that particular moment of bliss? She searched her memory. Most depicted the moments before a seduction—the outstretched hand, the bouquet of flowers, the teasing glances. But there was one painting: Antonio da Correggio's *Jupiter and Io*. She'd seen it in Vienna. In it, Jupiter, hidden in a cloud, embraced the naked Io, his hands giant, smoky paws on her bare back, Io's face transported in pleasure, her own hand encircling the god's. Io's face was lifted in rapture to accept the god's kisses. How would it feel to greet Clive as Io had Jupiter? To accept his touch, his kisses, his warmth all the way to the core of her being? She sighed, more a swoon than a sigh, knowing Clive's embraces would feel glorious. Stretching against the expensive bedding, she let herself imagine it, and the imagination made her wonder . . . why not? Why not enjoy their partnership fully, until it ended?

Unfortunately, now that she was awake, she couldn't allow herself more than a moment of indulgence. Sighing, she steeled herself for another day heavy with responsibilities. She draped a Chinese silk dressing gown over her shift, the fabric shimmering in the firelight. Such elegance. She hadn't worn a silk dress in years, and to have worn two in less than a day was a delicious excess.

They had returned from the Masons so late that she couldn't have slept more than a few hours, but somehow she felt rested and refreshed. Her room was still dark, save for the light of the fire on the hearth. The curtains fell in heavy puddles, blocking light and cold. It was a room crafted for those who wished to sleep in luxury, not those who had jobs. The house wasn't yet stirring, though a servant had recently fed her fire. How had she not heard them?

Outside, dark would still be resting on the city, the sun just starting to make its way across the sky. She relished the city in its last quiet moments before the day. In the fire's half-light, she walked to the windows and drew the curtains back.

She recoiled, blinking against the bright light. Not dawn. Not even early morning. No, noon or later. The cries of the street vendors hadn't reached her ears because the duke's house sat back from the street behind high walls. Her comfort and ease disappeared in an instant, replaced by a near panic. The Rotunda! The crew would have come to work, and, not finding her there, gone home with no work done. Panic turned to fury, welling up from the bottom of her belly and filling her chest and throat.

How. Dare. He? Each word was a condemnation. Letting her sleep the day away! That wouldn't help her finish the exhibition! Didn't he understand that? But what did she expect? Men often thought that help was the same as control. She'd merely hoped Clive was made of better stuff. She blinked away the beginnings of tears—she had no time for regret.

She ignored the fashionable walking dress laid out on a chair for her. Normally she would have marveled at the softness of the fabric and the delicacy of the colors. But she had no time. Finding her freshly laundered clothes tucked in the wardrobe, she pulled on her blouse, Turkish trousers, and skirt as usual, and tucked a plain fichu around her shoulders and into the front of her blouse. She caught a glimpse of herself in the mirror: with no night cap, her long hair had escaped its plait to form a heavy mass around her face. She began to repair it, then stopped.

She'd already spent too much time considering how her appearance might please him.

She needed to confront him and call her crew back to the Rotunda. If she hurried, they could still accomplish something today.

She slipped Horatio's note into her pocket, then rushed into the hall and down the stairs. A servant, shocked at her haste and rough hair, directed her to the morning room where brunch and Clive waited.

She refused to notice the buffet laden with cheese, eggs, jellies, and meats, though her stomach rumbled at the smell of freshly baked bread.

Clive sat at the table, absorbed in work, surrounded by neat piles of paper. His back to the window, the winter light diffused around his head and shoulders, making him look like a saint or a god.

"Good morning, Miss Frost." He glanced up for barely an instant, then scribbled intently on one of his papers. "Help yourself to the buffet while I finish."

His face was intent, his lower lip caught between his teeth as he concentrated, and she forced herself to look away from the beckoning fullness of his lips. Instead, she waited with a cold patience, her hands fisted at her sides. She wanted her complaint to receive his full attention.

"Aunt Agatha insisted that we let you wake naturally." When his eyes met hers, they widened in surprise, then acceptance. "One doesn't argue with Aunt Agatha, but I should have anticipated you would be displeased."

"I'm not displeased: I'm angry." She held out her palms, rejecting his words. "You and your peers may sleep away the day, but thanks to your aunt Agatha, I've lost a full day's work."

"In that accounting, you must balance the lost work

hours against the improvement in your health." He stood, examining her with the concentration of a physician. "Your face is less drawn, your color much improved, and your hands appear to be healing nicely."

Lena looked at her hands. The scrapes were sealed over, the skin a healthy pink.

"When was the last night you had a healthful sleep?" Clive's voice was gentle, and his brows furrowed.

"It doesn't matter." She refused to be mollified. "*I* don't matter. All that matters is opening my panorama on time."

"I would disagree, Miss Frost, *you* matter a great deal. I would say . . ." He paused as if uncertain how to proceed.

"You would say what?" she prompted.

"Without you, there would be no panorama, so you can't separate the problem into *it* and *you*." He answered as if proud of his logic.

It wasn't the answer she'd expected; in fact, it wasn't any answer she'd expected.

"Though you were not present this morning, your very detailed instructions were," he continued matter-of-factly. "From before sunrise to about an hour ago, I and my brother Seth, with the help of your man Louis, directed your crew to complete the tasks you had outlined."

At the buffet, Clive filled a plate with various foodstuffs.

"What happened an hour ago?" Watching him, Lena felt her stomach rumble. But to eat might suggest she was accepting his rationale, and she'd learned long ago to be suspicious of any man's control, even one as seemingly well-intentioned as Clive. Even so, Lena's anger began to subside.

"My cousin brought my sister home. Your crew is used to taking orders from a woman: Judith and Ophelia are used to giving them. It seemed a perfect match."

Clive held out the plate he'd just prepared. When she refused it, he placed it on the table beside her. "Judith could have beaten Napoleon years before Wellington did, so you may find all your work for the week done in a single day. But do not worry: Judith is following your instructions to the last detail."

Lena couldn't imagine how her crew would respond to four strangers telling them what to do. "But your relations know nothing about a project of this sort. My crew—"

"—cheered when we explained that you would be taking the morning to recuperate."

"They cheered?" Lena felt confused. Somehow her world had turned upside down.

"Your crew wish—as much as you—for the panorama to be a success, but they believe you have pushed yourself far harder than is wise or healthful."

"It's . . . I . . ." She brushed her hand through her unruly hair. Somehow he had anticipated all her objections. Finally, she blurted out, "I can't have strangers in the exhibition hall. We've worked too hard to generate public curiosity to let the subject become public knowledge now."

"The curtain remains in place. There's no need to move it to arrange the gutter or clean out the space beneath the platform for the musicians." He pushed the plate toward her. "Sit and eat, then we will go to the Rotunda."

"I need to go now." She tapped her foot in pent frustration.

"Yesterday, I was too caught up in finding Calder to realize you hadn't eaten. Today, as a physician, your physician, I will not make that mistake again. We have tea, coffee, or hot chocolate?" He turned back to the buffet, ignoring her with a calm civility. "Which is your preference?"

She felt thwarted. How he had managed their conflict

baffled her. He should have railed back in response to her anger. But he'd treated her with a straightforward politeness, addressing one concern after another. He had taken care that the crew was working at the Rotunda, that her instructions were being followed, that her secret was protected, and that she was being fed. Worse yet, he offered her chocolate. The smell of the rich drink stole away the last of her resolve. "Chocolate, please."

"You may, however, have some difficulty dislodging my relatives from a useful task." He held out the chocolate.

She sipped the thick warm liquid, then sitting, she spread butter and marmalade on the thick bread. Once mollified, she couldn't resist the foods Clive offered to her. Somehow he'd selected a plate of her very favorites, and every bite was a delight.

As she ate, Clive remained attentive, refilling her chocolate when the first cup was done, and, before she'd finished her first plate, providing a second with those items she had seemed to most like. It was a little disconcerting to be pampered so assiduously by a powerful, handsome man, but she wasn't going to refuse. At least not for now.

As she ate, Clive placed some paper and pencils beside her. "When you have had your fill, could you sketch your Mr. Calder? That way, while you are at the Rotunda, I can search for him."

She stopped short, her hand holding a piece of jam-covered bread inches from her mouth. "What do you mean *search*? Are you leaving me out?"

"No, I would not do that. While you are at the Rotunda, I'll investigate where Calder might be. Then, once you have finished for the day, we will review what I've discovered."

"Why can't we search together this evening?" She set the bread down.

"Yesterday, we found two people dead. Calder's information may well be vital to stop more murders, and that requires finding him. Besides, I would prefer to do this bit of investigating alone."

"More murders." She paused, realizing he had told her very little about his investigation. "Yesterday you told me that you were chasing a murderer. *A* murderer suggests *a* murder, a murderer who was provoked into two more to avoid discovery. But that's not the case." She worked through her thoughts aloud. "You *expect* more murders. How many have there been already?"

"I don't know." His face grew solemn, but his eyes avoided hers.

She leaned back in her chair, watching him stare into the distance. "That suggests you've found a pattern of killings. If Horatio saw a murderer in London that he recognized from some other place, then the killings may have been going on for some time. What do you know? Perhaps I can help."

"Not anything I can prove. I was working in the icehouse where we store the cadavers."

"Icehouse? I would have imagined a dark and dank cellar—or dungeon," Lena said, without thinking, then added, "Ice is difficult to paint—all milky and layered."

"Ice cellar then." He nodded acknowledgment. "Ice, even in summer, preserves a body for almost three weeks. I was examining some neck bruises that indicated strangulation. A fellow surgeon recognized the pattern from his work the day before. We kept looking and found others. But since surgeons and students acquire their cadavers independently, we had no record of who might be at fault.

If the murderer had delivered the bodies to different schools, no one would have seen the pattern."

"If selling a body is a crime, why is buying one allowed?" she wondered out loud.

"No one *owns* a cadaver, so neither buying nor selling is a crime. But removing a cadaver from the grave is a misdemeanor, and stealing clothes or other objects is a felony. That's part of the outcry. Everyone agrees that having cadavers for experiments will produce better doctors, and by extension save lives. But, to avoid the felony, resurrection men must strip a body naked, and *that* offends sensibilities."

"Ah, foolish sentiment impedes progress every time." She mimicked his tone.

He raised an eyebrow at her mocking. "No one wants their aunt's or cousin's body stolen, stripped naked, sold, and dissected. For that reason, the wealthy buy iron coffins or mort safes, to keep their—as Byron says— 'memory whole and mummy hid.'"

"Why don't you want me to help you?" When he didn't answer, she added, "I deserve to know."

"Yes, you do." He brushed his hand through his hair, clearly choosing his words. "I need your drawing to search the surgery schools for Calder's body."

She felt all her vitality drain to the floor. "You're trying to protect me. You think Horatio dead."

"It's a possibility to eliminate. If he isn't dead, we must find him before our murderer does."

"I'm coming with you." She rose, setting her serviette next to her plate.

"You just argued quite convincingly that you are needed at the Rotunda."

"And you just argued quite convincingly that I am not." She stared him down, watching how the changing light influenced the color of his eyes. "If Lady Judith and Mrs. Mason can supervise my crew for the afternoon, then I can help you find Horatio. I owe him that much."

"I've spent months investigating these crimes on my own."

"And?"

"I've succeeded in compiling a list of bodies we believe were murdered." He looked at his feet. "But nothing I've discovered has put me one step closer to solving the crimes, and every week another body arrives at the surgery school to accuse me of failing them."

Lena searched for words to comfort him. But what could she say that would balance his sense of responsibility for so many deaths? She looked at her hands, and then she knew. "You saved me. I'm not gravely injured or dead because of you, because your investigations led to my Rotunda and you are fearless."

"It wasn't intentional." Clive looked abashed. "I mean it was merely instinct."

Lena smiled. "Instinct isn't all of it. You risked your life to save mine. I won't forget that."

Lena had hoped they would take one of the duke's carriages. If they were alone, there was no reason—now that she understood him a little better—not to enjoy more of his kisses. But all the carriages were being used by the duke's other relations. Clive offered to hire a hackney, but Lena refused, not wanting him to spend any more money she couldn't repay. Besides, in London she walked everywhere, and there was no reason to grow lazy now.

The crowds on the street were too thick for conversation, so they walked in near silence to the surgery school.

Even so, she found herself stealing glances at him, noticing the confidence in his stride and the gentle way he negotiated the crowds for her. He continually surprised her. He wasn't always forthcoming or even tactful, but he seemed to respect her opinions, and he answered each of her questions thoroughly. His presence—so calm—soothed her, even when she didn't want it to. She found herself wanting to savor each moment with him, so that when their time together came to an end, she wouldn't be too disappointed.

Once at the school, Clive greeted the porter with genuine affection. "Good morning, Harner."

"Sun's been up for hours, your lordship. But you lot trade day for night so often, you don't know the difference." The old man laughed.

"True." Clive gestured toward Lena. "Miss Frost has come to visit the icehouse."

"Are you sure, miss?" The old man looked her over carefully. "The dead aren't a sight for the faint at heart, even when the death is natural."

"I have seen my share of death during the wars, and as an artist, I study the human form," Lena explained.

Clive winked at her, and she felt warm with his confidence. "You won't need to worry about Miss Frost, Harner. She is as unflappable in the face of death as any of our most experienced physicians."

"I'm also in search of a lost friend, though I'm hoping we don't find him."

"Ah, I hope so as well. It's not the same as drawing them, if you know the body, I mean." The porter led them to the end of the hall and down several flights of stairs. "It's harder to see a friend dead than a stranger."

The air grew colder the farther they descended, and the passage darker. Periodically Harner stopped to light a wall lamp, illuminating the next set of stairs. They grew quiet, and Lena's mood began to darken.

"I remember my first cadaver quite well, though I doubt he remembers me." Clive broke the silence and the growing gloom. "Johns was his name, a pockmarked fellow with a withered arm."

"I'm not sure which word troubles me more: *first* or *cadaver*." Lena laughed. "Did you dig him up yourself?"

"He was a murderer sentenced to dissection and hanging—though not in that order—so his body was delivered to me." Clive sounded amused at her questions. "The law disallows students from participating in exhumations."

"That's a pity," she continued, emboldened. "I was already imagining how to paint the scene: you—your back to an ash tree—watching the gravediggers raise a shrouded body from the grave."

"Are we robbing the grave at night? If so, how will I see them?" Clive played along.

"The moon will be full, and its light will illuminate the gravestones and mausoleums, but not so much that it obscures the light of the night watch, entering the scene from the lower right corner. I would call it 'Clive's First Cadaver.'"

"Do you always convert people's stories into pictures?" Clive asked.

"It depends on the story. Some lend themselves to pictures better than others."

"What about this story: us descending to view the dead?"

"Except for the bodies, this scene lacks drama. These stairs, for example, are entirely too wide and even."

"Students need wide, even stairs to carry the litter up and down," Harner added, lighting the next wall lamp.

"Ah, but if I were to paint them, there would be no litter in my picture, and the stairs would be so narrow that the students would have to turn their feet sideways to fit." Lena warmed to the story. "John Boydell's Shakespeare Gallery exhibited a picture much like what I'm imagining."

"The scene from *Richard the Third* where the conspirators carry the murdered princes down the stairs?" Clive asked.

"You know it!?" Lena was delighted. Typically only other artists recognized her references. Clive, she kept discovering, was an exceptional man. "My scene would be much like that: the medical students, all cramped together into a narrow space, awkwardly passing down their cadavers."

"Except with fewer lamps and narrower stairs," Clive added, and she could hear the amusement in his voice.

"Is this gallows humor?" She found herself amused as well. "Here I am, going into a charnel dungeon to see if my business partner has been murdered, and all I can think of is how I might paint the scene. How do you do it?"

"Do what?" Clive slowed before her as Harner's lamp stopped descending.

"Take a human body and study its various parts? Is it as the poet Wordsworth says? 'We murder to dissect.'" At the bottom of the long staircase, Lena inched her foot down to the floor. Her breath misted white.

"I've been told—quite often, in fact—that to be able to do it requires an unhealthy distance from one's humanity." Clive stepped to the side and directed her forward.

Lena glanced at him as she passed. Even in the half-light she could see that his face had shuttered. In an instant she saw her behavior toward him with new perspective. She had been afraid, and that fear had made her suspicious, frustrated, and angry, yet he had treated each change of her emotions with an equanimity her behavior didn't merit. She touched his arm, gently. "Or perhaps such research requires a man with a more poignant sense of the value of life."

He stared at her hand, as if it had just conveyed a great gift, and his face transformed with relief.

"Why do you do it?" she asked.

"I assume for the same reason you paint. I have a talent for the research, and using that talent satisfies something deep within me. Without its animating spirit, the body is only a shell, but that shell can reveal much about the nature of life, health, and illness. I treat the body as a gift from the departed spirit."

"That's very philosophical," Lena observed.

"More practical than philosophical. To treat an illness, a doctor must know what lies underneath the skin. What is more *un*healthy: Learning from a cadaver how blood circulates through a limb? Or amputating a living man's whole arm, when, with adequate training, you could have stopped at the elbow?"

"In France, the vivisectionists claim that adequate training requires experimenting on the living as well as the dead." She'd read *Frankenstein* and been horrified by Victor's headlong pursuit of knowledge at the risk of everything dear to him. She needed to know how far Clive was willing to take his experiments in the pursuit of knowledge.

"I do not—will not—cause such suffering to living animals." His answer was swift and decisive. "In that, however, I am somewhat alone."

"Then I approve—of all your researches." She smiled, breathing out in relief.

His returning smile, spreading slowly across his face, warmed her despite the cold of the room.

Harner held up the lamp to reveal a long, narrow room with sconces down the wall, which he proceeded to light. The room was filled with giant slabs of ice, each one covered in straw and sawdust to keep it from melting. Where the ice was visible, it looked dark and murky. Piled neatly on top of each slab were rows of cadavers (as she reminded herself to think of them). Thirty or more, she estimated quickly. Covered in white linen, the bodies looked like the mummies she'd seen at the Louvre before Napoleon lost at Waterloo and the stolen works of art were returned to their home countries.

"Where do these come from? Thus far, you've mentioned executed prisoners and grave robbers." She rubbed her hands on her arms to warm them. She made sure her tone was inquisitive, not judgmental. "It's hardly a reputable group to deal with, before or after death."

He ignored her jibe. "It's not all skullduggery. We receive bodies from families who can't afford even a cheap burial, or from the poorhouses to save the parish the expense. In those cases, we are actively helping the community—not just with the results of our research, but with the fact of the research itself. That's why this group of resurrectionists is so dangerous: they steal lives as well as bodies. If their activities became widely known, Parliament could act swiftly to end all dissection. If that happened, we could still do research using dried specimens and those preserved in spirits, but we would have no way to improve our practice."

The porter uncovered the bodies, and she stepped forward, not wishing to appear unwilling or afraid. She considered the features of each body, the signs of occupation or dissipation. Some of the bodies gave up the story of their deaths easily, from the failed farmer's calloused hands to the drunkard's red-veined nose.

"It's not hard to tell how this one died," she said, almost to herself. "Stabbed."

"Knife fight at the docks. He was brought to us by the magistrate." Clive sounded approving. He pointed to the other bodies. "What else do you see?"

Lena stepped to the next body. "Poison?"

Clive nodded, looking pleased. "How did you know?"

"Burned lips, shrunken body." Lena walked to the next alcove, with Clive at her side. "I had a teacher once, who made me dress as a boy, and go to the charnel house with him to draw. Some say you can paint a body without knowing how it works. Perhaps that's true in portraits of the aristocracy where the important details are the face and the clothes. But you must know how the muscles and veins lie under the skin to paint an arm or a torso right." She looked into his face, trying to read his thoughts. "If we had met under different circumstance, I likely would have offered to pay to attend a dissection."

"Then you understand how important it is for doctors to understand how the human body works."

"Was it difficult? Being the son of a duke and wanting to work with the dead." She looked at him with new appreciation, wondering how much his path had cost him.

He glanced toward the porter, returning from the opposite end of the room. "Let's say—for now—that the challenges were different than you imagine."

"A conversation for later then." She moved to the next alcove, but was caught off guard. It was filled with the bodies of children, chimney sweeps with their hair and skin blackened by coal dust. She wiped away the tears with the back of one bandaged hand.

Clive stood by her side. "Suffocation or the coal dust. Chimney sweeps breathe the dust in and swallow it. From the stomach, it circulates through the body, blackening the organs, particularly the lungs."

"You should look over here for grown men," Harner called out, having lit all the lamps. Though still dark in the corners, the room had lost most of its gloom.

Blinking back tears, Lena walked to where Harner waited.

Harner pulled the linen back from the faces one at a time, waiting for her determination, then moving on when she said no. They repeated the action at each slab. Every time Harner revealed a face, Clive was at her side, reassuring her. But Horatio was not there.

"Is your friend recently missing?" Harner asked when they'd finished looking through the cadavers he'd suggested. "This week? Or last? Or longer?"

"This week, I think."

"Ah, then you won't be needing the bodies over there. They've already been examined." Harner clearly thought she should stop looking.

She looked up into Clive's kind face. "I'd rather know," she whispered.

"We should be thorough, Harner." He placed his hand supportively on the small of her back.

Harner grunted assent. "Give me a moment. These need a bit of arranging. The students never put their work back as they found it." He pulled and tugged the bodies, laying them out shoulder to shoulder, then he carefully pulled back the linen, showing only their faces.

Lena gasped.

"Calder?" Clive stepped closer to her side, ready to console her.

"Not Horatio." She shook her head no. "But these three." Through the linen, she touched the shoulder of the towheaded man with the long scar on his cheek and chin. "This is Maxim Cardolet, portrait painter, able to make the most ordinary face memorable." She pointed at the long scar that ran across his face from temple to cheek. "He got that scar when he protected his employer's artworks from an angry French mob." Maxim's face was bruised and cut, and she was grateful the sheet obscured whatever had killed him.

She moved her hand to the next man's shoulder, offering a eulogy of sorts. "Hugo Cardolet, Maxim's cousin, who painted machinery, ships, rigging, all with an amazing detail. Hugo was deaf from a fever, but even so, he sang robustly as he worked, a lovely baritone." Bruises lined Hugo's neck.

"This is Armaud Bonheur, who traveled with the Cardolets and painted birds—all kinds—so lifelike you expected them to fly." She touched the third man's shoulder as she had the others. "Once he discovered I could speak French, he refused to speak anything else." Bonheur showed no indication of what might have taken his life.

"Were they with you long?"

"A month, perhaps a little less. The Rotunda is known for hiring émigrés. One day they simply didn't return. I thought they had found more lucrative jobs. They were saving to open their own atelier. They had such plans. . . ." She stopped, uncertain she could trust her voice. Her throat thickened with unwept tears, but she held them back.

"*Someone* had plans." Clive's voice was hard and cold, a tone she'd never heard before, but she understood it. He touched Maxim's shoulder. "We will find that person." She could almost hear him add "I promise."

He nodded to Harner, who covered the men's faces.

"I'll be sending the magistrate, a man by the name of Thacker. He'll need to see these three bodies."

"I've had enough death for a day." Lena waited until his eyes met hers, then she walked with Clive toward the stairway. "I had steeled myself to find Horatio, but not the others. I'll need some paper to draw Horatio for you."

Chapter Fourteen

At the street, Clive hailed a hackney. Lena's face was drawn, whether from the cold or the shock, but in either case, it pulled at his heart. He wished he could tuck her somewhere safe until he'd uncovered the scheme that put her in danger, and he was more and more certain the Rotunda was the least safe place Lena could be. But how could he broach it in a way that his self-reliant, resilient Lena might listen?

His. He liked the sound of it, and he wondered what Lena might think. Would she say she thought of him as *hers* as well? He hoped she would.

He gave the driver the address of the duke's residence and climbed into the carriage. "When you are satisfied with your drawing, I'll send it to Thacker and ask him to search the other surgery schools." He took the backward-facing seat. "You and I will take a different approach. Of your craftsmen, how many are émigrés?"

"I don't have a number. We hire the best craftsmen, regardless of nationality, and we advertise here and abroad. 'Wanted: the best craftsmen for the most important painting in the last decade.' Horatio used every opportunity to stimulate public interest. We had dozens of applications, but Horatio handled it all. He even fashioned some accommodations in the storehouse behind the Rotunda for those new to London." She paused, worrying her bottom lip with her teeth. He tried not to focus on the fullness of her lips, but he wanted to kiss her again.

"I was in Paris during the years of the Musée Napoleon." She seemed to change the subject.

"The museum Napoleon made for the works of art he'd stolen from across the Continent," he prompted.

"Before the works were returned to their homes, the Musée Napoleon offered an unimaginable opportunity: all that art in one place to study and copy. It gathered a rich community of artists and craftsmen from across Europe. I had hoped to rebuild something of that community here, but the continental craftsmen move on too quickly, sometimes as soon as we hire them."

"Do they find other employment or simply disappear? Do they leave anything behind?"

"Horatio would know better than I do." She shrugged. "But a month or so ago, he was upset that two craftsmen—both Belgian—left after only a week to paint theatrical backgrounds in Brighton. They asked us to store their belongings until they returned." She paused. "Horatio read the note they sent several times before he stuffed it in his pocket."

"Do you know where he might have put that letter or their belongings?"

"If Horatio kept it, we might find the note in the hatbox. As for their belongings, Horatio boxed them up, and he may have left them in the storeroom." She grew silent for a moment. "You think they didn't leave."

"Would you recognize the missing craftsmen if you saw them again?"

"Probably. Why?"

"I've kept sketches of all the bodies suspected of

having been murdered, and it would be useful to see if you recognize anyone else. I'll bring them to the duke's residence tonight."

Lena looked him over, and he felt her examination as a warm sun. He studied her eyes, her brows, her mouth, her full, inviting lips, but it was more than her physical charms. He thought of her hand, touching the three dead artists, and her impromptu eulogies. She was willful and stubborn, thoughtful and talented, and ingenious and independent, but under it all he saw glimpses of a vulnerability that she wouldn't even admit to herself. She was an enigma, and if he wasn't careful, he might risk losing his heart.

He was about to touch her knee, when something out the window caught her eye. She looked past him, watching the passing buildings, then pulled her body away from his.

"This isn't the way to the Rotunda." Her voice was hard and suspicious.

Clive looked out the window and cursed inwardly. "A mistake of habit. Please forgive me. I must have given him the duke's address. I'll have him turn the carriage at the next opportunity." Clive started to tap the ceiling, but paused. "At the same time, until we know why Calder is in hiding, you must consider staying away from the Rotunda. Judith and Ophelia can manage your crew during the day while you and I search for Calder, and at night you can advise them what to do next. It's the only way to keep you safe."

The look on her face told him he had compounded one error with another equally grave.

"You withhold information, parceling it out when you can't gain my help otherwise." Lena studied him intently, as if trying to read his character in the lines on his face. "You tell me the Rotunda is so dangerous that I must stay away, but your relatives—your *female* relatives—can safely remain there day in and day out. Whose interests are you protecting? Yours, the duke's, or the surgery school's?"

"In solving a murder, I'm protecting the interests of the *state*. I've withheld information, yes. That's how one conducts an investigation. As for the safety of my *female* relatives, they are protected by a raft of the duke's servants."

Clive watched her face for any reaction, but saw none. He continued, "Earlier, you offered to help me. Now you must let me help you. Or if not me, have you no family, no community, to call upon?"

The look on her face, somewhere between sorrow and anger, told him a great deal. "No."

"But you aren't dead."

"What?" She gave him a look he couldn't interpret, both surprised and defensive and something else.

"In this world, people without a community end up dead." He wished she could trust him. "Who is your community?"

"I told you already." Her eyes were dark. "I was building a community of craftsmen here, refugees—like me—from the Continent."

"You describe yourself as a refugee but you are clearly British, and your English shows no hint of your years abroad," Clive observed. "Do you feel that distanced from the land of your birth?"

"Have you heard me speak French, *monsieur*?" At the word *monsieur*, she became French in accent, posture, and mannerisms. She offered a short tirade on London fashion. Clive pretended not to understand, knowing it was a test, but of what, he couldn't be sure. He managed not to react—or smile—not even when she described an embroidered waistcoat one of his cousins had worn to Ophelia's dinner as a "violation of all that Beau Brummell held holy." Underneath her words was an anger he hadn't seen before, a hurt that went years deep.

Her manner changed back to English. "Or perhaps you would prefer Italian, *signore,* as the Romans speak it?" She performed the trick again, her voice, body, and gestures becoming Italian. This time he didn't have to pretend. He only caught her meaning in bits and snatches, enough to know that she was complaining about the quality of wine available in London.

"My German changes with the country. In Austria, I speak like the Viennese; in Switzerland, like those from Bern. Anywhere I have lived, I have listened for the smallest distinctions and practiced until no one could tell I was from anywhere else. The British are notorious for speaking every language in their own dialect: they make Cádiz rhyme with ladies, as Lord Byron points out. But not me. If I were to meet you on the street in Naples, or Villach, or Montpellier, you might not know which country I was from, but you wouldn't pick England. The Continent took me in when England failed me, so, though I was born here, I am also a refugee."

He wanted to draw her into his arms; her wounds clearly still ran deep. But he knew a show of sympathy would be unwelcome. Instead, he spoke without thinking, "You are quite good at that. You'd be an excellent spy." He wished he could call back the words as soon as they left his lips.

She stared at him, disbelieving. "Are you always so . . . accommodating? I lie to you at the Rotunda office. I challenge and bait you. I disagree and refuse your suggestions. I show you that I can pretend to be from any number of countries, and every time, you respond as if I'm being perfectly reasonable."

"Perhaps I find you fascinating, Miss Frost, utterly and

completely fascinating." She stared at him with a look he couldn't interpret, and he breathed in before continuing. "Besides, you have had several very trying days. It seems only fair . . ."

She put her hand on his lips, stopping his words. "Stop acting as if I'm some piece of Dresden porcelain, liable to break at the most inconvenient moment. I do not break."

He took her hand in his. Never letting his eyes leave hers, he kissed her gloved palm, reveling in the electricity that arced as if they were touching flesh to flesh. "I've never thought you were liable to break."

With one hand, he held hers, while the other pulled on the tips of her glove. She watched his hand, as if the motion of his fingers mesmerized her. With each tug, he named her attributes. "You are strong. Resilient. Brave. Inventive. Daring." He began again with her forefinger. "Clever. Charming. Devious. Headstrong."

"I preferred the first set." She tried to pull her hand away, but he held it tight and continued, one finger at a time, releasing each from the fabric inch by inch, then beginning again as he drew the material slowly off her hand. With "honest," the glove released completely. He laid it on his knee, never letting her hand go. Raising her palm to his lips, he watched her eyes widen, but rather than kiss her again, he instead breathed warmth onto her cold fingers and palm.

With his index finger, he traced the slender length of her forefinger lightly, barely touching her skin. He moved from forefinger to second to third, his touch a whisper. She shuddered, but she never pulled her hand from his. All her attention—and his—was focused on that singular meeting of their flesh.

It was a long seduction, a single hand, five fingers, a wrist. By the time he finally pressed his lips to her palm, the air between them shimmered with energy. She stretched out her other hand and cradled his cheek. Her eyes never left his.

She leaned forward. He lowered her hand from his lips, clasping it to his heart. Their lips met, as they had the night before, but with more conviction. His free hand curled behind her neck, supporting her head. His fingers, slipping beneath the soft fabric of her cap, felt the silky twist of her hair.

The kiss ended, only to be followed by another, and another. The world existed only in their kisses, and each parting brought a new apocalypse.

With one elegant movement, he changed his seat, drawing her closer. His hand slid down her spine, settling against the small of her back, holding her close to him.

She shifted, pulling away so that she could meet his eyes with hers.

"We haven't time." Her voice was husky with desire. "We are nearing the Rotunda."

"If you wish, I'll tell him to drive us somewhere else." He brushed a stray curl back with his forefinger.

"Somewhere else." She repeated the words as if she'd never heard them before. She gave him one last long kiss, but her face indicated the moment was gone. "Actually, there is somewhere else we should go." She looked through the window at the passing streets. "It will take less time to walk than to turn the carriage. But it's not the best of neighborhoods, so I must caution you to be brave." Her words were serious, but a smile played at the corner of her mouth.

Clive tapped for the coachman to stop, then he kissed her once more. "With you at my side, how could I be afraid?"

She rolled her eyes in response. She straightened her

clothes and bonnet. "We will hurry. I don't wish to take advantage of your family's goodwill in helping a perfect stranger."

"No one is a stranger who has been to a family dinner. And you garnered extra goodwill for entertaining Ophelia's chemistry lesson." He gently straightened her bonnet, tucking in the escaped hairs.

She ran her hand down his chest, then readjusted his cravat. The gesture was intimate, as if their kisses had shifted the landscape between them. "Are we suitable?"

He curved his palm around her cheek, and she covered his hand with hers. "Quite."

The carriage stopped, and Clive stepped down, then lifted Lena out. "Where are we going?" The address, several blocks away, lay in the direction from which they had come. Clive paid the driver, then returned to her side.

"My studio. It's the sort of place Horatio would hide if he knew about it."

Clive followed. "But he doesn't?"

"I inherited it before I met him. But I have a box there that I was keeping safe for one of the craftsmen. It might hold nothing interesting."

"Or it might give us a clue we need."

She led him down a short block, then through an alley. When they came out again, they stood on a street lined with buildings to either side and a large cemetery before them. "We are going to that row of buildings on the other side of the cemetery."

Clive sniffed the air. "Is that the smell you mentioned to Ophelia?"

"Yes. It's so pungent in summer that it's driven away most of the trade and many of the residents. Even thieves stay away." She pointed at the churchyard gate. "It's quicker to cut through, and if Ophelia is right, we should be safe enough during the day."

"I see why you were so interested in Ophelia's chemistry lesson."

"One can learn a great deal from another person's passion."

Clive held the churchyard gate open, gallantly. "After you, my dear ghoul."

Chapter Fifteen

The interior of the cemetery was desolate. To their left, long expanses of exposed dirt alternated with strips of barely rooted grass. To their right rose hills of displaced earth, and before them stood several trenches, twenty feet wide and equally deep. Clive studied the trenches as they passed, the dirt held back by walls made of wooden slats. They walked in near silence, trying not to breathe in too much of the noxious air.

"Lena. Stop," he whispered, pulling her back into the shadow of the mounded earth. In the distance, a group of men lifted a body from the ground, then stripped it of its clothes. Grave robbers. "We need to leave and quickly."

"But we are almost there. It's just to that gate." Having not seen the robbers, she pointed toward the gate. One of the men caught sight of her movement. Yelling to one another, two men ran across the yard toward them, and the other two to the gate.

"They're cutting us off." Clive examined their surroundings, and picking up a nearby tarp, he threw it in the closest trench. He took her elbow. "Sit down."

"On the edge of the pit?" She sat, but unhappily. He flung himself flat on the ground beside her. "We haven't

much time. I'll lower you as far as I can, but when you hit
the bottom, try to roll with the impact. Give me your hands."

The men, yelling to each other, were drawing closer.
She grabbed his wrists, and he hers, closed her eyes, and
slid off the edge. When she was hanging the length of
his arms into the pit, she let go. She fell, rolling naturally.
She landed next to a skull sticking up from the earth, and
she recoiled away from it, pushing back into the wall of
the pit.

Clive lowered himself from the edge, then let go. Covered in mire, he picked up the tarp and pressed it into the
mud at the base of the trench wall. "Sit there, on the tarp,
as close as you can to the wall."

"I'm going to hate this, aren't I?" she whispered, sitting.

He sat beside her, pulling the tarp over them like a
blanket. "You can bury your face in my chest, but we're
going to have to lie down— if they can see anything in the
pit, we want them to think we are just another pair of
bodies."

She pulled her fichu up from her bodice and over her
head, then followed his instructions. She felt him lie down
beside her and pull the tarp up to conceal them.

"Are you sure you saw something?"

"No one came out the gate."

"No one passed us neither."

"I saw someone. I'm sure of it."

"Are they in the pit?"

"Can't tell. Nothing but dark down there."

"We'll give them a bit o' help, if they are."

The retaining boards made a wrenching sound, and the
earth came crushing down. Clive pulled her against his
chest, sheltering her between his body and the side of the
grave. The weight of the dirt was heavy, terrifyingly so.
What if they sent more dirt down—would it bury them

alive? She thought of the skull lying in the dirt, and she started to press against the tarp.

Clive breathed the word "quiet" into her hair, and she forced herself to be calm. Another rain of dirt fell down.

"That's enough. Anyone down there much longer won't be telling what they saw."

Lena, to distract herself from the stench and the weight of the dirt, tried to listen to the men's accents.

"We should take what bodies we have now, then come back. With tomorrow's burials, we should be in better stead with . . ." The voices grew distant.

Lena and Clive waited, unmoving.

The smell of decay surrounded them, and she tested how her body felt against Ophelia's symptoms of gas poisoning. She wasn't yet faint or bilious. To control her anxiety, she focused on the rise and fall of Clive's chest against hers and his even breathing. How could he be so calm when the circumstances were so threatening?

They waited a long time, bodies pressed close, the weight of the dirt bearing down on them, listening for any sign of danger.

After what seemed like an eternity, Clive whispered into her hair, "I think they are gone." He pressed against the weight of the dirt, pushing the tarp down from above their heads. Dirt fell down between them. Above them, the boards on the sides of the pit hung down. Luckily, the men could only loosen the slats at the top of the trench, leaving the lower wall still in place. If more than the upper wall had collapsed, Lena and Clive would have been buried, perhaps permanently. As it was, they could still make their way free.

Clive used the tarp to push back the dirt, then pulled himself free. She let him pull her out, then tried to shake the muck from her skirts.

"How do you anticipate getting out?" Lena stood beside him examining the walls.

"I hadn't fully considered that. I simply realized this was our only escape. Perhaps you could stand on my shoulders and pull yourself out? If that fails, I am counting on your ingenuity."

"On your shoulders. Like a circus act?" Lena looked at him, then at the side of the pit.

"I assumed you would prefer to be on top." Clive's voice was matter-of-fact, but his eyes danced. A long silence drew out between them at his double entendre. She thought of his kisses and of the weight of his body next to hers under the tarp.

When she finally spoke, she kept her voice level. "I suppose I would prefer that."

"Then we should try to escape." Clive knelt before her, and she used his knee to try to climb up on his shoulders. But he couldn't see through her skirts. She took off her skirts down to her Turkish pantaloons.

They tried again. This time Clive could see, but she couldn't get her balance, and he caught her as she fell. He held her against his chest, both breathing heavily from the exertion. They stared into each other's eyes.

"How long do you think we have to get out?" Lena wrapped her arms around his neck.

"What do you mean?"

"Before we succumb to the vapors."

"The dirt was dry and crumbling, so I risked that it had already aired sufficiently." He looked abashed. "Had it not, we would be dead already."

"Well, that's a comfort." She signaled he should put her down. "I suppose you thought of that before hiding here."

"I decided we would prefer dying by vapors than by the

hands of grave robbers who attack rather than run." He set her on her feet.

"That seems reasonable, given your investigations. Should we try again?"

"What do you have in mind?"

"If you make a cradle with your hands, I'll run toward you, like the circus vaulters at Sadler's Wells. Then if you can throw me far enough up, I might be able to catch the palings they pushed down and pull myself out. But you'll need to catch me if I fall."

"Always." His voice was like chocolate again, urging her to trust him fully.

The next few moments were more like a farce at the theater than a real escape. Lena would run, leap, then slide down the dirt wall, or fall against Clive's strong chest. She preferred his chest.

On the fifth try, the plan somehow worked. Lena dug her feet in above one of the fallen palings, and from there, she worked her way slowly up the wall.

It took what felt like forever. Her hands, still wounded, struggled to make handholds in the packed soil.

At the top, she pulled herself up over the edge. She lay on her stomach, watching for the men. Once she was convinced she and Clive were the only living bodies in the cemetery, she allowed herself to lie on her back, panting and looking for a way to help Clive escape. Luckily, a wagon with a variety of ropes and tools was not far off. She tied one end of a long rope to the wagon and lowered it to Clive. Soon after, Clive pulled himself out of the pit.

Relieved, she pressed herself against his chest, and he wrapped his arms around her. They stood alone in the churchyard, holding each other, their clothes torn, covered in mud and muck.

After a few moments, they parted, and Lena tried to

repair her clothing. "These clothes will have to be burned— there's no hope of getting the stench out."

"If we aren't careful, someone will think we've risen from the dead," Clive joked, brushing the worst of the mud from his trousers.

"If we aren't careful, someone will think *we* are grave robbers and call the magistrate," Lena countered. "If you agree, I'd prefer to collect the box from my studio later. I don't know what I'm wearing, but I want it off me as soon as possible."

Clive had asked the carriage to wait for them at the cemetery's address. But when the pair of them arrived, dirty and foul smelling, the driver clearly wished he hadn't. Lena had thought he would refuse to transport them, but Clive's promise of an additional reward from the Duke of Forster eased the driver's qualms, and they set out for the duke's residence without any further delay.

Chapter Sixteen

"If Dan had done his job, we wouldn't be in this trouble." Sparks looked around the Blue Heron for eavesdroppers. An old drunk sprawled facedown across the next table periodically twitched and mumbled like a dog having a bad dream. No one else sat near enough to overhear.

"I don't know why you're mad at me." Dan, a strongly built man, leaned forward over the tavern table. "You gave me the key and told me to kill her."

"*Her* meant Calder's *partner*, not the landlady's cousin." Sparks punctuated the *her* with a finger.

"The cousin was in the room, keys in hand, rummaging in the wardrobe," Dan growled back. "How was I to know she was thieving?"

"Should Dan have asked her name before he bashed her head in?" a third man, taciturn and normally silent, spoke up.

"Henry's right." Dan nodded. "If I'd hesitated, I might have ended up like Jim."

"Jim was a fool." Sparks looked around the room again.

"A dead fool now." Henry calculated how much more beer was left in his tankard.

"He thought he could bribe Calder . . . gain us some time." Sparks shook his head ruefully.

"Bribe him with a pistol? Calder was already suspicious." Henry refused the explanation.

"I paid Abbott plenty for that key." Sparks shook his head in frustration. "She'll want more now that Dan's killed her cousin. And we don't have any more money."

"We should sell the body," Dan suggested.

"The magistrate has already had it removed," Sparks countered.

"The cousin, yes, but not Jim. His body is still in Calder's room, waiting to be found—or sold." Henry took another swig of his beer. "We could splash him with liquor to manage any smell, then carry Jim out between us as if he were drunk. No one will be the wiser."

"A big man like Jim, healthy—except for being dead— we'll get prime rates," Dan added. "But we'd have to act today."

"I still don't know how it went wrong. Jim is—was— twice Calder's size." Sparks shook his head mournfully.

"Calder may know what we did in Edinburgh and here. But as Mr. Georges told us, the law needs bodies to pursue the crime."

"I'm not afraid of the law. I'm afraid of Georges. He won't like it if we've brought the eye of the law, and he won't care about bodies or trials. He'll simply slit our throats. . . ."

"If we're lucky," Dan interjected.

"And feed us to some pigs." Henry waited for Sparks's response. Getting none, he continued. "We should leave. Manchester, Liverpool, even back to Scotland. Start over. New place, new bodies."

"And Calder?"

"Do you think the woman in the cemetary was Calder's partner? Killing her would send Calder a message, wherever he is."

"Too bad we won't know until tomorrow if she and the man went into that pit."

Sparks rose, drinking his remaining beer in one gulp. "There's plenty of light left. I say we collect our last set of bodies for Georges, so we're even with him. Make sure Calder didn't leave any other messages. Then we leave town before anyone's the wiser, particularly Georges and Charters."

The other men rose, following his lead. "I wouldn't even drink here if it weren't for the discount Flute always gives us."

The trio left, and shortly after, the drunk, mumbling to himself, stumbled out into the night.

Sometime well after midnight Flute bolted the door to the bar and climbed the stairs to his apartment. As he expected, Charters was sitting before the fire, whiskey in hand.

"Did Midshipman Timpson enjoy his evening?"

"I've never understood men who discuss their sins in a public house." Charters, out of any costume, looked like a half-befuddled aristocrat, cravat badly tied, waistcoat years out of date. "Henceforth, anytime we are interviewing additional help, we will first ply them with discounted drinks at the Blue Heron and see who can hold their tongues."

"What did you learn?"

"That Sparks and his crew have a great many secrets. But more importantly, they mentioned the name Calder, and I remembered this." Charters held out a letter. "The writer contacted us on the recommendation of one of our clients."

"*Clients*." Flute snorted, then read over the letter's first page. "Let's see: stepmother wants us to find a missing stepdaughter. The inheritance is tied up, waiting for the girl's reappearance. Ah, I remember now, the stepmother wanted us to *confirm* the girl's dead, but too much time had passed to be worth our while."

"True, but read the last sentence on the second page."

Flute read the last sentence aloud. "'A Mr. Calder told my husband he'd found my stepdaughter and would bring her home, but I have heard nothing since my husband's death.' So?"

"The proprietor of the Rotunda in Leicester Square is named Calder, and his assistant is a young woman the same age as the missing stepdaughter."

"That changes things, doesn't it?" Flute whistled through his teeth.

"It certainly does. I believe we need to investigate this assistant on our own."

Flute poured himself a glass of whiskey and settled before the fire. "What character will you play?"

Chapter Seventeen

At the duke's residence, Clive called for baths and new clothes, and within the hour, the pair was back in a carriage, headed to the Rotunda.

"Do you want to predict what the crew will have accomplished in your absence?" Clive asked as they walked down the long hallway onto the Rotunda's stage.

"I'm afraid to have expectations." Lena didn't resist when Clive took her hand.

On the stage, several women clustered around her plans, none of them noticing that she or Clive had arrived. Lena examined the gutter. Everything was unpacked and was placed beautifully, just as she'd imagined it. Instead of losing a day, she might even be ahead of schedule. Strangely, however, the women had left one narrow portion of scaffold partially intact, its height level to the exhibition floor.

"Ariel, did your group finish making space in the storage room for the extra stage sets?" Lady Judith's voice rose above the group.

"Yes, they are already moved there."

"Kate? What about the area for the musicians?"

"It's cleared, and we've already set up the chairs, according to the diagram. But we can't find the music stands."

Lena dropped Clive's hand and stepped forward. "The music stands will be delivered on the day of the gala. I'm renting them, and we had to work around the Royal Opera's own performances. Of course it helped that I hired most of their musicians."

"Miss Frost, we have had a delightful time." Lady Judith motioned to the plans she had been marking in pencil. "I believe we've put you ahead by a day."

The women parted for Lena to see her plans. "But how? I don't have enough workers to do this much in a single day."

"Since the duke insisted that most of his footmen and postilions accompany us as guards, I saw no reason for them not to help."

Lena felt stricken. Lady Wilmot's advance provided just enough money to pay her own crews, and not a penny more. "How much do I owe them—you?"

"Oh, no, Miss Frost! These are the duke's men. Months ago, after Lady Wilmot began the Muses' Salon, the duke asked if any of his servants would be interested in 'an occasional day's levity.' Those who volunteered have become our staff. But we kept your curtain in place, so the subject of your painting remains secure."

"As for us, we enjoy being useful," Ophelia interjected. "It's our purpose in the Muses' Salon to act as a support and inspiration to those who might need our help. It would defeat that purpose to expect payment."

Lena looked at her plans, noting each one of Lady Judith's decisive ticks. "You appear to have gained me more than a day."

"We had hoped as much." Lady Judith paused, nodding to the other women who withdrew to the opposite side of the large exhibition platform. Lady Judith placed her hand on Lena's shoulder. "But I'm afraid the exhibition has also experienced a setback."

"Is it Horatio?" Her throat closed around the words.

"Oh, no, dear, we have no news of your partner." Lady Judith met her eyes and held her gaze. "Your painting has suffered some vandalism." Lena turned toward the shortened scaffold. "Your man Louis discovered it this afternoon."

Kate returned to their side. "All the men are outside, and Louis is ready to lower the curtain."

Lena, still staring at the scaffold, nodded yes.

In a few moments, a portion of the curtain behind the short scaffold lowered to the floor. As the damage became visible, Ophelia gasped, and her sisters, Kate and Ariel, made exclamations of horror and dismay.

Someone had smeared paint over half a dozen faces, then cut the canvas in angry swaths, slicing most of the damaged faces. Clive stood beside her, waiting to offer whatever comfort she would accept. Another setback in a series that included the disappearance of her partner, her own accident, and the deaths of her men. Did someone want the panorama to fail? And were the murders tied to that aim and not some larger scheme?

Clive watched Lena's response to the ruined canvas. He expected her to rage and rail against the destruction. But she did none of those things. Instead, she stood silently, every muscle preternaturally still, the only movement the rise and fall of her breath. For a single moment, her shoulders fell slightly, but then she straightened her back. Only her strength of will seemed to hold despair at bay.

"What will you do now?" Kate whispered.

"Repair it, then paint." Lena, her jaw set sternly, sounded calm and practical.

"How can you repair the cuts?" Ariel, always interested in how things worked, asked.

"I'll bond a piece of linen to the back of the canvas with melted beeswax." Lena's eyes narrowed as she examined the damage. "I can't use gesso over paint, but I can fill the repair lines with lead white, sand it, and paint again. Since none of the damaged portions will be viewed at an angle, the repair shouldn't show. As for the painting itself, it's the temperature that matters. As it is now, the repairs could stay tacky for a week or more. If I am to repair this before the gala, I have to do it today."

Behind Lena, Judith motioned that the other women should go, and Clive nodded his approval. Judith stepped to Lena's side. "Miss Frost, we are happy to remain and help you, but I fear that since none of us are painters, we will prove more of an impediment than a help."

Lena tore her gaze from the painting to face Judith. "You have already helped a great deal—more than I can say."

"Then we will take our leave. I promised my wards, the Halletts, a game of hopscotch in the nursery." Judith placed a reassuring hand on Lena's arm. "If you need help tomorrow or any other day, the Muses are at your service."

Each of the women took their leave, and Louis, who had joined them after he raised the curtain, led them out. "The ladies have left, and I've locked the door tight behind them. But can we trust the locks?"

"I suppose we must. Go home to your wife. There's no reason for you to stay." Lena stared at the painting.

Louis raised an eyebrow at Clive, asking without words if Clive intended to stay with Lena, and Clive nodded agreement.

"Then I'll be going; my Ella will be waiting. By the

way, the canvas maker sent round a boy to collect his last payment." Louis cast a sympathetic look at Lena.

Lena stiffened, but did not reply, appearing to be completely engrossed in her examination of the damaged painting.

"I'll see Louis out." Clive followed Louis to the back door of the Rotunda.

"I hate to say this, but it has to be one of the crew doing this damage. Harald never leaves the door unattended, so someone couldn't sneak in repeatedly. But someone could hang back and hide until the Rotunda is closed." Louis rubbed his chin. "You stay close to her."

"I intend to do just that."

Louis stuck out his hand, and Clive shook it.

Clive watched the older man until he reached the street and disappeared into the heavy pedestrian traffic. No more Rotunda craftsmen were going to be losing their lives, not if Clive could stop it. Clive examined the door of the Rotunda, its hinges, latch, and lock. Everything seemed sound, but whoever was tampering with the exhibition had found a way in.

Back inside the Rotunda, Clive found Lena under the exhibition platform near a large supply closet built into the back wall. She'd already filled a basket with two lanterns, matches, various paints, brushes, and solvents, and she was loading wood into what appeared to be a kiln. Beside her was a narrow wheelbarrow holding a pot, a bucket of wax, an iron, and several large strips of linen.

"I understand that you must repair the damage yourself, but could none of your craftsmen paint?"

"The portrait painters are all gone." She flung kindling

into the kiln, her movements sharp, even angry. "I paid them their last wages before Horatio disappeared. Those who remain are builders, like Louis, not painters."

"Can you call them back?"

"I haven't the money to call them back." Instantly, her fury became visible. "Horatio took it, every penny that we hadn't yet spent, all that remained of the subscription fees, everything. Without Lady Wilmot's advance, I'd have had to ask everyone—my crew, my suppliers, the musicians at the gala, and a dozen more contractors—to extend me credit, hoping that the fact I've paid so promptly before would vouch for me." She flung more wood into the pile.

"Why didn't you tell me?"

"And confirm that I have a motive for killing the man in Horatio's bedroom? You said it yourself: 'The only way this could be worse would be if Calder's absconded with all the money.'" Lena brushed her cheek with the back of her hand and met his eyes defiantly. "How would you have responded if you'd known?"

"I would have done exactly as I did." He stepped close to her, close enough to feel her frustration, rising in waves. "I don't know what is going on. I don't know why you seem to have become a target. But I don't believe you killed your partner, or your crew, or that you are responsible for any of this." He watched as her shoulders lowered and her tension seemed to abate. Helping her to her feet, he enclosed her in his arms. "However, I do believe this: we will find the answers together."

She leaned her head forward into his chest, forehead against his breastbone. He put his hand against the back of her head, cradling her in his arms. They stood still for several moments, him offering her the kindness and support that she needed. She lifted her head, looking into his eyes, searching for the answer to a question she hadn't yet asked. He waited for the question, but after a moment, she tapped his chest with her fingers, letting him know their embrace had ended.

She returned to the fire, lighting it with skill. She placed the iron directly on the wood, then hung the pot of wax above the flames. As the wax melted, she brushed it onto the linen, permeating the fabric. When all the strips were waxed, she moved them to the wheelbarrow, then she placed the iron, now red-hot, in a deep iron bucket in the cart.

Pushing the wheelbarrow, she quietly made her way to the back door. There a split in the canvas gave her access to a three-foot-wide space between the canvas and the exterior wall. The narrow wheelbarrow fit perfectly. He respected her silence, recognizing in her deliberate movements the concentration of an artist. He followed her, not because he could help, but because he needed to be near her and needed to ensure she was safe.

The damage was obvious: each long cut let in a stream of light from the exhibition platform. Lena worked quickly, placing the linen strips on the cuts, then using the iron to melt the wax and meld the two fabrics together. By the time the iron had grown cold, she was done. She ran her fingers around the edges to ensure they were well-affixed. Satisfied with her work, she nodded him back the way they had come.

Back at the storage case, she let him help her empty the wheelbarrow, then she put in her basket of supplies. This time, he lifted the handles before she could. She started to object, but instead, she led him to the scaffold. There, she tied a rope to the basket and then climbed up, pulling the supplies behind her. By the time he'd climbed up, she'd lit the lanterns.

The damaged section presented a group of British

soldiers helping their wounded peers from the field. To accommodate the distance between the viewing platform and the painting itself, Lena had designed the figures to be more than life-size.

Clive examined the repairs that now appeared like long cracks in the painting. "With just the wax and linen, you might not notice the repair from twenty feet away."

"That's what I'm counting on. In an easel painting, I'd never repair it this way because eventually the surface will craze."

Clive sat beside her as she mixed paints on her palette. "I know you like to work in silence, but would you mind explaining how the repair will work?"

Lena's face softened. "I'm mixing lead white with flesh-colored pigments to match the parts of the face. Eyebrows. Lips. Skin." She pointed at the blobs of paint with the palette knife. "While it's still wet, I'll wipe on a lean damar varnish mixed with turpentine. That will give enough of a shine to hide the repair."

Where the linen had been joined with the wax, Lena began to fill the crack with the various paints, then when done, she took a stiff bristle brush and smoothed out the textures so that it matched the surrounding surface.

Clive watched her complete the process twice. "I can't paint, but I could do the final smoothing with the bristle brush."

She looked torn, but interested. "Show me."

She watched his every movement, giving him tips along the way, and when he had finished, she agreed to move on to the next repair, letting him do the final smoothing.

They worked in tandem, him smoothing the previous repair, while she moved on to the next face. In between, he watched her paint, her sure skill transforming each long crease back into a face.

She looked up, clearly pleased with her work. Once more, he felt the pull of her, a deep sense of connection that went beyond anything he'd ever imagined. She wet her lips with her tongue, its pink tip fascinating him, and he imagined kissing her. She blushed as if reading his thoughts.

"This one will be ready for you in a few minutes." She waved him away with her paintbrush. "Go look at the rest of the panorama. You are distracting me."

"My dear, *you* are the distraction." Clive resisted the impulse to lean down and nuzzle her hair.

"Go." She pressed her brush into the paint, dismissing him. "I'll call you back when I'm ready to move on."

Though reluctant to leave her side, Clive stepped back to examine the section. He considered every detail: the uniforms of the British soldiers; the eyes of the horses, wide with terror; the sky filled with gun and cannon smoke. Past that, at the far end of the section, two officers consulted a map, one pointing the viewer's attention to the center of the painting (still hidden by a curtain), where, Clive assumed, the central part of the battle was depicted. "This section is magnificent. If the rest is half as good as this, your panorama will be the talk of the town for months." He moved closer to her, focusing his attention on one of the wounded men. "Who is this?"

"It's just a face." She rubbed out a bit of chin and started over. "Horatio joked that we should sell the faces for a bit of extra profit. But I didn't want to depict a known coward as a hero merely because he'd paid for it or to show a man at the battle who hadn't served. We agreed that the only identifiable faces would be Wellington and the other officers, though sometimes we do include the face of a man known to have died heroically."

"Well, this man didn't serve. He's the proprietor of a poorhouse near Lincoln's Inn Fields and completely lame." He pointed to a man binding another man's wounds. "And this man here. He just opened a new anatomy school near Covent Garden. Why would Calder include these men?"

She moved to the next damaged face. "I've given up trying to figure out what's going on."

Clive stepped back, looking at the painting at large. "How many faces were destroyed?"

"Eight."

"Eight," he repeated. "Could your Horatio be sending us a message? I've been searching for a single villain, but after our experience at the cemetery, perhaps it's an entire gang." He returned to the scene with the two officers examining a map. "And what's this?"

"A map of the field of Waterloo from the British perspective." She didn't look up.

"It's not Waterloo; it's England, though a distorted England." He leaned in. "The midlands are enlarged, making the west of England bulge badly toward Wales."

"That can't be." She lowered her brush and looked down toward the map. She rose and touched the paint of the map. It was still tacky, but not overly so. "This has been repainted, three, maybe four days ago."

"A vandal would destroy, not paint."

"But if this map is a message, I'm not sure what it means."

"We can review Calder's notes once you've finished here. But for now, think. Did Calder say anything about the midlands, Lena? Anything at all? Did he leave you any other message?"

Without thinking, she touched her bodice where she'd hidden Horatio's note. She closed her eyes, trying to remember anything Horatio might have said or done before he disappeared. She worked her way forward in memory, from the last time she'd seen him, to his note, his rooms, the body, the lemons.

The lemons. She removed the tightly folded piece of paper from her bodice.

Clive tried not to let his eyes linger on her generous bosom. He recognized the packet—it was the one he'd saved from the laundry without reading.

"Horatio left me a note."

"When?" He walked back to meet her.

"I found it a moment before you arrived to burgle his office."

"I wasn't burgling."

"Did you take anything away?" She searched his face.

He avoided her eyes.

"That's a confession. Burglar." She began to unfold the note, but stopped. "What did you take?"

"A wood carving of a bird was wedged in the back of a drawer—I practically had to take the desk apart to get it out."

She grew very still. "It's not a bird. It's a tavern called the Pelican, or the Albatross, some seabird. Horatio bought the carving there several weeks ago, and he'd sit at his desk for hours, just turning it over. Whenever I would ask about it, he would change the subject." She unfolded Horatio's note and held it out. "Perhaps it was meant to accompany this."

Clive read "RUN" written large in the middle of the paper and remembered her in the office, shoulders back, spine straight, defying him. "No wonder you pretended to be someone else. You must have been terrified. I wish we'd met under better circumstances. Perhaps if I had been introduced to you by a trusted friend at a crowded ball, you might believe that I wish only to help you." When Lena didn't respond, he added, "Were you supposed to run to or from this tavern? I believe the bird is a heron. Does that sound familiar as its name?"

"I don't know. I never went with him." Lena pulled the two lamps close together to create a bright pool of light. "But Horatio might have left more than that one word. Remember the lemons?" She held Horatio's note carefully over the lamps, her face narrowing with concentration.

The lemon juice darkened into an image, drawn in thin lines. At the top was an ornate gate, flanked with a row of trees on either side. Yews, for Horatio had sketched a leaf beside them. Beneath one yew stood an angel, hands clasped in prayer. A line led down the page, past a series of hasty, short lines in rows. Some of the lines squiggled upward. He'd numbered the rows: eighteen. Near the bottom of the page was a sort of building.

"What is it?" He watched over her shoulder.

"I'd say it's a graveyard."

"Any indication of which one?"

"No. It's not a pauper's cemetery: pauper's graves don't have markers. The angels, oaks, and gate could narrow the options down. But why leave me an image of a cemetery?"

"Would Horatio leave you a memento mori?"

"No. He's more likely to leave me a statement of which tailors have yet to be paid for his suits."

"Might I have a closer look?"

She pushed the note into his hand, frustrated and scared. Horatio's original message was bad enough. But to find the image of a cemetery on the back of his note was even more disturbing. What did it mean? Was it, as Clive suggested, a memento mori reminding her that death was always at hand? Or some other message? She had no idea.

"Lemon juice isn't a medium for much detail. The gate, yes. We can see something of an unusual design, but it would help to know what sort of trees flank it. At least he's numbered the rows for the graves. May I heat it a bit more?"

She stepped back from the lamps.

"I think there might be something more here." Holding one corner of the candles, he teased out additional lines.

"Why not simply tell me an address?"

"Perhaps he was afraid someone other than you might find the note." He turned the note face up. "Have you noticed *RUN* is spaced unevenly? Look at this odd, long ornamentation before the downstroke."

She leaned in close, breathing in the comforting scent of him. "Is that a *D*?"

"Then we have the *R* in *RUN*, but there's an odd mark I can't make out behind it."

"The *U* is bisected to become a *B*."

"I can see it now. Look here." He pointed at the *N*, where a faint line from the back made it into an oddly shaped *Y*.

"DRBY." She repeated the letters. "Between the *D* and the *R*, that squiggle could be an *A* or an *E*."

Looking away from Horatio's note, he pointed to the panorama. "The map the officers are holding is distorted to emphasize Derbyshire. That map leads us to the shire; your note leads to the city and, using these details, to a particular cemetery."

Lena suppressed a niggle of discomfort. At least the map didn't lead to Kent or to Gravelines in France. She pressed her fingers to her forehead. "Horatio would know that I can't leave the panorama to find some crypt just because he has told me to run and given me an ambiguous clue."

"I could investigate for you, but whatever is hidden in that crypt might be something that only you will understand."

"How? I know almost nothing of Horatio's past before coming to London, except that he's originally from Edinburgh. Where he's been in between, or even recently, I have no idea. He wasn't a man to share his secrets easily—and we've never spoken of Derby." Her voice broke, but she did not cry.

"We know this: he's left you two maps." He held Horatio's note up to the map on the canvas. "He wants you to go to Derby, and once there, to a cemetery."

"And still we know nothing." She sat down in front of the fourth face, her lower legs dangling off the edge of the scaffold.

He sat beside her, watching her mix the flesh tones. Her colors were impeccable, her technique flawless. He watched and waited.

"There," she announced as she finished the fifth face.

"We need to go to Derby, Lena." His voice was gentle. "Derby may be smaller than London—only about thirteen thousand residents—but it's still too big to investigate alone."

She sat unmoving. He took her paintbrush from her hand and set it on her palette, then he drew her close to him. He simply held her, her body tucked into his side. Eventually, the tension in her back and shoulders began to release into his embrace. "Trust me, Lena. Let me help you. . . ." When she didn't respond, he added, "As a friend."

"What if I don't want to be friends? What if . . ." Her voice trailed off. She lifted her face to his. Then without waiting for his response, she pressed her lips against his, replacing her fear and frustration with desire. He returned her kisses each for each, matching her pressure, her pace, until neither of them could think past the next sweet touch. He pulled off her mob bonnet and released the pins holding her hair. It fell around her shoulders in thick waves. He ran his fingers through the heavy mass, cradling her head, as he plundered her mouth.

Lena focused on the feeling of him, his firm shoulders, solid chest, muscled belly. Without thinking, she let his kisses pull her forward until she was half lying on his chest. Their legs were entwined on the platform, and her passion rose as she realized she could have him under her. She placed her hands on either side of his head, then with one quick motion, she positioned herself over him, her chest to his, her legs to either side of his narrow hips.

"Ah, Lena." He whispered her name with such longing that her heart ached. He ran his hands down the sides of her body, holding her against him.

Their hands were greedy, feeling each other's bodies as if there weren't layers of clothing between them.

She realized a moment before he did that her typical work uniform left them few options, short of undress.

"Trousers." He groaned against her mouth. "For all the appeal of a woman in breeches, I discover a disadvantage."

The Rotunda had grown cold and dark around them. The only light remaining was that of the two lamps beside them and a distant one marking the stairway to the platform.

He pulled away. "It would be unwise for us to proceed."

"Are you always so formal when you reject a woman's desire to take you as a lover?"

"I have rejected nothing. If someone has a key to the Rotunda, we must be alert, rather than exposed and vulnerable." He helped her up. "I wish merely to delay until we are somewhere comfortable, warm, and certain of safety." He brushed her clothing smooth, retrieved her mob bonnet, and gently—very gently—put her hair back up.

"Where might such a place be? Certainly, not your brother's house or your club. It is here . . . or nowhere." She kissed his lips once more.

"Or a quiet hotel on our way to Derby."

She shook her head decisively. "I cannot leave the Rotunda. I've told you. My future rides on the success of this exhibition."

"You *have* told me, and I have heard you. But what if you have been thinking of it from the wrong angle? How well does your partner Calder know you?"

"As well as anyone in London." She shrugged. "As well as anyone."

"Then, he knows your commitment to the panorama and its importance for your future career in London, perhaps even in England."

"Yes." Her face grew solemn. "No one knows the stakes better."

"What would you have done—in response to his note—if he'd left the money. Would you have run?"

"No." She pulled back from kissing him.

"Calder knew that. If he left you any resources at all, you would finish the panorama, hold the opening, and largely ignore his warning."

She said nothing and began to repair her clothes.

"Even now—after your accident, two dead bodies, and

an almost-burial—you refuse to let the panorama go. You took Lady Wilmot's commission merely for the funds to pay the crew. Even *without* the subscription money, you are doing exactly the opposite of what Calder instructed you to do."

"He left me very little choice."

"That's my point. What if your partner took the money to give you only one choice—to run? He even knew you well enough that he left you a map, painted into the one thing he's telling you you must leave behind."

"I won't do it." She shook her head resolutely. "I can't abandon it."

"You don't have to. Horatio left the note when you had no support but him. But you have Lady Wilmot and the Muses."

Her eyes met his, afraid and hopeful.

"And me." He traced the line of her jaw gently with his fingertips. "I can investigate this in Derby without you. But I think Derby holds answers to questions you haven't yet asked. With the painting repaired, there's nothing the Muses can't oversee."

She stood quietly, weighing everything he had said. "I was surprised that he left me without even money enough for another week's lodging. He'd been so insistent that I remain at a respectable boardinghouse, and he always insisted I take out my rent before any other payments." She paused again. "But it's the kind of thing he would do, especially if he felt that waiting put me more at risk."

"It's a long ride to Derby. We could enjoy getting to know one another better," he offered carefully, waiting to see her reaction to the suggestion of a tryst.

Her face grew more solemn, then lightened. "Does *better* include kisses?"

"Would you find that appealing?"

"How long do you think it will take?" She eluded the question.

"A day there, a day back, and however long it takes to decipher a crypt in between."

She stared at the canvas, calculating. "Three days if we are lucky, longer if we aren't." She turned her gaze to him. "Promise me: if we haven't found Horatio's crypt in a week, we'll return here to open the panorama."

She watched his face, waiting for any sign of hesitation, and saw none.

"No more than a week, it is."

Lena exhaled, surprised to find she had been holding her breath. "Then, I suppose we should hire a carriage. But first I'd like to consult with the Muses."

"Of course, Miss Frost, we can oversee the work for the grand gala. I formed the salon to help those in need." Lady Wilmot gently embraced Lena. Surprised and oddly touched, Lena allowed the embrace. "Tell us everything."

Lena laid out two pages: Horatio's plan for the gala and her list of tasks. While Sophia and Judith—as they insisted she call them—reviewed the documents and asked questions, Lena noticed that Clive had stepped aside to consult with the duke. Both Clive and his brother were handsome men, but the duke was reserved and austere, while Clive was kindness embodied. Even from across the room, she felt drawn to him. He looked up from the conversation and winked. A slow wink that warmed her cheeks and twisted her belly.

He was a contradiction. An aristocrat who devoted his life to curing the ills of his fellow man. A gentle man resolute enough to dissect the dead. *Does he apologize to the corpse before he begins every examination?* She had defenses against every sort of man. Charming men, manipulative men, deceitful men, she'd learned how to keep them all at bay. But a kind man, an honest man—*that* she hadn't expected. He'd slipped into her heart before she'd realized her danger.

She had no hope of a future between them. A man of his rank married a suitable woman, and she was wholly unsuitable. And she would be no man's mistress. Soon she would have to leave him before her heart couldn't bear the loss. Perhaps, as he'd said, if they had met under different circumstances . . .

"Have you considered a pantomime to entertain the gala-goers?" Sophia's question pulled Lena's attention back to the plans. "Perhaps a bugler in uniform calling the soldiers to arms."

"Or for a little more drama, an English and a French soldier could engage in a mock battle," Judith suggested. "A little something to engage viewers right at the start."

"Either would add a lively bit of showmanship," Lena agreed.

"We'll add them to your lists." The two women jotted down notes.

The men returned to the group, and Clive's smile warmed her chest.

"My brother, the duke," Clive announced with a mock half bow, "has lent us his third-best carriage, the coach we brothers affectionately call Old Red."

"Old Red?" Sophia raised a stern eyebrow at the duke. "The one you called a 'shabby conveyance suitable only for a funeral cortege'?"

The duke lifted his palms in supplication. "Clive chose Old Red. I can't *make* him take a finer carriage."

"Old Red is quite comfortable, with features we might

find useful on the road," Clive intervened. "Without the duke's crest, we'll travel less conspicuously."

"If I may point out," Lena interjected carefully, "any private coach—however shabby—is hardly *in*conspicuous." The whole group laughed good-naturedly, the duke heartiest among them, another surprise in her dealings with the duke and his family.

"Then we will leave *conspicuously* at dawn, to arrive in Derby by nightfall." Clive acknowledged her objection with another belly-teasing wink. "I don't wish to add highwaymen to our list of villains."

"You will not be disappointed on your return, I promise." Judith touched Lena's upper arm reassuringly, then gathered up the plans neatly into a single pile.

"Miss Frost." A small voice called to her, and the group parted for Lilly to join them.

"What will I do for my lessons?" the child asked plaintively, holding out a sketchbook. "I've finished all the work you gave me already."

"If your mother agrees, we can have another lesson now." Lena looked at Sophia, who nodded approval.

The child, delighted, spread out her drawings. Lena was impressed at her raw talent. Lilly was already prepared to undertake more difficult tasks.

"Do you have a favorite painting?"

Lilly nodded enthusiastically. "Sophie painted our family before Papa died."

"Then examine it very carefully. Look not at what she painted but *how* she painted it."

The child had tilted her head, trying to understand.

"Have you seen any of William Turner's paintings?"

"The duke has one of his landscapes. I like the colors."

"To add a light accent, Turner scratches the paint with

a long fingernail to reveal the white canvas underneath; and when he wants to create a sense of haze, he drags the paint around with his fingers. To paint like Turner, you have to use the same techniques."

"That makes sense." Lilly squinted as she thought.

"Copy your mother's painting. Draw the shapes as exactly as you can, but after that, paint it, trying to make the paint itself look like your mother's."

"Yes." The child smiled broadly. "I'm supposed to make you wonder if I painted it, or if Sophie did."

"Yes and no. There's no better way to discover how you wish to paint than by learning how others do. But when you copy another artist's work, you must always make it very clear which one is yours. Your copy must be different in some way, larger, smaller, round when the original is square. Anyone seeing your copy should know it's not the original, even if it's perfect in every other way. Does that make sense as well?"

"Yes." The child leaned into her mother's leg. "May I ask Sophie how she did something if I can't tell for myself?"

"Of course. Every great artist learns from the artists who have gone before."

Lilly threw her arms around Lena's waist. "I want to be a great artist, like you and Sophie."

"Then you must practice, Lilly. Make it a game: when you look at an object, consider how you might make a particular color or effect."

Chapter Eighteen

The next morning, Lena arrived in the coach yard just as dawn began to spread over the sky. She took shelter from the winter drizzle under the porte cochere. Her sleep had been disturbed by dreams. In them, Horatio and her crew, all dead, chased her through a cemetery and into an open grave. In the distance she could see the Rotunda, and she ran toward it, but the landscape was not London but the hills and valleys of Derbyshire. Her father had been in the dream as well, but when she'd begged him for help, he'd simply turned away. By the time she'd reached the Rotunda, it was engulfed in flames. She woke, gulping air in big swallows and trying to calm her heart. In the end, she'd simply given up, and read until she could reasonably go downstairs.

Old Red was being readied for their trip. In the half-light, the carriage seemed perfectly serviceable, even luxurious, though its once-brilliant red enamel was faded. Clive was already in the yard, examining the carriage with the stable master. He occasionally motioned for the postilion to hold up or lower the lamp. He moved deliberately, but with a natural grace, as he inspected the wheels, wheel hubs, spokes, and springs. Taller than every other man in the yard, Clive could have served as the model for any number of ancient Greek statues.

Lena enjoyed watching him. His long coat, perfectly tailored, hugged his shoulders and back until it fell straight down over narrow hips. How satisfying would it be to have an entire day with him, alone in the carriage? They would start with kisses, and—this time—before the day was out, they would enjoy other pleasures. She had learned in France not to be shy about passion, and there was no harm in discovering each other's body. For a little while at least, she could wake up beside him. What would it be like to be Clive's wife? To have the pleasure of waking up to him, day after day, year after year? She turned the thought away; she knew not to hope for impossible things.

For the first time in years, she longed to sculpt. No matter how talented she was as a painter, some subjects deserved—no, required—more than a single dimension. She imagined how she would shape the sinews of his muscles, the curve of his mouth, the kind set of his jaw. The challenge would be to give a sense of his character, to make a hard medium like stone show the generosity and tenderness of his personality. She knew his face would haunt her, when they eventually parted, but that day had not yet come. No, she would enjoy him while they were together, not thinking of how much she would miss him when they weren't.

While she watched, the duke approached Clive from the carriage house, speaking privately into his brother's ear. Clive's expression changed to one of resignation. The two men looked her way, and Lena's heart clenched. Had they found Horatio? She waited for their faces to grow solemn as they approached her with bad news. But they didn't. The duke merely nodded. When Clive, noticing her, smiled widely, she felt relief to her very bones. No bad news. The duke and Clive, in deep consultation, walked into the carriage house, and once the men disappeared from sight, she felt strangely bereft.

In the yard, a groom strapped her luggage to Old Red. Mrs. Tracy had provided her with a small chest to carry with her, and she had packed conservatively. Planning for a day or two's journey, she'd brought bedclothes, a riding habit, and a blue wool walking dress, serviceable and flattering, and a velvet dinner gown, on the remote chance that she might have need of it, all from Aunt Agatha's collection. From the house, two postilions carried pans of hot coals to fill the carriage's foot warmers. In a flash, Lena could once more feel Clive's lips pressed to hers, his hand warm on the side of her breast. Her cheeks flared with heat.

Lena felt torn. She needed to work on the gala, but it wasn't safe. She needed to find Horatio, but going to Derbyshire, even to a city she barely knew, reminded her of why she'd sworn never to return. She wanted to learn more about Clive and his kisses, but she knew there were some secrets she couldn't afford to reveal, and the thought of deceiving him distressed her.

"If you wish, I can make the necessary inquiries alone." Clive's voice gave her a start. "The duke will provide you guards until I return."

She turned to face him, grateful he had returned to her side. "You convince me to go; then, as I'm watching my bag being strapped to the coach, you offer to leave me behind," she teased. Somehow when he was near, her tension lessened.

"Uncovering secrets can be a dangerous business. The duke has more men in London than we will have on the road. I wish for you to be safe. Whatever it is, I could discover it alone, then deliver it to you. . . ." His voice rose at the end, as if he were uncertain of how to complete the sentence.

"*Gently?* You could deliver it to me *gently*, or *discreetly*, or any other dozen words that suggest I need coddling." She let her voice have a hint of steel, a reminder he should not discount her.

"Coddling?" He caught back a laugh. "Of all my acquaintances, you are least in need of coddling. If you were anyone else, I likely would have left before you woke, and asked Aunt Agatha to inform you. I decided to leave the decision to you, rather than take it on myself."

"I do prefer to make my own decisions, but, having said that, I'm unused to having anyone give so much thought to my preference." Lena watched his face, appreciating the kindness in his expression. "You are entirely too thoughtful."

He laughed out loud. "I'm sure my brothers would disagree, and heartily."

"Family doesn't often see us truly. Save for your unfortunate tendency to say exactly what you mean at the least advantageous times, I begin to think you are a man of few faults. Is there at least a broken engagement or two in your past? Or perhaps a trail of mistresses?" His face clouded, and she felt oddly abandoned. "Ah, so there is a trail of mistresses."

"Not mistresses per se."

"A mistress who isn't a mistress *per se*," she repeated.

"Tell me about *your* experience, Lena." He shifted the subject. "I know almost nothing about you."

"Perhaps I like being unknown." Lena wished she had stopped the words before they left her lips.

He put his hand on her shoulder, an uncharacteristically solemn gesture. "No one should be entirely unknown."

"Then I suppose eleven hours or so in a carriage will give us ample time for mutual discovery." She kept her tone light, even provocative, to distract him from her unintended revelation. "But I must apologize in advance of our leaving. Knowing Horatio's penchant for drama, we might well discover the goal of his map, and it will turn out to be instructions on how to visit his fourth cousin once removed to apologize for some prank he played as a boy."

"Well, if we are to embark on apologies, I should offer mine now. When my great-aunt Agatha discovered that we would travel to Derbyshire, she arranged for an old friend of hers to accompany us."

"Is your aunt afraid that a lowly painter might compromise your reputation?" Lena tamped down her disappointment.

"My aunt's ways are like those of the gods, inscrutable to the mortal mind. I doubt she gave much thought to us at all. It's the carriage traveling through the midlands that she wants. Apparently her friend needs to return to his estate, but his carriage is being reupholstered."

"How will he return to London for the carriage?" She leaned toward him, both careful not to touch in the sight of the servants.

"I have no idea. But he's promised us a pair of fresh horses to finish our journey. He will be meeting us here shortly." Clive watched as another carriage pulled into the yard, then leaned down to speak into her ear. "So, any compromising of reputations will have to wait a few hours."

"I take that as a promise." Lena was surprised to find she meant the dare. Whatever was to be discovered in Derbyshire, she wished to enjoy his company until then.

A postilion, all efficiency, announced the arrival of

their traveling companion, then, as Clive went to meet him, the boy guided her to the stairs and up into the coach. The postilion handed her a warmed blanket, and she settled herself comfortably, feet on the warmers, waiting for Clive and the squire to join her. Her thoughts for the first time since she'd found Horatio's note had nothing to do with the Rotunda, or the murderers, or even her own future as a painter. Instead, she was imagining all the ways that she might seduce Clive, and every thought made her deliciously warm.

"Are you certain you haven't a taste for delicacies?" Squire Averill dug into the basket filled with wine and food sitting between him and Lena on the forward-facing seat. "Perhaps you'd like some stewed eels or potted eggs?"

Clive, sitting backward across from Lena, mouthed *no*. Averill looked up, holding out a veal cake, and Lena shook her head with a polite smile.

"Speak up, girl. I broke my spectacles yesterday, and I can't see a thing without them. I can see your head moving, but whether it's yes or no, I'll be damned if I can tell." From the basket, Averill took out two jars with paper labels and held the jars close to his face to read the labels. "I think they are both marmalade, but I can't read the flavors. I'd taste them to be sure, but the lemon one is for my daughter and I can't stand the taste of it."

Lena took the jars, and giving the one he liked to the squire, returned the other to the basket.

"Lived in France during the Revolution, did you?" Averill dipped his head into the basket, then waved a bottle of wine emphatically.

"I traveled to the Continent first around 1805, and I

remained in France until after Waterloo." Lena slipped her foot out of her slippers and ran her foot up the inside of Clive's leg, making sure that her skirts hid her movement. Clive's eyes widened, then he smiled broadly.

"So you weren't in residence during the Revolution itself, but for ten years after and at the height of Boney's reign." The old judge returned the bottle to the basket. "Are you one of those revolution-loving, king-hating Jacobins?"

"Squire Averill!" Clive tried to catch her foot between his calves, but she slipped her foot to the outside of his leg instead.

"Old men ask impertinent questions. Old judges expect to be answered." Averill waved Clive's objection away.

"An artist travels where commissions take her, and my benefactor traveled widely." Lena answered only the question about her residence, paying most of her attention to the progress of her foot up and down Clive's calf.

"If you won't tell me your politics, I will have to predict them." The judge leaned across the basket, staring at Lena with the gaze of a man who expected to be answered. "What is your full name?"

"Lena Frost." She dropped her foot back to the floor.

"Just the two names? No middle one?" he quizzed, then ducked his head back in his basket.

"Just the two." Lena lifted her foot and resumed her caresses.

"I have a theory, my dear." The old judge leaned back, the wine in his glass sloshing wildly. "Regardless of profession, if a man—or woman—uses three names, then invariably that person is a government-by-the-people, king-killing Jacobin. We see it in every profession: Charles James Fox, the politician; Richard Brinsley Sheridan, the playwright; Theobald Wolfe Tone, the revolutionary;

Samuel Taylor Coleridge, the poet—I can list a dozen others."

"I'm not certain that there's an identifiable relationship between one's name and one's politics. A number of political radicals use only two names: William Pitt, the politician; Thomas Paine, the revolutionary; and William Wordsworth, the poet," Clive interjected, but the old man ignored him completely, focusing only on Lena. Clive, in response, gave Lena a slow, assessing look, beginning at her face, and roaming slowly down her body, until she felt flushed and warm.

"I'm sure you have considered your position very carefully, Squire Averill." Lena renewed her caresses, letting her toes curl around the back of Clive's calf. "But perhaps those share some other commonality that causes political radicalism? A taste for Flemish wine? A tendency to gout?"

Clive hid a laugh under a cough.

"No, no, my dear, there's no other connection. I've considered it from every angle. Take my name: Wyman Averill, both good Anglo-Saxon names, meaning fighter and wild boar. My name tells you that I'm a strong opponent, dangerous when threatened."

"I never realized one could learn so much from a name," Lena replied absently.

"Are you Helena?"

Startled, Lena looked quickly at Clive, but his attention was focused on their slow seduction. "It's just Lena. Why?" When the judge tucked his head into his giant basket of provisions, she wet her lips with her tongue, slowly, and Clive's face flushed.

"Helena, Magdalena, Madeline, Ellen—all the same name. But is your name drawn from Helen of Troy or Mary Magdalene? Are you the seductress or the penitent?"

Clive mouthed *seductress.*

When Lena didn't answer immediately, the squire began to laugh. "You must think about it, girl. Our names make us, whether we know it or not. Your man here . . ."

"He is not *my man*," Lena corrected, her foot making another descent down his calf. "He is an associate, helping me to address some business arrangements."

"Ah, right, your *associate.*" The judge refused to acquiesce. "But don't underestimate him, Miss Frost. He may be clumsy when it comes to polite conversations, but he's got quite a reputation for sport, this one does. Other men's wives—a right harem."

"Averill!" Clive sounded every inch the son of a duke.

Lena let her foot drop back to the floor.

The judge shrugged. "Have you heard that he once had three mistresses at one time? More troubling, none of them have been seen in the ton since they took up with him. We'd call him a regular Bluebeard, my dear, but mistresses don't count in the same way as wives, do they, my dear?"

Lena slid her foot back into her slipper.

"So you be wary," the Squire continued. "When I'm not with you, you make him ride outside. Isn't that right, Somerville?"

Clive looked angry and ashamed at once, and she wondered what the truth was behind the judge's only half-jovial accusations.

The judge continued, unfazed. "That package in front of your *associate* is a genuine Titian. Though Somerville's great-aunt tried to dissuade me, I had to have it, and the price was unimaginable before the wars. As an artist, you must look it over."

"Of course." She kept her attention firmly on the judge, refusing to meet Clive's eyes.

"Unwrap it, Somerville." The judge tapped Clive on the knee, then turned back to Lena. "All those continental hereditary houses need funds, and I'm happy to help—if it means I have a Titian on my walls. It even came framed."

Clive, still avoiding her glance, unfurled the wrapping as one would a mummy. Soon one corner of the frame appeared, painted gold with a green vine trailing down the edge.

Lena's stomach turned. *Not here, not now.* That frame and its painting were supposed to be destroyed long ago. If she were lucky, the frame—itself a work of art—had merely been repurposed.

Clive balanced the large painting on his knees, holding it in front of his face, as he revealed the artwork itself. She wasn't in luck. The revelation caught her breath. At least Clive couldn't see her face.

"Take a good look, my dear. How often do you see such work?"

How often indeed? This must have been what Horatio discovered. She should have run.

"Look at it closely, dear, the workmanship, the masculine strength of the brush strokes. If I had my glasses, I'd give you quite a treatise."

Masculine strength indeed. She leaned forward, as if to examine it. She hummed appreciative noises, as her belly twisted tighter than rigging on a ship. "How did you find such a . . . gem?"

"Someville's great-aunt and I were at a showing of Old Masters prior to their auction. I was admiring one of the Nicolas Poussins. Another man was admiring it as well—Austrian, very knowledgeable." The judge took a long drink of his wine and, picking up one of the stewed eels, dropped it into his mouth.

And he confided in you. She already knew the story.

"Eventually he confided that he was the agent of various, impoverished royal houses, selling their works of art very confidentially. I'd heard of him through my club, but could never arrange an introduction. Then to meet him by chance, what luck!"

By chance. Lena could imagine exactly how the meeting had happened. Whet the appetite of the victim. Tease him with being excluded from the game, then, when the victim threatens to give up the chase, arrange a chance meeting.

"I couldn't wait to get it home. In the country it will be safe from London's robbers and cheats." The old man preened. "What do you think, my dear?"

"You are wise to protect it. It is a very rare painting indeed."

"My thoughts exactly! How many others might want it, if they knew where it was?"

"This dealer"—she tried to make the question sound offhanded—"how many paintings was he selling?"

"With him in London, fewer than twenty. All very fine, though not all to my taste. I gave him the name of other men of discriminating taste—the duke among them."

"My brother has somewhat eclectic tastes." Clive twisted his head around to see the painting.

"Even he will not be able to resist such an opportunity. By the time I met the dealer—Tenney by name—he had taken orders to bring back at least twenty more from the Continent."

"So, he's gone then." Lena wasn't sure if she was relieved or angry. Perhaps both.

"Ah yes, for several days now."

"Tenney. I may have known such an art dealer during my stay in Paris." Lena tried to sound offhanded. "Would you mind describing him?"

"Tall man, thin, but not overly so, dressed neat, shock of gray hair over his left ear—but the most piercing eyes. They reminded me of a bird of prey. Does that sound familiar?"

"No, not at all." Lena would never admit she knew Tenney, or that she had trusted him until she'd discovered she couldn't. She had no interest in being the one the squire tracked down if he ever discovered his painting was a fake, a forgery painted by her own hand. She'd already paid for the sin of knowing Tenney.

She looked up to find that Clive was studying her face. A moment later, he changed the subject to another of her host's enthusiasms: fishing. She began to rewrap the painting.

Chapter Nineteen

Four hours later, the carriage deposited the squire and his painting at his home. While Lena had tea with the squire's wife and daughters, Clive and Fletcher, the coachman, oversaw the change of horses. An hour later, all were refreshed and ready to be on their way.

With the help of the postilion, Lena climbed the stairs to the carriage, leaving the door open for Clive to join her.

Clive, however, motioned for the postilions to remove the stairs, then he stepped into the doorway. "I thought you might enjoy one of the Old Red's more delightful features. Lift your legs to the opposite seat."

She obeyed. He reached under the seat and pulled out an ottoman, as wide as the well between the seats, but only three-quarters as long, so that two travelers could sit upright at one end.

"It locks into place," Clive demonstrated. "Inside it, you'll find a thick pallet that covers the seats to create a level sort of bed. You might find it more comfortable than sleeping with your head tucked into the corner."

"What if I wish to be more comfortable *not* sleeping." She met his eyes, and he looked back to the house, where the Misses Averill watched them prepare to go.

"That, my dear, will simply have to wait." A look passed

across his face that she couldn't quite decipher, then he shut the door decisively behind him.

Alone in the carriage, Lena found that the long drive to Derbyshire made memories, long suppressed, rise to the surface. She tried to push them aside, wiping the frost from the window to look outside, but the desolate winter landscape gave her little to enjoy. Soon, she was unable to do anything but let her thoughts carry her into a past better left forgotten.

"You are a disgrace to your father and your name." The headmistress's voice had been taut and shrill, as she rapped the back of Lena's knuckles with her cane. Lena refused to flinch, refused to make any motion at all. She sat with her eyes forward, focused on the front of the room. Mrs. Edstein liked submission, and Lena would not submit.

The other girls tittered to themselves, grateful that Lena always drew Mrs. Edstein's ire.

"Silence!" Mrs. Edstein rammed her cane into the floor, and the girls fell silent. "What is this?" Her finger tapped the edge of Lena's work where Lena had sketched a very pretty bird.

"A titmouse, Headmistress."

"Why would you draw a titmouse? This is not natural history."

"I skipped a line, Headmistress, when copying from the book. So I wrote the line at the bottom of the page. The titmouse's beak points to where the line should go."

"You must copy it out again. You might think a bird carrying the line to its proper place is amusing, but it isn't." The headmistress turned Lena's page a one-quarter turn, so that the already-written lines ran vertically instead of horizontally. "But you will get no more paper, and I must be able to read every letter."

"Might I please go outside with the others? I promise to copy it out clean before class tomorrow."

"Do you intend to use a candle?"

"Yes, Headmistress. I have a candle from home."

"That wouldn't be fair to the other girls who have no candles from home. If they must miss a walk in the garden, then so must you."

"But no one else made the mistake."

"That's correct. None of the other girls are so careless with their work that they miss the reward of a walk in the garden." Mrs. Edstein turned to the other students. "You may walk in the garden until dinner."

The girls rose together and walked in neat lines out of the classroom.

Lena watched them from her seat.

Mrs. Edstein turned her attention back to Lena. "Hold out your hands. Keep them still."

Lena held them out, watching the cane tap the floor. She was surprised then by the hard slap of Mrs. Edstein's palm across her cheek, hitting her jaw so hard that she felt it snap. Without thinking, she wiped the tears from her eyes.

"Did I say you could move your hands?" Mrs. Edstein struck her again, this time with the cane against the back of her hands. "You. Will. Learn. To. Follow. Instruction." Each word accompanied a blow.

Lena couldn't keep the tears from running down her cheeks, but she wouldn't respond. She would not concede. She would not be a prize pupil, compliant to Edstein's face, but mean and petty behind her back. Edstein preferred the pretty girls, girls with perfect English complexions, pale skin, sloping shoulders, narrow chins. She liked nothing about Lena, except her father's money.

"Your father has entrusted you to my care, Helena, and I will not fail in that mission. As a punishment for your inattention, you will copy out the whole chapter, not just the first three hundred lines." Mrs. Edstein hit the book with the top of her cane. "You will not leave this room until you are done. And do not rush. Each line must be evenly lettered, or you will do it again, and again, until you have it right. You may ring the bell when you are done."

Mrs. Edstein walked away briskly, locking the door shut behind her. Wiping the tears from her eyes, Lena traced the wings of her long-tailed titmouse. If only she had wings to fly . . .

Her hands ached, her fingers were swollen, and lettering each shape hurt. But she moved slowly, carefully, ignoring the bruises growing on the backs of her hands.

Shortly before the last glimmers of sunlight left the schoolroom, Lena finished. She rang the schoolroom bell for someone to let her out and waited. But no one came. She rang again. No one came, and the dark grew heavy around her.

She was about to ring the bell a third time, when she saw two of Edstein's pets, outside the window, pointing at her and laughing. The test, she realized, was to see how often and how loudly she rang the bell.

She moved next to the classroom door, where the girls could not see her. From there, she could hear Mrs. Edstein and one of the under-teachers, standing outside the door. She pressed her ear to the keyhole.

"When should I let her out, mistress?"

"A few nights in the dark will be good for our little hellion. It may do nothing to improve her behavior, but it ensures the other girls will follow all our directions. She's our little scapegoat, if you will, punished for the sins of the group."

"A few nights for one offense?"

"Oh, she will do something wrong every day this week. Every day, her punishment will be to remain alone in the schoolroom until dawn."

"Will her father approve? He dotes on the girl."

"Her father believes that only my methods can redeem his little monster."

"Will they?"

"Eventually. But more importantly, I have gained the baron's ear."

The voices moved away from the door, and Lena pulled her knees to her chest and buried her face in her arms. She let the tears fall, silently, until she had no more.

The darkness grew deeper, and the night sounds surrounded her. Creaks and thumps and groans left her wary and afraid. Curling her feet under her skirts, she wrapped her arms around her chest, already feeling the chill of night.

There, she plotted her escape. She would not suffer in the dark for predetermined failures. She would run.

Lena wiped the tears from her cheeks, but the sorrow remained. Typically when the memories refused to let her go, she enumerated all her accomplishments. Things she could not have done if she'd remained at home. But all those things seemed tenuous and fragile. She could only hope that she escaped before the rest of her sins found her.

To distract herself from heavy thoughts, she stared at the countryside and made a catalogue of all the painters and other artists who had tried their hand at the British landscape. But counting painters was better than counting sheep, and somewhere after Constable, she fell asleep.

Her sleep, however, was troubled with dreams, dark dreams of a French mob throwing her into an empty grave and burying her, not with dirt but with paintings, until the weight of them suffocated her.

She awoke to Clive beside her, the carriage door open, and the coach at a stop.

"Lena. Wake up." He sat next to her, legs in the narrow well left by the ottoman, having pulled her to his side.

She shuddered, pushing off the last remnants of the dream.

"You were dreaming. From the terror of your cries, we thought you were either having a very bad dream . . ." He wrapped a caring arm around her shoulders, and she allowed herself to welcome the strength of him. "Or you had discovered an asp in the carriage."

"An asp." She thought of Mrs. Edstein and stiffened under his arm. He removed his arm from her shoulders. "You have a vivid imagination." She couldn't help the bitterness of her tone.

"Well, then, seeing you are unhurt, I'll leave you to your thoughts." He began to pull away. "You have slept a long while. We should reach the inn in Derby shortly."

"Clive." She put her hand on his arm. "Don't go."

He looked at her hand, then her arm, then her lips, and finally her eyes. What she saw in his was pure desire.

"I suppose your dream gives us an excuse to travel together." He leaned out and called up to the coachman, "All's well, Fletcher, merely a nightmare. But I'll remain here till Derby." He pulled the door shut.

The moment the coach began to move, Lena pulled Clive close, pressing her lips hungrily to his. Lonely and sad, she wanted Clive's touch. She was not the abandoned girl she had been, but a woman able to forge her own path and make her own decisions. And she had decided to love him.

"This isn't wise." Clive stopped her kisses, pulling back to read her face.

"Are you always wise?" She pressed forward once more, insistent. When he refused her his lip, she settled for his jaw, then ear, then the space between his jaw and neck not covered by his cravat. She felt the groan deep in his chest. "Do you really wish to refuse me? A man known to keep a harem?"

"You are in trouble. You are vulnerable."

"I make my own way. I do as I wish." She nudged the cravat down, kissing the underside of his jaw. Pulling out the knot of his cravat, she made her way lower, teasing the side of his neck with her tongue.

He pulled her away, hands on her upper arms, and searched her eyes. His face was hungry, but solemn. "What do you want, Lena?"

"I want this, now, here. Nothing more." She waited for his reaction.

They stared into each other's eyes for a long moment. She leaned forward, putting her lips closer to his, but not touching. She could feel the warmth of his breath on her skin. Then his lips were touching hers, slowly, sweetly, as if he wished to savor each one individually. She met him, kiss for kiss, mirroring his pace. She ran her palms up his chest, feeling the muscles beneath his clothes. He followed her lead, tracing the lines of her body, shoulders to hips.

Pulling his cravat, she leaned back onto the pallet. He followed. Soon his body covered hers. The welcome weight of him rested between her legs, and she pressed her hips upward, feeling his desire against her own. His hands found her breasts, caressing, and heightening her desire.

Their hands grew greedier, their kisses more insistent, their tongues more abandoned. Suddenly kisses and touching were not enough to satisfy her growing desire. She wanted him naked, flesh to flesh, laid bare before her.

Her fingers began unbuttoning his waistcoat. She had undone three of the six buttons when his hand stopped her. His kisses stopped as well.

He breathed into her ear. "We can take our pleasure here, but we will do it with our clothes on."

When she started to object, he touched one finger to her lips. "I will not be rushed. At the inn, I intend to call dinner to our drawing room. After we have eaten our meal, I wish to undress you, slowly. I wish to see each inch of you before we couple."

"Why?" Lena pressed her hips against him again, causing a deep growl. "We have time and a perfectly serviceable bed here."

"An hour at best. My plans involve a seduction of several hours." He breathed against her neck, taking little bites on the lobe of her ear. "That can *begin* here." He slid his hand between them, pressing against her sex, rocking back and forth until she squirmed in delight.

He rolled off her, never stopping the caress of his one hand, while the other made its way under her skirt. His fingers felt the inside of her ankle, then, finding the opening in her drawers, teased her thighs. When he finally touched her, flesh to flesh, she almost cried out, but his lips stopped the sound.

Kisses and caresses together heightened her desire. His fingers expertly found the exact spot that made fire burn up her spine. And she let him, let his kisses claim her lips, ear, neck, breasts. Without removing her clothes, he'd found a way to reach the tender flesh of her breast, and his mouth paid homage to her there. Soon she could think of nothing but his touch. She felt the rhythm of her body increase. Felt everything, his lips, his hand at her breast, his fingers on her sex, each one urging her to release. Then she found it, a shattering joy that left her spent in his arms.

When she came back to herself, he was smiling, a rich genuine smile that warmed and caressed her heart. "There, my sweet." His voice was like chocolate, deep and full. She could drink it in—him in—forever.

"Now you." She put one hand to his crotch, feeling the strength of his desire, and the other pressed him back against the pallet.

At that moment the coachman tapped twice on the roof.

"We are within sight of the inn." He began to repair her clothes, and she his.

"When we retire to my drawing room, you will *not* be removing my clothes." She paused as she began to button his trousers, but his hand stopped her.

"If you have changed your mind about our liaison . . ." For the first time since she'd known him, his voice sounded uncertain.

"Stop being so conciliatory and let me finish. You will not be removing my clothes until I have removed each piece of yours. We are unequal now, but we *will* be equal then. Remember: I grew up in France after the Revolution. Liberty, Equality, Brotherhood were the values of my youth."

"I grow to appreciate your Revolution more each moment."

The inn Clive had chosen was quiet, near the Derwent, but north of St. Mary's Bridge, far enough from the silk and china mills that the neighborhood was still quite rural.

The innkeeper—a stout, garrulous man who'd lost an arm in the wars—met them at the carriage. Clive descended to talk with him, and soon the innkeeper ushered them through an exterior door and up a stairwell.

"Lord Edmund's paid for his regular suite through the end of next month. Quite a nice note he wrote, telling me to give you the suite, though I certainly wouldn't have questioned that you and he are brothers. On a tour, he said you were. Newlyweds."

Lena started to object, but given her intentions for the evening, she decided against it. Instead, she took Clive's arm, as if she had every right to do so. His arm was strong, and she let her fingers trace the firm contours of his muscles. The innkeeper led them to the end of the hall, then turning right, he started up another short flight of stairs. Each one creaked loudly.

"I've tried to remedy that creak, but there's no fixing it. We're going through that door at the end there, then around the corner into the hall where your rooms are." The innkeeper led them, talking the whole way. "They are our most secluded rooms, past all the other guests, so no one should disturb you. Your brother likes that when he's in residence, private he is. He even asked me to install that locking door at the top of the short stairs. I'll lock it on my way down. How long have you been married?"

Lena looked up at Clive, smiling as if the sun and moon rose in his face. "Just a fortnight." She let her voice go a bit breathless, and Clive, arm around her shoulders, drew her body into his side.

"Ah, newlyweds. I remember them days." The innkeeper nodded. "It's four bedrooms in all, two front, two back, and two sitting rooms in between. You'll find fires already on the hearth in the suite at the back."

"I was going to suggest we take the back rooms, in case my brother returns while we are here."

The innkeeper handed Clive a set of keys. "You and the missus will want dinner in your rooms?"

"And a bath for my wife," Clive added as the innkeeper was almost to the door. "If it's acceptable to you, we'll take dinner in the front sitting room, and the bath in the back one."

"Certainly, my lord. That will be no trouble at all."

The pair listened as the innkeeper walked to the end of the hall and down the short stairs, which creaked with every step.

"I would wager you that Edmund likes that creak best of all."

The sitting room was nicely appointed, if plain, and the window looked out over a robust kitchen garden at the back of the inn. "If we need to escape quickly, we can always climb out this window. There's a low roof here, but it's still a bit of a drop to the ground."

Clive stood behind her, his hands on her upper arms. "Already looking for a way to escape?"

She turned in his arms to face him. "If I were looking to escape, I wouldn't tell you that the grape trellis below looks fairly sturdy. How does your brother know about this place? And how did he send our innkeeper a note if we only decided to travel yesterday?" She began to untie his cravat.

"My brother Edmund keeps a log of every posting inn and tavern from Liverpool to London, and since I know his handwriting as well as my own, it wasn't difficult to write a note recommending us." He stood still, watching her face as she worked.

"So *you* told the innkeeper we are married, not your brother." She raised an eyebrow.

"I did. It seemed the most reasonable decision—if your enemies followed us from London, they would be looking for a single woman, not a married one. And Edmund praises this inn for its cook, its relative distance from the main thoroughfare, and its discretion."

"Discretion? That's an interesting word." She began to undo the buttons on his waistcoat.

"How so?" Clive tried to help, but she batted his hand away.

"A man wishes for discretion when he is traveling with his mistress, not when he is accompanied by his wife." She pushed the waistcoat open, starting on his shirt's buttons.

"The day Edmund marries, a line of women will weep at the church door." He watched each deft movement of her fingers.

"Do you suppose that will prove awkward for his bride?" She untucked his shirt to reach the lower buttons.

"The Brothers Grimm tell a story about the Pied Piper of Hamelin, whose music was so captivating that he stole away all the village children. Perhaps, if he ever wishes to marry, I could do the same, drawing away all Edmund's old lovers, until the bride is safely at the altar." Clive watched as she undid the last of his shirt buttons, then pushed his shirt open.

"Wasn't it rats?" she asked, her fingers tracing a shape on his chest.

"Rats?" The slide of her fingers across his flesh made his brain move slowly. "Yes, rats. Then he stole the children."

"Ah, yes, taking the children was a punishment when the mayor refused to pay him. I remember now." She leaned forward and kissed his bare flesh. "Do you play the pipe?"

"The pipe? No." He watched her head, kissing one spot, then another.

"Do you play any instrument?" She lifted one of his wrists and unbuttoned the shirt sleeve, then repeated the action on the next.

"No. I thought perhaps charm would be enough."

She pushed his shirt and waistcoat back off his shoulders in one motion, pulling his shirt off at the wrists. "You certainly are charming." She kissed his chest again. "I find this particularly charming." She kissed his nipples. "And this." Then standing on her toes, she kissed the base of his neck. "And this. I like this line here between your neck and chest, very much."

Just as he was about to pull her toward him, she stepped back. He waited, watching her expression, intent, focused, and somewhat devious. He wondered what game she was imagining they might play.

She rubbed the rim of his trousers between her fingers, but did nothing. Without intending to, he moaned aloud. She responded quickly, rubbing his flesh through his trousers. He tensed with pleasure. Never letting up the pressure, she quickly unbuttoned the flap on his trousers, freeing his member. She smiled at the length and girth of him.

"We are not yet equal." She let her fingers move against his flesh.

Groaning, he stopped her hand. "I would prefer to pursue equality, more . . . equally."

She stepped back, watching him watching her. Then she began to disrobe, slowly, first fichu, then bodice, then skirt, until she stood before him in only her shift.

"Don't stop."

Smiling, she shook her head. "We are now equally undressed. For me to remove more of mine, you must remove more of yours."

Clive tore at his boots, his socks, his trousers, until he stood before her entirely nude.

She had imagined how he might look without his clothes. She'd rejected Donatello's *David* as too soft, Michelangelo's as too static. Eventually she'd settled on a Roman copy of a Greek statue she'd seen at the British Museum: a discus thrower—his body in motion, his muscles engaged in the instant before a burst of power. But even the lines of that stunning statue seemed a failure when compared to Clive. In one instant, she wished she had her pencil to capture his perfection. In another she wished never to move, never to stop gazing at his perfect proportions and his obvious desire. In the third, she ran into his arms.

As her shift met the rest of her clothes on the floor, Clive stopped, gazing at her, just as she had gazed at him. "You are so beautiful."

His words warmed her cheeks, her breasts, her belly. And soon it wasn't merely his words, but his hands and his body.

She stared into his eyes, seeing her reflection in them. Was she part of his soul, or just a passing fancy to be replaced when he found another puzzle to solve? Did she care?

He couldn't be hers, but she could love him. And in that way she could make him hers, if only for the moments when his body was buried deep in hers.

She lifted her hips to him, pressing her lower body against his. Their rhythm was as old as time, a dance lovers had known since Adam met Lilith in the garden. As an artist she preferred Lilith to Eve, the rebel to the wife. She bit his neck teasingly. Their joining was a burst of color, emotion, sensation, and she wanted to cry *mine*

mine mine, but instead she only called his name, a guttural sound, full of her ecstasy as it took all thought away.

"If this is how you treat a lover, I envy your wife." Sitting up, she pulled the sheet toward her and tucked it under her arms, covering her breasts. "I can see how women might wish to be part of your harem." She brushed his hair back from his face.

"There is no harem." Clive pulled the sheet away. She let it go, both relieved that the judge had been wrong and surprised at her relief. He kissed her arm to her shoulder, and she reveled in the sensation. "Not really."

"Not really," she repeated, her desire fading abruptly. She pulled her arm away. She shouldn't be hurt that he'd had other lovers—perhaps still had other lovers—but she couldn't deny the sick feeling high in her stomach. "Either one has a mistress—or twelve—or however many one must keep simultaneously to make a harem—or one doesn't."

"It was three, but it wasn't a harem." He tugged at the sheet to see her body again.

She put the pillow between them and wrapped her arms around it. "Am I the fourth?" She kept her tone light, teasing, but inside she wanted to run. Why did three matter more than one? It was the nature of his sex and his class to take a mistress, even to keep a series of mistresses. Was it the fact that his appeared to be simultaneous, rather than sequential?

He brushed back his hair and rolled out of the bed onto his feet in what seemed like a single motion. "The situation is a little bit complex."

She watched as he pulled on his trousers, one glorious leg then the next disappearing under his clothes. He fastened his trousers, but he kept his chest bare, even though the room had suddenly grown cold. He picked up her shift, and Lena held out her hand.

She pulled the shift quickly over her head. "You are not obligated to tell me anything about your life."

"But I am obligated. If nothing else, this"—he pointed to the rest of their clothes still in a pile on the floor—"obligates me."

"Then I free you of that obligation." She walked to the pile and began to separate out her clothing. "Like my French sisters, I am an emancipated woman. I am beholden to no man for my wages or my employment. I support myself with my own labor, and I choose who I take to my bed."

He pulled her toward him, holding her at arm's length, so she was forced to look into his face. "I am obligated to you by affection and by passion. I have hesitated because only the duke knows the truth about my 'harem.'" He said the word with distaste. "I trust that you will not reveal it."

She nodded her head as she spoke. "You have my word."

"When I was a younger man, I had a sweetheart. Her family promoted the match, but my father refused, calling it a schoolboy infatuation and denying me any form of communication with her. I sent her one last letter, telling her I would never stop loving her, and that if she ever needed my help, I would come to her side."

Lena's heart fell. It was worse than she'd imagined. He loved another.

"Her family moved to London for the season. At first, I grieved, but my father was right. After a few weeks, I barely thought of her, and by the time she was married, I felt merely embarrassed that a few kisses stolen in the garden had led to such overblown declarations of undying love."

Lena felt her heart lift a little. "This sounds like the opposite of a harem."

He turned away, pacing the room. "I didn't see her—think of her—for six years. One day, I encountered her and her two sisters in the park with her husband and the suitor of one of her sister's, a man known for having a vicious temperament. My sweetheart was changed—her face drawn and aged beyond her years—and her sisters were timid. I spoke to her husband briefly, watching him treat her and her sisters with deliberate cruelty. I did not interfere, not wishing to do anything that might worsen their lot at home."

"What happened?" Lena was afraid she knew the end of the story—that the woman died unexpectedly of a fall or something else.

"That night Aidan and I were at the ducal residence working on some accounts, and her youngest sister—not yet twelve—came to the door, begging for my help. My former sweetheart's husband had in a drunken rage beaten her quite badly, and when her middle sister had tried to intervene, he'd turned—with the help of the fiancé—his rage on her. The youngest, with the help of her mistress's maid, had been able to steal her sisters from the house, hiding them in a potting shed in the alley behind their house. The child held out a worn piece of paper, its edges frayed, its ink faded. I almost didn't recognize it."

"Your letter."

"My old sweetheart had kept it, hidden, believing that I'd meant every word. She sent it to me, hoping that I would fulfill its promises."

"And you did, even though her husband had every right to beat her if he wished."

"We did—Aidan and I. He was the cool-headed one. He collected witnesses: our family solicitor, a magistrate, another peer, and our family doctor. To avoid being inter-cepted, we left our carriage at the end of the alley on the main street. Aidan even brought a litter, in case she was too injured to walk. I never saw my brother in battle, but I could see something of who he had been as an officer under Wellington." Clive's voice trailed off, and Lena waited for him to finish.

He picked up the story several moments later. "We found her, face bruised and bloody, several ribs and one of her arms broken; her sister in no better shape. And we took them. The next day the five of us—Aidan, me, the magistrate, the peer, and the doctor—called on her husband, encouraging him to grant her a separation and a settlement. He refused, saying that if we didn't return her and her sisters, he would take me to court, accusing me of criminal conversation."

"What did you do?" Lena watched his expressions, seeing sorrow, betrayal, and resolve in the lines of his face.

"We went to court. Everywhere the newspapers described me as the childhood sweetheart who had been recently reunited with his love . . . with the implication, of course, that we were not only reunited, but lovers."

"Was there any other way?"

"No. But helping came at a price. When I went to balls, I was largely shunned, except by those who wished to redeem me. Being the brother of a duke might make up for dissecting bodies, but it can't remove the scandal of a trial. Even worse, I had to tell my childhood sweetheart that in all those years she'd clung to my letter, I hadn't given her a single thought, though I said it more kindly. I had been a foolish young man who had made foolish promises."

"That you kept."

"She'd believed I would love her. Instead, she found only scandal."

"But she's alive."

"Certainly she has come to realize that, but I'd been her one hope during years of abuse. Losing that dream was not easy for her."

"What happened to her and her sisters?"

"They live on a ducal property, using different names. But we are still cautious. Her husband is a cruel man who was embarrassed publicly when the judge granted the separation, and we must remain vigilant to ensure that he never discovers where she lives."

Never letting her eyes leave his, she joined him at the fireplace. Wrapping her arms around him, she placed her head against his chest. At first he made no motion, but eventually he conceded, wrapping his arms around her as well.

"You kept a childhood promise," she told him gently. "You saved a childhood acquaintance and her sisters, and despite great personal cost, you have protected them, supported them, even for years. I find those the actions not of a disreputable man, but of an honorable one."

"I only did what had to be done."

"What is that if not honor?" She placed a kiss on his lips. "But if you'd rather be disreputable . . ." She led him back to the bed once more.

Some time later, Clive rolled onto his side, watching Lena sleep. The tension she carried in her jaw and at the edges of her eyes had disappeared, leaving her looking younger, less worldly-wise, more vulnerable. This Lena would be easy to love, but the other Lena—driven, ambitious, suspicious—had stolen her way into his heart. Yet what did he know of her beyond her name and her employment? She wanted to tell him her secrets—he knew it—knew from the way she twisted the corner of her mouth and paused, staring into the distance for a second before she told him something that was at best half true. If she could only trust him . . . Very gently, he brushed back a stray hair from in front of her face.

"What are you doing?" She didn't open her eyes, and he was pleased to see that the tension didn't immediately return on waking.

"I'm watching you sleep." He traced the line of her nose with his finger.

"I'm not sleeping." She batted his hand away from her face. "I'm thinking."

"Your eyes are closed. It looks like sleep."

"I could be dead."

"Unlikely, though we both died several times last night." He placed his fingers on the side of her neck, feeling her pulse strong against his touch. "No, it beats still. 'We *die* and rise the same, and prove mysterious by this love.'" He watched for her reaction to the word *love*, but her only response was to open her eyes and examine his face.

"John Donne? 'The Canonization.'" She stretched, like a cat on warm, summer grass. "Don't look surprised: when I'm not painting, I read."

"I wasn't surprised, I was pleased. Few people of my acquaintance know Donne as well as I do."

"I prefer Shakespeare: 'I will live in your heart, *die* in your lap, and be buried in your eyes.'"

"Benedick in *Much Ado about Nothing*," Clive added. "But Shakespeare said 'thy' instead of 'your.'"

A broad smile spread across her face. "Yes. We are both readers, it seems."

"Both readers, but still unequal." He waited for her reaction.

"How?" She looked into the distance, clearly counting.

"No. By my tally, we are delightfully, perfectly even. Me in the carriage, then you in the drawing room, then the two of us together in the bedroom, then . . ."

"You are counting the wrong thing. I confided in you something I've never told another person. Yet you haven't confided anything of the same importance. We are unequal, and there is only one remedy." He watched her reactions play across her face: surprise, chagrin, acknowledgment, and finally acceptance.

"I'm unused to confiding in others. But I am committed to equality." She shrugged. "When I first arrived in London, I had the privilege of a letter from a very famous painter to a wealthy English aristocrat. That letter, which I sent ahead for the lord to review, made the mistake of referring to me only by my last name. 'I commend Frost to you, the best painter between Ireland and St. Petersburg.'"

"Are you?"

"What?"

"The best painter this side of St. Petersburg."

She smiled. "Why, of course."

"Then go on with your story."

"The aristocrat invited me to his country house to demonstrate my skill in painting three of his sons. The invitation included a fortnight's food and lodging, and travel to and from my rooms in London in his private carriage."

"Promising."

"I thought so. But I didn't realize I was one of four painters invited, and the aristocrat didn't realize that Frost was a woman. He would have sent me home before my bag left the coach, but his mother insisted I remain."

"I apologize on behalf of my sex and class, but sadly I'm not surprised."

"I had lived in France—my mentor had been a painter

to the royal court—I *was* surprised. The aristocrat had set up four identical easels in the gallery, canvases already prepared. Each day three sons would sit for us. One of the younger boys carried a ring and stick, his favorite game; the other played with his dog. The eldest, however, brought nothing that would indicate his personality or that he will grow up to be one of the most powerful men in the nation. How we presented the heir was part of the test."

"You aren't going to tell me who he is, are you?"

"No," she said. "The aristocrat had hired a judge from the Royal Academy. The prize was a commission to paint the whole family, twelve portraits in all, enough work for a year at least, in addition to the fame of having one's work displayed in that lord's open gallery."

"What happened?"

"We painted. The younger boys came to us in short intervals, playing on the lawn outside our windows in between sittings. One day, one of the younger brothers fell. The oldest boy picked him up, then checked his elbows and knees for scrapes. That tender moment shaped my portrayal of him. I had already sketched him in the center of a triangle between his brothers. After that, I showed him with one hand on each brother's shoulder. His face looked directly at the viewer, earnest and kind all at once. It was one of the best paintings I'd ever done."

"And then?"

"The judge came in. We stood next to our easels."

"The paintings should have been judged without the painters or the aristocrat in the room."

"Then you already know the end of the story. The judge spent a great deal of time praising the skill, wit, and mastery of the male painters. In both, the younger boys appeared as part of the background, distanced from their brother. One painter put a whip in the heir's hand and painted him in riding gear. Another had him looking out over the estate, with his hand extended to show the extent of his domain. The last painted him looking sternly at the viewer, a map of England under his right hand."

"Those are fairly conventional choices. What did the judge say about yours?"

"The judge never looked at mine. He chose the stern-faced boy with the map, and I received ten pounds for my painting."

"At least they bought the painting."

"The other painters received thirty-five each. Had my painting been judged unworthy, I could have stomached it. Had he critiqued its strengths and weaknesses, I could have learned something. But he took one look at me—a woman—and turned away. At that moment, I decided that I would have to find another path."

"The panorama."

"Yes, I've thrown my future on the low entertainments of the middling classes, and I made up a man to run my company, H. Calder and Company."

Clive stared at her long and hard, his head spinning. "I don't understand. I've been corresponding with Calder. We've been searching for him. But *he* has been *you* all along?" Some investigator he was turning out to be.

"No, I have a partner who *calls* himself Horatio Calder. I told you I advertised for an assistant. What I didn't imagine was an assistant who took to the role quite so enthusiastically."

"What is Calder's real name?"

"I have no idea—I made the name up. H. Calder, that is. Out of whole cloth. Famous Scottish painter from some little town that I had no risk of anyone ever being from. It seemed like a good idea. Then he walked into my office—this short, jolly, dapper man, all 'hale fellow well met.' I was painting a small commission at my easel. He put his hat and coat on the rack, then seating himself behind the desk, he began to critique my painting. Horatio missed his calling. He should have reviewed paintings for the periodicals."

"What did he say?"

"Some version of that I'm the most talented painter this side of St. Petersburg, but with more advice."

"So, you hired him to pretend to be the name."

"No, he introduced himself as Horatio Calder—and he's never budged from that position. Suddenly I had a partner. I could do nothing but confess the truth to all of London. I preferred to have a partner."

"What's so wrong with the truth?"

"A woman of no background or standing masquerades as a man, at least in name. No, I know how that story ends. Think of Chatterton and his poems. The ton would demand I be punished for deceiving them so. For all Horatio's odd ways, I have found life easier with a partner. There you have it. Does the story of my reasons for starting the panorama make us equal?"

"Did you learn nothing about me from spending time with my family?" He raised an eyebrow, waiting for her answer. When she said nothing, he added, "Then we are not yet even. I deserve another story."

Lena threw a pillow at his head.

"Ah, my prickly darling, you don't yet trust me."

"I told you: I don't trust anyone."

"But why? Who hurt you so deeply that you reject all tokens of esteem and friendship?"

"I suppose, if anyone hurt me, I did it to myself. Early on, I learned that those you should be able to call upon for succor or aid often refuse to help you. The greater the protestations of love or affection, the more likely those protestations are a lie, a deception."

Clive grew silent, and when he spoke, his voice was resigned. "When I was young, my eldest brother was still alive. He was cruel, vindictive, and mean spirited. His only motivations were pleasure and control. When we were young, he would trick us into doing as he wished us to do. He would always claim it was a test, of our strength, our cleverness, our dedication to the family, but it was never any of those things. It was always a test of how much he could deceive us, of how much we wished to believe that someday he would treat us like brothers. One time he had Edmund and me climb the turret walk. We didn't fall, but if we had, he would have blamed the whole idea on us. I was ten when I realized that I would never measure up to whatever standard he had made up at the moment."

"That sort of betrayal takes a long time to heal." She paused. "And mine hasn't. I don't know if it ever will. I trusted someone to have my best interest at heart, to understand my concerns, and I was banished for my pains."

"Banished is a strong word."

"But apt."

"Who is this person who thwarted your expectations and desires?"

She was about to answer when a tap at the sitting-room door drew him away. When he returned to the bedroom, Lena had begun to dress.

"While you took your bath last night, I sent Fletcher and the postilions to gather intelligence at various taverns."

"Was that wise? Whoever damaged the canvas could have seen Horatio's map as well as we did."

"Fletcher served with Aidan in the wars, and he's as savvy an investigator as any of us. If anyone can find a fact without revealing his interest, it's Fletcher. But even so, we will still be better off with a directed search than a haphazard one."

"How many church cemeteries can there be in one town?" She folded her arms over her chest.

"The Anglicans have five parishes. The dissenters another four: two Baptists, one Methodist, and one Quaker. The men have spent the morning searching for an ornate gate between two tall trees. But they've found nothing."

"Then why are we here?" Lena groaned.

"To discover what is behind Horatio's disappearance and your other troubles." Clive pulled her into his arms. "I've sent the men out to examine the churchyards in the nearby villages, in case Horatio didn't mean Derby."

"Lord Somerville?" The innkeeper's voice called to them from outside the door. "My wife sent up some victuals."

Lena pulled out of Clive's arms and returned to the bedroom to finish dressing.

"One moment, Mr. Burrell." Clive crossed the room in four long strides. Outside the door, the innkeeper held a heavily laden tray.

"I can set it on the table there." The innkeeper hurried to place the tray down and return to the hall. "If you and the missus need anything . . ."

Clive held up a finger. "One moment, my good sir." He picked up Horatio's scribbled map. "We're looking for a cemetery with an elaborate gate, perhaps of wrought iron, between tall trees. My wife wishes to visit the grave of her great-grandfather, but we seem to have gotten the name of the town wrong."

"A wrought iron gate in a churchyard old enough to

hold her ladyship's distant relations." The innkeeper scratched his head. "If you've tried all the Derby church-yards, you might consider looking in Denby. If I remember right, the Church of the Virgin Mary there dates to the fifteenth century, and it has an iron gate. It's about seven miles away, but the road is good, and in a coach like yours, it shouldn't take more than an hour."

Clive clapped the innkeeper on the back. "We will do that, Mr. Burrell, this morning."

With the innkeeper gone, Clive looked at Horatio's scribbled map once more. The *A* could easily be an *E*, and the *R* an *N*. He hurried into the bedroom. But Lena looked sullen rather than excited.

"You heard?" Clive questioned.

She nodded, hugging her shawl tight around her shoulders.

"I can go alone."

"No. I should go, but do you think we could ride?" She pulled a riding dress out of her luggage. "I can't stand another hour in the coach."

"It's a cold day to ride, but if you wish, I'll arrange it."

She picked up her clothes, then stared at him until he made his retreat to the coach yard.

Mr. Burrell had a fine pair of horses, steady and reliable, available for rent, and, by the time Fletcher gave his approval of their quality, Lena had joined them in the yard. Mrs. Burrell offered Lena a heavy cloak and fur-lined gloves and Clive a knapsack filled with food. Lena did her own inspection, running her hand down the horse's back, withers, and legs, all the while talking to him in low, calm tones. Once she mounted, Mr. Burrell gave them directions for a shortcut using an ancient right of way through the property of an absent landlord, but Clive assured him they would keep to the road.

"You have some experience riding." Clive kept his comment matter-of-fact.

"When I was just a girl, I rode a bay. I spent days on her back, racing over the hills, jumping fences and fallen trees. There's nothing quite like riding a strong, fast horse."

"How young were you?"

"Young enough that I should have ridden something less powerful." She leaned down to pat the neck of her horse. "I haven't ridden for the joy of riding since I left France."

She looked over her shoulder. The inn was out of sight. There was no one on the road, ahead or behind them. The air was crisp, the ground firm. Lena spurred her horse forward, leaving Clive behind. Even a decade or more later, she still knew the land, and when she reached the cutaway described by the innkeeper, she pointed her horse onto the well-marked alternate route, reaching the churchyard in barely half an hour.

She'd raced ahead both for the thrill of a fast horse and to give herself a few minutes alone at the churchyard. When the innkeeper had said Denby, her stomach had twisted into a tight ball, and nothing—not painting herself mental pictures or casting the servants as characters from famous novels—helped. She had only one choice: to face the truth, whatever that was, and bear the consequences. She'd believed she'd met Horatio by accident, but if he knew to send her here, well, she didn't want to think about what that meant.

Clive was wrong: the Rotunda was far safer than this

pretty rural cemetery. As she stood at the gate, she felt
nauseous, but not from marsh gas. She had to face a past
she'd been running from almost her whole life. She
should tell Clive, but he was too kind, too gentle for that
confession—at least not before she knew what revelations
Horatio had left her.

Chapter Twenty

By the time Clive caught up with Lena, she was talking to a village boy about the horses. For a few pennies, Clive hired the lad to walk their horses in the lane while they visited the churchyard.

With heavy clouds and old trees blocking the sun, the churchyard was gloomy. The chill in the air made it even drearier.

At the churchyard gate, Clive held up Horatio's map. "That structure must be this squiggle with a box around it." He stepped into the churchyard from the lane. "If these lines here are headstones, then we have to go that way, toward the hedge."

"No, the church should be at our back, and the crypts should run along the bottom of the churchyard." She turned the page in his hands, but she didn't need the map, not any more. "This way." She walked to the edge of the churchyard.

Clive followed, counting off the rows of gravestones that Horatio had scribbled into the map as if they were exact. There had been no wrought iron gate when she'd left the village, and the trees beside the gate had been striplings her father had planted when her mother had died. Seeing them grown thick and strong made her eyes water with unspent tears.

"Yes, you are right. I believe that's the crypt there." He pointed at a large monument, square with columns. It was a gaudy thing by any measure. Angels blowing trumpets, putti looking to heaven, and a great variety of styles and ornaments. The crypt door was a heavily ornate iron, with giant yews carved into the marble on either side.

"It's the door to the crypt, not the gate to the cemetery. We're lucky to have found it." Clive tested the door. "Locked," he called back to her.

"I'm going to investigate the other sides." He walked around the crypt, describing each of the sides as he encountered them. "A long poem here. What you would expect: loss, grief, regret, hope for reunion." He rounded the next corner. "Just decoration here: ornamental yews, columns, putti." He continued on to the next side. "Ah, here it is: the inscription to the dead. Family name is Winters. One body." Receiving no response from Lena, he read the rest silently.

Lena stared at the pile of marble, more in shock than anything. The old man had always been one for pomp, and she should have expected he would bury himself in style. He'd probably spent months designing it, then several more overseeing its installation. The only surprise was that he'd thought that far ahead.

Clive picked up the knapsack and placed Horatio's note inside. Then, starting at the entrance door, he ran his fingers across the edges of the crypt, working his way down the front of the monument.

"What are you doing?" Lena stood, arms across her chest, holding herself in. She'd known the old man had died, and she'd mourned in her way, but she'd never expected to be looking at his grave. She found the experience unsettling.

"I'm looking for something that's out of place. When I was ten or so, Judith's husband invited us to his country house, and to entertain us younger boys, our brother Benjamin explained how to find the secret passages. This occasion seems to warrant the technique."

"That line there is wrong." She pointed but kept her distance.

"You can't have discovered something that fast—and from a distance. It requires touch to find the secret places."

"I'll wait." She sat on a nearby stone. "I'm sure you'll work your way to it eventually."

He sighed. "Which line is wrong?"

"The border near the bottom."

He bent down to the ground, examining the course of the line with his fingers as well as eyes. He felt a small bump along the edge of the egg and dart design. "How did you see that?"

"I'm an artist. I've spent my life looking at patterns." Lena sounded angry, and she bit her tongue. There was no reason to be difficult with Clive. He'd been kind, more than kind. She added apologetically, "That's where Horatio's arrow pointed."

"What arrow?" Clive looked up from the crypt.

She carried Horatio's note to Clive, positioning herself so that the crypt's inscription was too oblique to read. "That one."

He looked the note over, shaking his head. "You didn't mention it?"

"I wasn't certain we would get this far, and an arrow would have given you incentive." Curious about how the old man had described himself, she stepped in front of the inscription. The words were like a hit to her stomach.

"Incentive." He tested the area around where the arrow pointed. "Keeping you alive wasn't incentive enough?"

"I've managed that quite successfully on my own, though you have proved helpful." Silent tears ran down her cheeks in salt-wet trails.

"You're crying," he observed, surprised. "You never cry, not when we discover dead bodies or damage to your panorama. Is this the crypt of someone you know?"

"A friend. I expected it to be someone else's, not hers." One tear reached the edge of her mouth before she brushed it away with the back of her hand. "I don't know why I'm crying. She's been dead a long time."

"Ten years." He pressed above and below the indicated corner, but nothing happened.

"How did you know that?" Lena felt exposed by her tears.

"The date of her death. It's on the epitaph. 'Here lies Frances H. Winters, beloved daughter. 1793 to 1805.'"

"Her death notice in the papers said much the same thing: 'beloved daughter.' Then it made me angry."

"And today?"

"It merely makes me sad. After her mother died, he was mercurial, and she was the one who suffered for it."

"Sometimes grief cuts both ways. A child loses one parent to death and the other to grief."

"If he grieved, it was for something other than the loss of love."

"You cannot measure all griefs on the example of one bad father and his mistreated child. What of your own parents?"

"I was a child of the streets, adopted by chance and luck, and grateful for both."

"Then your guardian—the one who adopted you— surely he taught you the power of friendship."

"*She* was my friend, yes, but having lived at court, she

taught me to be wary of others, even as you enjoyed their company."

"That's a bit pessimistic." When she didn't respond, he continued. "Why would Calder send us to the tomb of your childhood friend?"

"I don't know." She wiped the tears from her cheeks and tried to sound matter-of-fact. "But we haven't searched his hiding place yet."

Clive, taking the cue, returned to his search.

"The egg and dart don't line up exactly here, and this dart is thicker than the rest." He pushed in. Below it, a drawer jutted out, and he pulled it free. In it was a document folded over to resemble a little book. Lettered on the outside in her father's hand was her name: "Lena Frost."

Lena felt the ground shift under her feet, and for a moment she thought she might faint. She struggled to breathe. But the moment passed.

As she tried to regain her equilibrium, a silver-haired man approached, dressed in old clothes, carrying a book and a trowel. Clive stepped in front of Lena, giving her time to slip her father's note into her sleeve.

Clive held out his hand in greeting. "My good sir! Can you tell us something of this monument?"

The man assessed Clive, then Lena. "A bright, sunny child, Miss Helen was. She died at boarding school, and her father was heartsick at her loss."

"We can tell that from the monument." Clive noticed that Lena was standing very still. "We were wondering if there were more to the story."

The man grew silent, clearly unwilling to tell tales.

Lena spoke up. "Helen and I were bosom friends at Mrs. Edstein's school in Nottingham. She was always begging her father to go home."

"Ah, then you knew her. Some think that a fancy tomb

can make up for all manner of guilt." The old man shook his head. "Baron Winters was a changeable man, excited one day, desolate the next, and drunk in between. Even as a wee girl, Miss Helen managed him, so when he sent her to school in Nottingham we thought it would be a blessing for the child."

"Mrs. Edstein's school was more like a hell." Lena rubbed the cuff of her sleeve, using her thumb to keep the document out of sight. "And Helen could never submit when the headmistress was unfair or capricious."

"Aye. That were our Miss Helen, a just child, as different from her father as milk from water. As long as she was docile, her father indulged her in every whim. But his pride couldn't allow her to oppose him. I was a groom then in the baron's stables, and I helped ready the carriage that took her to school that last time. It broke me heart: the poor child threw herself, weeping, at her father's feet, and begged him to let her stay."

"What happened then?" Clive studied the old man, noting his clothes, his hands, his book.

"A sin it was. Her father kicked her aside, then dragged her by her clothes through the gravel to the carriage. It wrenched all our hearts to see her treated so. Soon after we heard she had died at that school, and within the year, he'd married again."

"Who did he marry?" Lena's voice was narrow and strained.

"The headmistress, Mrs. Edstein, herself. The baron was quite taken with her, even started her a school for mill children when she grew restive. But when the children started refusing to go, we all realized—the baron included—that Miss Helen had not exaggerated Edstein's cruelties. At least the old baron did right by his child in the end."

"How, if she was dead?" Clive looked from Lena to the old man.

"His will cut Lady Winters out, giving her only a pittance to live on." The silver-haired man pursed his lips and nodded his head slowly. Then staring solidly in Lena's face, he added, "The rest is in trust, waiting for Miss Helen to return."

"In trust? For a dead girl?" The answer offended Clive's logical sensibilities. "Surely he knew that was impossible."

"Shortly before he died, the old baron confided in the curate and his housekeeper that Miss Helen didn't die. She ran away. The old man was so angry she defied him, that he announced she was dead and gave her this tomb. But he left her the estate, and for another five years, she can claim it—if of course she can answer the questions the baron left with his solicitors. He left the curate with a list of clues to jog Miss Helen's memory, but the clues have gone missing, and we think her ladyship paid for them to disappear. She isn't an old woman, Lady Winters, and five years isn't that long to wait."

"Where is Lady Winters?" Clive put his arm around Lena's shoulders, rubbing the outside of her arm as if she were cold.

"She's lady of the manor and a bitter one. None of the local girls will work in her kitchen, so she brings in servants from London or Manchester, but they never stay more than a month or two. She has a companion now, and the whole town pities the poor woman."

"How do you know so much about her?" Lena ventured quietly.

"Secrets are hard to keep in a village. My wife—generous soul that she is—invited her ladyship to tea when she first arrived, and Lady Winters treats it as a perpetual invitation. Arrives each week at the same time, expecting tea and cakes, she does. On those days, I visit Miss Helen or the baron—over there under that yew. He used to sit by Miss Helen's crypt for hours, and I would join him. He was a kinder man in the years before his death, perhaps even a father Miss Helen could have been proud of, but t'were too late for that."

Lena turned toward the monument once more, her hand clenched at her side, her back rod straight. "That foolish old man. He could have . . ." She let the words trail off. She felt dizzy, out of sorts, inexpressibly sad, and angry all at once.

"He could have what?" Clive asked.

"You wouldn't understand." She picked up her reticule and walked away, the stiffness of her shoulders and the tilt of her head revealing more of her anger than any words.

Clive took a few steps, then paused, uncertain of what comfort he might offer.

"You should follow her, boy, if you love her," the old man said.

"I'm not certain she wishes to have company." Clive watched as she walked farther into the churchyard.

"Aye, that might be so. She can send you away, if that's the case, and then you can stay away. But it's better for her to tell you to go than for you to assume she doesn't want you."

"That makes no sense. You're telling me to ignore her express wishes to be left alone."

"I'm telling you that girl is upset and angry, and she doesn't know how to accept help or even kindness. Her hurts run deep—betrayal, abandonment. She was cast out on her own before she could understand what that meant."

"What hurts? What betrayal?" Clive stared at the old man as if he were a fortune-teller.

"Ah, that's for her to tell you, if you decide to follow her."

"And if I decide not to? If I decide to listen to what she *says*?"

"Then she might come back to you."

"Might?"

"If you follow her, you might learn what she's thinking. If you stay here, it's certain you'll never know. But if you stay near to her, even when she pushes you away as now, she might come to believe that you aren't going to leave her or let her go without a fight."

"I don't understand." Clive shook his head, furrowing his brow.

"But that's the beauty of it: you don't have to. If you love her, you only have to be present. You don't have to ask questions, or give her solutions. You simply have to be available for her."

"I think I can do that." Clive felt the knowledge that he loved Lena deep in his bones.

"Then you should go. The longer you wait, the harder it will be for her to believe you are sincere."

"Your congregation is very lucky in their parson."

"Oh, I'm not the parson, my boy. I'm the bell ringer. But I've listened to whatever parson we've had for the last fifty years, and more than that, I have a wife of my own."

"Thank you." He shook the bell ringer's hand. Turning down the path Lena had taken, he saw her back in the near distance. Two men, large and unsavory, stepped into the path before her. He couldn't hear their words, but he could tell from the way she recoiled that they had accosted her.

"What ho!" Clive called out, gripping his walking stick with both hands. A present from his brother Colin, the walking stick pulled apart to reveal a rapier. But he delayed showing it. Weapons always made a situation more dangerous if the opposition was prone to take offense. "May I offer my aid?"

The men looked from Lena to Clive and back again. Lena took advantage of Clive's distraction to step backward, out of immediate reach. She pulled a thin blade, not much longer than a penknife, from her reticule. Immediately—as Clive had feared—the men's stances grew more belligerent.

She pointed the narrow knife toward them. "Don't underestimate the power of my blade."

"You can't possibly think we are afraid of a little knife or a little woman." The youngest of the men stepped forward menacingly, though the older man stepped back.

"Then you aren't very wise." Lena let the light glint on the blade. "A small blade can easily puncture a lung or kidney. If I aim for the right place, you will be in the grave by nightfall."

The older man pulled the younger man back. "Our employer wants information, and he hasn't any patience with those who don't give it."

"Information about what?" Clive motioned Lena to step farther out of reach.

"We're looking for our former associate, Mr. Seamus Byrne." The older man assessed Clive's strength.

"I know no one of that name." Lena stepped closer to Clive.

"He's Horatio now, Horatio Calder. We saw his map at the Rotunda, and we followed it here." The man leered at Lena. "He's got a partner supposed to look like the lady here."

"I've met his partner," Clive interjected. "She's severe, sharp-tongued, and demanding, not the kind of woman a man would want to spend time with."

"Perhaps." The older man nodded in agreement. "But Seamus told her information that puts our employer at risk, and our employer doesn't like being at risk."

"Does my friend here look like such a woman?"

The three men examined Lena, who tried to look demure, while holding her penknife. Taking the opportunity, Clive stepped closer, intending to put himself between the group and Lena. But he stepped on a dry branch. The loud crack caught the youngest villain off-guard, who, pulling a rock from behind his back, lashed out at Clive. Hit in the head, Clive reeled with the blow, then fell to his knees. His walking stick dropped to the ground beside him.

From the top of the churchyard, the bell ringer, seeing the violence, called out an alarm: "Magistrate! Magistrate! Call the magistrate!"

For a moment, the men debated whether to finish the fight. But seeing the bell ringer, magistrate, and a boy leading a pair of horses run toward them, they retreated into the fields beyond the churchyard until they were out of sight.

Clive, his hands cradling his bleeding head, sat roughly on the ground. The laceration above his temple was sticky with blood. Clive felt the edges of the cut. "The blood makes it look worse than it feels."

"It looks bad enough, regardless of how it feels." Lena brushed his hair back to inspect his wound, then pulled a handkerchief out of her reticule. "We should return to the inn and treat this. Can you ride?"

"How did you survive?" Clive stopped her hand, holding it to his chest.

"What?" Lena touched the handkerchief to his head, her stomach still twisting.

"When you ran away, how did you survive?"

She looked over her shoulder toward the church, where the bell ringer, magistrate, boy and horses were almost upon them. She couldn't risk them overhearing, but she needed to give him an answer. At the same time, she needed to determine how much she was willing to tell him. "I'll tell you. I promise. But can you ride back to the inn?"

"No need." He closed his eyes against the palm of her hand, his words slurring. "I had Fletcher follow in the carriage." He fell unconscious to the ground.

Chapter Twenty-One

It took only a few minutes to call for Fletcher, who was waiting down the lane. He, the postilions, and the magistrate lifted Clive from the ground, each man taking a limb. Lena followed helplessly, the handkerchief covered with Clive's blood still in her hand.

At the carriage, she entered first, then the men handed in Clive, back first. He was too long and lean to position easily on the seat, so Lena sat with him in the well between them, holding his head in her lap. *I will die in your lap, and be buried in your eyes.* The line from *Much Ado* echoed in her head, and she whispered softly, "Please don't die."

The laceration was still bleeding badly, and she pressed the handkerchief to his head. She wished he would awaken, so she could tell him how much he meant to her. But she knew that even if he did, she didn't have the courage. Instead, she sang children's songs to him softly, hoping they would comfort him.

At the inn, Fletcher arranged for Clive to be carried to his room and placed in the bed. The other men withdrew, leaving Clive to the ministrations of Lena and Fletcher. They loosened his clothing and washed his wound with fresh water from the basin.

"Don't worry, Miss Frost. Somerville men have heads as hard as granite." Fletcher patted her shoulder. "He just needs a little rest. He'll be well in the morning."

Lena wasn't so sure. But she treated his head with the salve the innkeeper sent up, and she waited beside the bed, watching for any fever or change of condition.

Several hours later, Lena woke to a room grown cold. At some point in the night, she'd curled up in the bed beside Clive, both of them almost fully clothed.

Clive was breathing evenly, his forehead cool. He woke when she tried to cover him with the blanket.

"Ah, my prickly darling, you haven't answered my question."

"That's the second time you've called me that." Lena examined his wound and was pleased to find it closed. "Prickles, thorns: either way it suggests I'm disagreeable."

"No, a thorn is part of the structure of a bush, like a branch, and if you remove it, you destroy the limb. But a prickle is only part of the skin, and you can remove it with no damage to the plant. Now tell me before I fall asleep again . . . how did you survive?"

She tucked her head into his shoulder. In the dark, she couldn't see his face. It made telling her story easier.

"Mrs. Edstein flattered my father, telling him she could make his daughter into a deferent miss, if he only supported her methods unwaveringly. At the end of the first month, I ran away from the school, having saved my pin money to buy a coach ticket. My father sent me back without hearing my complaints. The next time I ran away, I had no coin, so I walked home, keeping to the forest, fields, and countryside where I could scavenge food and sleep unmolested. It took me a week. When I arrived home, my father locked me in the nursery and sent for Edstein. He called me to his study to hear Edstein outline her plan for my next year under her tutelage—increased confinement, additional chores, no visits home for a year. He threatened that if I ran away again, I would be dead to him.

"We were to return to Nottingham in the morning, and I knew if I returned to the school, I would be lost. I took my mother's jewels, as much coin as I could find in the house, and I sewed it all into my skirts. That night, I ran to the Roma who camped near the village, asking them to let me travel with them to London. To take an English child into their caravan was dangerous, but they knew me—and my father's temper—so they agreed.

"Once in London, I tried to get work hand-coloring the illustrations in expensive books, but all the jobs were taken, though the women who did the coloring felt sorry for me and let me sleep in their apartments by turns. About that time, I ran out of money. I found a ragged copy of the London *Times* with the announcement my father had placed, 'Dead, the daughter of Baron Winters, Denby, of a short illness.' Since Helena Winters was dead, I became Lena Frost."

"A clever choice of name," Clive murmured. "Go on."

"I spent my last halfpenny buying a ticket to the British Institution exhibition. There I met Vigee Le Brun, and she was moved by my plight. I became her protégée, and I left with her when she returned to France. I remained with her for over a decade."

"Thank you for trusting me with your story." He nuzzled her neck. "And we're still not even." And he fell asleep.

Chapter Twenty-Two

The next morning Fletcher insisted the group return to London, and Lena agreed. Clive, his head still aching, slept most of the way, leaving her to her thoughts. But rather than thinking on the past, she considered her present, and in a small way, her future. She brushed back Clive's curly hair with her fingers. She couldn't get enough of the feeling of it between her fingers.

She'd grown to love him, his kindness, his solicitude. He'd seemed to burrow his way into her heart and set up housekeeping. She felt as if she had known him forever, and her need for him already went bone-deep. Worse yet, she trusted him, more than she'd ever trusted anyone. But dukes' sons did not marry businesswomen, and certainly not those with no true name or fortune.

No, the only way to remain near him was to be his mistress, and she couldn't do that, not even for Clive. Lover, yes, but not a mistress to be bought, whose love was merely another commodity to be bartered like her clothes, her food, her apartment, or her jewels.

Lena studied his face, memorizing every detail: the small scar over his right eyebrow, the freckle at the corner of his eye, the indentation at the bottom of his earlobe.

She wanted to remember each detail so thoroughly that when they were through, the memory of his face would comfort her when she was lonely or sad. She tried to think of a portrait or sculpture that was like him, but she rejected each one. Somehow Clive had replaced all her models with his own face and form.

She hadn't dared yet to open the document that Horatio had left hidden in her tomb. When they had left the inn, she'd shoved it to the bottom of her carpetbag. Certainly, a baron's daughter was closer in rank to a duke's son than a nameless painter, but she needed resources to prove her claim. But pursuing her inheritance could cost her the one dream she still clung to: that with hard work and luck and an assiduous avoidance of notoriety, she might one day be a painter to the queen. Her life couldn't bear the public scrutiny of a chancery suit wending its way slowly through the courts. And Clive wouldn't want to be the subject of another public scandal.

Perhaps if she could talk to Constance, her friend might help her imagine a future where Lena and Clive could be together. But Constance was hours away, and Clive was sleeping beside her.

Whatever time they had left to spend together, she wouldn't waste it. And when they were through, she would slip away and never see him again.

They'd arrived in London that night, too late to do anything but retire to their rooms. Clive had slipped into her bed sometime after the rest of the house had grown quiet, holding her in his arms until daylight. But when she'd awoken, Clive was gone, and a note from the duke summoning her to his study had been slipped under her door.

She'd dressed slowly, choosing the nicest of Aunt

Agatha's morning dresses and a pair of matching slippers. Though the duke and her father were nothing alike, she felt the same dread as when her father called her to his study. Since visiting her own grave and her father's, she'd found herself remembering more of her childhood than she'd allowed herself to in years.

She'd measured her father's mood by where he'd directed her to meet him. The house was a thermometer of his shifting temper: the morning room, genial; the stables, hardy; the estate office, practical; the conservatory where the gardener tended her mother's plants, maudlin; and his study, imperious or drunk.

On a good day, he would want her beside him. She would receive a note telling her how to dress and to meet him at the stables. Sometimes, she would ride across the estate with him, jumping fences and logs, until they raced back to the stables. Sometimes, clad in her best morning dress, she would accompany him as he inspected the work of the cottagers, delivering baskets of food to their wives as he met with the men. He would be proud of her then, patting her back and calling her "my good girl." On other good days he taught her how to fish and hunt, how to evaluate a failing roof and a fallen fence. On bad days, he sequestered himself in his rooms, staying in bed and calling for his meals to be sent up on a tray, until the mood passed.

She preferred the consistent days, either jovial or brooding, because then she knew her limits.

The worst days, though, were those when he left his room and nothing she could do could please him. He began those days convinced that she was a useless child, good for nothing but the rod and work. If he called for her to read to him, he would criticize her diction; if he told her to write a letter, he would criticize her handwriting, no matter how carefully she formed her letters. On those days, she usually ended up dressed like a common maid scrubbing the floors or dishes, or even raking the stables as if she were no better than a groom. Those days, if they hadn't begun in drink, always ended in the bottle. The worst of the bad days ended with her bloody and bruised, hiding from him and the servants. Those nights, when he fell down in a stupor, she would sneak up to his body to make sure he was breathing. She would call for the butler to move him to his bed, or they would cover him with a blanket where he lay, unwilling to risk another one of his rages.

The only good thing about the worst days were the presents she would receive after them. A new horse, a new saddle, her mother's jewels when she was far too young to wear them. On two occasions, when a bruise purpled her cheek, he'd handed her a pound coin—more than he paid her maid for a month—and promised he would do better. It might take a month or two, but he always broke his promises.

As a result, she grew up an observant child, watching for any sign of a change of temper, and learning as best as she could how to change a mood with a smile or a bon mot and how to disappear when she couldn't. Those skills had served her well on her own, when she was dependent on the goodwill of patrons and fellow artists for her food and shelter.

She paused awkwardly before the door of the duke's office, reminding herself that the duke was not her father, and she had no obligation to him, other than her business relationship with his fiancée. It had been more than a decade since she'd felt the back of a hand across her cheek or the toe of a boot in her stomach. When she had left her father's house, gold coins and jewels sewn into her skirts, she had told herself she would not ever again be that afraid. And she wouldn't. Not today. Not tomorrow. Even if the panorama failed, she would not be afraid. If necessary, Lena Frost would disappear, and she would reinvent herself again.

She straightened her shoulders and knocked on the door, entering when she heard the duke's "come in." She could predict why he wished to speak to her: he'd seen her with Clive when they'd returned from Derby after all. The only question would be whether she would take the money. Certainly she could use it, but if she agreed . . . She turned her mind away from the question. A week ago, before she had come to know Clive, she might have been able to do it, but now, knowing him . . . Even if she disappeared, she did not want their friendship—if that's what it was—to make her fortune. She could ill afford the scruple, but it felt right.

"Ah, Miss Frost, it is kind of you to agree to a conversation." The duke, seated before the fireplace, gestured her to sit.

"I could hardly refuse my host." She chose the chaise longue directly across from him. In dealing with patrons, or possible ones, she always sat herself in a nearby comfortable chair, presenting herself as being at ease and attentive.

"Most would say they could not refuse the request of a *duke*."

"I lived for many years in France," she elided.

"And you have imbibed the revolutionary spirit. Rights of man, equality, and all that." He appeared to be teasing her, but she couldn't be certain.

"No, I merely was thinking of the Terror, and how aristocrat, merchant, and laborer are all made of the same blood."

"You are too young to have seen the Terror." He leaned forward, studying her face for signs of age.

"Yes, but I knew those who did." She mirrored his action, a tactic she'd learned early on to put a patron at ease.

"Then we have that in common. Glass of wine?" He gestured to a nearby table that held carafes of various wines. "I have mountain if you prefer a sweet wine."

"Claret will be sufficient."

He poured, his movements smooth like his brother's, but she felt no attraction to him. He handed her the glass. "I suppose you are wondering why I've asked for you to join me."

"I can think of several possibilities." The lightness of her tone belied her interest.

He nodded acknowledgment that she hadn't answered his question. "My brother is fond of you."

"And I of him." She waited, for the inevitable litany comparing his brother's place in society to her obvious unsuitability: a woman in trade, who had lived in France under Boney, and who had no name or family. She predicted the objections easily, but was surprised at how sad the recitation made her.

"I know, from my own experience, that the course of true love never does run smooth." He leaned back, enjoying his glass.

"Shakespeare?" She sipped the claret.

"Midsummer Night's Dream. It seems suitable."

"Is this the moment when you try to warn me off? Given that you are a diplomatic man, you might even offer me money to break off whatever affair we are having."

"Are you having an affair?" He raised an eyebrow, clearly expecting an answer.

She shrugged. "I would not tell you if we were."

"Hmm." He thought for a moment. "If I offered you money to let him be, would that work?"

"No." Her soft answer was quick and decisive.

"No explanation of how your affections are more pure than any filthy lucre could sully."

She gave him her best cold stare.

"Simply no." He set down his glass and stared up at the ceiling for a moment. "It's good that you are unwilling to reveal—or sell—your *friendship* with my brother, because I wasn't offering to buy."

She felt surprised but said nothing, hoping he would explain further.

"I've found in the last several months that I'm a terrible judge in matters of the heart." His expression grew serious. "In fact, several months ago I had a conversation much like this, with another young woman who appeared by rank and class to be as wholly unsuitable a match for my brother Colin as you appear to be for Clive."

"Lady Colin."

He nodded, still somber. "She told me in no uncertain terms that whatever decision she made would be entirely her own. I believe our conversation encouraged her to hide—even from my brother—a secret that later caused her great harm. As a result, I've determined, in matters of the heart at least, to avoid giving my brothers advice."

"That's very un-*duke*-like of you," Lena assessed blandly.

He smiled, and suddenly Lena could see the man that Sophia loved. "I hope that where my siblings are concerned, that I never act as the duke, but only as their brother."

"Are those things separable?"

"In most cases, yes."

"How were your objections to Lady Colin resolved?"

"Any objections based in rank and class were eventually proved moot, as she was revealed to be an heiress in her own right. I don't suppose you are an heiress in disguise, Miss Frost?"

"You would have to resurrect me as another person for that to be the case."

He turned his attention on her, looking again very much a duke. For a few seconds, he said nothing, just examined her, head to toe, as if he had never seen her before. She sat under his gaze unflinching, then his face softened. "As to the purpose of our conversation."

"That wasn't the purpose?" She felt confused.

"No, I merely took advantage of having you here to see how you might respond to a conversation about my brother. My real purpose in this meeting is twofold. The first quite easy." He held out a letter. "Your friend Constance Equiano sent you a letter while you were in Derby, and Lady Wilmot asked me to deliver it to you."

"A menial task for a duke." She opened the letter, a request for her to visit the African's Daughter on her return.

"I tease Lady Wilmot that I am more her *cavalier servente* than a duke. But having almost lost her, it's a role I am grateful to play." He laughed. "Which brings me to my second task. I was hoping you might be willing to paint my Sophia, surreptitiously of course. She has refused to sit for any of the London painters, but she seems to like you."

"Then why must I be surreptitious?" Lena found it amusing that the pair each wanted her to paint something for the other surreptitiously.

"Because she doesn't wish to have her portrait painted."

"But she is an artist herself, and she has commissioned portraits for her salon already. Is there a reason?"

"Oh, yes! When she was quite young, her uncle commissioned a family portrait from a very famous artist. Sophia, her aunt and uncle, her multitude of cousins, all sat together for three long afternoons with three greyhounds and a tabby cat while the artist took sketch after sketch. While the artist worked on the painting, her beloved aunt Clara died. The family, missing her desperately, clung to the idea that the painting would allow them to see Clara once more. Months after the funeral, the painting arrived, but none of the faces looked much like any of the sitters', particularly her aunt Clara's. So, even though she has commissioned portraits she likes a great deal, she refuses to endure the process again."

Lena returned to her room, relieved and delighted. She didn't expect that she and Clive could marry. Even if the duke didn't enumerate them, she knew all too well the many obstacles to such a liaison. But to have the duke question neither her integrity nor her affection was somehow exhilarating.

The door at the short stairway was open, when she remembered specifically having shut it. She quickened her pace, eager to see Clive and feel his lips on hers.

As she approached the front suite, she heard Clive laughing, and she stopped to enjoy the sound of it, his full rich laugh that she loved so much. She walked to the door, wondering if they were moving to the other pair of rooms, when she heard a woman's voice, and more laughter. Her stomach turned, but she told herself there had to be a good explanation. He might not have told her, but she'd seen he loved her in his eyes.

She stepped to the outside of the door and put her ear to the crack. None of the sounds were distinct enough to identify. Eventually, when the room had grown silent, she opened the door an inch. Her heart fell into her shoes. Clive. A woman in his arms. Kissing. A long ardent kiss that tore her very guts out. She could not mistake their feelings.

She pulled the door to the jamb, not risking shutting it fully, and walked, then ran to her rooms. Only an hour ago, she'd wondered how long she might stay; now she couldn't leave fast enough. She flung her few belongings into her carpetbag. As she still hadn't retrieved her other clothes from her studio, she allowed herself the walking dress Aunt Agatha had lent her, but nothing else. Luckily, her boots had already been returned to her, buffed and polished.

She slipped into the hall, passing the front suite, where the sound of laughter had turned to something more erotic. Wiping the tears from her eyes, she found her way out of the house, into the stable yard, and from there, into the street.

"She's a blasted annoying woman. Refuses to do anything for her own good, except what she has already decided to do. Insists on putting herself in harm's way all for that blasted panorama." He punctuated each objection with a long stride across Sophia's library. "She's gone there now—packed her bag and left, without even telling me she was leaving."

"You care for her," Sophia offered gently.

"Of course I care for her. She's stubborn and hard-headed"—Clive paced in the opposite direction—"but she's also charming, witty, and smart."

"No, I mean you *care* for her." Sophia put a stronger emphasis on the word.

He stopped in midstride. "I have known her for less than a fortnight. I might find her company exhilarating, but one needs a longer acquaintance to care for someone."

"Or not." Sophia shook her head. "Sometimes *love* takes no time at all. After all, love often grows from a meeting of congenial minds."

"Attraction, yes." Clive stopped at one end of the room. "It's a function of our chemistry. But love, no, love takes time."

"I would have to agree with my fiancée. I fell hopelessly in love with Sophia on a bright summer day, when she wore a blue muslin dress with flowers embroidered around her ankles." Aidan smiled at Sophia from across the sitting area.

Clive stared at the ceiling, thinking. "Well, that explains a great deal." He looked from Aidan to Sophia and back again. "I remember that dress."

"You couldn't," Sophia and Aidan objected together. Their eyes met, and the room fell silent.

"No, I do. It was after you had left for the wars, Aidan. Seth, Edmund, and I were traveling to London to meet Father, and on the way, we called on Sophia and Tom at his estate. I remember because whoever had embroidered the peonies had left out the ants that the peony needs to bloom. I was quite disappointed."

"You were a natural philosopher even then," Sophia said lightly, but her brow was furrowed.

"I must tell you, Aidan." Clive shook his head slowly. "All these years I've thought you were distant and difficult out of grief for Benjamin and Father coupled with the pressures of the estate. But now I understand: your best friend married your girl."

The silence in the room lengthened.

"It's no wonder you went away to the wars. Seeing Tom

and Sophia together—so devoted to one another when your love went unrequited—must have been unbearable."

"I hope you will keep my secret." Aidan's voice was measured. "I would prefer that the ton not catch hold of that piece of old news."

"Of course. I only wonder if Tom knew of your unrequited love when he made you co-guardian of Ian and Lilly. It would be like him to matchmake from beyond the grave."

The growing tension between Aidan and Sophia evaporated in an instant. "I would like to think so." Aidan smiled, and Sophia's face brightened. "But we were discussing your love for Miss Frost. What are you going to do?"

"But even if she loves me, it's impossible, isn't it?" He sat on the chaise longue across from Aidan. "You and Sophia are of equal rank. Lena—Miss Frost—is a woman of business."

Aidan didn't answer immediately, and when he did his face was solemn, even stern. "From the time I was a young boy, our father taught us that our obligation as sons was to make the best possible match for the dukedom, choosing for rank, alliance, or funds, preferably all three. Had you brought this question to him, he would have told you to marry inside those considerations or forfeit your income from the estate." Aidan paused, letting his words sink in. "Would Miss Frost be worth such a sacrifice?"

Clive's belly twisted. Would he have the courage to oppose his brother? If he were cut off from the family fortune, would he have the wherewithal to survive? Stipends at the surgery school had never been large, and those with families struggled, taking on more and more patients, until they had no time for research. His whole life would change: *he* would have to change.

Suddenly, he understood, if only in a small way, how brave Lena had been to remake herself, time after time. When her expectations and hopes had been thwarted in one area, she had found the personal resources to shift to another. She would learn a new language or a new culture, find a new patron or enterprise. With no resources but her own ingenuity and talent, she walked a tightrope, like the acrobats at Sadler's Wells, but if she fell, no net would catch her. She was wary about offers of help, not because she wasn't grateful, but because she didn't have the resources to survive the loss of help she'd grown to expect. He'd never seen the terror of her situation so fully. But could he be like her?

"I understand." He rose. "Whenever I've considered being without the resources of our family estate, I've done so from a position of strength. I could imagine not having them, but I've never had to actually do without them. And it's frightening to consider what doing without them will mean."

Aidan looked disappointed, but Clive hurried on before he could interrupt.

"But if my choice here makes those supports disappear in a single instant, then my sense of comfort and protection has been no more than an illusion." He rose. "And to lose a woman like Lena to protect what is only an illusion would be foolish beyond measure. So, yes, Lena is worth the sacrifice."

"Does she care for you as you care for her?" Sophia asked.

"I don't know," Clive answered soberly. "I can only hope she does."

Aidan leaned back, his face inscrutable. Then he rose, facing Clive. "Our father's attitudes were shaped by his class and his upbringing. A great many in the ton still think as he did. For choosing below your station, you will likely be criticized, perhaps even ostracized. But that's a pill you have swallowed once already, and a second dose may be less painful." Aidan held out his hand. "But you will not lose me and my support. I lost a decade of happiness by following our father's rules. By any measure that matters, Miss Frost strikes me as a singularly good match, and we will welcome her."

Clive felt tears well in his eyes, but he blinked them back and shook Aidan's hand. "I never expected . . ."

Sophia joined them. "You forget, Clive, I'm only Lady Wilmot by marriage. Before that, I was the orphaned daughter of a country parson, a poor relation living on the goodwill of my uncle. Your father did not consider me an appropriate match even for Tom." She smiled softly. "What are you going to do?"

"Go to the panorama and see if she will have me."

Chapter Twenty-Three

At the Rotunda, Lena found the building dark and locked tight. Her stomach—already aching from hurt and disappointment—twisted tighter. If only the Muses had kept her on schedule, she could bury herself in work. She'd done that before. But even the thought of working filled her with despair.

She made her way through the dark to the storage closet. The doors hung open, and she slung her carpetbag on the floor. For an instant, she wished she could crawl in and hide, weeping all her tears until she was spent. But what would be left?

Taking one of the lamps and some matches, she climbed the stairs to the platform. She waited until she was standing in front of the task chart to light the lamp. Then taking a long breath, she looked up.

Every task was marked through. She brushed tears from her cheeks, grateful tears for the Muses and their help. If she'd had even a crumb of that support as a child, how different might her life have been? How different would it be as an adult to have friends to aid her when her needs exceeded her resources? Was this what it was like to live within the circle of a family's goodwill?

Sure, she had an affectionate circle among her crew,

but it was the affection of coworkers, not of friends. She might see them irregularly, even hire them again for the next panorama, but she couldn't call on them for the sort of help the Muses or Clive had offered so willingly.

Clive. The name stopped her tears. She'd never told him she loved him, nor he her. But somehow she wished she had, if for no other reason than to make the break clean between them. But it was lucky she hadn't. If she had, even painting on top of Lady Wilmot's scaffolding might not be distant enough to protect what was left of her heart. Sadly, the breach with Clive would extend to the Muses, and she felt the loss of their friendship—and Clive's—bitterly.

How could she have been so foolish? She'd known he had a harem. She'd known he had obligations to other women. But she had thought those obligations were in the past, or at least platonic. She hadn't expected him to love another, as he obviously did. No, she'd expected him to love her, as she did him. She couldn't deny that she loved him, at least not to herself.

She told herself all the things she would tell Constance if the situation were reversed. Yes, she would heal. Yes, eventually she would forget him. Yes, she would eventually love someone who could love her as well. Even as she affirmed the sentences, she knew that healing, forgetting, and loving again were years in the future. She'd guarded her heart so carefully, so long. Then she'd lost it to a man who . . . She tried to create a list of his faults. She got no farther than *he dissects bodies* before the list turned to virtues. *He tended my wounds. He listened to my concerns. He treated me as an equal. He . . .*

She wiped the tears from her face. It did no good to remind herself of all his positive characteristics when all that mattered was that he loved someone else.

Tacked to the wall was a long note from Lady Judith and Ophelia, detailing everything completed in Lena's absence. Only two items remained: to set up the music stands for the musicians, and to paint over her list of tasks. She'd hoped to bury her sorrows in work, but the Muses had left her with nothing to do.

Picking up her lamp, she climbed down the stairs to the lower level. She was almost to the supply closet when she heard the sound of men's voices above her and the sound of the door being forced. How had they found her already? And what did they want, breaking into the Rotunda again? Would they damage the painting again or do something worse? She doused her lamp and hid it behind some boxes against the wall.

The sounds of movement were followed by a crash and cursing. "Raise the damn lamp. I think I'm bleeding." The voice was raspy and coarse. One of the men from Denby.

"I thought we were going to surprise her." The second man spoke with a rural accent, but she couldn't place the area.

"Not with Ned falling over his own feet, we aren't. Raise the lamp." The third man was clearly the leader.

The wood of the platform creaked above her head, and she shrank against the wall.

"Just because she wasn't in the office doesn't mean she's not hiding here." Ned's coarse voice carried in the round space.

"In the dark? This place is dead silent—no one's here. She must have slipped past us." The rural voice sounded petulant.

"If Ned hadn't fallen asleep, we could have followed her. Eventually she'll lead us to Seamus. We must simply be patient."

"She could still be here, hiding in the dark, hoping to deceive us."

"Then we search, every nook and cranny. If she's not here, at least we'll discover if Seamus left anything else that could point to us."

"Why'd Seamus paint that map of Denby, if not to send her to him?"

The other men groaned. "Why does Seamus do anything?"

"Perhaps we'll find something we can sell to make up for the trip." The leader shifted his weight, and the floor creaked above her head. "Find more lamps."

"Forget the lamps. There's a canopy under the skylights. Once I find the rope pull, we'll have all the light we need."

Lena bit back a gasp. The canopy had only been installed a fortnight ago. She strained to identify the voice, but the man was moving away from her, the light from his lamp moving across the wall.

The floor creaked as the two remaining men met nearly above her on the platform. "We should have killed them when we had the chance," Ned's voice glowered.

"There's time. But not until we know everything Horatio saw." The leader's voice was hard and angry. "Then, we kill him and by the time someone thinks to miss him, he'll be no more."

"No body, no crime." The rural voice snickered, and the other man with him.

Lena covered her mouth, biting back her horror.

"If Charters discovers we've run into trouble, he'll kill us, then them to make sure no one talks. But shut the door." The leader walked away from his position above Lena's head. "We don't want to let anyone know that we're here."

The light from the leader's lamp slipped through the cracks between the boards on the platform above her. She rose slowly, her position still hidden. Turning toward the door, she held her hand over the latch to muffle the sound. The men were making no attempt to search quietly. She raised it, the click barely noticeable in the noise the men were making. Opening the door would let in some light, but perhaps they wouldn't see it.

She pressed her back to the wall next to the door, intending to open it only just enough to slip through.

"Do you think Seamus told the girl about us?"

She stopped, her hand still on the latch. Staying was dangerous, but leaving before she knew what they had planned was more dangerous still.

"Whether he did or not, we use her to get to him. Then we kill them both—and that man who's been helping her."

"He wasn't with her today."

"Then perhaps he'll be lucky. If he keeps away from her, he can live."

Kill them both—and Clive. She felt the fear pulsing through her body. But she forced herself to breathe and wait. If she gave in to panic, she would be lost.

"Here we go, boys, all the light you want."

The canopy over the high windows creaked as the rope pulled on the gears. As the canopy pulled from in front of the skylights, she waited, watching the light approach her slowly. To hide her escape, she had to open the outside door at the moment the light from the windows reached her location. The men began to search again. She couldn't allow herself to wonder what mess they were making; she could only think about timing the door and the light.

As the light struck her position, she slipped out the door and ran.

* * *

She'd almost reached the end of the Rotunda yard when a tall figure stepped from the shadow of the alley. Strong arms pulled her back. She bit back her scream, not wanting to draw the other men from the Rotunda. Instead, she raised her heel and rammed it hard into the man's instep.

"Ouch. Lena." Clive let her go. "What's the matter?"

She started to tell him, about the men, their threats, but the confession died on her lips. She walked swiftly out of the view of the Rotunda. He followed.

"Lena! Stop!" As they reached the street, he grabbed her arm, pulling her back to face him. With her free hand, she slapped him across the face, hard.

"I want nothing to do with you, Clive Somerville." She took advantage of his surprise to pull out of his grasp once more. But Clive caught her elbow, herding her toward a waiting carriage.

She looked back into the Rotunda yard. The men hadn't yet left the building. If she wished to get away quickly—to get Clive away quickly—her best option was the carriage. So be it. She could both save his life and have her say.

She pulled her elbow out of his grasp, and forgoing the stairs and Clive's help, she pulled herself into the coach. Clive didn't interfere.

"How could you?" She sat as far from him as the coach seat would allow. "I trusted you. I . . ." She sputtered to a stop, finding no words to convey the depth of her anger.

"You have me at a disadvantage." Clive watched her face. Somehow the ground had shifted between them. The expression on Lena's face, angry and belligerent, suggested no hint of affection or even of friendship. The realization made his chest tight. "What have I done?" Clive spoke cautiously, testing his words against her emotion.

"You lied to me."

"Only when it was necessary." A misunderstanding, but Clive knew her too well to be relieved.

"Then you admit it." She crossed her arms over her chest. "I'm surprised."

"Admit what?" He hadn't felt so helpless since his childhood. "I told you from the first that I was conducting an investigation. I wasn't at liberty to give you every detail."

"I'm not talking about your investigation. I'm talking about her. Your mistress . . . in the very suite we shared together."

"If I have a mistress in that suite, it would be only you." Somehow his world had tilted on its axis, and he needed to right it, but how?

"I saw you—with her." Her voice was trembling with anger. "I will not be a member of your harem."

"Don't let an old scandal ruin . . . this, us."

"An *old* scandal? That places it in the past. But I saw you with her only this morning. Don't deny it."

"But I must, Lena." He dragged his fingers through his hair. "Caroline and her sisters never come to town—it is far too dangerous."

"Then who was that dark-haired woman you were kissing in the guest wing?" She shook her head and tightened her lips.

"You are the only dark-haired woman I have kissed. There's only you."

"More lies." Lena crossed her arms tight over her chest. "I wish to go to the African's Daughter. After that, I wish never to see you again." She looked out the window. A part of her hoped that he could offer some reasonable explanation, but she knew it was impossible. She'd seen the kiss with her own eyes, and no explanation could erase her betrayal.

"I will take you to the African's Daughter."

His agreement stung, a confirmation of her every accusation.

"Excellent." She refused to look him in the face. All that mattered was getting him far away from the Rotunda. She might not wish to see him anymore, but she didn't wish him dead.

"But only on one condition: you must give me ten minutes to prove that I haven't lied to you about Caroline, her sisters, or any woman."

"You can't convince me to reject what I saw." She was lucky he'd betrayed her. It made leaving easier.

"But I can give you cause to look again. Ten minutes, and if I haven't convinced you, I'll have Fletcher deliver you to the African's Daughter and never trouble you again."

She stared at him hard, then agreed with a curt nod.

They rode in silence to the duke's residence, and once there, Clive settled her in the main drawing room. "Remember: you promised me ten minutes."

Near the window, a pile of books sat on a writing desk, and she picked the top book up, rubbing her thumb down the spine.

A few moments later, Clive returned, wearing the clothes he'd been wearing when she'd seen him embracing his lover. The door closed behind him.

"You came all this way to change clothes?" She laced her words with hostility.

"Clive tells me that I've caused a rupture between you." He shrugged half apologetically and ran his hand through his hair.

"*Clive* does, does he?" She flung the book, hitting his chest. She threw another. He stared at her with surprise.

"Wait!" He held out his hands in submission. "I'm not Clive." He looked over his shoulder at the closed door. "I neglected to tell anyone I was in the house and with company."

"You admit it then." She flung another book, this time barely missing his head. "Why do you waste my time?"

"Apparently my brother wishes for me to suffer." Dodging the fourth book, he strode to the door. "Come in, you devil. It's not fair to make me bear her wrath alone."

A second man—identical save for his clothing—stepped into the room. The only difference between them was their clothing and the part of their hair. Lena studied the two men's faces, their hair, the set of their shoulders, the lines of their bodies. They submitted patiently to her examination, even when she poked each man in the chest, as if to test if he were real.

"You are a twin," she said flatly.

Clive nodded apologetically. "My brother Edmund concealed his arrival in order to address some business that he keeps entirely to himself. He chose the Rowan suite for privacy, as we did, without asking if anyone else might already be in residence."

"You aren't Clive." She pointed at Edmund, dumbfounded and relieved in the same breath.

"Are you satisfied?" Edmund waited until Lena nodded. "Then I must ask my brother to accompany me briefly.

My own lady will not be satisfied with throwing only books."

Lena watched the two brothers leave, even their strides identical. Learning that Clive had a twin left her dissatisfied. Certainly, he hadn't betrayed her with another woman, but how could he neglect to mention something so fundamental as having a twin? She'd been a fool to trust him, but the truth was that she'd wanted to, and now she loved him. With every fiber of her being she loved him. His calm kindness had soothed her soul in a way she'd never expected, and never imagined possible. When she was with him, she had no desire to wander, and she'd never felt anything that could soothe her wanderlust.

But she was a danger to him, somehow, even if she didn't understand why—and she had to remember that. If she told him of the threats, he'd feel obligated to remain by her side. The duke would send men to protect them, but for how long? And from what enemies? Eventually they would chafe at the restrictions, then one or both of them would die. If her heart ached now at the prospect of living without him, how much more would it break if he were to die for being her lover? But if he stayed away from her he might live—that's what the men said.

Breaking it off with him would have been easier, cleaner, if he had betrayed her. Instead, she would have to destroy any hope they might have of a future together.

He returned all too quickly.

"I assume you pretended to be each other when you were young." She tightened her shawl around her shoulders.

"I'm not terribly good at dissembling." He grinned, clearly thinking that all was resolved. "But we once had a dancing master—a Mr. Quince—who believed we were the same boy for almost a year. We never tried to deceive him; we would simply alternate who attended the lessons. It quite confused him because I prefer my left side, and Edmund prefers his right."

"How did he discover?" She paused, extending their remaining pleasant moments.

"Father invited him to a family dinner. He glared at us until Father asked if he had indigestion."

"I would have received a worse punishment than a glare."

"If you are a possible heir to a dukedom, no one, other than your parents, dares punish you. We boys had to learn for ourselves how unbridled self-interest leads only to cruelty."

"If you had no teacher but your father to guide you, how did you learn?" she prompted. Now that their minutes were numbered, she wanted to learn as much about him as she could.

"Our eldest brother was a textbook in cruelty. Aidan and Benjamin bore the brunt of his misuse, but none of us escaped."

"Benjamin? You mentioned him before." She regretted the question almost immediately, as his expression turned inexpressibly sad.

"My second eldest brother, lost in the wars. I still miss him."

She resisted touching his arm. She couldn't afford any motion that might appear affectionate.

At the tender expression on Lena's face, Clive shook off his sad memories. Sophia was right: he was in love. In love with her strong will, her creativity, her intelligence, her kindness. In love with her. Thanks to Aidan's blessing, that love was no longer in conflict with his duty to his name or to his family. He could—if she would have him— remain with Lena for the rest of his life. The realization buoyed his spirits. The misunderstanding with Edmund had almost ruined that future, and he was no longer willing to risk it.

"I quite enjoyed you throwing the books at Edmund. He richly deserves it, and not just for today. He's a scamp, though not a scoundrel." He closed the short distance between them. "Would you like to know an easy way to tell us apart?"

She stepped away. "Other than the part of your hair and the way that you walk?"

"Yes, other than those things." He stepped back as well, giving her whatever distance she required.

"The hair on your crown curls to the left. You have a slight scar beside your right earlobe, and your left eye crinkles more than your right when you smile."

"As I have no fear of any further confusion with my brother, I must ask you another question." He felt the pressure of his heart increase. His blood pounded so loudly that he heard it as a tide. His knees felt as if they might fail him. "It is a question vital to my happiness as I hope it will be to yours."

He paused, but she said nothing, merely stared at him with a look that seemed equal parts affection, pity, and regret.

He rushed forward, forgetting the words he had planned. "I can't offer you the wealth of a duke. Unlike my brother Seth, I have no interest in business, so I'm unlikely to become an industrialist. But I'm well settled, thanks to Aidan and Judith's management of the ducal estate. I wish only to do my researches and have you beside me."

"Clive, no. Our affair . . ." She held up her hand to stop him, but he took it and held it against his heart.

"I don't want an affair, Lena. I want to marry you, if you will have me." He kissed her palm, watching her face as she weighed the question.

"You don't know me." Her eyes filled with tears, and she pulled her hand away. "You can't want to marry me."

"I can, and I do. I know it hasn't been long since we met, but sometimes love takes no time at all. I know you will consider my proposal from every angle, just as you considered every task at the Rotunda. We are alike in that." Something was wrong: the way she bit the inside of her lip revealed confusion, not delight. "But I don't wish to marry you because we are alike. We notice the same details when we look at an object, but we put those ob- servations together in marvelously different ways. We complement one another. We . . ." He stopped, realizing his words had somehow gone astray.

She looked away, as if she were blinking back tears. Her voice when she spoke was filled with regret. "I'm not who you think I am, Clive."

"I know your heart, your mind, your courage. I love you, Lena, or Helen, or whatever you wish to be called . . . as long as it's also Lady Clive Somerville."

She folded her arms over her chest, holding herself tight. She closed her eyes for a moment, as if weighing a heavy decision, then, sighing, she looked him directly in the face. "Remember when I told Lilly that she should practice painting like other painters, learning their tech- niques?"

"Yes." He felt his heart grow tight.

"I studied with Le Brun for almost a decade. But when she retired from Paris to her country estate, I stayed behind, living in the house of a well-connected patron of the arts, an Austrian count named Remberg, decades my senior. The lure of the Musée Napoléon—all those shapes, colors, materials, and textures—was irresistible, and I spent every day, morning till night, there. It became my whole world." She looked into the distance.

He stood silently, knowing that at the end he would discover her reason for rejecting him, and he prayed he could convince her it didn't matter.

"Eventually, Tenney—though he went by a different name then—invited some of us students to compete against each other. I was the only woman he invited. Each week, we received canvas, paints, and a masterwork to copy. But, to judge us fairly, Tenney insisted that we paint in exactly the same dimensions of the original canvas. I was intent on becoming known for my skill, not my sex, and soon my copies were almost indistinguishable from the originals."

She sat down on the couch, as if exhausted, and he sat beside her, wanting to pull her into his arms, but knowing it would be unwelcome.

"You became a forger."

She nodded. "I believed it was a competition until I found my pieces on sale in several gallery windows, and I discovered that others had already been sent to Gravelines."

"Gravelines? To be smuggled to England?"

"There was then, as there is now, a steady trade in contraband between Gravelines and Kent. I begged the count for help, and, though I hadn't expected him to, over the next several weeks, Remberg bought all my copies, even those already intended for the English market. When I tried to destroy them, he stopped me, saying he saw in the paintings a heart that could not otherwise be his. I realized he loved me, and when he asked for my hand, I did not refuse."

"You are married." His heart collapsed into his belly. He'd imagined she loved him, but he was wrong.

"I was grateful. The paintings could have destroyed my career before it began, and he bought them simply because I asked." She shrugged, lifting her palms in a sort of penitence. "He was to travel to Austria that week, but he insisted we marry before he left. He even invited fifty of his friends to the ceremony." She shook her head sadly. "He was a kind man. His only fault was in loving me."

"Was? Is he dead?" Clive hated that he hoped her husband was dead.

"After he left, I returned home to find the house ransacked and the paintings gone. One of the smaller paintings ended up in the hands of the police, accompanied by a note accusing Remberg of the forgery. When they stopped him at the border, Remberg admitted to the crime to protect me. He was executed before I knew he'd been arrested." She looked into the distance, wiping away her tears. Her voice was flat, as if she were confessing to a crime she'd committed long ago.

"Within days, rumors began to circulate that Remberg's *English* wife arranged his arrest and execution. I had to flee. I sold his property and all his things, and to honor him, I used the funds to purchase the Rotunda."

"This means that attacks on the Rotunda could have nothing to do with the resurrection men." Clive followed her story to one possible conclusion. "One of Remberg's friends could believe you deserve to be punished."

"Don't I? I should have known the competitions were staged. Then later, I could have let the paintings be sold—my name wasn't on them—but I was afraid they would surface in the future and thwart my ambition to be a painter to the royal family."

"Or Tenney didn't wish to let such an accomplished forger go. He certainly went to great lengths to remove you from Remberg's protection. It seems suspicious that he would show up in London now—before you could open the Rotunda exhibition—and begin selling your forgeries."

"But I'm Frost here, not Le Givre, and I only used Madame Remberg for a few weeks. Everything for the Rotunda is billed to H. Calder and Company." She sighed. "But you see, Clive, why marriage to me is impossible?"

"What if I don't see that?"

"Then let me make it perfectly clear. Elene Remberg caused the death of her husband and stole his money. Lena Le Givre is a criminal, a forger whose paintings were intended to be part of the contraband that travels from Gravelines to Kent, whose sins are even now pursuing her to London. Helena Winters destroyed her own reputation. She traveled in a gypsy caravan, begged on London's streets, then lived in France during the wars. I am as wholly unsuitable to marry you as any woman alive. I've already lost one kind man. I will not lose another. I cannot marry you and I will not remain your lover." She rose. "I promised you ten minutes, and we have taken almost an hour. Would you please call Fletcher to deliver me to the African's Daughter?"

"I'll escort you." He rose as well.

"I would prefer if you didn't."

"If we are dissolving our liaison, you can hardly refuse me a twenty-minute drive across town." His voice

broke as he spoke, and he made no attempt to cover it.
He loved her. He'd told her, and she'd rejected him, but
at least she would not be able to lie to herself about his
feelings.

Her chest fell. "If you wish."

Chapter Twenty-Four

They sat far apart on the same seat, neither speaking. Occasionally she would steal a glance at him, and each time she found him watching her intensely. She could tell from the slope of Clive's shoulders that she'd hurt him, and her own heart hurt to see him so dejected.

If she hadn't overheard the men—if they hadn't threatened his life if she remained with him—she would never have told him her truth. She would have held her secrets close, until he had grown tired of them. And their affair would have died a natural death, leaving her to mourn, but preserving his life. As it was, she could only console herself that by separating from him, she kept him safe.

She'd had few illusions about marriage when she'd accepted Remberg's proposal. Given their long friendship, she had expected a pleasant sort of companionship but no real passion. And she'd experienced nothing of married life, save for widowhood. But marriage to Clive would have been a different thing entirely. She hadn't realized how much she wanted it until he was lost to her.

The carriage seemed to travel immeasurably slow, then suddenly it had arrived. He followed her, without asking her permission, into Constance's shop.

The sound of women's laughter met them as she stepped

through the door at the African's Daughter. As usual, Constance met her near the front of the store, embracing her with a relief that bespoke the depth of their friendship.

"I've been so worried, even though Lady Wilmot assured me you were in good hands."

"I'm sorry. I should have sent you word myself. But . . ." Lena stopped as Clive entered the shop after her.

Reading both their faces, Constance wrapped her arm around Lena's shoulder. "I understand *but.*"

Lena refused to cry. Tears would only give him hope. "The duke gave me your letter this morning. I came as soon as I could."

Constance leaned into Lena's ear and whispered, "Horatio. He's here."

Some of Lena's fear and worry lifted. "Take me to him."

Constance looked back at Clive, who was standing awkwardly at the door, neither in nor out of the shop. "And Somerville?"

Lena sighed. "He should come as well."

Constance led them past the laughing women to her office, a room in the middle of the shop, above which were her lodgings. "Above my apartment is another bedroom. He'd been hiding at your studio for days, thinking you would go there when you found his note. While you were in Derby, he came looking for you here. He's been scared for you, but I'll let him tell you the story." She unlocked the door that led to the stairs. "There's a way to escape over the roof, so call out when you reach my apartment, or he might run."

The reunion with Horatio seemed to cheer Lena somewhat. The old man clasped her to his breast over and again, repeating, "Oh, my sweet girl, my sweet girl, you're safe!"

Clive stood watching, saying nothing until the old man dried his tears and motioned them both to chairs. Clive felt like he was watching the scene from a far distance. Even if he had no hopes for a future with Lena, he still had murderers to catch, and Horatio was the key.

"Mr. Calder, or should I call you Mr. Byrne?" Clive's voice sounded harsh even to his own ears, and Lena winced.

"Lena here named me Calder, and I prefer that name to the one my father gave me."

"On the day you disappeared, you wrote that you had information regarding the murders."

"Didn't you see it? I painted the culprits into the panorama."

"Someone destroyed the faces, Horatio." Lena petted the old man's arm. "But we found the map, and we went to Denby."

Calder shook his head slowly, racking his fingers across his bald pate. "Ah, I see. And you found the crypt."

Lena nodded, her eyes never leaving the old man's face. "I did."

I. Not we.

Suddenly resentful, Clive took control of the conversation. It was no longer *their* investigation; it was *his*. "Can you tell us about the murders, Mr. Calder?"

Lena began to object, but bit the words back.

Horatio sighed sadly. "We'd been losing men. Continental craftsmen all, and them the least likely to give up a paying job without having a better one. I'd known there was sentiment against them, so I searched for them, wanting to know if someone working for the Rotunda was at fault. But they'd simply disappeared."

He paused, patting Lena's knee. "I've been so worried,

my girl. I would never have left you alone if I'd realized you wouldn't come to your studio."

"How do you know about the studio?" Lena furrowed her brow.

"Ah, that's another part of the story. But you found the packet—the papers I left you in the crypt."

"Yes."

"You haven't read them?"

Lena shook her head, apologetically.

"Ah, then, when your friend here is gone, we'll talk about what you've found." He turned to Clive. "The papers have no relation to the murders."

"Then can we focus on the murders, Mr. Calder?" Clive said coldly.

"Of course, of course. After my inquiries, the disappearances stopped, and I chalked the losses up to bad luck. But last week, one of our newer carpenters came to my office to tell me the names of other émigrés who had disappeared. He left, and I went back to my work, but I noticed that he'd left his cap on my desk. Thinking I could just throw it down to him, if he were still in the yard, I looked out the window." The old man stopped, his voice close to breaking. "And there, in the yard, were four men loading his body into a cart. I must have made a sound, because they looked up, and, in the moonlight, I could see each of their faces. I'll never forget their faces." Horatio fell silent.

"Oh, Horatio, what did you do?" Lena's voice was full of affection and concern.

"I hid, my dearie, hid like a small boy scared of the banshees. That's when I wrote to you, Mr. Somerville, arranging a meeting."

"*Lord* Somerville, Horatio," Lena corrected.

"Ah." Horatio looked from Lena to Clive, pursing his

chin. "I see the way it is." He patted Lena on the knee comfortingly.

"The rest of the story, Mr. Calder," Clive pushed. "You wrote to me arranging a meeting that you didn't keep."

"No, I came to meet you, but when I arrived, one of the murderers was already speaking to you. I heard you call him Calder, and I knew they were waiting for me, so I ran again, and I wrote you a letter asking you to meet me at the Rotunda in two days' time.

"Sadly, the night before we were to meet, another of our crew asked if he could work late for extra pay. I gave him some work painting faces, and while he worked, I climbed the high scaffold to check the work on the upper curtains, as Lena had asked me to do. When I looked down next, I saw the murderers emerge from under the stage, come to remove their witness."

"Oh, Horatio!" Lena leaned into his arm, and Clive felt a raw fury at her obvious affection.

"Please continue, Mr. Calder. I have murderers to find."

"Before I could shout a warning, one of the men bashed our painter's head in. They rolled the body up in canvas and drug it outside. By the time I reached the back door, they were carrying him away in a cart. So I followed them, then I returned to the panorama and painted them into it: the murderers, the murdered man, and even the man who bought the body."

"Can you sketch them again?" Clive asked.

The old man pulled out a roll of paper. "Already done, my boy, already done."

Clive threw the sketches onto Joe's desk and himself into a chair.

He'd left Lena patting the old man's knee and cooing

over him as if he were a found puppy. In the long walk from the African's Daughter to the secret division of the Home Office, he'd replayed every word Lena had told him, trying to recapture every hint of her emotions. He thought of her hands, clasped, one thumb rubbing the back of the other hand, and of her eyes, refusing to meet his. But most telling, he thought of the way her whole body had gone still, as if she were speaking to her confessor or a judge. She would have him believe she didn't care for him, but her very refusal to let him see her emotion made her a liar.

By the time he'd arrived at the Home Office, he was certain both that she loved him, and that he had no chance on earth of convincing her of it.

"Why are you in a foul mood?" Joe carried a carafe of wine to his desk. "Does it relate to your investigation or that interesting girl?"

Clive pushed the papers toward his supervisor. "The top five are your murderers; the bottom ones are the men they are suspected of killing. Apparently, they frequent a tavern called the Blue Heron."

"We know. Your murderers are dead." Joe picked up the pictures.

"What?! No! They can't be."

"Their bodies were left in a cart in front of your surgery school not an hour ago, with a note pinned to the top body." Joe separated the sketches into murderers and murdered.

"A note?"

"There." Joe pointed to a slip of paper on the corner of his desk: "They killed our men. We killed them."

Clive read the note silently and shook his head in disbelief. "Something's wrong here. Calder said that the murdered men had no family here. That's how their crimes went unsuspected for so long."

"Well, someone cared enough about the killings to poison the murderers."

"Poison." Clive pressed his lips together in consideration. "Poison seems an odd choice here. It's neither a political assassination nor a family member unwilling to wait for an inheritance."

"Perhaps it was a weapon of opportunity. We've gotten reports that our murderers left a local tavern, with a local beggar, half drunk and carrying a bottle of gin. Let's see . . . I have the name of the tavern here." Joe shuffled through a pile to his right.

"The Blue Heron," Clive predicted, retrieving the wooden carving from his desk. "That's what Horatio meant by this. He was directing us to where we might find the murderers. Do you think the beggar or someone at the bar poisoned them?"

"Given the poison's speed, they were likely poisoned elsewhere." Joe shook his head. "The surgery schools are watching for the beggar's body."

"I can understand a revenge killing, but to advertise that you've done it seems a bit too neat to me."

"We'll keep an open file, but without the beggar—or his body—we haven't much to investigate. Besides, we have more pressing work here. We'd like you to go to Scotland to look into an unusual death there. The local magistrate is holding the body for you."

"Are you trying to get me out of London?"

"Did the girl throw you over?"

Clive grew silent.

"Then, yes, we are trying to get you out of London. We almost never got the office back to its comfortably cluttered state after that Morley girl rejected you."

"The situations are not the same. I didn't love Morley."

Joe sat silently for a few moments. "You love this woman?"

"Don't say it like that!"

"Like what?"

"Like you're surprised and pleased and gloating all at once."

Joe placed his hand on Clive's shoulder. "Perhaps I'm merely happy that you have found someone to love. After all the publicity you suffered, I thought you might deny yourself the satisfaction of a real love."

"I wanted—want—to marry her, but she won't have me. She says our future could never be free of her past. And I don't know how I can convince her that's not true."

"Is it? Not true, I mean. Or rather, is there anything that can be done to make it not true?"

Clive thought for a moment. "Why not send Michaels to Scotland, and give me the resources to investigate a merchant bringing forged Old Master paintings from the Continent?"

Chapter Twenty-Five

"Lena, will you consider my advice?" Constance stood at the doorway to the room where Horatio was staying.

"We are friends. I will consider anything you suggest."

"When you arrived, the Muses' Salon had just begun their meeting." Constance paused. "They were hearing requests for their help. Perhaps you might wish to talk with them?"

"If they will entertain one more request, then yes." Lena held out her hand to Constance. "But will you stay with me?"

Constance looked surprised for only a moment. "Of course." The pair made their way to the heart of the store.

While Constance held her hand, Lena told her story. She knew—though she asked anyway—that the Muses would keep her secrets, if only for Clive's sake. She detailed the whole of it, from her childhood as Helena Winters and her escape from Mrs. Edstein's school to France under the protection of Le Brun, her art career as Lena Le Givre, including her forgeries and her marriage to Remberg, to her return as Mme. Remberg, then as Lena Frost to build the panorama and make her fame. She outlined the mysterious losses, the missing and dead craftsmen, the threat of some agent known as Charters, the attempts on her life, and her fears for Clive's. She was on trial for her sins, and they were her jury.

"You were so young when you left, and France was in such turmoil; it must have seemed like another life," Lady Wilmot said gently.

"That ten years could have been a hundred. I returned to a city I barely recognized, with no friends and only the money I had from Remberg's estate." Lena searched their faces for any indication of their responses.

"But you hired craftsmen from the Continent? Wasn't that a risk?" Ariel asked.

"I hired the crews." Horatio stepped from the shadows of the bookcases. "I took anyone who applied—men and women alike—to a tavern. After a filling meal and some drink, I asked about their lives, where they'd worked and for whom, what projects. Lena only saw the ones I felt comfortable hiring." He put a protective arm around Lena's shoulders, and she suddenly regretted all the times she'd begrudged him those meals.

The Muses nodded at his answer, seemingly satisfied.

"Clive will not allow a woman to be in danger without acting to protect her, and I cannot bear the thought of him being harmed—killed—because of me."

Lady Wilmot raised a finger. "Do you love him?"

Lena blinked away tears. The question hit her in the gut. She should have expected it, given the duke's unorthodox position on his brothers. "Even if I did . . . love him"—she paced out the words to keep from crying—"as long as he is associated with me, he is in danger."

"Clive since his boyhood has chosen to help when another is in trouble. He helped Mrs. Sinclair and her sisters with a full knowledge of the possible costs." Judith's voice was soft. "Shouldn't you allow him to choose here as well?"

"Then he would be choosing to die. These men have no qualms about killing."

"A wound to the soul can be worse than a wound to the body, Miss Frost, even a mortal one." Lady Judith leaned forward, studying Lena's face.

"That's why I'm asking for your help." And she began to outline her plan.

"I have come for your help."

"Then we are your men. It's about time for us to help you." Carlin leaned forward toward Clive.

"It must be a woman," Battenskill interjected.

"Why do you think that?" Clive felt exposed.

"Because if it were anything else, you'd ask one of your troop of brothers," Battenskill explained, and the other men nodded agreement.

"The Somerville women have formed a salon to help others, and we should do the same. They are the Muses," Garfleet, more foxed than the others, exclaimed. "We could be the Night Terrors. Unmarried men only, and all paying into a pot to keep us that way. It's a sort of tontine, with the last bachelor collecting."

"What do you need?" Stillman put his hand on Garfleet's arm, drawing the man's attention back to Clive's business.

"Tomorrow night, I'd like you to attend the opening gala at the Rotunda in Leicester Square." He pushed five tickets across the table, and each man picked one up.

"Langdon has a bet on that at White's. He thinks the subject is Thermopylae." Battenskill tucked the ticket into his breast pocket.

"How much do you have on it, Roland?" Clive asked.

"Thirty quid."

Stillman whistled.

"If you are going to help me, I need you to withdraw your bets," Clive said somberly. "As it stands now, there's little chance she will forgive me. But if it looks like I've told anyone about her business, I'll have no chance at all."

"She?" The men leaned forward, even more interested.

"The proprietor of the Rotunda, Miss Lena Frost." Clive started cautiously, uncertain how to explain what he needed without revealing too much of Lena's situation. "You all have experience in difficult situations."

"Look at him—become a diplomat after all these years," Garfleet joked.

"Let him talk, Robert. If this were a public bar, you'd be more discreet," Battenskill chided.

"Go to the opening gala and make sure nothing happens." Clive looked at them hopefully. "She's warned me off strongly enough that I don't dare anger her more by going myself."

"What do you expect might happen?" Stillman asked, and Clive overviewed the murders and his investigations, ending with the discovery of the gravediggers' bodies.

"If the men you were searching for have been found, so to speak, why do you think she'd be in danger?" Langdon asked quietly.

"It's a feeling that I can't shake." Clive shrugged, feeling helpless and frustrated. "There's an inheritance, but I don't know if she intends to claim it. And a stepmother who might wish to do her harm to keep it."

"An inheritance that she doesn't intend to claim? What's the story there?" Stillman waited for an answer, but Clive didn't offer one. The truth was that he hadn't asked when he had the chance.

"I just need you to be there. My eyes and ears—and hands—if anything goes wrong."

"We will be there, watching and intervening. But if we fail, you might never forgive yourself—or us."

He remembered the old bell ringer's words, but shook them off. "I asked her to marry me, but she refused me. Told me she never wished to see me again." His voice almost broke with the emotion, and he focused his attention on the glass in his hand to steady himself.

The men fell silent.

"You asked her to marry you," Stillman repeated softly.

"I love her." Clive shrugged. "I thought she loved me, but she believes an alliance with her will harm my reputation."

"A woman who is concerned about *your* reputation." Garfleet whistled. "In other circumstances, I'd tell you to stay away, to respect her wishes and find a woman who welcomes your attentions. But after the Sinclair trial, you could marry the scullery maid and do no harm to your reputation. She must love you."

"I agree with Garfleet. Go to the gala or don't, but before you let her go, you should find out what's behind that excuse."

Chapter Twenty-Six

Charters removed his makeup, watching as with each brush of the cloth his own face appeared. The scar that etched the side of his face in front of his ear faded, then emerged pink and irritated.

"It's strange to see you as your true self." Flute stared.

"My true self. I've often wondered which one of my characters that is." He gestured at his study. "Even this setting is just another role—Lord Montmorency, collector of antiquities, scholar of ancient Greece and Rome. But tonight you shall wear a costume as well, Flute."

"Me?"

"Yes. I'll need your ears and eyes with me tonight."

"Who am I to be?"

"What would you think of a sea captain? I found a uniform at a secondhand clothier's some months ago. It's about your size."

"Was my captain prone to take on cargo from other ships? A pirate turned country squire. I'd like that."

"That's the beauty of these characters, Flute. We make them anything we wish."

"What's my name?"

"What will you answer to?"

"My first name is Henry. I'd answer to that."

"Then Henry it is. What last name?"

"Speedwell. It was a flower my mother loved."

"Captain Henry Speedwell. I like the sound of it. Do you have your knife, Captain Speedwell?"

"Always." Flute patted his belly. "This narrow pocket you had sewn into the side of the waistcoat is perfect to conceal it."

"Very good."

"What is the plan?"

"Miss Frost must die. I have just signed a nice contract to do away with her."

"What about Somerville?"

"With the deaths of Sparks and his crew, Somerville should grow less of a problem. But we can't risk that Frost knows something, even if she doesn't realize it. She dies."

"You're letting Somerville live because you don't like killing within your own class."

"It's not a matter of social class; it's the resources that give me pause. A poor man might suspect his friend was murdered, but he has few avenues for redress. Whereas the pockets of a duke, grieving the death of a beloved younger brother, are bottomless. But Frost's circle, thanks to Sparks and his crew, has grown used to disappearance and deaths. Her death will be the sensation of an hour or less."

"How will we do it?"

"We take what opportunity arises. When we find them together, we'll see what we must do. We may find, in the crush of the crowd, that you can slide your knife between his ribs, and steal his purse, and that will be fine. Just slip away before the body drops to the floor. But one of them, perhaps both, will die tonight."

Chapter Twenty-Seven

Clive sat in front of the fire in his brother's study, alone in the house. Forster had given the household the evening off as well as provided each servant with free tickets to the Rotunda for the next day. Clive's own ticket lay on the table beside him, next to a half-empty bottle of claret and a tray filled with the remains of his dinner.

Judith had been the only one to take her leave of him, the rest having avoided him and his bad temper for days. She'd refused to advise him, telling him the choice whether to go or not had to be his.

So, he sat, watching the fire and wearing a dark suit to match his mood, waiting for the clock to finally reach the hour that the gala would begin. What else could he do?

The sound of someone at the door dragged him from his chair. Without the butler, Clive had no choice but to answer the door for himself.

Outside stood Joe Pasten, and behind him a carriage with the curtains pulled.

"Ah, Somerville, Edmund said I could find you here."

"Is there trouble?"

"No, we've found Tenney on the docks with a crate

filled with forged Old Masters. I thought you might like to go with us."

"Us?"

"Mr. James is in the carriage. On the way, he'd like to talk to you about whether it would be possible—or even advisable—to reset the leg that was crushed at Waterloo."

The musicians were practicing their program, alternating sets of martial tunes with more melancholy laments. Lena had planned the musical settings to convey the pomp and pageantry of war along with its sorrow and loss.

But for the last ten minutes, the musicians had been playing the melancholy pieces, and all Lena could think of was Clive. The way his face had looked when she'd told him to go haunted her, creating a bone-deep sadness that she knew would never leave her. Each expression—from surprise, to disbelief, to confusion, hurt, and betrayal— she felt as a stab to the heart. Even now, days later, her heart felt numb, even dead.

What if Lady Judith was right? A blow to the body might kill, but a blow to the soul thwarted healthful life forever. Lena turned the thought away, but it came back, this time as a memory. She was twelve again, and her father had just forced her into the carriage that would carry her away from her home for the last time. Had her face in that long-ago moment looked like Clive's when she told him to stay away forever? She wiped the tears from her face.

Clive would eventually thrive, she told herself. He was too practical to hold on to memories of a woman who had rejected him. Though she wished she could have told him she loved him, that would have made parting unbearable for both of them, even if he had agreed to leave. No, he would eventually heal, but she would regret losing him until her last breath. She'd never imagined that such a man existed, one who valued her intelligence, her talent, and even her insistence on doing for herself.

"Lena, my dear, it's time." Constance set her hand on Lena's shoulder, having barely left her side for the last two days. Lena turned to find the Muses gathered at the front of the platform, all waiting to wish her well.

"It's going to be a crush, Miss Frost," Kate, who had been helping at the box office all day, announced happily. "The line waiting for the doors to open already circles Leicester Square."

"The duke's men have organized the gala-goers into a neat queue by rank and will let them in slowly," Ariel added. "All you must do is give the word."

Lena faced the painting, already unveiled so that the guests could be amazed as they entered. It was the Battle of Waterloo in all its horror and glory. The product of three years' work, it was magnificent. She looked to the spot where the murderers had cut the painting, but even her trained eye could barely discern the repair. All her preparations were about to come to fruition, and she should enjoy it, even if only for a single night. The only thing that could make it better would be if Clive were by her side, but that was impossible.

As scheduled, the band began to play "The Plains of Waterloo," accompanied by a single strong voice:

> *"The ancient sons of glory were all great men,*
>   *they say,*
> *And we in future story will shine as bright as they;*
> *Our noble fathers' valiant sons shall conquer*
>   *every foe,*
> *And long shall fame their names proclaim who*
>   *fought at Waterloo."*

A veteran of the Peninsular Wars, the Duke of Forster, wearing his army uniform, listened for a moment, then joined them. Lady Wilmot took his arm. "Are you certain, Miss Frost, that you wish for me to moderate the ceremonies? London should see the artist behind such a breathtaking painting."

"No, it's best this way." She shook her head. "It will make clear that Horatio is not in London. And I have my own performance to manage."

She took a deep breath, then turning back to the Muses, she smiled. "We should let our subscribers in."

Clive pressed his way through the crowd. But a block away he gave up trying to reach the main entrance in good time. He made his way to the alley and the Rotunda yard. A carriage stood in the alley, blocking the entrance to the yard, but he made his way around it.

At the entrance, Harald, on guard as usual, gave him a curt nod and opened the door into the lower level. Clearly Lena had not told her men of their falling out. Once under the platform, he maneuvered his way around the orchestra to the wall ladder, now covered by a heavy curtain. He climbed onto the platform, but the crush was too great to find Lena quickly—or at all. Taking advantage of the wall ladder, he climbed higher, surveying the crowd, until he found her at the front of the platform, dressed like a French soldier and surrounded by adoring patrons.

It took him almost a quarter of an hour to reach her side.

"Lena." He pulled her away by the elbow. "I almost didn't recognize you. Why French dress at an exhibition celebrating the victoy of the English allies?"

"There's to be a marshaling of arms, and I play the French soldier." She looked skittish, glancing over her shoulder as if expecting someone to accost them. "Why did you come?"

"I came to wish you luck. But it's clear you don't need it. Soon, I predict, you'll have your first commission from the royal family, and no one deserves it more."

She blushed. Her eyes met his only for a moment, but long enough to reveal a depth of sadness that equaled his own. He wanted to enfold her in his arms, to whisper "all will be well." But he knew such actions would be unwelcome. Instead, he looked away, to avoid blurting out a sentiment that would make them both unhappy.

"Your help and that of the Muses was invaluable. I will always be grateful to you—and them." She stepped back, as if to walk away. But he held her elbow.

"Wait. I'll leave you alone as you wish, if you will simply hear me out."

She didn't pull away. He lowered his voice to a whisper.

"Tenney's presence in London was a mere coincidence. He's returned to France on the last packet. I doubt he will return to England; he already exhibits the hectic red of one dying of consumption. Your paintings are safe at the duke's house."

She blinked away tears but did not cry. He continued speaking, lest she stop him before he could finish. It was his one chance to change her mind. "As for Madame Remberg, I asked for her in Soho. The few émigrés who remember her name say she died of grief shortly after her husband's execution. So there is no obstacle, Lena: we could marry—if you will have me."

She looked stunned, then sad. "It's too late." She shook her head slowly. "I'm sorry, Clive."

"For what?"

"I didn't believe I would see you again, and certainly not here tonight."

"How could I miss this? It means everything to you, more even than I do." He put his hand on her arm, feeling the warmth of her, wanting to pull her into the circle of his embrace. In the press of the crowd, no one could see.

"No, not more than you. Nothing means more to me than you. But I've made plans, plans that can't include you." From under the platform came the sound of a bugle, and she pulled her hand out of his.

Turning her face to the sound, she looked past him at the painting. Some of the scaffolding had been draped in green cloth to give the illusion of rolling hills.

"I want to be with you," he pleaded. "I'll fit in to whatever plans you have. I'll leave the surgery. I'll go wherever you need."

Her eyes filled with tears, but she blinked them away. "It's simply too late." She shook her head slowly, as if dismayed by his confidences.

"What do you mean?"

The bugle sounded a second time.

"I must go." She touched his hand. "Forgive me." She slipped away into the crowd.

"Is that Miss Frost?" Clive looked over his shoulder to find Lord Montmorency, an odd sort of man Clive had never trusted. Everyone insisted he was a good sort, having returned home from his Grand Tour to find his brother dead, and his father ailing. But Clive had never liked him. Something about his eyes spoke of avarice, not generosity, even when he was donating significant sums of money to various causes.

"My associate and I are acquainted with Mr. Calder, the proprietor. But we haven't yet had the pleasure to meet his assistant. When I bought my tickets, Calder said she was the talent behind his throne, so to speak. Isn't that true, Captain Speedwell?"

The larger man spoke little, but nodded in time to Lord Montmorency's words. Speedwell held his hand close to his side, his arm hidden by Montmorency's body. Clive instinctively took a step back, too close to the two men to feel comfortable. Something about them didn't ring true. But his retreat was stopped by the press of the crowd. There was nowhere to go, and he wouldn't leave, not before he could talk to Lena again.

The doors opened, and the sound of the marshaling of arms drifted down the darkened corridor. The roll of the drums and the call of the clarion came closer, when a voice cried out, "Look up there!"

A lone French soldier—Lena—stood at the edge of the scaffolding. Behind her a British soldier approached. The dance was to be a pantomime between the two soldiers. But Clive knew something was wrong. Lena's face was pale, her expression forced. Then the whole audience heard the sound of wood breaking under her weight—and her stifled cry as she fell two stories to the ground.

He tried to rush forward, but the crowd held him back. He could hear Aidan's voice from the area below the platform, calling for their physician, Lucy. A few minutes later, Aidan, from a ladder at the front of the platform, announced regretfully that Lena Frost, the co-proprietor of the Rotunda and the actor playing the soldier, was dead.

Exclamations of shock and horror rippled through the room. Clive stood, unable to move, unable even to think, or feel. Lena—vibrant, witty, infuriating Lena—was dead. He could still feel the warmth of her breath against his cheek, hear the timbre of her voice. But she was gone.

Lord Montmorency and Captain Speedwell were talking to him, but he couldn't quite make out their words. Slowly, they came back into focus.

"Terrible shame. Talented girl. Will you be well, if we leave you?"

Clive nodded, and the two men left him standing in the press of the crowd, alone. The crowd moved about him, more subdued at first, then regaining its animation when the band began to play again. Eventually, he'd begun to attract attention for the tears streaming down his face, but soon after Stillman found him, and his friends took him home.

Lena's death garnered almost no attention in the press. "Died. The female assistant to Horatio Calder, proprietor of the Rotunda panorama, by falling from a large scaffolding the night of the grand soiree. As she was dressed as a French soldier, many present at first believed the accident was part of the grand pageant, a marshaling of arms complete with old soldiers."

The story didn't give her name. It provided no sense at all that the panorama had been her project, not Horatio's. In death, she was reduced to Horatio's assistant. A nameless woman dressed up in a costume. For the first time, perhaps, he understood the cruelty of history, how it ignored or reassigned the accomplishments of remarkable women. She had been remarkable. And nothing he had done had made any difference.

He still loved her. It didn't matter any longer if she'd had one name or fifty. All that mattered was that she was lost . . . and so was he.

Chapter Twenty-Eight

Clive kept the covers over his head. For a fortnight, he hadn't left his room at his club. Each day, a maid came and drew the curtains, and he would draw them again. Why be reminded that the world still turned when she wasn't in it?

He ignored the tray of food left him each day, ignored the servants, ignored his family come to check on him, even ignored his brother, the duke, who (uncharacteristically) begged him to come home. He hadn't needed to ignore Boatswain, Lucy's dog, when someone let him into the room—the dog, sensing his sorrow, had merely curled up at his feet, until someone called him away hours later. He'd drunk himself senseless each day, until his brother had given instructions to the majordomo not to bring him any more whiskey, and no one refused the order of a duke. The servants came and went, stoking the fire, leaving or removing his food, refilling his basin and pitcher, and he never said a word. He hadn't spoken to a soul in so long that he wondered if he could still speak. But why would he want to? The only person he wanted to speak to was Lena.

Lena. The thought of her gone bowed him to the earth.

He had no interest in going to the laboratory, no interest in his cases, no interest in the promotion Joe had offered him that would take him somewhere new, somewhere that wouldn't remind him of her. He had no interest in his friends who came and sat by his side. They had been unable to keep her safe, and they felt the failure, though he didn't blame them. He should have known that whoever killed the resurrection men wasn't acting out of altruism for the community. He would find the killers, ensure they were punished, but not now. No, he would do it someday, when the giant gaping hole in his chest didn't make it hard to breathe.

He'd begged to see her body, but his family had refused, and he hadn't the energy to fight them. Aidan arranged the burial, placing notices of her death in the newspapers, making arrangements for Lena to rest in her tomb in Denby. He'd insisted on a guard to ensure that no one disturbed her body; the grave robbers' remaining crew had stolen her life, but he wouldn't allow them her body.

He heard the door open and close and the sound of movement in the room. The servants. They would be gone soon. He made no movement. This time the room remained dark—the way he liked it.

"I wish I'd met the woman who turned Clive Somerville into a lover."

The voice startled him. He felt the frustration rise. Lena wasn't any woman: she was his heart.

He growled his way out of bed, throwing back the covers, and ran into his aunt Agatha.

"How did you get in here?"

"I bribed the porter with an exorbitant fee, which I expect you to repay." Agatha threw open the curtains, and he recoiled from the brightness of the day. "You will not stay in this room or at this club for another hour." She strode to the hall door and opened it to a crew of maids and footmen, carrying a tub and water. "You will bathe. You will dress suitably for leaving your rooms. And you will go out," Agatha commanded, in a tone Clive (her favorite) hadn't heard in years, and certainly never before directed at him.

"Are you quit pining?" Joe Pasten sat at his desk, across from the chair Clive had thrown himself into more than an hour ago.

"Pining suggests a wayward or a juvenile passion. He'll object to that." Edmund looked up, then returned to his reading.

Joe placed a long, unfolded document in front of Clive's face. "It's time to decide. Do you want this assignment or not? A dozen other men have asked for it. If you are going to retreat to your bedroom or your surgery for the rest of your life, I might as well make one of them happy."

Clive read the assignment papers. Scotland. "It's so far away."

"We thought perhaps being far away for a while would provide you with some time to . . . recover. You need something to keep you from thinking, from dreaming of her fall," Edmund said gently.

"How do you know that?" Clive growled again.

His twin merely raised an eyebrow, and Clive turned his face away.

"Then that's it." Joe took the papers from Clive's hand. "I'll give it to Picket or Hatchett."

"No." He raised bloodshot eyes. "I'll take it. When do I leave?"

"The next mail coach to Edinburgh leaves in an hour." Joe checked the wall clock.

"I have to collect my things."

"It's done already." Edmund pointed at a large trunk beside his desk. "Aidan has made a cottage available for you. The servants are already in place. The gatehouse is occupied by some charity case of Sophia's, but there's no need to engage with them, except to give them this packet." Edmund placed a thick leather case on top of Clive's trunk.

"It's a six-month posting. But if you wish to extend it, you have only to ask."

Clive stared at the trunk. "How long has that been here?"

"A week." Edmund placed his hand on Clive's arm. "Go, brother. I'll follow next week to see if you need anything."

Clive looked into his twin's eyes and found a depth of sympathy he couldn't endure, not even from Edmund. The duke, his family, his friends, all wanted to talk to him about what had happened, but he needed to grieve where no one could watch. "I'll go."

The cottage was a distance from the center of town on a large acreage, and the coach driver was anxious to get back, unloading Clive's trunk to the porch almost before Clive had alighted from the coach, and heading back down the drive before Clive had even knocked at the door.

Clive looked around for a few moments. The cottage was more a manor house than a cottage. But what else would he expect from the northern property of a duke? Two stories, with large drawing rooms on either side of the front door. More house than he needed.

No one answered his knock, though the housekeeper had set a light in the window. He had assumed the servants were in residence, but apparently they came in from the town. But he had no key.

He looked around. The drive was carefully cleared, but everywhere was snow, heaped into tall piles along the sides of the drives and the path around the house. He walked around the house, trying the doors and windows, but all were locked tight, and no sign of any servants anywhere.

He returned to the front door where his trunk waited on the porch. On top sat the leather packet for Sophie's lodgers. Perhaps they held the key for him. He could deliver the packet, retrieve the key, and never engage with them again.

The walk to the gatehouse was a long one, and desolate, the landscape snow-bound and devoid of color. By the time he reached the gatehouse, he was chilled to the bone. The windows were all well lit, and he could hear the sound of children. A family. Hopefully, not a happy one. That would be more than he could take, especially if the children were girls with raven hair and dark eyes.

He used the knocker, but no one came. He knocked again, harder this time. The door opened, revealing a short, fat man, with long whiskers and red cheeks, wearing an apron covered with paint.

"I'm the duke's brother, come to deliver these papers and collect the key to the cottage." Clive held out the package.

"Ah, then come in, come in." The old man gestured with his paintbrush toward the drawing room where a portrait stood. The smell of the paints turned his stomach. An image of Lena laughing, a paintbrush in her hand, filled his memory. He needed to escape, but he looked for the old man, and he was gone to retrieve the key. In the hour before he'd left, Sophia had told him she'd found a new painter, but he'd been unwilling to hear the words, so he'd brushed her away with an angry hand. Now he realized she'd been trying to warn him that her painter was also the Scottish lodger.

He drew near to the painting. Even he could tell it was a masterpiece. In it, Aidan sat in the garden behind his London house, Lilly on his knee and his hand on her shoulder. The pair looked directly at the viewer, both smiling. In her hand, Lilly held both a pencil and a piece of drawing paper. Clive drew close. The paper showed what appeared to be one of Lilly's drawings from the nursery, a fort with the ocean beyond it. The old man was a fine painter, able to capture Aidan's affection for the child as well as the child's energy and enthusiasm.

Clive turned to the old man. "In recent years, I've seen that expression on my brother's face far too little, and I'm grateful you captured him in that pose."

"You'll need to tell the painter then." The man waved to the back of the house with his paintbrush.

"Are you not the artist?" Clive gestured to the man's apron and brush.

"Oh, no! I'm a student. Paint heather, I do, and thistle. Always wanted lessons, but we never had the luxury of a teacher here before." The old man held out his hand. "I'm Squire Potts. Not a very useful or fancy name, but it's mine. It's my teacher you want, though. In the kitchen making tea. Come along."

Clive followed the squire to the back of the house, toward the kitchen. He could hear laughter, children's voices, and the sound of pots clattering. Exactly the sort of noises he'd always imagined for a home of his, but that wasn't part of his future, not with Lena gone.

"Mary, Susan, come along now," Squire Potts called out as he pushed the door open. "We must go home. We can return tomorrow." Two small, blond girls curtsied good-bye to those in the kitchen, but Clive, standing somewhat back in the hall, couldn't yet see his brother's lodgers. "I've brought you a visitor."

He stepped to the side to let Squire Potts and the girls leave.

The kitchen had grown quiet. He stepped inside to find a woman turned away from him facing the window. She turned to him, and when her eyes met his, tears streaming down her face, he began to weep as well.

Neither of them moved, neither of them spoke, as if to move would break the spell that allowed them both to be in the room together.

After several minutes, a voice broke their silence. "Well, what are you going to do, boy? She's not dead. Kiss her!" Clive tore his gaze from Lena to find Horatio sitting at the far end of the table.

In the next moment, Lena was in his arms.

"That's why I had to die, you see. I knew you would never be safe, as long as we were together."

"After Lena asked the ladies of the Muses' Salon for help, it was your brother, the duke, who planned how to manage it all, the fall, the removal of her body," Horatio explained. "I was waiting in a carriage in the alley, and we left for this place that night."

"My brother?" Clive suddenly remembered Aidan, demanding, then cajoling him to listen. Clive had turned his face to the wall and covered his head with a pillow, until Aidan had given up.

"Yes. We've sold part interest in the Rotunda to him, and together we have hired a manager. So far the proceeds have been more than sufficient to look forward to another exhibition in a few years' time, when we are certain that the danger of the remaining resurrectionists has passed."

Lena's hand covered his, and he didn't dare move for fear if he stopped touching her, she would disappear, and this would prove just another cruel dream.

"That's when I come into the story." Out of the adjoining room, Aidan joined them, followed by Sophia and the two Gardiner children.

Lilly flung herself into Lena's arms. "I brought my last lessons to show you. We had to come see you, so I could have another one."

"And I look forward to seeing them." Lena hugged the child. "I have some easels set up in the morning room. Perhaps you and your brother would like to paint?"

Sophia nodded to Ian, and he took his sister by the hand. "We would like that very much."

Horatio rose. "Then I'll get you started."

Clive shifted his chair closer to Lena, and she leaned into his side. When Horatio returned, they picked up the conversation again.

"When you discovered that Helena Winters had an inheritance waiting, I began to wonder about the requirements of that bequest," Aidan began. "Horatio was able to offer us some information about Helena's father."

Clive raised an eyebrow in question.

Horatio took up the story. "You met my brother in the Denby churchyard—he's the bell ringer now, but when we were young, we both worked in Baron Winters's stables. I left home as soon as I was able, and I performed for some years in the regional theaters. That was all before

Lena's mother died. I didn't return even for a visit until long after Lena had run away. I renewed my acquaintance with Baron Winters one day when he was talking to Miss Helena's crypt."

Clive looked at Lena to see her reaction.

"Horatio and I have had some time here to tell each other our secrets." Lena smiled warmly at her business partner. "He has helped me reconcile, at least somewhat, with my father."

"We found each other good companions, and Baron Winters told me he knew his daughter was still alive. Madame Le Brun's tender heart couldn't bear the thought of a parent agonizing over a missing child, so she sent Winters regular notices, along with news of Lena's success as a painter. Winters, by the time I met him, had taken the full measure of his wife's character, and he'd kept those notices to himself. He asked me to find his girl, and I agreed. By the time I reached Le Brun, Lena was in Paris. But by the time I reached that city, she had already run home to England. I lost the trail."

"What happened then?" Sophia asked. "How did you find her?"

"Purely by chance. I was drinking chocolate at my favorite shop, and Lena walked in, looking the very image of her mother. It didn't take long to realize her partner in the Rotunda was a fiction, and it took even less time to become him."

"Did you tell Baron Winters you'd found Lena?" Clive caressed the back of Lena's hand.

"I traveled to Denby, but the baron had died while I was away. Her ladyship—having learned of Lena's inheritance— demanded to know if I had found her. I agreed to work for her, in order to gauge the extent of her ladyship's ill will for my girl." Horatio gave Lena an affectionate grin.

"Horatio knew that the baron had hidden papers in the crypt proving Lena's claim to his inheritance," Aidan added. "Lena gave her answers to me, and I have served as her agent in chancery. Sadly, the status of the inheritance has changed even since Clive left London with the papers." Aidan picked up the portfolio and pulled out some of the pages.

"But I only left London three days ago."

"You were in no hurry to arrive. We were," Aidan explained, then turned to Lena. "Though I know you have been ambivalent about your inheritance, I still regret the news we bring you." He gave Lena a tender look. "Your family's manor house and stables have been destroyed by fire, though the livestock escaped unharmed. There is nothing left but rubble."

Lena gasped, and Clive wrapped his arm around her shoulders.

"Several days before the fire, your stepmother posted a note to her solicitor, warning him that if anything were to happen to her, you would be to blame." Aidan removed a letter from the portfolio, but Lena made no attempt to take it. "This is a copy. I included it in Clive's packet because, at the time, neither I nor her solicitors believed that Lady Winters was in any danger from Lena."

Clive took it, reading over it carefully. "This is evidence certainly, but not of Lena's guilt. Her stepmother's madness is evident in every line. It's rambling, incoherent, and nervous. The magistrates can't seriously believe Lena is at fault." It couldn't be true; he couldn't bear losing her again.

Lena looked stunned. "As a child, I often wished her dead, but I didn't kill her. What can I do?"

"Nothing at all." Aidan put the letter back in the portfolio.

"Nothing!?" Clive interrupted, but Sophia placed her hand on his arm.

"There's nothing to do, because no one believes Lena is at fault. Squire Potts can confirm that she was here when the house burned."

"He has had a lesson every day," Lena added in a voice somewhat dazed.

"But even if Squire Potts didn't have a fondness for drawing thistles, Lady Winters's companion saw her ladyship methodically setting fire to every textile in the house. The companion didn't appreciate that Lady Winters apparently intended for her to die in the conflagration as well," Aidan explained. "The worst part, however, is that without the house and barns, your purchaser is no longer interested in the property."

"Clive appears to be exhausted from his journey." Lena placed her hand on Clive's shoulder. "Perhaps we can discuss the next steps in the morning."

Clive felt wrung out. In the space of an hour, his emotions had run from despair to elation to fear to relief. But with his brother, Sophia, and Lena in the same room, he had one question that couldn't go unanswered.

"Why?" He felt suddenly angry, as if they had all betrayed him. "Why didn't you tell me your plan?"

The three looked uncomfortable, but finally Sophia spoke. "You weren't supposed to be at the gala."

"Judith left me a ticket."

"You might have found it odd if we didn't." Sophia looked at Aidan for help.

"When Lena asked for the Muses' help, she said that the resurrection men were working for a man called Charters. Sophia recognized the name as the man the Home Office believes murdered her late husband. So, we believed Lena when she said you and she were in danger."

"I've read Joe's file on Charters—all the agents have." Clive turned to Lena. "By all accounts he's a very dangerous man."

"Then you understand how carefully we had to guard our plan and how important it was that you didn't know it," Sophia explained. "At the same time, you didn't act as we had predicted."

"Had you come to the main entrance of the panorama, my men would have kept you out," Aidan explained. "Edmund was waiting at the door to escort you home. We wanted it to look like you weren't welcome or that your family disapproved of your interest in Lena. We hoped such a strategy would convince Lena's enemies that you and she had fallen out."

"I wanted you to be safe. I couldn't have borne it if you were hurt or killed on my account." Lena put her hand on his chest, and it felt . . . like peace.

"But you took the back entrance, and once you were in, you had to believe it was real, all of it." Aidan shook his head ruefully. "We needed for everyone associated with Lena's enterprise to believe she had died."

"Your shock and grief cemented the story as nothing else we could have done," Sophia added. "If you had remained home, we would have told you after the event, spirited you off to the assignment Aidan had arranged for you in Scotland, and no one would have needed to observe whether you were grieving or not."

"Or if you had come home after the gala, instead of

going to your club, we could have done the same, though we would have had to put you in the coach for Scotland before we told you, so the servants didn't question your immediate change of spirits," Aidan watched his brother carefully.

"But, instead, your friends took you to your club, where you refused to see us or, when you did see us, to listen." Sophia explained gently. "We kept thinking you would come out, so that we could intercept you. But your friends stayed too close, and we didn't know who might say something to the wrong person and defeat all our work."

"So you sent Aunt Agatha."

"That was a bit of a masterstroke. We knew no one would refuse her." Aidan reached out to take Sophia's hand.

Lena pulled out of the circle of Clive's arms and rose. "We can discuss more in the morning. But you have all had a long journey, and are, I'm sure, anxious for some dinner and a good bed. Squire Potts has had fires lit in the cottage bedrooms, and his cook should be there shortly to prepare something to eat."

Aidan, Sophia, and Horatio rose, but Clive remained seated.

"What name are you using now?" His eyes never left Lena's face.

"I don't need to hide anymore." Lena smiled. "I am Helena Winters, daughter of the late Baron Winters of Derbyshire."

He slipped down onto one knee. "Helena Winters, would you be willing to change your name once more—to Lady Clive Somerville—and be my wife? I will be happy watching you paint for the rest of my days."

"I will marry you, but on one condition." Lena clasped

his hand and drew him to his feet. "We must always be equal: if I paint, you must continue your researches and your investigations, and when they catch my attention, you must allow me to work beside you."

He grabbed her up in his arms and swung her around in a circle, kissing her, a long, passionate kiss that felt like it touched their very souls.

When Clive set Lena's feet back on the floor, Aidan, Sophia, and Horatio had slipped from the room, leaving them to kiss, and kiss again, until they both felt equally satisfied.

Epilogue

Four years later

"It *is* stunning." Clive gestured toward the frescos above their heads. "It's a quite different experience to see it piecemeal as you worked than now when it's finished."

"I'm still grateful that Sophia and Aidan were willing to let me work on it in stages, rather than hire another painter, even though it took far longer that way." Lena studied the ceiling, making sure, for the four hundredth time, that all was as she had wished it to be.

"They had no choice really." Clive studied the six putti surrounding the center medallion.

"Did you threaten them, darling?" Lena stretched out her hand and found Clive's.

"I don't threaten. I merely point out the options."

"What were the options here?" Lena squeezed his hand.

"Hire an inferior painter, and forever regret it. Or extend the timeline, allowing the finest painter this side of St. Petersburg to come to London for a month at a time to work."

"You remembered that?" Lena's eyes grew wet with joy and gratitude.

"I remember everything. Every moment." Clive pointed to the medallion. "I quite like the putti here in the center. Is that our Elisabet Louise on the right and our Charles Laurent on the left?"

"Actually, if you look closely you'll see that all the putti are Elizabet and Charles. For some reason, when I imagined the faces of the putti, I could only imagine our darling children in various moods."

"I can see giddy, silly, and joyous." Clive brought her hand to his lips and kissed each of her fingertips.

"I thought it better to preserve those than their other moods, both for the sake of Sophia's ceiling and ours when Elizabeth and Charles are old enough to discover the cherubs wear their faces." Lena leaned her head on Clive's shoulder. "Do you really like it?"

"I thought that your Waterloo panorama was spectacular, but this—it is a tour de force. After Sophia's grand ball tonight, you will be offered more commissions than you can paint in a lifetime, and soon you will find yourself a painter to the royal family."

The doors at the end of the great hall swung open, and Sophia walked toward them.

"Should we get up?" Lena rolled on her side and studied her husband's face, still as handsome as the day she'd first met him.

"Why? You painted much of it lying on your back. We are just following in that tradition. Besides, after this, we'll have fewer opportunities to lie on the floor in my brother's dining hall. But lying here with you is so delightful— perhaps you should paint a fresco in our bedroom!"

Lena swatted his shoulder, laughing. When she looked up, Sophia stood over them, smiling.

"I can't tell you how many hours I've lain on this floor

staring at our ceiling," Sophia confided. "It's simply too much to take in while standing."

"Then join us, Sophie." Clive held out an inviting hand. "It's hours yet before your guests arrive, and it's not as if you've already dressed for the ball."

Sophia shook her head. "It's good to know that Clive will never lose his candor." She looked to the door, then at the ceiling. Without another word, she lay down beside Lena. "It's more beautiful than I could ever have imagined. You couldn't be in London for the great success of your first panorama, but you will be here for this unveiling. And it will be the start of your new career—no one in the ton will be able to ignore such a performance."

The doors swung open again, and in a few moments, the duke joined them. He didn't ask why they were lying on the floor; he merely took his place by Sophia's side.

They lay in silence, taking in the richness of the colors and the vibrancy of the designs.

The duke spoke first. "I've never noticed before—perhaps because of the scaffolding—but the design of the ceiling seems to have shifted."

"How so?" Clive asked, noting that Lena had grown strangely quiet.

"I thought this was to be a ceiling in praise of extraordinary women. And it is. The portraits of the ladies of the Muses' Salon are exceptional, and the historical figures are depicted with grace and wit. But some of the stories—there along the edges—seem to include men."

"Are you referring to the section over the far doors? It's a family portrait—but in Ophelia's sense of family—depicting your siblings, their spouses, children, friends, and pets."

"No, I mean the long scenes over the windows." The

duke's voice grew suspicious. "In particular, I mean that section where someone who looks like me appears to be . . ."

Lady Wilmot cut him off. "It is such a large space, that as the ceiling developed, Lena and I decided to ask the Muses to tell their stories in the panels along the upper wall. Lena and I chose to depict each of you in a heroic act that reveals your character, albeit that depiction is somewhat metaphorical."

"How have I never noticed that before?" Clive looked pleased.

"Which is yours?" Aidan followed the line of Clive's finger. Aidan studied the image carefully: a man lifting a woman into the sky. "Are you a circus performer?"

Clive smiled broadly. "I quite like it. If I read the metaphor correctly, I provide a ground from which Lena can soar, as she does for me."

"That's exactly right." Lena smiled radiantly, then she kissed him as if she hadn't been kissing him every day for the last four years.

Aidan studied the other panels. "Why are some of the panels still unpainted?"

"Why darling, that's easy." Sophia tucked her head into the curve of his arm. "This room is, in part, a record of the Muses' Salon, and our work is not yet done."

Books by Bestselling Author
Fern Michaels

7304

Romantic Suspense from
Lisa Jackson

Absolute Fear	0-8217-7936-2	$7.99US/$9.99CAN
Afraid to Die	1-4201-1850-1	$7.99US/$9.99CAN
Almost Dead	0-8217-7579-0	$7.99US/$10.99CAN
Born to Die	1-4201-0278-8	$7.99US/$9.99CAN
Chosen to Die	1-4201-0277-X	$7.99US/$10.99CAN
Cold Blooded	1-4201-2581-8	$7.99US/$8.99CAN
Deep Freeze	0-8217-7296-1	$7.99US/$10.99CAN
Devious	1-4201-0275-3	$7.99US/$9.99CAN
Fatal Burn	0-8217-7577-4	$7.99US/$10.99CAN
Final Scream	0-8217-7712-2	$7.99US/$10.99CAN
Hot Blooded	1-4201-0678-3	$7.99US/$9.49CAN
If She Only Knew	1-4201-3241-5	$7.99US/$9.99CAN
Left to Die	1-4201-0276-1	$7.99US/$10.99CAN
Lost Souls	0-8217-7938-9	$7.99US/$10.99CAN
Malice	0-8217-7940-0	$7.99US/$10.99CAN
The Morning After	1-4201-3370-5	$7.99US/$9.99CAN
The Night Before	1-4201-3371-3	$7.99US/$9.99CAN
Ready to Die	1-4201-1851-X	$7.99US/$9.99CAN
Running Scared	1-4201-0182-X	$7.99US/$10.99CAN
See How She Dies	1-4201-2584-2	$7.99US/$8.99CAN
Shiver	0-8217-7578-2	$7.99US/$10.99CAN
Tell Me	1-4201-1854-4	$7.99US/$9.99CAN
Twice Kissed	0-8217-7944-3	$7.99US/$9.99CAN
Unspoken	1-4201-0093-9	$7.99US/$9.99CAN
Whispers	1-4201-5158-4	$7.99US/$9.99CAN
Wicked Game	1-4201-0338-5	$7.99US/$9.99CAN
Wicked Lies	1-4201-0339-3	$7.99US/$9.99CAN
Without Mercy	1-4201-0274-5	$7.99US/$10.99CAN
You Don't Want to Know	1-4201-1853-6	$7.99US/$9.99CAN

Available Wherever Books Are Sold!
Visit our website at **www.kensingtonbooks.com**